ONCE A KILLER

A WARHAMMER CRIME ANTHOLOGY

WARHAMMER
CRIME

WARHAMMER
CRIME

ONCE A KILLER

A **WARHAMMER CRIME** ANTHOLOGY

JONATHAN D BEER | MIKE BROOKS | VICTORIA HAYWARD
DENNY FLOWERS | NICK KYME | MITCHEL SCANLON
GARETH HANRAHAN | JUDE REID

WARHAMMER CRIME
A BLACK LIBRARY IMPRINT

'Grit in The Wheels' first published in *White Dwarf 467* in 2021.
'Chains', 'Slate Run' and 'Clear as Glass'
first published digitally in 2022.
'Once a Killer, Always a Killer' first published digitally in 2022 as
'Once a Killer…Part 1' and 'Once a Killer…Part 2'.
'Habeas Corpus' first published in *White Dwarf 479* in 2022.
This edition first published in Great Britain in 2023 by
Black Library, Games Workshop Ltd.,
Willow Road, Nottingham, NG7 2WS, UK.

Represented by: Games Workshop Limited – Irish branch,
Unit 3, Lower Liffey Street, Dublin 1,
D01 K199, Ireland

10 9 8 7 6 5 4 3 2 1

Produced by Games Workshop in Nottingham.
Cover design by Jamie Gibson.

See Warhammer Crime on the internet at

blacklibrary.com

Find out more about Games Workshop
and the worlds of Warhammer at

games-workshop.com

Printed and bound in the UK.

WARHAMMER
CRIME

*It is the 41st millennium, and far from the battlefields
of distant stars there is a city. A sprawling and rotting
metropolis of ancient hives, where corruption is rife and
murder a way of life.*

*This is Varangantua, a decaying urban hellscape, full
of fading grandeur and ripe with squalor. Countless
districts run like warrens throughout its cancerous
expanse, from greasy dockyards and factorums to gaudy
spires, decrepit slums and slaughterhouses. And looming
over all, the ironclad Bastions of the enforcers, the
upholders of the Lex and all that stands between the city
and lawless oblivion.*

*To be a citizen in this grim place is to know privation
and fear, where most can only eke out a meagre existence,
their efforts bent to feeding an endless war in the void
they know nothing about. A few, the gilded and the
merchant-barons, know wealth, but they are hollow and
heartless creatures who profit from suffering.*

*Violence is inescapable on these benighted streets, where
you are either a victim or a perpetrator. Whatever justice
exists can only be found through brutality, and the weak
do not survive for long. For this is Varangantua, where
only the ruthless prosper.*

CONTENTS

CHAINS

JONATHAN D BEER

Rakove looms over her, impassively watching her struggle as the gas fills her narrow prison.

It is not pride that drives her to fight, because she has never known the luxury of pride. The privilege of dignity. Nor is she trying to free herself – she's learnt that the tough synthweave cuffs are beyond her malnourished strength. And a part of her welcomes the relief that the gas brings. The shrieking cacophony of other people's thoughts only abates when her gaolers render her unconscious. She fights just as hard when they wake her, fingers scraping at the transparent interior of her coffin cage in a desperate attempt to claw her way back to the peace of narcotic-induced slumber.

No, she fights as a chained animal fights, and for the same reason. Her limbs thrash against the bonds that encircle her wrists and ankles, that press tight against her chest and forehead. She spits and hisses, screaming the curses she's learnt as a vagrant thief of Varangantua's pitiless streets. She even tries to lash out with her witch sense, imagining her body's pain as a dagger that she hurls at Rakove's inscrutable form. But she has never really controlled the power that afflicts her, and if her mind's blade lands, he shows no sign of feeling it.

The agony collar bites, its barbs flooding her veins with punishment for her pointless resistance. Her body arcs, muscles locked with pain, tears streaming from her eyes.

Finally, she slumps against the coffin's bare steel, though the collar continues to scourge her. She has had the strength to fight stolen by the gas that hisses from inlets beside her head and must now endure in mute misery.

As the soporific takes hold, Rakove continues to watch her. She looks back at him through the thick plex, his fleshy face turned into smears of colour by the curve of the coffin's lid. Desperation drives her to plead, though she knows there's nothing she can say that will lead him to free her. She can feel his thoughts, hot and cruel behind bloodshot eyes. There is no compassion in him, not for her.

Only contempt.

Melita lurched out of her chair, flailing at the phantom sensation of cuffs on her wrists and fire blazing through her limbs. She scraped her hip against her metal desk's hard edge as she stood, yelped and staggered away. An errant step caught a pile of paper and data-wafers, spilling them in a rippling cascade across the office floor.

She stood in the centre of the room, chest heaving, fists balled. It was dark, and though Melita wanted to snap the lumens on, she couldn't make herself move. She forced in one breath after another, reaching for calm even as her heart thundered. She swore, shuddered and swore again. Each curse was jarringly loud in the near silence, but they helped her shed the cloying, aching touch of the memory that was not hers.

It had been the sound of her cogitators this time. For a moment, the rhythm of valves switching, the hum-click of magnetic coils engaging and disengaging within the steel and brass bowels of the machinery that crowded the room's far wall, had synchronised into the same warbling pattern as the engines that had pumped the soporific gas into her cage.

No. Into Alim's cage. Not hers. It had been the boy who had endured that torture, not Melita.

All at once, the tension left her body, taking her strength with it. Melita collapsed back into her chair, grateful as ever for the embrace of its cracked, welcoming synthleather. As it always did, a headache had begun to bloom behind her eyes, sharp and bitter as the memory that had assailed her. She swore once more and put her head in her hands.

A pale finger strayed to the skin of her throat, remembering the barbs of the hateful collar. The sight of red weals around Alim's neck from their punishment. That had been how Melita had found him, chained and caged by the cruel cabal who had been using him for his unnatural powers.

Melita sighed, guilt and anger adding their sour edge to her throbbing headache. She had saved the boy from their clutches, and, in return, Alim – that was the only name he had given her, and despite furious research she had been unable to uncover any record of the boy's existence – had used his unnatural abilities to thrust his memories into her mind.

That was how the mutant psyker had forced her to shoot him. He had begged for it, pleaded for the las-bolt that would put an end to his misery. She had only pulled the trigger to stem the awful tide of pain and indignity that he had violently shared with her.

But they had stayed with her. Even after two months, the memories were as vivid as ever, triggered by stray sights, sounds or scents. Three days ago, she had nearly bolted from a meeting with one of her informants. A juve had rounded the street corner tossing a handball from palm to palm. Instantly, she had lapsed, overcome by the recollection of sudden shock and pain as a rock struck Alim's scalp. The jeers and curses of the encircling crowd. It had taken all her self-control not to set off running, driven by survival instincts from another person's life.

Melita uncovered her eyes and kicked her chair into a slow spin to take her back to face her desk.

More data-wafers and folders littered its surface. One – the only one that mattered – sat beside her primary runeboard, caught in a pool of yellow light from her desk-lumen.

A face glared at her from a pict fixed to the cover, hard eyes almost lost amid puffy features and a cobweb of broken veins. The image was from Jorg Rakove's service record, taken just a few years before he retired from the enforcers. There were others inside the folder, pulled from the data archives of joy house monitor picters and district Administratum residency records, and even a still from a propaganda reel in which he'd featured some thirty years ago as a young sanctioner. They sat alongside a detailed biography, constructed over weeks of arduous research. Melita had traced the path of Rakove's life, learning all she could about Alim's tormentor as she hunted him.

The man had gone to ground, hiding from the justice he deserved. The Valtteri Cartel – Melita's new employers – had tasked her with running him down. Rakove was the only link to whoever had orchestrated Alim's capture and the attacks that had brought the all-powerful alliance of merchant-combines to the brink of civil war. Such elaborate hostility could not be ignored, and Melita had been given access to a seemingly bottomless well of slate with which to pursue him. She doubted there was a single snitch or ganger from Dragosyl to Setomir who didn't know Rakove's face.

It was the Valtteri's wrath that Rakove ran from, but it had been Melita's need for vengeance that had driven her through the long nights at her cogitators. She doubted Rakove had ever heard her name, but she knew him, intimately, and not merely from her assembled notes. Alim had been his captive for weeks. The boy had known the taste of Rakove's thoughts, and he had forced that on her along with so much else.

Melita stared at the pict, meeting the sanctioner-turned-torturer's gaze. Revulsion and rage churned within her. For Rakove, and the hateful torture he had inflicted on Alim. For the boy, for obliging her to know that agony herself, and his violation of her innermost self.

The office's door chime made her jump.

She steadied herself and checked the feed of the external picter on one of the boxy imagifiers on her desk. A familiar face was illuminated by the reflected glare of the street-lumens. Melita thumbed a switch on the desk to deactivate the electro-magnetic locks holding the heavy steel closed.

Edi Kamensk loomed in the doorway, his broad chest and shoulders made wider by a heavy synthleather coat and a thick woven jersey beneath it. Varangantua's wet season had thrown up one last squall before it gave way to the stifling heat of the dry months, and cold, wet air blew in around him to further upset the papers on her desk and floor.

He studied her warily. She hadn't told him what the psyker had done to her, but the former sanctioner had worked as Melita's bodyguard for four years. His look of mute concern had become all too familiar over the past few weeks as she stalked Rakove with single-minded zeal.

'What's wrong with your face?' Melita snapped.

Edi's expression dropped into its more typical, reassuring scowl. 'You ready?'

She was. After weeks of hunting, Rakove had finally been revealed to her. Tonight, she would expunge the debt of pain owed to Alim and lay to rest the ghost that haunted her. Melita was not a violent woman, but the visceral hate she had inherited from the psyker had only grown as she hounded his tormentor. Before the night was over, she would see Jorg Rakove delivered into the Valtteri's ungentle custody, or to the city's crematoria fields.

'Melita?' Edi prompted.

She looked down at Rakove's porcine glare and felt barbs pulling at the skin of her throat.

'Let's go.'

The twin beams of the groundcar's headlamps cut bright streaks through the pouring rain as they drove along deserted arterials and across pitch-black junctions. They had driven deep into the heart of the Spoil, following a route Edi and Melita knew well. Her business took them to every corner of the dilapidated sprawl, although it would have been foolish for either of them to let their familiarity turn into complacency.

'That's coming along,' said Edi as they crossed a span of elevated highway. The object of his comment was hard to miss. An expansive collection of rockcrete and brick buildings rose from a patch of derelict land half a mile to the south. The compound was lit by bright sodium lamps that shone in the darkness, illuminating dozens of men and women who were working despite the lateness of the hour.

In contrast to the districts surrounding the Spoil, construction was a major employer for the region's itinerant labourers. So few basic utilities were available to the unfortunates that eked out their lives within the Spoil's borders, but every year a little more seemed to be added. In this case, the furnaces were intended to pipe power and heat into the nearby habs, although only for those who could pay for such a luxury.

'Sorokin wants it running before the end of the year.' Melita had been paying close attention to the erection of the furnaces. Every brick, bolt and cable was provided by Andreti

Sorokin, the ganger-king of the Spoil. The city had abandoned the region to its squalor, and the Har Dhrol gangs had filled the void.

They drove on, leaving the builders to their task. The roads were almost empty, but that was typical. The Spoil's nightlife was a coy, tense affair. Those with the slate to spend freely were typically gangers, and were a liability to any revel house they frequented, as well as to anyone who happened to be sharing it with them. Most denizens of the Spoil kept to themselves after Alecto's wan sun had set, or else hid from their miseries in tiny drinking dens converted from the basement rooms of hab-blocks. Those found roaming the streets were usually stumbling to or from narco-pushers' corners.

But while venues for higher-class amusement were rare in the Spoil, they were not non-existent.

The Teseralde was a joy house, although like everything in the neglected morass of abandoned foundries and rotting hab-stacks of the Spoil, the revelry was a faded echo of what that title could mean in a true district of the city. Where a Dragosyl joy house might blaze with kaleidoscopic neon, the Teseralde's grime-hazed windows flickered with greasy yellow light, where they were not boarded up. Where Melita would have expected armour-clad private securitors standing sentinel over a carefully corralled queue of off-duty clerks and administrators, here gangers shook down the vagrants and dispossessed labourers who approached the entrance for proof they had sufficient slate for the night's amusements.

It wasn't even a purpose-built joy house. The Teseralde was set back from the street and had the look of a merchant-baron's townhouse. Three storeys of time- and toxin-etched stone reared above Melita as Edi steered their groundcar into the building's courtyard. Streams of chem-rich water fell from the mouths of gargoyles atop its eaves, and sculpted cherubim leered from the columned portico. The stone columns between which Edi and Melita drove would have once held iron gates to ensure the manse's occupants were undisturbed by the rabble, but the gates and the rest of the courtyard's railings had likely been wrested from their foundations and sold for the value of their metal by enterprising Spoilers long ago.

They were stopped just inside what remained of the joy house's boundary by a pair of gangers, who shone hand-lumens into the groundcar's interior. They glanced inside, then, evidently satisfied they were not a stub-gun-toting crew of rival gangers, pointed towards a covered depot.

Melita climbed out of the groundcar as soon as the engine died, bracing herself against the biting wind and torrential rain. Edi climbed out more slowly, one hand resting protectively on the vehicle's roof. He had not wanted to bring Katuschka, his prized antique Dymaxion Model 34, into the Spoil, fearing the jealousy of the gutter, but Melita had insisted. Everything that happened from this moment forward would be an exercise in projected status. In pretending at confidence and composure no matter what obstacles were set in her way.

She had dressed with that goal in mind. Though Melita rarely made an effort at her attire, she had made her living as an info-broker for four years, and experience had taught her that appearances mattered on the street just as much as in the offices of a merchant-combine executor. Her expensive real-leather jacket, cut high above her hips, tight breeches and thick-soled calf-length boots were what she thought of as her armour. The face with which she met the world and its trials.

She hadn't brought Oriel, as much as she had wanted to. As much as she would have been reassured by the servo-skull's proximity, she knew that her quarry's paranoia would not permit her to bring so lethal an entity into his presence.

Edi rounded the groundcar's frame, shoulders hunched against the downpour, the hand-cannon at his hip visible beneath his coat. That would have to do.

They started for the joy house's portico, but a huddle of gangers in grey synthleathers loomed out of the shadows to bar their path.

'What you want, upclave?'

Melita didn't blink. 'I'm here to see the King.'

The lead ganger's facial tattoos contorted as he made a gesture of derision. 'You and half the scum of the Spoil. Piss off.'

'He'll want to see me.'

'Is that so?'

Melita dipped a hand inside her jacket and withdrew a blue slate. She held it between thumb and forefinger for a moment to ensure she had the ganger's attention.

'My name is Melita Voronova. He'll want to see me.'

She flicked the chip to the ganger, who smartly plucked it from the air. The bribe was on the high side for so small a thing as getting through the open door, but Melita reasoned that a flash of slate now would set the tenor for the conversation to come. Besides, it wasn't her money she was giving away.

The man sniffed, then stepped back to let Melita and Edi pass, but not before sending a member of his crew inside to warn of their arrival.

Heat billowed from the joy house's interior, foetid air steaming where it met the night's storm-blasted chill. The wet slap of humidity was foul, and Melita fought to keep her face neutral. It wasn't just the heat – the rain had blunted the Spoil's usual reek of refuse and open sewers, and so the ripe fug of compacted humanity was particularly sudden and repulsive.

They forced their way through the press of bodies, Melita leading but with Edi close behind. They passed from the vestibule into a larger reception hall, where the crowd thinned sufficiently for Melita to catch her breath.

The hall was dominated by a pair of staircases that curved from opposite walls up to the second level. The stairs formed an arch through which most of the crowd were trying to move, but the hall also branched left and right towards other, evidently less popular entertainments.

The joy house retained enough of its character as a former gilded manse to feel strangely dissonant. Vendors served pitchers of slatov from stalls set up beneath ornate coving. Bill papers advertising the joy house's diversions were pasted over discoloured patches of plastered wall that should have held portraits of the owner's kin. Men jostled one another in ill-tempered disagreement on a tiled floor that must have been the work of a dozen skilled artisans. An Imperial aquila carved from black marble crowned the apex of the arch under the stairs, a common affirmation of loyalty in the homes of the gilded. But in this house, the heads of both eagles had been hacked away, and the aquila's wings were similarly chipped back to nubs.

Melita couldn't see Edi's face, but she was sure he noticed the casual desecration of the Imperial emblem and was grateful that he kept his disapproval to himself. Despite accompanying her on almost all of her sojourns into the Spoil for the past four years, Edi had never lost his strangely innocent dismay at how far the sprawl and its denizens had fallen from the Emperor's light.

Both staircases were blocked by more knots of gangers clad in grey, who snarled at anyone that, either through curiosity or the accidental motion of the crowd, came too close. One man dressed more like a clerk than a street-blade stood halfway up the right-hand side, evidently waiting to catch Melita's eye. They pushed their way forward as he descended to meet them.

'I'm Nurem Babić.' He had to shout over the din of voices that suddenly roared from beneath the arch. 'This way.'

'Weapons first,' grunted one of the guards. Melita nodded

in mute acceptance and held open the lapel of her coat to let the ganger reach in and withdraw her snub-nosed laspistol from its holster. Edi, with far less grace, gave up his enormous Sulymann Engager, his smaller backup autopistol and his jawsnapper. The last of these was handed over with particular reluctance – Melita was sure he carried the knuckleduster as a proxy for the shock maul he had worn for every day of his thirty-two years as a sanctioner.

They were led up the curve of the staircase and through a synthwood door. The cacophony of voices was reduced to a tolerable level for only a moment as Babić led them along a short corridor and opened the door at its end without knocking.

Many people claimed to rule areas of the Spoil. Even the lowest crew of street-blades could call a particular corner their territory. But, just like the rest of the city, true ownership was found much higher. A crew of narco-pushers might occupy a street, but a clave-captain controlled the block. And while the clave-captains might squabble amongst themselves, and even wage brief and bitter wars for particularly valuable tracts of land, they were all bound within the Har Dhrol, the alliance of gangs that had transformed the Spoil from a divided, catastrophically poor urban wilderness into a single, semi-coherent whole.

The man at the centre of that whole was Andreti Sorokin, the King of the Har Dhrol.

He bore a passing resemblance to Edi, in that they were both big men, powerfully built, but for whom time's knife had begun to cut. Sorokin's hair and beard were closely cropped, both more grey than black. He had a slightly hunched posture, but this emphasised rather than diminished the air of menace that bled from him. Sorokin was a hulking, ageing brawler who had built a throne for himself atop the bodies of every other Spoil ganger who had made the mistake of opposing his rise.

She knew from her informants within Sorokin's household that his eyesight was fading, but he wore no lens or other aids tonight. He stood as they entered, gesturing with a hand holding a glass of what looked like amasec to beckon them inside.

'Mistress Voronova, what an unexpected pleasure.'

Andreti Sorokin's voice was unlike any other. It started in the great barrel of his chest, deep as a grave, hoarse from a lifetime of whispered threats and bellowed curses. He spoke in a strangely wandering manner, lingering on some words and biting off others. It was deeply disconcerting, like almost everything about the King of the Har Dhrol.

'Messr Sorokin.'

'Andreti, please.'

Melita inclined her head. 'I was grateful for the invitation.'

Sorokin blinked, apparently nonplussed. 'Did I invite you, Mistress Voronova? Far as I see it, you have appeared suddenly before me, waving your masters' slate about, to interrupt a rare night of leisure.'

Melita registered his note of disapproval regarding her bribery of the doorman, but pressed on. 'You let it be known that you have Jorg Rakove. And that you'd be here tonight.'

'Yes, I did.' He abandoned his pretence immediately and waved a hand at one of the chairs that occupied the box. 'Well, come on then. Sit. Have a drink. Talk to me about Jorg Rakove.'

The fighting was a distraction Melita could have done without.

They sat in a pair of overstuffed armchairs at the edge of his private box, with Edi and Sorokin's own bodyguards standing near at hand. The box had evidently once been a balustraded landing overlooking one of the townhouse's receiving chambers. The enterprising operator of the occupied manse had sectioned off the landing into discrete spaces, like the private booths of a theatre, and Sorokin had occupied the largest of these, as was his right and privilege.

Beneath them was the fighting pit. The box overlooked the main hall, and at least three hundred people had crammed themselves into the narrow space. Whoever ran the joy house had prised up the flagstones at the hall's centre to create a shallow square, and this pit was hemmed in on all sides by a roaring crowd of gangers, labourers and other Spoil dregs.

Above them were more boxes, like Sorokin's, and from these more men and women cheered and jeered. The Spoil's makeshift joy houses and other venues of salacious entertainment were heady temptations for a certain class of gilded sensualist, drawn to the illicit substances and unlicensed flesh found at civilisation's edge. All of these were readily available in Setomir's and Dragosyl's own dens and alleys, but in the Spoil they were accompanied by the alien thrill of true poverty. Several knots of these gaudily dressed rakes occupied the boxes opposite Sorokin's, though they were outnumbered at least three to one by more sober companions – only the most foolhardy hedonist ventured beyond the Rustwater Canal without a sizeable contingent of their family's lifewards.

Melita watched as two men, stripped to the waist, emerged from the crowd and stepped down into the fighting pit. As odds were called and bets taken, Melita wondered how purposeful was Sorokin's choice of location for their meeting. Immediately, she dismissed the question as naive. Everything was a test.

A ringmaster was calling the fighters' names to roars of approbation, while another lifted a length of chain perhaps three yards long from the sand of the pit. With a surprising amount of ceremony, the ringmaster fixed each end of the chain to the fighters' wrists with a heavy metal cuff. Then he withdrew a pair of long-bladed knives from a case held by another assistant and spun them for the crowd's appreciation.

With one final shout, he tossed the knives into opposite corners of the pit, and the fight was on.

Melita leant back as cries erupted from beneath her. Almost instantly, the tang of blood cut through the choking miasma of sweating humanity and noxiously sweet body scents. Melita kept her face in an impassive mask and fought down the sensory bombardment.

'Where is he?'

Sorokin took a slow swallow of amasec before replying. 'Safe. Contained.'

'Rakove is scum,' she said between cheers. 'The Valtteri want him, and they'll pay to have him.' There was no point being coy. Both of them knew why they were there, and the rest was merely haggling over the cost.

'Before we get to that.' Sorokin leant back in the chair. He combined his odd mode of speech with a roaming, inconstant gaze, looking from the fighting pit to Melita to the crowd to his drink and back to the pit. 'What's a smart young thing like you doing in hock to that band of usurers and idolators?' His voice dropped low in his condemnation of the cartel.

Melita had assumed this would come up and had an answer ready. 'They pay well.'

'Is that right? Well, that is a shame.'

'How so?'

Sorokin's eyes stopped their roving and met hers. Melita felt the sudden force of his attention and judgement. His was a fierce, angry stare, a challenge to whatever or whomever he turned it on.

'We know each other of old. I thought better of you.'

She turned, uncertain how to take that. Melita and Sorokin had met perhaps three times in the past few years. Each encounter had been a moment of high tension for her, but Melita was surprised he remembered her at all.

She swiftly considered how best to respond to his apparent disappointment. 'You don't seem to mind being seen to deal with the Valtteri.'

That was a risky play. It was common knowledge that Sorokin, the warlord who had built an empire from the ashes of the Spoil, was backed by the Valtteri Cartel. He had reined in the excesses of his clave-captains, outlawed the engine-gangers that preyed on Valtteri convoys, and in return they kept him in power, with a steady flow of slate, weapons and whatever else he desired. Or, at least, that was the rumour that had become the truth on the street.

Melita saw that her jibe had landed. 'Dealing's one thing. Being at the end of their leash is another. I'm beholden to nothing and no one. I don't think you can say the same.'

They sat in silence, or the closest thing to silence with howls of glee and derision heaving up from the pit.

'So, why is it your *employers*' – he put a special emphasis on the word – 'want him?'

Melita was relieved to be back on easier ground. 'What has Rakove told you?'

'Told me? I haven't spoken to him. The bastard doesn't even know that I'm the one who has him. He thinks he's holed up in a safehouse used by a bunch of bliss-pushers.'

That was a lot of information to give away, and Melita wondered how much of it was true. In a place as vast as the Spoil, it would be almost impossible to narrow down a list of locations that narco-pushers might use to stash their goods.

'You didn't answer me,' growled Sorokin. 'What's Rakove to the Valtteri?'

Melita had gone back and forth on just how much truth to give him. 'He harboured a psyker. Inside the Spoil. Used it to attack the cartel's interests.'

Sorokin made a face, a pious scowl at the mention of heretic witchery, but Melita could see that he had already known everything she had told him.

Another gale of hoots and whistles erupted from the fighting pit. Sorokin gestured over the balcony's edge. 'Who'd you favour, hmm?' he asked, suddenly switching topics.

'I'm sorry?'

'Let's say I give you the mutant-hoarding scum if you pick the winner.'

Melita scoffed. 'You're not going to do that.'

'I might.' He stared back at her. Insincere though the offer clearly was, his challenge was very real. She frowned and leant forward to look over the balustrade's lip.

The two new fighters could not have been more different. One was a mountain of a man, his upper body one vast slab of scarred muscle. He looked like a foundry worker, or perhaps a stevedore for the shallow-bottomed hulks that crossed the Rustwater with cheaply made goods turned out from the Spoil's workshops.

The other was a woman, also tall but surely no more than a third of the man's weight. She wore a cut-down bodyglove, exposing lithely muscled arms. Her hair was shaved to a finger's width all over, and she spun her knife with rapid flicks of her wrist, watching for her opponent's reaction.

Despite herself, Melita tried to gauge which would be the victor. The crowd evidently favoured the woman, cheering at each flash of her knife, jeering the giant's caution as he turned in the centre of the pit, moving as quickly as he could to follow the woman's dancing motion. In less than a minute, both of them were bleeding from thin cuts and off-hand blows. Melita winced. The pain from those wounds must have been immense, tugged and jarred as they were by the demands of the fight.

The woman changed direction with an elegant spin, but the man read the move and was ready with a clenched fist swung backhanded. She rolled away from the blow, but only as far as the chain that bound them together would allow.

He started to heave. The woman's heels left trails in the blood-wet sand as she resisted, strength set against strength. But then she darted in, left hand rising quickly to twitch the sudden slack in the chain that bound them together. The curl of metal leapt up, but at the last second the man jerked his head away so that the chain lashed across his temple, rather than blinding him as the woman had intended.

She was on him in a heartbeat, blade moving like quicksilver as the giant backpedalled. She caught him three times with shallow cuts to his massive torso, but the man's roars of pain made her overconfident. As she stepped in for the kill, he checked his backward motion. She ran straight into his hugely muscled hip, staggered away, and in the brief second of confusion the giant reached forward, almost casually, and dragged the length of his blade across her bicep.

The woman reeled back, blade abandoned so she could clutch at the horrendous wound that had laid her arm open to the bone. The crowd groaned as the giant raised his hands in triumph. The motion jerked the woman's hand from her mutilated arm, and blood sprayed in an arc into the faces of the front rank of the crowd. Melita lurched back, sick to her stomach.

Sorokin half stood from his seat. 'Nicely done!' The mob roared back, their bias towards the stricken woman forgotten in the face of Sorokin's approval. The victor, for his part, tapped the flat of his wet knife against his chest in salute, then waited for the ringmaster to remove the chain from his wrist. The woman's crew had already freed her and were pushing their way to the opposite side of the hall.

He settled back into his seat. 'Well, too slow there. Shame, too. It's in no one's interests to have a man like Rakove walking the street.'

Melita's pulse quickened. She was almost certain that he was teasing her, looking for another angle from which to test and probe her. But the fear of losing Rakove when she was so close was palpable.

'It is a shame.' Melita managed to keep her voice level. 'Since I'd have picked him.'

'Easy to say so now.' Sorokin's eyes glittered with amusement, glad that Melita was keeping up with his game. 'But, for argument's sake, why?'

'"You can be quick and you can be canny, but being tough enough to ride the blows is what sees you through a fight."' That had been one of her mother's pearls of wisdom, hard learnt from a life spent warring with other smuggling clans beneath the massive stanchions of the Dragosyl voidports.

'Is that so?' Sorokin seemed to ponder her words. 'So you'd always bet on the big man?'

'Usually.' Melita had a premonition of approaching horror but was powerless to stop it.

'Right, then. I have a new proposal. You can have Rakove if your man wins a bout in the pit on your behalf.'

Melita froze. Behind her, she felt Edi stiffen.

'I mean it.' The mockery was gone, or at least it had disappeared behind a mask of rigid intensity. 'Blood for blood, the way everything is settled out here beyond the world's edge.'

Melita's heart pounded, loud enough to hear. She was paralysed. She had been so clear that Sorokin had come intending to make a deal, but his careless jibes and goading had thrown her off balance.

'I...' She trailed off. She would never allow Edi to set foot in the pit, but she could not let Rakove evade her revenge. 'There's no way you'll–'

Edi twitched the coat from his shoulders. 'I'll need to borrow one of those knives.'

She spun in her seat. 'Edi, don't.'

As soon as she said the words, an involuntary whisper, something changed in Sorokin's eyes. Triumph. He'd got what he was looking for. He'd cut through her layers of front and indifference and forced her to let slip something real, something true about herself.

Melita cared about Edi. He was probably the only person left in Varangantua who still mattered to her, and Sorokin had effortlessly drawn her into giving that vulnerability away.

'Maybe there's no need,' said Sorokin, leaning back. 'After all, folk are lining up to fight in front of me. I wouldn't like to deprive some young talent their turn in the spotlight.'

Melita seethed. She had lost all patience with Sorokin's antics, his casual jests and jibes. 'You didn't come here to gamble. You're holding Rakove because you're looking to get paid. What's your price?'

His eyes narrowed, either with amusement at her temper or anger at her insinuation. 'Make me an offer.'

The cartel's agents had given her close to a free hand to obtain Rakove's head. She could offer him the deeds to land and property in half the city, off-world treasures, immunity for his agents and allies beyond the Spoil or enough slate to bury anything that could still trouble him. But Melita's blood was still up, and she gave into a reckless impulse.

'Rejuvenat chems.'

Sorokin's stare turned brittle, just slightly, enough to know that she had struck a nerve in return.

The King of the Har Dhrol was an old man in a world that punished weakness. For the gilded, age was nothing but a number, their careless immortality bought with the labour of the millions who toiled at their command. Sorokin was undoubtedly as rich as any three merchant-barons Melita could name, but the Spoil was not the place to find the exclusive, highly secured therapeutic clinics one needed to enter in order to achieve rejuvenat's full results.

He gave a rough sort of laugh, a recognition of a point landed. 'Nice try, but no. Those I can source myself, if I were ever to be so vain as to want them.'

'Then what?'

Sorokin said nothing for a long time. Then he slowly stood, all of a sudden wearing the years that Melita had mocked. He rounded his armchair, ignoring the cries for his attention from the pit below, and crossed the box to a narrow shelf that held an array of glass bottles.

'I am constantly disappointed by you upclavers' low regard for what I have done. What I'm trying to do.' He lifted a bulb-like decanter of amasec and poured himself a tall measure. 'Don't get me wrong, I understand it. Everyone needs somebody to look down on. But it does... irk me.'

Realisation dawned. In the thirty years since Sorokin had risen to command the length and breadth of the Spoil, he hadn't merely exploited the people still trapped inside it. He had built. Cut off from the city's infrastructure, Sorokin had set about creating his own, like the furnaces she and Edi had passed on their way to the Teseralde. For all that the Spoil's facade was broken and its bones rotten, Sorokin was doing what he could to graft, piece by piece, the muscle and sinew of a functioning district onto the Spoil's decaying frame.

But there would be so much beyond his reach. Bricks and mortar were one thing, but to build generatoria, sanitation plants, data-junctions – that required complex equipment and refined parts, machined to the exacting templates of the Adeptus Mechanicus. Such things would be difficult to acquire in the quantities that the Spoil needed, even for the King of the Har Dhrol.

She spoke slowly and carefully. 'I'm certain that the produce of the Valtteri's manufactoria can be made available to you, Messr Sorokin.'

He turned, glass half raised to his lips. He grinned. 'Not bad. I had to walk you right up to it, but not bad.'

Sorokin made a summoning gesture with his free hand. Babić, the ganger who had led them in, crossed the box quickly and handed him a pasteboard card. Melita could see the tight alphanumerics of a loc-ref stamped onto one side, and nothing else. She fought the desperate temptation to try and snatch it from the old man's hands. Sorokin flicked the card with a thick finger.

'I'll have Babić send you a list. If everything on it – and I mean everything, to the last bolt and rivet – is delivered to my crews by midnight tomorrow, then I'll see to it that Rakove will be here the following morning.'

'You'll have it.' She made the promise instantly, carelessly.

'Mess me around and he'll vanish beyond even your powers to dredge up.'

'They won't.'

Sorokin, conscious of her stare, continued to toy with the card. 'What's Rakove to you, Mistress Voronova?'

Melita tried to affect nonchalance, although it was far too late for that. 'Do you care?'

Sorokin drew out the silence for several rapid beats of Melita's heart, then shrugged. 'I suppose not.' The ganglord tossed the loc-ref to her like a card sharp, and Melita plucked it from the air. She had him.

Melita caught the tremor in her hand as it started, but too late to stop the surge of sensation that overtook her.

The control stave for the agony collar was in Rakove's pocket. She was inside his mind, and she could feel the bulge of the stave against her hip. The hatred polluting his thoughts was a bitter heat, a fever that set her limbs trembling as much as the collar's barbs. There was nothing about her that he considered human, no shred of pity or guilt for the torment he inflicted. What pity he had was for himself, forced to taint his soul by proximity to her abhuman existence.

She tensed, mewling pleas rising to her lips, as he withdrew the stave and thumbed it on.

Sorokin was still talking. 'I have four men keeping an eye on him. Don't kill any of them.'

Melita breathed out, trying to control the violent shivering in her chest. She sensed Edi place a hand against the armchair's back, as close as he dared to a comforting grip. Melita leant away from him and instead pressed a thumb against the edge of the card.

Rakove had lost. She had freed Alim, and now she would trap him in his own cage. She would show him where the limits of *her* mercy lay.

If Sorokin noticed her distraction, he didn't comment on it. 'Do you know why I'm giving Rakove to you? Other than the fact that he brought a witch onto my ground, and I won't harbour any man who trifles with their kind.'

It took her a moment to stammer a reply. 'Why?' Melita itched to leave, to escape the stink of blood and sweat and the changeable warlord whose word was law.

'Because you asked.' He drained his glass, placed it on the table between them and flicked it onto its side, where it rolled back and forth. 'I let you learn I had him, but you'd have found out eventually. You're a smart one.'

Melita was still too caught up in the aftermath of the memory to register his compliment.

'But you came here to ask me for him. I like that. It shows respect. Shows we understand one another.'

The old man picked up his glass, turning it one way and

another in the greasy light. 'But, on the other hand, the Valt-teri sent you. Not that any of the top men would ever come here themselves – I've made my peace with that. But they have an army of faceless worms to fetch and carry for them, and yet they sent you. Why'd you think that is?'

Melita knew exactly why, and it had nothing to do with Sorokin. It had been a test. The cartel had adopted her into their organisation because she'd been the one to find Alim when every other organ of their will had failed, and because she had been desperate enough to sell her skills to them.

The test hadn't been to track Rakove down – her masters had been entirely confident that she was capable of that. No, the true test had been this night, in whether she could acquire him and for what price. They had given her a free hand to spend as she had to because their coffers were that deep and their wroth that great, but she would be judged on what she had given away in return. It was impossible to know how well she had done by that metric – she was sure that Sorokin's list of demands would represent an extortionate price for the sale of one man.

Sorokin needed to hear none of this. She forced a smile. 'Because they knew you'd like me, Messr Sorokin.'

He laughed at that, with a sound like a canid's bark. 'That could be it, right enough.'

He lifted the decanter and poured himself another measure. 'Go on then, clear off with your prize. Let me see if I can't sal-vage something from this evening.'

Melita stood, grateful to be away, still shaken by the flash of memory and the fear of almost losing Edi to the pit.

She clutched the card in her hand. She had stumbled at almost every hurdle Sorokin had placed in her path. She was leaving with what she had come for only because he had wanted to give it away. She had failed by almost every measure, except the one that mattered.

Sorokin rapped his glass against the decanter's side to stop her as she reached the door. 'Good to see you, Mistress Voronova. Until next you need something.'

Melita said nothing, and slipped out of the box.

The previous day's storm had not abated, and the sound of freezing rain breaking against the groundcar's bodywork was the only sound in Melita's world.

She and Edi sat inside Katuschka's carefully maintained interior, two blocks from the loc-ref Sorokin had provided. The Valtteri had moved quickly, marshalling their considerable resources to meet Sorokin's price. A well-guarded convoy had rumbled across the Rustwater Canal a few hours earlier, loaded with the future of the Spoil's hesitant restoration.

Now, all that was left was to collect what they had bought.

Her vambrace pinged as Oriel registered the Valtteri's approach. She was wearing the lattice, her home-made rig for transporting the guardian servo-skull. The chromed skull squatted on her shoulder, its needler lurking at the corner of her sight, its suite of sensors feeding information to the curved data-slate that was clamped around her forearm.

They came in two of their enormous Shiiv Hegemons, each closer in size to an enforcer riot-wagon than a civilian groundcar. Their huge flanks showed the insignia of the Reisiger Company, a band of mercenaries who handled much of the cartel's security and related activities.

Melita and Edi had no role in what was to come, but there had never been any question that she would be there for Rakove's capture.

The two Hegemons came to a stop at the end of the street, surprisingly quiet for vehicles of such size. The rear of one of the groundcars opened and a quartet of mercenaries emerged. With professional efficiency, they trotted towards the hab-block's door, which was opened for them by an unseen figure within. They disappeared inside.

The seconds ticked by, agonisingly slowly.

Melita couldn't sit idle. She opened the groundcar's door and leant out, and the servo-skull detached from the lattice with a purr of its suspensors. With a flurry of tapped commands, she sent the skull up into the darkness, pursuing the mercenaries who had begun their climb through the levels of the hab-block, raindrops rolling from its silver plating.

Watching through the skull's thermal sensor on her vambrace, Melita could follow the progress of the Valtteri men as they rose through the hab-block's stairwell. Other smears of colour showed residents retreating into their rooms, no doubt fearing the sudden tramp of heavy bootsteps outside their habs.

Melita panned up. The first of the Valtteri men had reached the third floor, and they were evidently stacking up outside the target hab. Inside were a clutch of figures, but Melita had no way of knowing which was Rakove. They were evidently sitting in the hab's communal area. She made a note to try to speak to the gangers who had been Rakove's minders – anything he might have told them could be relevant to tracing his elusive backer.

One of the shapes twitched around, its limbs a smear of colour as it stood. There was just enough time for dread to settle in Melita's stomach, and then gunfire shattered the night.

Melita's head rose on instinct towards the sound, in the same moment that Edi pressed her protectively down into her seat. She struggled under his weight, desperate to know what was happening.

More shots rang out. The harsh bark of a large-calibre stub pistol and the chatter of autoguns. She awkwardly twisted her body to bring her vambrace up in front of her and refocused the imagifier. Melita switched from the thermal sensor to Oriel's picter, but the skull saw nothing but the flash of multiple muzzle flares.

'Fuck!'

She pulled herself from beneath Edi's weight and pushed open the groundcar's door. She leapt out and raced the length of the block. She rounded the corner, almost falling on the slick, broken paving.

The mercenaries were emerging from the hab-block, surrounded by others who had appeared from the Hegemon's passenger compartments. Slung between two of the armoured bodies was a heavy-set figure, knees scraping on the steps, head slumped forward to almost touch the rockcrete.

Melita ran on, reaching for the laspistol holstered beneath her shoulder. She struggled to clear it from the synthleather, swore as she stumbled, and then stopped short as one of the mercenaries stepped into her path.

'Out of the way!' All rational thought had fled with the first gunshot. The Valtteri's need for what Rakove knew had ceased to matter, if it ever had to her. Melita would kill him, here and now. For Alim, for herself. For all his crimes, against her and whomever else Rakove had wronged in his brutal life.

But he was already dead.

The mercenaries laid Rakove on the street, blood flowing into the puddles of acrid rainwater.

Melita gaped, thoughts misfiring to the rapid tempo of wasted adrenaline. 'What the hells happened?'

The mercenaries ignored her, busying themselves with unloading their guns and pulling off their armour. They seemed far from happy – one of them would have to explain to the Valtteri's executors how they had so catastrophically failed at what should have been the simple collection of an unarmed man. But first they would have to explain it to her.

'Well?'

One of the Reisiger men stopped peeling the sections of plate from his chest. 'The target grabbed the weapon of one of the gangers that were with him. We had to drop him.'

An overwhelming weight settled on her shoulders. She'd hoped to feel a measure of relief, but all she felt was frustration. The Valtteri's questions would go unanswered – whoever had supported Rakove's operation would evade their grasp and perhaps make use of some other unfortunate to try again. Alim's torturer was dead, but justice would have seen him suffer as Melita knew the boy had suffered. A quick death was not revenge enough for her.

'By the damned Throne!' Melita tore the data-slate from her arm and hammered it into the asphalt. Shards of plex and arcane electronics flew away into the darkness. The mercenary turned back to the Hegemon's interior, ignoring Melita's outburst.

She suddenly became aware of Edi's grip on her shoulder, pulling her away. Melita shrugged him off and turned, choosing Edi to be the target of her frustrated rage and confusion.

'Why were you going to fight last night? Back at the joy house?' She'd been holding in the question for the entire day, but now it erupted unbidden. The former sanctioner said nothing.

'Answer me.'

'Because you needed this,' he said finally. He turned to look at her, face streaked with rain. Melita felt oddly alarmed by the strength of feeling that filled his eyes.

'Whatever that witch did to you...' Edi looked like he wanted to spit, but instead he silently made the sign of the aquila over his chest. 'Whatever it did, it got inside your head. I've watched you. You always work like you're possessed, but these past months you've been manic. Hyper-focused, like only one thing existed. You needed to see this done, and I wanted to help you do it.'

Melita gaped. Without a word spoken between them on the subject for two months, Edi had cut to the core of her turmoil. She felt exposed, laid bare just as she had been by Alim's casual penetration of her mind.

He was right, of course. It might not have been the catharsis she had hoped for, but she had needed to see Rakove broken, one way or another. She glanced back to watch the Valtteri men load the body into one of their vehicles.

'What do you want to do now?' Edi asked.

Melita sighed. She knew it was too much to hope that she would be rid of Alim's implanted memories. They were a part of her now, a parallel life of trauma and fear that she would have to endure, just as the psyker had. But perhaps, if she was lucky, she might finally have a night of unbroken rest.

'Take me home.'

SLATE RUN

MIKE BROOKS

I frowned in confusion. 'A what?'

'A *lifeward* job,' Mirea Scairns said. She took a swig from her bottle, then pulled a face and looked at it suspiciously. 'Throne of Terra, what *is* this?'

'Booze,' I replied flatly. 'It's all I've got right now.'

'Did the label corrode, or is no one prepared to take responsibility for making it?'

'Did you come here just to insult my hosting?' I said, not a little testily.

'No,' Mirea said. 'Like I said, I heard about a job that might interest you. And Angel knows it looks like you need the work.'

I bristled, but she was right. I'd been seeing more of the inside of my very modest hab-unit lately than I would have liked, keeping my head down after the Targus Syndicate tried to have me killed and I responded by blowing them sky-high and murdering Tanid Targus in his own manse. However, I was now down to carb-bars and the nameless rotgut about which Mirea was so dubious.

She'd been part of Targus, a sacrificial rat who would have been collateral damage, but we both survived, and she helped me take them down. We split the profits from robbing Tanid's place – such as they were – and whatever she did with her share had paid dividends. She was young, and a touch too naive when I met her. I wasn't quite sure what she was now, but she'd had the corners knocked off her fast, and was making her own way and forging her own connections.

She was one of very few people who knew where I lived, as opposed to contacting me through go-betweens, message drops or my known haunts. I was suddenly wondering if this was a mistake.

'You haven't mentioned me by name, have you?' I asked. Mirea tutted a laugh and shook her head.

'I know better than that, Sorena. Haven't mentioned you at all. Got asked if I knew of any ex-Militarum who fancied playing watchdog for a gilded at a fancy party. Apparently it's the fad to have your lifeward look like they were a soldier, and the Contessa Taverlinn wants the real thing.'

'A one-off?' I asked. 'Wouldn't she have an actual lifeward?'

'Maybe they don't look the part,' Mirea replied with a shrug. 'Although I heard the contessa took a big hit from the Korsk incident, so maybe she can only hire someone on a night-by-night basis.'

I grimaced. Half of Korsk district had been flattened when a starship of some sort – or possibly more than one, by some rumours – crashed into it. Even here, in neighbouring Urgeyena, the impact ruptured water mains, brought down power conduits and caused far too many buildings to shift and sprout cracks. The vid-feeds had endless coverage of rescue efforts involving tunnelling equipment, humanitarian relief and rebuilding projects. They didn't mention the vicious conflicts as trade combines and criminal syndicates – the Vorozny, the Lowella Collective, the

Opira and others – smelled rival blood and went in for the kill. It was all too easy to believe that a gilded family whose assets were in the wrong place at the wrong time might have suddenly found themselves very low on slate.

Still, all things were relative. A down-on-their-luck gilded probably had more value on their person at any one moment than was in my entire hab-unit.

'A one-night deal, as lifeward for a gilded?' I said, thinking it over. I'd had worse jobs – my entire Astra Militarum career, for one – and I was hardly likely to run into vengeful remnants of Targus, or its disappointed business partners, at a high-society party. And as Mirea had so tactlessly mentioned, I did need the slate. 'Yeah, I'm interested.'

'Great,' Mirea said. 'I'll set it up.'

I eyed her. 'You get commission for finding someone, don't you?'

Her smug expression was so entrenched it even survived her next swig of booze.

Despite my appearance, I'm no stranger to the world of the privileged – I was chauffeur for a Navigator House for a while, and so far as a well-to-do Nav House is concerned, 'taste' or 'restraint' are concepts for paupers. So for all the crenellated splendour of Taverlinn Hall, a towering monstrosity of dark carved stone and intricate metalwork, I was not as impressed as someone else in my position might have been. The automated gates opened smoothly to let my groundcar into the vehicle bay, where maintenance servitors waited to attend to it. The aide with the Taverlinn crest on his breast who greeted and ushered me into the main building had the exact sort of oiled hair and waxen expression I would expect, all personality subsumed and nothing but service remaining. However, I could see the alcoves where statues or carvings should stand,

and bare walls once covered by paintings or tapestries. The gilded liked physical things, not holo-art – it was tangible, and implied exclusivity through scarcity.

In this case, so scarce that it wasn't here at all. Somehow, I didn't think this was down to minimalism so much as trying to keep the coffers full.

'How long have you worked here?' I asked the aide. He was probably a bit older than me, mid-thirties by standard measurement and late-thirties in Alecto years. He barely glanced sideways at me.

'My family have served the Taverlinn estate for five generations.'

What do you say to that? I had no idea whether he viewed this job as an inherited curse or a glorious birthright.

'Your uniform for this evening is laid out within,' he said, stopping at a door. It was made of real wood, but with only simple panelling and no decoration, clearly a room for the use of servants. 'It conforms exactly to the measurements provided by your representative.'

'Mirea?' I said. I resented her being thought of as my representative but decided not to engage. I entered, closing the door on his slightly disapproving expression.

The chamber in question was as large as my entire hab-unit, with a significantly more sizeable bed than the roll-once-and-fall-off-it cot in my dorm. Even here, though, the slate-pinching was clear – there was no furniture other than the bed, which was not even possessed of sheets. My 'uniform', as the aide had called it, was laid out atop the bare mattress, and I gave it a quick once-over.

In truth, it wasn't awful. It wasn't my old Formund Scorpions dark green and purple – it wasn't any sort of Astra Militarum uniform at all – but you could see the inspiration. The deep navy chased with silver thread, the cut of the trousers, the collar and the buttons, the cuffs; it was what gilded who'd never seen an actual trooper might think a dress uniform looked like and therefore would commission a tailor to make.

I stripped off my casuals and tried it on. It fit perfectly and was easily the best-quality clothing I'd ever worn, even when working for the Navs. The shirt was thicker and stiffer than I'd anticipated, but this wasn't the bulk of a flak jacket – I'd have put money on there being some form of armour-mesh in there, which doesn't come cheap. The boots were real grox leather, supple and strong, the sort that's the envy of a platoon if the Munitorum actually coughs a pair up for some lucky individual. I won't lie, I wondered whether I could take it with me after the engagement, given it had been fitted for me *anyway*...

The aide hadn't moved by the time I emerged, and I wondered how he perceived me. Ex-soldier and current gangland fixer, someone who could, if she chose, very likely kill him within a matter of seconds? Or downclave trash, brought in from outside and therefore inevitably inferior? Someone there to perform a function, essentially nothing more than a servitor inexplicably allowed to keep its powers of cognition? I didn't know – his face gave nothing away. He was a servitor himself in some senses, moulded by more subtle tools than the brain-wipers of the Adeptus Mechanicus.

He led me over intricately patterned carpets which had seen too many years and too few cleanse-scrubs, and floors of mosaic tiles, many of which were now worn away or missing entirely. House Taverlinn had not just been the victim of a recent financial disaster – the decline had clearly been going on for a while.

Some parts still maintained their grandeur, however. The aide ushered me into a sitting room richly furnished with chaise longues and armchairs, hand-carved side tables, and padded footrests. A sideboard held a selection of finely cut glasses and decanters filled with different-coloured spirits. At least, I assumed they were spirits – perhaps they were coloured water, simply an embellishment. All the same, it seemed some dregs of wealth remained, and I could easily imagine that guests were kept to a small area of the building, not allowed to stray into the decaying greater whole.

'The contessa will join you in a moment,' the aide told me, moving towards a door in the far wall. 'Before she does, she instructed me to ask you to brace yourself for her appearance.'

I frowned. 'What?'

'Brace yourself for her appearance,' the aide repeated, speaking more slowly and clearly, as though it were uncultured unfamiliarity with his manner of speech which had caused my confusion, rather than the nonsense of his words.

'Fine, consider me braced,' I said, and he began to turn the handle. 'I've seen squadmates get blown apart and watched my major get eaten by something I don't even have a name for. I don't know what makes you think I'd be worried by–
What the fuck?'

'He did tell you to brace yourself,' said the Contessa Taverlinn from the doorway.

Contessa Taverlinn was the interesting side of plain, in that none of her features in and of themselves were particularly notable – she did not have large, languid eyes, a delicate rosebud of a mouth or cheekbones that caught the light – but when you put them together, you ended up with a face that many would consider worth getting to know. Her hair was an artful mess of spun-gold tresses – not blonde but actual shining gold, which had to be a treatment of some kind – and her eyes were ringed with dark powder in which glittered motes of silver. Her neck, chin and lower cheeks were encased in a high collar of a reflective, apparently semi-rigid black substance which fanned out over her collarbones to meet the fabric of her dress, mainly luxurious black velora, with two panels of night-green sateen rising vertically on either side of the lace-adorned front. Her arms were bare from the shoulder down, but her hands and forearms were shrouded in black gloves, over which she wore a mere two rings. She looked every inch the noblewoman, in fact, but the golden hair and fancy clothes couldn't fool me.

'Imora Tarsh,' I said, through stiff lips and a frozen throat. The combat knife tucked into one of my new boots suddenly seemed very far away. 'What by the nine devils is this?'

Imora Tarsh, sister of Piotr Tarsh and daughter of Cratton Tarsh. The Tarshes were criminals – violent, murderous and very successful criminals. Piotr and some of his thugs had tried to jump a cargo I was carrying, and I'd shot him dead before I even realised who he was. That was what nearly got me killed, because the Tarshes went into business with Targus and – so I surmised – asked for my death as a welcome gift. That ended badly for Targus, and I'd hoped Cratton would take the hint.

More fool me.

'That's "Contessa Taverlinn" to you, Varlon,' Imora Tarsh said. Her accent was pure Salt City drawl, absolutely laughable in these surroundings. She was watching me intently, and as the seconds dragged by and a host of gun-wielding goons failed to burst into the room, I recovered a little of my badly damaged poise. Imora was always reckoned to be the smart one of old man Cratton's children. Too smart to put herself for no good reason into a room with a woman who could kill her, and who might think that Imora wished her ill. There had to be more to this than met the eye.

'All right, I'll play,' I said, buying time while I tried to remember my route back through the house. 'You're a contessa now. That's a thing that just happens.'

'It doesn't "just happen",' Imora said with a sniff. 'But everyone's got a price, and if you're a gilded family who threw their dwindling resources into the Korsk district and ended up bankrupt after the disaster, that price can be surprisingly affordable. They cried, but the pain of losing their status to low-blood scum like me was apparently more appealing than the very real pain their creditors were threatening.'

I blinked. 'You're… *actually* a contessa?'

'Only recently,' Imora admitted. 'And I haven't publicised it. Hence why that Scairns girl had no idea who was sending out enquiries about hiring a lifeward for an evening. I specifically wanted you.'

'You wanted *me?*' My thoughts caught up with my mouth. 'Hang on, this is actually a job? You're expecting me to come and be your lifeward after you tried to have me *killed?*'

'That was father,' Imora corrected me sternly. 'He couldn't just let Piotr's death go, but I talked him into having Targus take care of it. They turned out to be a bad business decision for us, but at least we quickly found out how incompetent they were. I suppose we owe you thanks for that, of a sort. And you *are* ex-Militarum, and I know very well how capable you are, so…' She spread her hands, as though that explained everything.

I rolled my shoulders, unable to believe that trouble wasn't about to start at any moment, although Imora seemed very lacking in the sort of bitter invective I would have expected. 'A lot of people would take their brother's death personally.'

'Piotr was a brute, and far too fond of the blunt end of business,' Imora replied. 'We have grunts for that sort of thing, but he wanted to get blood on his hands. You shot his brains out instead and left me as father's heir apparent.' She shrugged. 'A good result for me. Father, as he's far too fond of telling everyone, carved his empire out of the guts of those he grew up with, but he doesn't have vision. We can be so much more than just the kings and queens of the gutters and manufactoria. That's what I'm trying to start tonight – I need to circulate in society.'

Someone claiming that Cratton Tarsh lacked vision was usually likely to shortly lack any vision of their own, but perhaps it was different if you were his daughter. I tried to think this through.

Firstly, Imora had made no moves to have me killed. Indeed, she'd had clothes made for me which included armour and had given a plausible reason for why she bore me no particular ill will for Piotr's death.

Secondly, unless something extremely odd was occurring, given that she was dressed in fancy clothes in Taverlinn Hall, I had to assume that she was actually a contessa now.

Thirdly, she clearly still had *some* money, as witnessed by my clothes, her clothes and the continued presence of the House Taverlinn aide (whose generalised disapproval now made more sense, given what he'd seen happen to the family that his own had served for five generations and to whom he now had to answer). It was entirely possible I could get paid after all.

Fourthly, this would be a *ridiculously* complicated way to have me killed, and watching Imora Tarsh try to fit in with Varangantua's gilded was going to be a sight to see.

I straightened. The familiarity of the clothes made it easy to fall back into the rhythms of the military, so I placed my hands behind my back and faced directly ahead in my own version of the aide's blank-eyed compliance. If Imora Tarsh was paying for an ex-Guard lifeward, an ex-Guard lifeward was what she would get, especially if it saved me having to make conversation with her.

'Where to, milady?'

Izkhana Surumir Fareltan's estate was everything the Taverlinns' should have been, and more. Not an inch of the wide, rolling lawns was untended, not a leaf out of place on the ornamental trees. The sun had dipped below the horizon and so the grounds were lit by the warm glow of heat-lumens, which cast pools of liquid golden light and patches of dusky shadow. I found my fists clenching around the steering wheel of Imora's groundcar – the *Contessa Taverlinn's* groundcar – as we purred gently up the long drive.

'You seem tense,' Imora observed from the back seat. There was a mirrored partition to give the gilded privacy from their driver, but to my annoyance, she hadn't raised it.

'It's the waste,' I said coldly. 'There are whole habclaves that don't have power, or if they do then the people inside can't afford to keep warm. And these bastards dump all this heat into the night just so they can flaunt some extra flesh?'

'That's the whole point of being gilded, isn't it?' Imora said. 'You've got to be wasteful, or people will think you can't afford the basics.' She snorted. 'It's two waterfront toughs comparing knife lengths, just on a much grander scale.'

'And you bought your way into this?' I asked. I didn't bother to hide my derision – most of it was for the gilded, but I had some to spare for Imora Tarsh.

'Darling,' Imora said, and suddenly her voice dropped the Salt City twang and became something far smoother. 'The society doesn't interest me, the *opportunity* does. The gilded commit larceny that would turn my father green with envy, and most of the Lex won't even look in their direction for it. Would you believe that this evening is a slate run for those *poor souls* made homeless and destitute by the ship crash?' She laughed nastily, and her voice reverted to normal. 'But most of the money will disappear into back pockets, or efforts that never actually happen, or equipment produced for one-tenth the stated cost that doesn't work properly. If we tried to pull that shit in the backstreets, we'd find ourselves in the gutters with our livers missing.'

I couldn't bring myself to reply. Emperor knew that my hands were far from clean in matters pertaining to the Lex, but that was a matter of survival – I could die from starvation, or I could sign up for a manufactorum or similar and work myself to death within a decade, or I could stray into the world of crime enough to keep myself fed, clothed and housed. On the other hand, I was an off-worlder who had come here from the Astra Militarum, where death might be waiting every morning, but at least until it arrived you had the right to a bedroll and rations. For Imora, who'd grown up in Varangantua, I could understand the mindset that since *someone* was making a fortune with immunity from the sanctioners, it might as well be you.

I pulled the groundcar to a halt on an expanse of gravel already littered with expensive vehicles. It seemed that rather than being ushered away into a parking garage until needed, the attendees' modes of transport were here to be judged just as much as their owners were. It was my first time driving anything as expensive as a Sullaina – it looked fancy, but the handling was only average and the engine underpowered for the size, by my reckoning – and it was still outclassed by most of the others on display.

'Is that a platinum-plated Marvus?' I asked incredulously, taking in the sleek lines of probably the most expensive make of civilian groundcar on the planet, two bays over.

'Don't gawk,' Imora said. She had switched back into her aristocratic voice, all carefully modulated vowel sounds and light consonants. 'Your role this evening is to remain expressionless even at the most outrageous displays of wealth, in order to imply that you regularly see similar extravagances in my employ.'

'I thought my role was to be your lifeward,' I said, looking over my shoulder at her.

'Your role is to make me look good,' Imora said. 'No one here has any *need* of a lifeward – it would be an insult to the host if we felt that. The point is to show that we can hire someone lethal and pay them well enough to follow us around like a tame canid. It's all appearances.' She grimaced, and I realised to my surprise that she actually shared my distaste with the whole thing. For her, this really was just the logical next step in the journey out of the gutter that her father had started. 'Look, all you have to do is follow me around and look bored but alert. Do that, and you earn your slate.'

'Fine by me.'

I got out of the Sullaina and opened Imora's door for her. She alighted without even looking at me, but I'd had several years of being ignored by senior officers, so I was used to it. I fell in behind her as she made her way towards a gathering of shining, glittering dandies beneath the drooping branches of a truly enormous silver zillow – the cost of keeping such a tree alive in Varangantua would be staggering, and it was one amongst many – but we were brought up short by two liveried servants.

'I have an invitation,' Imora said, her tone one of quiet steel wrapped in soft outrage, but the left-hand servant just shook her head and pulled out a handheld weapon-wand.

'Standard precaution, milady,' she said in the leaden voice of one who has a job to do and is going to do it no matter how much high-born fury is directed her way. Her sweep of Imora came up negative; her partner's sweep of me unsurprisingly registered my combat blade, which was now sheathed on my left hip, as well as the laspistol holstered on my right. It was Mons pattern, but a high-quality one, probably worth a month of meals if I sold it on the street. It and the gun belt had come from the Taverlinn armoury.

'What are you doing?' I asked as the servant brought out two thick, bright red bands of what looked like sturdy, flexible plastek and reached for my belt. Imora shot me a look, but being protective of my weapons was perfectly in character for my role – which was lucky, because it was going to happen whether she liked it or not.

'All weapons must be peace-bonded,' the servant said, although he at least paused in the face of my glare.

I raised my eyebrows. 'And if there is a threat to milady's life?'

'The izkhana is able to release all peace bonds by carrier wave,' the servant said. He glanced at Imora. 'This is a condition of entry, milady.'

Imora waved a hand dismissively and looked away, apparently not wishing to waste her breath on a mere flunkey. The servant, well versed in interpreting gilded expressions and gestures, took that as consent and locked the bonds in place to secure my knife in its sheath and my pistol in its holster. I tested them both and nodded as though to express satisfaction that he had at least completed his task competently, but the truth was that I felt suddenly uncomfortable. I never went anywhere without my combat knife, a Formund Scorpions 'Stinger', and although it was still technically on my person, the inability to draw it was already weighing on my mind more than I would have anticipated.

Imora set off across the lawns without waiting to see whether I was done, and I shadowed her, doing my best to look boringly intimidating while I scanned our surroundings. The dark grounds were a nightmare from a lifeward's point of view – the deliberate aesthetic contrast between light and shade left any number of places where even an amateur assassin could lurk. The estate was protected by void shields – honest-to-Emperor void shields set up for a private dwelling! – with a narrow aperture at the gate for vehicles to come and go, but I had no idea whether they were calibrated to stop a person climbing over the boundary walls.

I tried to dismiss it as none of my business, but I had been

hired as a lifeward, even if the job was essentially being a per-
ambulatory ornament. Besides, what hadn't even occurred
to me as I'd been wrestling with the notion of Imora Tarsh
becoming a gilded and also *not* wanting to kill me was how
her father would react if something happened to her. He would
be out for blood, no question about it. The ranking of this job
in my brain abruptly dropped from 'profitable and worth the
risk' to 'do not touch with a dredge pole', but it was too late
to back out now.

Best make sure she didn't die, then.

The group of chattering, giggling gilded looked like they'd
clothed themselves in stars or shadows, depending on how
the mood had taken them. Their loose circle deformed slightly
as Imora approached, in the manner of a cluster of scab rats
when a new one arrives, at least until they've sniffed each
other's cheeks and arseholes to work out who the new arrival
is. I could sense the same sort of enquiry here, the narrowed
eyes, the unconsciously bared teeth instinctively disguised as a
smile, the shifting of position to make themselves more or less
obvious, depending on rank and temperament. Imora was right
about the whole thing being essentially the same as any gathering of gangers coming together in a revel house, swaggering
and bragging and keeping their weapons obvious.

'A good evening to you all,' Imora said softly, as though her
arrival were nothing to remark upon. I appreciated her playing
it cautious at first, but it seemed that was not going to work –
several of the gilded turned away from her, some with obvious
snorts of disdain. The ones who still acknowledged her seemed
amusedly curious, disdainful or a mixture of both.

Imora was not the only one coming under scrutiny. The
gilded all had lifewards, and *they* were inspecting *me*. I glanced
between them, returning the favour, and sized them up.

Mainly big, generally physically impressive. Mostly male and good-looking as well, or bordering on it – the image of the heroic Astra Militarum trooper as depicted on peeling recruitment posters or dragged out of their regiments to appear in vid-captures. I dismissed half of them out of hand as nothing more than showpieces there to look good in embarrassing amounts of gold braid – they lacked the posture or alertness to be the real thing. One or two of the remainder struck me as dressed-up street gangers, twitchy and uncomfortable in these surrounds but possibly handy in a fight.

Then there were a handful who probably were professional, trained lifewards, maybe two of which were actually former Militarum. Both of those were men, one with warm bronze skin and his black hair worn so short that his scalp showed through it, and the other pale and lean, with a ring of blue tattoos around his left eye and his red-gold hair shaved and braided in a queue. The redhead was attached to a young man in a beautifully patterned long vest and loose trousers of diamond-silk which might have cost as much as my entire hab-block, and whose supercilious expression directed towards Imora gave the impression that he was primarily composed of nostrils and teeth. The other lurked behind a woman whose diaphanous, billowing gown of the palest ice blue accentuated the curves of her exquisitely tailored white bodystocking more than it obscured them, so she looked like some sort of cloud-wreathed winter goddess. She was regarding Imora with the expression one might give an eight-year-old announcing they'd just devised a way to improve the stability of Geller fields.

'And who might you be?' the diamondsilk gilded demanded, his tone suggesting he felt the need to disinfect his mouth after addressing her.

'Contessa Taverlinn,' Imora replied. She looked nowhere near as furious as I knew she must be, but the Tarshes were used to being sneered at – they just gutted you in the shadows for it afterwards.

'My dear,' the woman said, 'I have met the Contessa Taverlinn many times at such events, and I can say with assurance that you are not her, and nor are you either of her daughters.'

'You met the former contessa,' Imora said levelly. 'Perhaps you had not heard that the title changed hands?'

'Ugh, you *bought* it?' the man declared, his words dripping with quite genuine horror.

'God-Emperor, no!' Imora laughed, a more delicate sound than I thought a Tarsh was capable of making. 'I was privileged enough to be in a position to help the family out of an unfortunate situation, and they were so grateful that they positively *insisted* I accept their rank.'

I couldn't prevent my lips from twitching at that piece of first-grade groxshit. The man spun on his heel and stalked off, and most of the rest of the crowd began to subtly fade away with the air of scab rats who'd decided that the new arrival wasn't an easy meal after all and not otherwise worth their time. The winter goddess, however, seemed amused at Imora's riposte.

'Dovolira was always a little incautious, I thought,' she mused. 'It is a shame that she found herself out of her depth, but these things happen. Eja, Margravaine Peralka.' She extended one hand; Imora took it and pressed her lips to it.

'Imora.'

The margravaine returned the gesture. 'Not entirely without manners, then. Merchant-combine background?'

'Nothing so respectable, I am afraid,' Imora said, with a flash of her teeth. It was a daring ploy, to hint at being an outright criminal, but perhaps the double bluff would work in company like this simply because gilded would never believe it. Peralka smiled anyway, as though Imora were a charming rogue rather than the remorseless killer I knew her to be.

'You seem interesting, dear, so I will give you a tip. At such events, it is courtesy to present yourself to the host first.' She extended one swirling sleeve to point towards yet another enormous tree. I'd seen more trees than I could count during my Militarum career – unlike Varangantuan natives, for whom they were both novelty and status symbol – but only as cover for either us or the enemy, so I wasn't great at identifying them. However, the dark red, almost black leaves of this one reminded me of a blood oak. 'The izkhana is over there,' Peralka continued. 'If you go now, you may reach her before she notices your gaffe.'

'Much obliged,' Imora said, ducking her head. She strode off in the direction indicated, and I followed her. It did not escape my notice as we crossed the grass that the diamond-silk gilded was now talking earnestly in another small group a short distance away, and cast an ugly glance in our direction as he did so.

'That went better than it might have,' Imora said in a low voice.

'You do understand that if someone calls the sanctioners, I'm letting them have you?' I murmured in return.

'Call the sanctioners?' Imora said, amused. 'No one here would do something so… *crass.*'

If Margravaine Peralka was a winter goddess, then Izkhana Surumir Fareltan was a deity of summer. The warm brown skin of her neck and upper arms was encircled by thick gold torques, her fingers dripped with golden rings and her wrists with golden bracelets, and her white hair was pinned in place with a fan of golden needles to make her head look like a sunburst. Her gown, a tight sleeveless bodice above a hemispherical pleated skirt, was a rich, vibrant green chased with yet more gold. Even predisposed to dislike her as I was, given the massive waste I'd already witnessed, I had to admit that she looked amazing.

She cast no more than a glance at the curtseying Imora, and lazily extended one hand to be kissed. Notably, and unlike the margravaine, Fareltan merely withdrew her hand afterwards rather than returning the gesture.

'Contessa Taverlinn, milady,' Imora murmured. The izkhana simply nodded, and waved her hand in dismissal – not a banishment as such, simply an acknowledgement that courtesy had been fulfilled and Imora could now wander and mingle as she pleased, so long as it was somewhere else.

'Back to your new friend?' I asked quietly as Imora withdrew. I was more than a little amused at her getting so thoroughly rebuffed by high society in general, but felt I managed to hide it fairly well.

'It would hardly do to look so desperate,' Imora replied, barely moving her lips. It probably wasn't done for a gilded to be carrying on conversation with their lifeward, after all. 'No, I think that group over there–'

'You!'

The word was loaded with all the sharpness and malice of a gunshot. I whipped around towards it with the urgency of the lifeward I was pretending to be and stifled a groan as I saw diamondsilk and his red-headed guard approaching, flanked by two more gilded and their attendants.

'*You* are the one who drove my dear Dovolira away?' one of the newcomers bellowed. He was an older man, with grey moustaches that looked as thick as my wrist, and he leant on a cane carved from a wood so dark it seemed to drink in the light. 'I will not stand by and accept this! I demand satisfaction!'

Imora looked perplexed. 'I beg your pardon, sir. You are challenging me to… a duel?'

I winced. Imora might not favour the blunt end of business so much as her brother had, but no Tarsh clanner was a stranger to wetting their knives. She would carve up this grandstanding fool without breaking a sweat, or riddle him with holes, or whatever manner of combat he was proposing. Part of me was aghast at the prospect, but another part secretly wanted it. I had no fondness for Imora Tarsh, but the sheer outrage these people exhibited at an outsider gaining access to their privileged world made me want to see her break down the walls they tried to throw up and laugh at them.

'Typical low-blood ignorance,' the man said with a sneer. 'Ankov!'

His own lifeward stepped towards me and removed his jacket, just as Imora and I realised what was going on.

Imora turned to me. 'I didn't know they make their lifewards fight like snapfangs in the betting pits,' she hissed, in what I realised with shock was actually an apology of sorts.

'You didn't think that after you strong-armed a gilded out of her title, one of her friends wasn't going to take issue with it?' I shot back.

'I didn't think she had any,' Imora admitted, with a glance over her shoulder.

My first instinct was to refuse. There was nothing in it for me, and no actual threat to Imora's life. If she left here with her reputation in ruins before her high-society life had even begun, then that was no blood out of my veins, as we said back on Formund. However, other gilded were wandering over to see the show, lifewards in tow, and while I didn't give two shits about the aristocracy's opinions, I found that I didn't want to be seen as a coward by my supposed peers.

'Warp take it,' I muttered, and shucked off the armoured jacket Imora had provided, leaving me in a sleeveless vest and dress trousers.

My opponent – Ankov – was roughly my height but more heavily built, with a cushion of fat over functional muscle. He looked faintly disgusted by the whole affair but clearly wasn't going to go against his employer's orders. I couldn't get an easy read on him, so I erred on the side of caution and assumed he was dangerous until I saw evidence to the contrary.

'So how does this work?' I asked, stretching. 'First blood, or what?'

'Until unable or unwilling to continue!' the moustachioed gilded said, with no small amount of glee. I suppressed a grimace, because that was a recipe for broken bones or worse, but I had no time to reconsider my decision as Ankov came at me without warning.

I went to meet him, lunging to land a thrust kick in his midsection with the sole of my boot. The force of the impact brought him to a halt with a *whuff* of lost air but knocked me backwards to the ground. I rolled over and back to my feet as fast as I could, eager not to give him a chance to pounce on me. He came in more measured this time, firing a pair of left jabs at my face, then a right cross that I slapped aside. What I didn't see until too late was his left leg on the end of that combination, which landed just below my ribs and hurt like I'd been hit with a metal pipe – a sensation I was unfortunately familiar with.

Now it was my turn to be winded, hunched over to my right while I tried to suck in breath, but I had enough wherewithal to stamp downwards at his knee when he tried to follow up too eagerly. His leg buckled and he yelped in pain, and I slugged him in the jaw hard enough to put him on his backside on the grass and severely sting my knuckles. I hesitated – pile on top of him and put myself in the grasp of a larger, stronger opponent, or stand off but let him recover in his own time? – and that hesitation probably saved my life, because it was at that moment that the ground started to vibrate beneath our feet.

'Earthquake?' someone shouted, but it was too regular and rhythmic compared to the aftershocks triggered by the Korsk impact. Ankov tried to get up, then was jolted back down again as the vibrations increased in strength. He just had time to look confused before the ground gave way beneath him briefly, then erupted outwards in a searing blast of heat and whirling metal, vaporising and shredding him in under a second.

Everyone screamed and stumbled backwards, me included. It took me a moment to make sense of it – it looked like a tunnelling machine, such as had been used in Korsk when great swathes of workers were trapped under rubble or sheltering in tunnels that no longer had exits.

And it was not alone.

Two more burst out of the ground about fifty yards to each side of us, while another emerged behind me, at the base of the blood oak. The melta cutters on the front atomised the trunk with no more trouble than they'd had with the ground, and the giant tree began to fall towards us with an inexorable and deceptive slowness.

'Run!' I yelled, grabbing Imora's arm and hauling her after me, desperately trying to get out of the branches' impact shadow.

We failed. The tree's massive weight snapped the boughs that hit first and sent shards of wood flying in all directions, probably an entire hab-tower's worth of value smashed into splinters. I narrowly avoided being impaled by a branch as thick as my leg but was knocked to the ground by the sheer force of lesser ones. I experienced a moment of desperate panic, but despite cuts on my arms and forehead, I appeared to have escaped anything more severe than a battering. I struggled to free myself, hissing in frustration at the leaves slapping my face and the particles of bark working their way into my eyes, but froze when I heard the shouting and saw running figures carrying guns.

Gilded were screaming, and the sharp bark of an autogun – a single shot, fired in the air as a warning – made it clear that the new arrivals' weapons were not peace-bonded. Peering through branches, I saw one nobleman shot with a needler, while his lifeward was clubbed in the face with an autogun butt.

'What in the hells is going on?' I hissed at Imora, before remembering that she might not even still be alive. However, the branches behind me shifted slightly, and her hand found my wrist again.

'It must be the Vorozny,' Imora said, her voice low and tight. 'They've been getting bolder since Korsk – I heard they snatched a minor gilded or two for ransom – but nothing like this!'

I grimaced, but the question had to be asked. 'Not your doing, then?'

'I came here to make alliances, not enemies!' Imora snapped. 'Why by the nine devils would this be *my* doing?'

It would hardly make sense for Imora to put herself in a position where a stray round might strike her, so I tried to dial back my paranoia and consider things. We were largely out of sight where we were, certainly less obvious than the gilded currently being rounded up. The Vorozny wouldn't want to risk being captured by the security forces, which would almost certainly already be inbound – they'd want to snatch their prizes and withdraw as soon as possible. Perhaps we could just stay put?

'Sorena!'

I turned my head to tell Imora to keep her voice down, but the reason for her urgency quickly became clear.

Fire.

One of the heat-lumens that had been rigged up in the lower branches of this accursed blood oak must have smashed when the tree came down and had set light to the grass and the tree itself. It was spreading with ferocious speed, and I did not fancy our chances with it if we remained where we were.

The choice of facing an armed enemy or being burned alive

was no choice at all for a soldier. I began to fight forward and up, trying to force my way back to my feet without broadcasting to all and sundry that I was there. Thankfully, the panic sparked by the Vorozny's arrival and the fire meant no one was paying attention to shadows in the branches.

'Here!' Imora whispered. She was right behind me, and she pressed something soft but stiff into my hand – my armoured jacket, which she'd been holding when the fight started. I slipped it back on and reached for my weapons, only to find to my consternation that I still couldn't move them.

'What the–'

'They've already got the izkhana,' Imora murmured, reaching past my shoulder to point at where a distinctively golden and obviously drugged figure was being dragged limply between two Vorozny thugs. 'She didn't release the peace bonding in time.'

'We're dead,' I growled, looking back over my shoulder at the fire. I still knew which way I would rather die, but I would have preferred a fighting chance.

'They're coming this way!' Imora hissed. She dragged me back down to a crouch, then pressed so close that her breath tickled my ear. 'Can you take them?'

I blinked in surprise, then realised what she meant. The Vorozny dragging the izkhana were heading to the tunneller that had – presumably accidentally – felled the oak, and directly past us. If we could jump out and subdue them without getting killed, and find the control to release the peace bonds...

It was still a long shot, but it was better than burning to death.

I picked up a snapped-off branch and broke it so it was the length of my arm – I winced at the cracking noise, but the fire and general commotion seemed to cover it sufficiently. Then I crept forward, which involved a lot more stepping awkwardly over horizontal branches than I would have liked but got me to a point which I hoped would be close enough.

The Vorozny drew level with us, merely a few yards away. I could see the slumped head of the izkhana and the taut features of her captors, swearing at her and each other as one of them stood on her gown and caused them both to stumble. Then they were past, and I was slipping after them.

My adrenaline had spiked when I realised I was going to fight Ankov and had only risen with the arrival of the Vorozny and nearly being crushed by a tree, so I was riding the wave of it now, in the zone where everything moves in slow motion. I brought my makeshift club up with one step and down on the skull of the left-hand Vorozny with the next.

The impact to the back of his head dropped him, and the strong green wood didn't split in my hands, so as the izkhana slumped to one side I was able to smash my weapon across into the second thug's face. I heard his nose crack, and he went down with a cry of pain and a splatter of blood. He tried to raise his autopistol, but I slammed the branch down onto the hand that held it, knocking it from his grasp. I didn't dare try to scrabble for it, so I stamped repeatedly on his face in a desperate panic until he stopped moving.

When I turned around, Imora was withdrawing her thumbs from the eye sockets of the other thug with an expression of grim satisfaction. I hadn't even realised she'd followed me.

'I hope you know what the peace-bonder looks like,' I told her tightly, crouching down and grabbing the autopistol now its owner was in no condition to object. I didn't want to give us away by firing before I had to, but the first notice I was likely to get that we'd been seen was someone shooting me, so I wasn't particularly relaxed.

'Probably one of the bracelets,' Imora muttered. 'She gave me her right hand, so she's right-handed, so it'll be on the left wrist... ah!' She pressed her thumb onto a square ornament. It clicked inwards, but the bonds on my weapons did not deactivate.

'Her thumb?' I suggested urgently.

'I was going to try that next,' Imora snapped. It took her a couple of seconds that felt like weeks to manoeuvre the izkhana's right thumb onto the bracelet and press it down.

There was the faintest buzz from my weapons belt, and the bonds fell away. I passed the autopistol to my left hand and drew the Mons-pattern with my right, feeling a bit like a gunfighter from one of the unfeasible holo-vids that Mirea had insisted I watch on a couple of occasions, but I wasn't going to pass up the chance for twice the number of shots. 'Right, let's get out of here.'

Imora picked up the needler belonging to the thug she'd killed. 'Don't be ridiculous, and help me get the izkhana away from the tree.'

I stared at her. 'What do you mean, don't be ridiculous? *You're* being—'

There was a sudden explosion of gunfire, and we both threw ourselves down instinctively. The other lifewards had discovered that their weapons were usable again, and desperate, close-quarters fights were breaking out around us. Given that chaos had erupted, I took aim at a Vorozny lit up by the growing tree fire and felled him with a burst of autopistol rounds to the back.

'Anyone and anything coming to help is going to prioritise the izkhana,' Imora said, fiddling with the needler, 'so the safest place to be is next to her!'

'Only if they don't assume we're the ones who drugged her!' I snapped back, but the thought of running through a live firefight back to the groundcar didn't exactly appeal either. I cast a glance at the burning tree, the heat from which was increasing uncomfortably. 'Fine, we do this your way!'

I holstered the las again and we each grabbed an arm, then towed the izkhana across the grass behind us rather than trying to support her as her would-be kidnappers had. We both jumped when the bright flash of a stray las-bolt sizzled past our noses, but hurried on until we got to the slight shelter of a weeping frangia bush.

'There should be a counternarc setting on this thing to wake her up,' Imora muttered, fiddling with the needler.

'If you're wrong, you're about to kill her,' I warned.

'Then we go with your plan, and run,' Imora said with a shrug. She fired a dart into the izkhana's neck with a soft *thwip*.

Surumir Fareltan sat bolt upright with a gasp, her eyes wide and a trail of drool spilling from one corner of her mouth. She slapped the dart away and looked at us wildly. 'Who...? What...?'

'Attempted kidnapping, milady,' Imora said, fairly smoothly given the circumstances. 'We slew your assailants and revived you.'

'Taverlinn?' the izkhana said breathlessly. She glanced at me as well, but I obviously merited no such acknowledgement, since she looked away immediately afterwards. 'Good– I... Thank you.'

'Please tell me that your security forces are incoming,' I said, still not ready to give up entirely on my plan to run for it.

'My biometrics are constantly monitored by Bastion-U,' the izkhana said. She had somehow managed to regain her haughtiness despite sitting in a bush in a torn gown. 'Should I pass out or become unconscious without warning, then the sanctioners are automatically summoned and codes are transmitted for them to deactivate the void shields.'

I shared a glance with Imora. Neither of us had banked on actual sanctioners turning up as the first response. On the other hand, perhaps Imora's plan had been wiser after all – far better,

I assumed, to be found with the property's owner than fleeing the scene.

As if on cue, a droning noise and the first sweeping searchlights from the sky announced the arrival of the Zurovs, the sanctioners' six-person gunships. They must have scrambled to get here so fast, but that was the privilege of the gilded for you – a mass mobilisation of the Lex if you fell asleep unexpectedly – as opposed to the downclaves, where if your disappearance was even noticed then the only likely outcome was someone else getting fined for not reporting it to your supervisor.

The discrepancy was sickening. On this occasion, however, I reflected bitterly as the gunships closed in and the remaining Vorozny began to flee in panic, it was damned useful.

The only warning I got was the thunder of footsteps, and then a shape emerged from the smoke with the blunt shape of a crude stub gun clutched in one hand. Another Vorozny thug, trying to find a way out, eyes wide and streaming. He saw us – two gilded and an armed lifeward – and did the only thing you'd expect. He opened fire.

I might have been able to beat him to the trigger, although I don't know for sure. Instead, I threw myself in front of Imora and the izkhana, shielding them with my body. I heard the stubber's crack and felt the impacts across my spine and ribs, hard as hammer blows, but the armoured jacket held and his weapon clicked empty after four shots – he must have already fired some off.

He probably would have just run away, but I have a rule. I'm no contract hitwoman or hired soldier, but if someone tries to kill me once, then I make sure they don't get a second chance. I whirled around and fired, the autopistol burst tracking up his chest in small eruptions of blood and flesh before terminating with the one that blew a hole in his face. He fell backwards, dead before he hit the grass.

'My word,' the izkhana said weakly. She had definitely noticed me now – in fact, her eyes weren't leaving me. I glanced at Imora, wondering if I'd incurred future trouble by upstaging her in the izkhana's eyes, but my employer seemed slightly stunned herself.

'Come, milady,' I said, offering my hand to the izkhana and pulling her to her feet when she took it. Imora got up on her own and leant close to me as I ushered our host towards the incoming searchlights.

'Which of us is the more surprised that you threw yourself in front of a gun for me?' she whispered mischievously.

'Me,' I replied, without looking at her. 'Definitely me.'

What can I say? If you hire me to do a job, I will damned well do it.

I avoid sanctioners wherever possible. Anyone with any sense does, regardless of social standing. For downclave types like Imora and me, they're stimmed-up bullies. For the merchant-combines, they're nuisances who need bribing. For the gilded, they're stinking eyesores and a reminder that not everything is as pristine as they like to pretend.

I'd been beaten, spat on, harassed and shot at by sanctioners in the past. That evening, when they saw me as a contessa's ex-Militarum lifeward who had saved Izkhana Fareltan, I got respectful nods from one professional to another whose actions had made their own jobs significantly easier. No sneers, no fingers straying threateningly towards the activation studs of a shock maul.

I preferred it, and I hated that I preferred it.

Imora had voxed ahead. When we arrived back at Taver-linn Hall, her aide was waiting for us in the vehicle bay with a sleek synthweave purse which contained, I discovered when he handed it to me, my agreed fee and then some.

'The evening contained unforeseen challenges, to which

you rose admirably,' Imora said lazily before I'd even questioned it. 'A bonus seemed in order, particularly given that the izkhana now considers herself to be in my debt. Overall, quite a successful first night in society.'

I noticed her aide's surprise at the mention of the izkhana, and how he stood slightly straighter afterwards. Perhaps he was revising his opinion of his new mistress' ability to improve the fortunes of the name she had bought.

'I can offer a place to clean up,' Imora said, gesturing beyond herself to the bulk of Taverlinn Hall, and then at my scuffed and stained clothes and the various cuts, scrapes and bruises I'd suffered during the evening. 'All I ask in return is that you consider a permanent role with me.'

It was a baited hook, but the bait was sorely tempting. The adrenaline dump had left me cold and shaking, my ribs were probably already a fine purple colour under my vest, my cuts were stinging, I stank of sweat and woodsmoke, and I had particles of tree everywhere. I wasn't looking forward to trying to get clean in the dribbling, lukewarm water of my dingy ablutorial, whereas Taverlinn Hall would undoubtedly have enormous tubs, waterfall-like deluges, scented oils and relaxing salts...

But then I remembered how casually Imora Tarsh had plunged her thumbs into the eyes and brain of that Vorozny thug, and all the people who had been carved up by her family's criminal empire. She wasn't gilded, but that didn't mean she hadn't trodden on others to get to where she was. It just meant her shoes hadn't been as fancy when she was doing so.

'Thanks for the offer,' I said, as politely as I could manage, 'but I'll be fine.'

'A pity,' Imora said, not taking her eyes off me. 'I think we could be a great help to each other.'

Let no one say that I can't be diplomatic. 'Perhaps we will,' I said, making my way slightly stiffly to the Dymaxion Falchion

I'd 'liberated' from the garages of Tanid Targus. 'But at present, I prefer to make my own way.'

Imora watched me drive away until the curving rampway took me up and out of her field of view. My shoulders didn't properly relax until I'd passed through the automated gates and was back on the main-trans.

Criminals. Sanctioners. The gilded. Varangantua was just full of ways to make life more interesting, or at least shorter. But this was my home, and I'd saluted and stood quietly for too much of my life to be comfortable with that as my default way of living any more. It might not be true freedom in Varangantua, but it was as close as someone like me was ever going to get.

My life might be a mess, but damn it, it's *my* mess. And that's the way it's going to stay.

NO CITY FOR HEROES

VICTORIA HAYWARD

The people of Vorask district had more than a hundred different words for rain. Probator Agnar Ledbetere was being soaked by what Voraski called a 'dredge rain'. Her hands were stuffed into her greatcoat pockets, and her collar turned up against the downpour, but the water still had a way of getting in.

Indifferent to the weather, Agnar stared down at the corpse in front of her.

'He's got the most beautiful face I've ever seen,' the stocky sanctioner beside her said speculatively.

'You're getting soft, Sinter,' Agnar said.

The woman laughed. 'If I'd known the Avenging Son looked like this, I'd have tried harder to catch him.'

Agnar shot her a look. 'If you'd caught him, he wouldn't have laid down quite so many Lexbreakers.'

'You say that like it's a bad thing.'

'Sanctioners might be happy sweeping up the bodies, but it makes my job much harder. We tend to find gangers less forthcoming than usual when dead.'

Sinter shrugged. 'The less scum on the streets, the better. And people liked him,' she added.

'Of course they did. The rig, the theatrics. The fact he came down to the places enforcers won't.' Agnar sniffed. 'But let's see how much they like the new cartels he's made way for. I'm sure it all looked simple from the spires. A criminal is a criminal, right? Except one gang will farm a community for profit, another will burn it if they think it'll turn them a slate.'

Sinter gestured acknowledgement. 'It's all bad. Who decides which is better?'

'Not someone who doesn't have to live with the consequences,' Agnar said flatly, crouching down under the makeshift canopy, critically taking in each tiny detail of the corpse. 'Get me more lumens over here,' she added. Nobody saw daylight down in the dregs. The spires screamed upward above the filthy alleyways, vertical mountains of plasteel and ferrocrete. The rain rattled through downspouts and streamed out through the eyes of the granite skulls, turning the dirt of the streets into a cloying mud. This was far from the first murder this place had seen, but it was the first so many enforcers had cared about.

The Avenging Son had died impractically but gracefully. His head was thrown back with his full lips slightly parted, hair tousled across his head, flattened by the rain into dark curls. A single tear of blood sat on his cheek, like a garnet, emphasising the symmetry of his face. Sinter was right, Agnar noted impassively. He was young and beautiful, and likely had the resources of a wealthy dynasty to protect him, even though he persisted in disrupting criminal activities in the district. So how did this gilded boy end up in a storm gutter full of bullet holes? And who was he?

The flare of a flood-lumen heralded Sinter's return.

'Don't stand in the tyre tracks,' Agnar warned. 'That's evidence.'

Sinter grunted, stepping back to the exclusion ribbon surrounding the scene. 'Looks like Graviteer tracks. One of ours.'

'I know,' Agnar replied impatiently. 'Where's his rig?' The Avenging Son's equipment was notorious, with every enforcer in the district seeming to have a story about him stepping on their toes, some more convincing than others.

'Gone.'

'Gone back to Bastion-V?'

'Gone as in it was never here.'

Agnar frowned. 'He's wearing a combat-glove with powered connectors. Ruthven manufacture. He'll have been wearing the rig. I need a trace on the components through the underveil and monitor skulls looking for prototype rig tech. If someone's stolen it, they'll break it down to sell.'

Sinter nodded, then pressed a meaty finger to the comm-bead in her ear. 'You'd better get back. Castellan wants you.'

Agnar grunted. As she turned to leave, something caught her eye just outside the beam of the flood-lumen. A decontaminant servitor juddered uselessly on the spot, withered human torso jerking randomly atop the bulky, wheeled sweeper engine.

'What's this?' Agnar asked, frowning.

The sanctioner shrugged. 'Damaged unit. Lucky it was, or it would've swept the scene.'

Agnar glanced back at where the incriminating tyre tracks lay. A broken sweeper wasn't an unusual sight. Vorask's humidity and creeping lichens were unkind to all things mechanical, and although a Mechanicus subclave was right next door, they couldn't immediately recover all their malfunctioning kit. 'Lucky,' she repeated, and made a snap decision. 'Take it in.'

'Cogboys won't like that.'

Agnar shrugged. 'My scene, my evidence.'

Sinter looked around wearily. 'Yes, sir.'

Castellan Iseth Abawi cut a formidable figure. A former sanctioner who'd risen through the ranks, she possessed a rare combination of brute force and keen intelligence. She'd halted what had seemed the district's inevitable slide into becoming another Spoil. And right now, her attention was focused entirely on Agnar.

'Did you hear what I said, Ledbetere?' Abawi said, leaning forward on strong arms.

'Hmm,' Agnar replied. Abawi was terrifying when angry. It reminded you that behind the smooth political operator was a trained killer who could break a neck with her bare hands.

'Ledbetere,' Abawi growled. 'We've identified the Avenging Son.'

'I heard. So why do you need me?'

'Because he was Tullian Ruthven, the scion to the Ruthven Dynasty, and his family are claiming he was killed by enforcers.'

Agnar grunted. 'The Ruthvens? The ones who run half the manufactoria in the district?'

'Yes. They're holding Bastion-V responsible for the death of their heir.'

'Why?'

'They got wind that there were Graviteer tracks at the scene. A couple of anonymous reports dialled in of uniforms in the area.'

'No ID on the uniforms?'

'No. Monitor skulls went dead in the area.'

Agnar nodded. That tallied with what they'd seen the rig do in the past and confirmed he'd started out wearing it that evening. 'The family were quick to accuse us.'

'Because of Vermid Street. Can you blame them?'

Agnar nodded. 'Ten years of undercover work blown and six of our own dead? The motive's there all right. There's not an enforcer in the district who wouldn't have gladly seen the Avenging Son swing for that.'

'Something that is quite apparent to the Ruthvens. If we

can't identify the killer, Fenwick Ruthven is going to take this Bastion apart.'

'Can he? Without conclusive evidence?'

Abawi smiled grimly. 'When the aggrieved party is this close to the lord justicius? Yes. We're looking at half the Bastion getting shipped to Sacc-Five. If we're lucky.'

Agnar raised her eyebrows. 'So where are the other probators?'

'It's just you, Ledbetere. Ruthven's jaegers are already scrambling to find dirt on Bastion-V. I need to keep them at bay, and make sure they don't find anything else that might…' She paused. 'Mislead them. I only have until the justicius issues them a warrant.'

'And the Ruthvens know we're investigating?'

'In the interests of procedural justice, the lord justicius has granted us a day's grace to do so.'

'A day?'

Abawi glanced at the chrono. 'Twenty-two hours now.'

'I'd best get along.' Agnar stood, taking her greatcoat from the stand. It had left a puddle of dirty gutter water on Abawi's floor. 'Will I have any problems accessing Tullian's residence?'

'The family have agreed to cooperate, but I suspect there's a limit to how far. They've agreed to an interview, but that took my last favour with the justicius,' Abawi said, pushing a heavy dossier across the desk. 'And Ledbetere…' She held her gaze for a little longer than the probator would have liked. 'I'm relying on you to fix this.'

Agnar shrugged her coat over her broad shoulders. 'You see to the politics, sir. Leave the dead to me.'

Agnar flicked through the Avenging Son file Abawi had handed her as she walked. The Bastion's corridors were thronged with anxious diurnus-shift enforcers carrying documents back and forth, and filled with the susurration of nervous, hushed conversations. She preferred the quiet of the noctis-shift. Varangantua was never silent, but Agnar found it less frenetic at night. She heard the dawn thrum of the palumba that heralded the usual end of her shift and noted that she would normally be going to sleep shortly. It was going to be a long day.

She closed the file and tucked it under her arm as she strode. There appeared to be no obvious pattern to the Avenging Son's activity, although he'd obviously annoyed someone enough to end up getting killed, which given his family, had been a high-risk enterprise for whoever was responsible. There were also numerous furious notes from enforcers who'd witnessed his particular brand of justice.

She could understand their anger. Tullian Ruthven had decided that in his gilded wisdom he knew better than the enforcers what justice meant, and who it applied to, and how it would be applied. She could even see how people might think he'd done some good. But if one man got to decide what good was, it was no good for anybody.

She sighed. She couldn't interview Tullian, but she could do the next best thing. She voxed for a ride upclave. The gilded put a lot of themselves into objects. Mostly the meanings were for others of their rank – conveying taste, status, heritage and pedigree. But there was some of the owner in there too. Whatever Tullian had been doing, perhaps his residence could tell her something about it.

Tullian kept private apartments away from the family estate. That made sense, given his nocturnal activities as the Avenging Son. The hab-block was relatively respectable but must have seemed like a hovel to the Ruthven heir. She flashed her holo-seal to the porter and was admitted. Tullian appeared to have been using one chaotic chamber as an office and living space. Apparently cleaning staff weren't permitted, or didn't dare to enter, as utensils and half-finished meals and drinks lay wedged into the general clutter and disarray. Papers and machinery were piled all over the floor and surfaces, apart from in one corner, beneath a very fine hanging of Roboute Guilliman. The embroidery was adorned in precious stones, and Guilliman's eyes burned as brightly as his flaming sword.

'The Avenging Son,' Agnar muttered to herself. The originator of Tullian's moniker. But what had Tullian Ruthven been avenging when he hunted gangers? Some wrong that had been done to Fenwick Ruthven? Did his father know what he was doing? Could he even have been directing him? A pile of books lay on the clear area of the desk beneath the hanging. This was the only place Tullian had bothered to keep tidy, so it must be significant.

Agnar examined each of the tomes. They were an eclectic mix. Among the array of gospels and grimoires was the *Almanack Alecto*, an Ecclesiarchy book of sermons, a child's abecedarium on the glory of the Emperor's Angels, and a multi-folio collection of chronicles on the deeds of the Adeptus Astartes. Some of them were clearly very old, and Agnar handled the cracked bindings cautiously. As she moved aside the assorted principia and treatises, she uncovered a much newer book. Sliding it out from its position behind the others, she opened it to discover it was a journal. Tullian's name was inscribed in the front, almost as a child would label their primer in the city scholam. It was a mix of handwritten observations and catechisms with cuttings pasted into it. All seemed to focus on the wisdom and epithets of Roboute Guilliman. Tullian had painstakingly copied out extracts on victory, tactics and duty from diverse sources.

As Agnar ran her finger down the page, she came to an underlined extract that made her pause. *To the enemies of my father's empire, we bring death.*

'Hmm,' she grunted. The Ruthvens' interests could certainly be described as an empire, and power always attracted enemies.

But Tullian had been interfering with relatively low-level gangers. What could they have to do with his father's interests?

Agnar flicked to the most recent entry. '"The darkest places in the city are within human hearts,"' she murmured. '"This is where I must brandish my burning sword, to cut down those who would betray our father's great works."' Something buzzed past Agnar's head. She dropped the journal and spun to find a decrepit-looking servo-skull hovering by her ear, eye sockets glowing a dull red.

'"To conduct battle on two fronts is an act of either desperation or utter foolishness". Codicil nineteen twenty-three, *The Writings of the Master of Ultramar*,' it intoned in a monotone, reedy voice.

Agnar rubbed her head and squinted at the gold plate drilled into the ivory bone of the skull, which proclaimed this to be the brainpan of Tullian's former tutor. 'Are you where this started then, Master Gregorian?' she asked. The skull stared at her blankly.

There was a knock at the door, and a sour-faced man entered, with the porter hovering behind him.

One look at the livery he wore told her that he worked for the Ruthvens. She had been followed.

'You're interrupting a criminal investigation,' she said mildly.

'Lord Ruthven will see you now,' the aide said coldly. 'I'm to escort you to the estate.'

'I'm not finished.'

'Lord Ruthven will see you, *now*. There is a vehicle waiting.'

Agnar nodded. Abawi had been correct. His lordship only had so much patience for an investigation. Very well. 'Before we go, you'll want to find the venerable master's charging dock,' she said, gently pushing the skull towards him, sending its anti-grav motor whirring as it bobbed through the air.

'I'll attend to that later,' the aide snapped.

Agnar shrugged. 'Fine. If you consider it worth the risk to the recollection engrams of such an esteemed heirloom.'

The aide looked unconvinced, but sucking his teeth he gripped the skull in disdainful fingers and turned to find the charging dock.

Agnar quickly bent down and snatched up Tullian's journal from where she'd dropped it, stuffing it inside her coat before the aide turned back to usher her out.

The Ruthven estate was the largest privately owned mass of land in Vorask. The ancient family's manufactoria and forges kept a large proportion of the district's workers employed, turning out service weaponry for the Astra Militarum as well as higher-end armaments for the luxury market. Their wealth was writ large in the grounds that Agnar was driven through in a personal conveyor. Unlike the hectic, vertical sprawl of the rest of the city, the Ruthven estate boasted a conspicuous blankness. The seemingly endless walkways and plazas spoke of a dynasty with wealth enough not to use their land. Something about it made Agnar's neck itch. There was no cover here. It was too flat, too open, and there were barely any people. It didn't feel like Varangantua. And Agnar got the impression the visit had been choreographed more for the justicius than anything else.

She followed the aide to the main house, past formal fountains and pools. All were pristinely maintained, not clotted with the usual Voraski algae that propagated so rapidly it populated even small puddles of rainfall. Flowering trees lined the walkway to Ruthven's apartment. They didn't look indigenous to Alecto, although for all Agnar knew of such things, they could be.

Just as they were approaching the apartment's entrance, an inhuman, ululating cry caused Agnar to nearly jump out of her skin. 'What the hells was that?'

It was the first time the sour-faced aide escorting her had

cracked a smile, although it wasn't a pleasant one. 'The Ruthven bestiary. It's regarded as one of the most extensive zoological collections on Alecto.'

Agnar shook her head. Beasts and nothingness. It was a strange way to live.

Tullian's father, Fenwick Ruthven, was not what Agnar had expected. She'd pulled up information about the family via dataveil on the way over to the estate. Everything suggested he was simply a society boy brought in to inject some fresh blood into his wife's ancient lineage. Just the right genetic distance to be a sensible match, but from a mercantile house elevated enough to be financially sagacious. Agnar was certainly not anticipating the sharp intensity that she found in Fenwick when he received her.

He sat on a chaise at the end of a long room panelled in real wood. The air was chilled to a degree deliberately ostentatious in contrast to the humidity of Vorask. Ice roses bloomed in frosted glass chalices lining the room. Fenwick wore a sumptuous cape of white fur over robes of mourning-gold. His face was painted in accordance with gilded conventions for a grieving parent, and was radiant with brittle, raw anger. He appeared every bit the bereaved father, Agnar thought, shivering in the cold.

'Explain yourself,' Fenwick snapped as she approached.

He had the manner of the gilded, if not the bloodline, Agnar thought wryly.

'Condolences, my lord.' She dipped her head.

Fenwick sneered, his beautiful face contorted into a mask of hate. 'You dare offer condolences? When you animals murdered my son?'

'This is a difficult time, my lord. And it's only thanks to your grace that we're able to undertake this investigation to identify your son's killer.'

He pursed his lips. 'Ask your questions. Quickly. Although it's clear to me what happened.'

'Would you care to elucidate, my lord?'

He shot Agnar a glance, taking in her garb disdainfully. 'You people couldn't stand that he was doing a better job than you, so you eliminated him. It's as simple as that.'

'You're referring to your son's… interventions in the district?' Agnar said, flipping out a battered data-slate.

'Yes,' Fenwick said coldly, brushing a lock of hair away from his face. 'His service to the city. Would that Varangantua's so-called enforcers of justice knew what that meant.'

'Hmm,' Agnar grunted non-committally. 'And of course, he outclassed our equipment. That rig…' She smiled slightly. 'We could hardly compete.'

Fenwick nodded. 'The Ruthvens have been manufacturing the finest tactical equipment in the sector for centuries. It stands to reason our scion would ensure he had the best.'

'Yes,' Agnar agreed. 'According to our reports, flechettes, neurotoxins, impact jets.'

'And you lost it.' Fenwick waved a hand dismissively, sending the jewels at his wrist clinking. 'Through incompetence. Or deliberate theft.'

Agnar was really very cold now. She could feel the moisture in her clothes hardening to frost. It didn't help that she'd not slept. She cleared her throat. 'Your son was very interested in the Adeptus Astartes. Their deeds, their legend.'

'What young person isn't?' Ruthven snapped.

'It strikes me that he was idealistic. Perhaps not grounded in the realities of business, as you and the family matriarch must be.'

Ruthven regarded her stonily.

'Does the Ruthven matriarch know about her son's death?'

Fenwick's lips tightened. 'Yes. But she's away on business, elsewhere on Alecto.'

'I wonder,' Agnar continued, actually wondering how long it would be before he evicted her, 'whether his activities might have been inconvenient. Embarrassing even, for a house like yours? Something that you might have wished would stop?' She let the sentence hang in the air.

'Enough,' Fenwick said abruptly, rising to his feet and clutching his furs around him. 'I've tolerated this farce for too long. Get out.'

Agnar nodded mildly. 'My thanks for your indulgence, my lord.' She could feel Ruthven's stare burning a hole into her shoulder blades as she departed.

Bastion-V remained frenetic when Agnar returned. There were now a couple of grim-faced jaegers posted outside the entrance, presumably waiting for the moment they were granted the authority to enter the building and start taking whatever evidence they wanted. Agnar dodged frantic probators and rushing, hooded verispex as she made her way to the technicum lexi. She checked the dataveil for any alerts on the rig trace she'd set up. Still nothing. She frowned. Normally kit like that would be broken down and distributed as quickly as possible. Whoever had it was hanging on to it for some reason.

Agnar sighed and pushed open the mortuarium door.

'Mask,' commanded a rasping voice from inside the metal-walled room. Agnar complied, lifting a rebreather from the rack by the door.

'It would be the most unhygienic probator they send me,' grumbled the apron-clad verispex through a battered vox-grille installed in his neck. 'Don't touch anything,' he warned before bustling away. He might not be the most personable, but Jensem was one of the most experienced corpse-cutters in the Bastion.

'I'll try and restrain myself,' Agnar said, grimacing at the sight of an eviscerated body on a slab.

'He's through here,' the verispex called.

Agnar walked through to find the mortal remains of Tullian Ruthven laid out on a plasteel bench.

'It's just me here, no assistants for the necroscopy,' Jensem complained, waving a disinfectant-reddened hand.

'You're the only verispex, I'm the only probator. It's all on us, or Ruthven senior will see us all shipped to Sacc-Five.'

Jensem grunted. His vox-grille translated the sound into a blast of static. 'Enforcers don't do well inside the worm farm.'

'No, we don't. And we're running out of time. Have you got anything for me?'

'Yes and no. I'll start with what I don't have. Look here.' Agnar followed Jensem to Tullian's body. 'See these?' He indicated a series of dark rubber valves sunk into the young man's flesh. 'Flesh-ports. They're located near nerve clusters and up the spine. Designed to control an external device, like power armour.'

'The rig,' Agnar said, peering at the ports.

'That's right. He was wearing something when he died or the external injuries would have been more extensive, but it wasn't powered.'

'How do you know?'

'There should be data-ghosts in the ports, but there's nothing.'

'What does that mean?'

Jensem shrugged. 'There wasn't a last command.'

'He didn't send one?'

'Or couldn't.'

'Hmm,' Agnar said. 'So that's what's missing. What else?'

'I can tell you how he probably died, and that he was full of Tzarina rounds.'

Agnar swore. If the scion was full of enforcer lead, that was probably all the evidence the Ruthvens needed to send the whole Bastion down.

'Not so fast, probator. I didn't say that was what killed him.'

'Well?' Agnar glanced at the clock.

'He fell – I would estimate from a distance of thirty to fifty feet given the hyoid bone is fractured, but the thoracic cage is intact. There's very little external trauma, presumably thanks to the rig, but the pulmonary contusions and cardiac lacerations along with internal soft tissue injuries suggest the fall killed him.'

Agnar's mind flicked back to the scene. 'Where did he fall from?' she muttered.

'I thought you'd want to know that. The sanctioners couldn't see any evidence of weapons discharge on ledges or roofs of that height. Only the spent cases by the body.'

'So, he was shot after he fell,' Agnar mused.

Jensem shrugged. 'Why bother shooting a body with a burst heart?'

'If you wanted to make it look like an enforcer did it but didn't have time to think very hard about it. But why take the rig if it was broken?' Agnar shook her head. 'Anything else?'

'No.'

Agnar nodded. 'I'll get back to the files.' She paused. 'What about the decon sweeper?'

'Pulled a gutterhog slug out of it.'

'One of ours,' Agnar said. 'Any chance it could have come from the angle of fire directed at the body? Or was it a stray left for us to find?'

Jensem threw his hands in the air. 'As if I've had time for that.'

'Look next. Something tells me the scene isn't what it appears to be.'

A voxmitter at the side of the mortuarium blared. *'Attention all Bastion personnel,'* the voice crackled. *'This is Castellan Abawi. With immediate effect, you are to make your way to the atrium and present yourselves to the jaegers stationed there. The Bastion and all personnel within it are now under an extraordinary writ of seizure and investigation, as ordered by the Lord Justicius Vorask.'*

Agnar and Jensem stared at each other for a moment.

'It's over, then,' Jensem said. 'What's Ruthven got on the justicius to be able to force this?'

'I don't know,' Agnar said grimly.

'Can you crack this?'

'Maybe.'

'That's better than nothing,' he replied, as the sound of footsteps approached the mortuarium. 'Get out. If you're not in the Bastion, you're not under the writ.' He opened a door. 'Quickly.'

Agnar heard the jaegers enter the mortuarium even as she ran down the corridor and out into the slops alley.

So, she was alone now – no castellan, no verispex, no evidence. She felt Tullian's journal thump heavily inside her coat as she fled. Well, *almost* no evidence.

In the absence of anywhere else to go, Agnar made her way to a grubby local taverna at the corner of her habzone. How far the writ of seizure extended she did not know, but it seemed sensible not to return to the first place they'd look for her. She ordered a slatov from the gruff barkeep.

'If anyone comes looking for me, I'm not here. All right?'

The barkeep nodded. 'Understood, sir.'

Agnar had been a patron long enough to trust him. She made her way up a winding staircase to the first floor. The patrons knew her here, and she wouldn't be disturbed. The taverna was quiet at this time of day, and Agnar pushed a few tables together in a corner. She needed space to lay everything out.

There was no functioning airflow system in the taverna,

so she shoved the window beside her open. The air outside was close to one hundred per cent humidity, so thick you could almost cut it. She could barely see the buildings opposite. There was a square gap between them, a bright shaft of half-light leading down to a drain far below where stinking steelfern crawled up the ferrocrete, prising apart the foundations. Had it been a clear day, she could have seen the ooze of the Rask, the river that coiled through the district – an oily mass of skerries and barges. They said that once, the scum had been so dense that for a few weeks children had been able to play on it.

Agnar exhaled. She'd been awake far too long for this.

She placed the journal on the table in front of her, along with a greasy data-slate, and pulled up the available report on the antics of the Avenging Son. Then she sat back and closed her eyes. What did she have?

Tullian's interventions in gang activities didn't seem to be coordinated. And as far as she could see, the Ruthvens were all above board – as much as gilded families ever were. And even if they weren't, what problem with gangers could the Ruthvens possibly have? What filial vengeance was the Avenging Son exacting for his father?

And the missing rig remained a problem. Had it been functioning, she suspected Tullian would have survived the fall. The reports on his activities suggested he'd used impact jets to break long drops before. And whoever witnessed the drop would have seen that the rig had malfunctioned. Why steal something broken from a powerful house who'd surely track you down? And why attempt to frame enforcers for it?

Agnar rubbed her eyes. She was missing something, and she was exhausted. Her brain felt like overcooked boil-pot and the drink wasn't touching it. Stimms wouldn't help, she didn't need to be any more jittery than she already was. She set an alarm on her chrono. Twenty minutes of shut-eye might bring everything into focus. She rested her head on her arms.

There was a rustling near Agnar's ear. She blinked slowly as she drifted to consciousness. Something was moving in front of her, quietly purring as it did so. She jerked upright. 'Oh no, you little bastard...'

A sturdy palumba had flown in through the open window and was busily devouring Tullian's journal, its craw already bulging with masticated evidence. The wretched vermin were known to chew through any parchment they could find to build their sprawling, stinking nests across Vorask.

It flattened its crest in response to her movement and hissed, serrated beak open, before seizing another mouthful of parchment.

'Steady,' Agnar muttered, moving slowly towards it.

The bird tensed, gaudy wattles shuddering around its baleful eyes.

'Stay there,' Agnar said, in as calming a voice as she could muster.

The creature extended its wings, apparently sensing hostile intent.

Agnar reached for her empty glass. 'Stay there,' she repeated, before flinging it towards the palumba.

It moved faster than Agnar had ever seen one do so, shooting backwards out of the window with a beakful of evidence, spurting a jet of noxious guano in its wake.

'You bastard!' Agnar growled, and slammed the window closed. She turned back to the table, where torn and soiled sheets of parchment lay, trying to sort them back into some semblance of order. She found two pages that seemingly belonged together and began skimming over the words, when something caught her eye. Overleaf from the underlined quote she'd seen earlier, *To the enemies of my father's empire, we bring death*, was written a small annotation – one of Tullian's own entries: *The Master of Mankind tests His children, would that we be worthy to inherit His Imperium. We must all scourge sinners where we see them, but my trial is a great one as my father is the enemy of my father...*

Everything shifted in Agnar's mind. 'You idiot,' she said, standing abruptly. Of course. The Avenging Son that Tullian had styled himself on was Guilliman, the son of the Emperor. If the Emperor was whom Tullian was avenging, rather than his own father, that opened up a lot of possibilities. Possibilities that she suspected she could confirm with more time, and a little more evidence...

But Agnar didn't have either of those things. She had to get to Fenwick Ruthven before it was too late. She grabbed her coat. She was sure now that she could get him to stop this. She'd just have to figure out quite how on the way.

Readmission to the Ruthven estate had come surprisingly easily, although Agnar found herself escorted through the grounds with even less grace than the first time.

Ruthven received her in the icy room again. Still haughty, but smug now too.

He thinks he's won, Agnar thought.

'I thought you people had all been dealt with,' Ruthven said, glancing at a gilt chronograph on the wall. 'The time to investigate is up.'

'Almost,' Agnar said. 'But by your grace, my lord, I have concluded my investigation.'

Ruthven rested his chin on his hand. 'A little late for your castellan, don't you think?' He was taunting her. 'So, you've identified a killer?'

'No.'

Ruthven raised his arms theatrically. 'Then why are you here?'

'To tell you that your son's death was an accident. He wasn't murdered. He fell from a height, and his rig malfunctioned. Without functioning impact jets, he was killed when he hit the ground.'

'Impossible,' Ruthven snapped. 'Ruthven technology does not malfunction. Besides, they tell me he was shot with enforcer bullets, that tracks from your vehicles were at the scene.'

'Tzarinas and Graviteers can be procured for the right price.'

'If it was an accident, why would anyone try to hide it?'

'Why indeed.' Agnar smiled coldly. Ruthven had sprung the trap she'd laid for him. 'At first, I thought this was about your son's activities. I assumed he was working for you, but he wasn't, was he? He was working against you. He was an idealist, a true one. He thought he was carrying out the Emperor's work.'

'Why is that relevant?' Ruthven snapped.

'Perhaps it's not. Because you didn't care what he thought, only that he was starting to get in the way.'

Ruthven's face became impassive.

'Here's what I think happened. Tullian interfered with gang business and fell to his death. The gang recognises who he is, panics. They don't want to make an enemy of the Ruthvens, do they? So, they start to cover up the scene, badly. They dress the scene to frame the enforcers, knowing that we had motive enough to kill him after the Vermid Street incident. They disable a decon sweeper so the evidence they planted will be found, and shoot the corpse with enforcer bullets, not realising when we cut him open, we'd find that the fall had already burst his heart. You get wind of what's happening and tell them to take the rig before the enforcers arrive. How close am I, my lord?'

Ruthven's knuckles were white, clamped over the arms of his chair. 'This is just conjecture. You don't have any evidence.'

Agnar smiled humourlessly. 'Do you think I'd have come here without evidence? The problem with you people is that you don't know your own business. My mother was a seam welder, and she could tell a faulty part by touch. She caught a bad batch of components that would have blown a ship apart in the void had they been used. But you? You're so removed from your trade that you thought the only link to the mal-function would be in the rig itself, which is why you recovered it. The data-ghosts in his flesh-ports told us everything. That proves the rig failed, that the death was an accident.'

Agnar's heart thumped in her chest. She was sure she had this right, that she had the measure of Ruthven, but it was a gamble. 'Should anyone look closely enough, I wonder if they would find the castellan's crackdown on crime somehow con-nected to your eagerness to see her put away… She's been very popular with most other merchant-combines. And the gangers who killed your son, I think they came to you directly when it happened. That would be a strange thing to do if they didn't know you already. What's your real business, Lord Ruthven?'

After a few moments of tense silence, Ruthven sat back, face sour. 'What do you want?' he said flatly.

Agnar felt a surge of relief. But it wasn't over yet. 'Tell the justicius to drop the investigation and reinstate the castellan. Get me the ganger who shot the body, and we'll prosecute. The real culprit has been identified, and there's no damage done to your reputation.'

Ruthven exhaled through his nose. 'Fine.'

'And just so you know, my lord, if I fail to make my way off this estate, this information will be automatically released.'

'Understood,' Ruthven said coldly.

Agnar paused. Nothing about this felt right.

'What?' Ruthven sneered. 'You have what you want.'

'Do I?' said Agnar, eyes glittering furiously. 'What I want to know is what your son wanted to stop so badly he'd risk his life for it. "My trial is a great one as my father is the enemy of my father,"' she said, quoting from Tullian's journal. 'I know why you tried to frame the enforcers, but why did your son think you an enemy of the Emperor? What have you done, Fenwick Ruthven?'

He stood, stony faced. 'It would be best for you if you were to stop pushing your luck.'

'You're probably right,' said Agnar. She shrugged bitterly, and left.

Agnar stood behind Castellan Abawi as she announced the reinstatement of the Bastion to the crowded atrium, and the arrest of the ganger who had shot Tullian Ruthven.

But who hadn't killed *him*, thought Agnar flatly, as the rest of the enforcers and sanctioners cheered. The noise was overwhelming, and Agnar slipped away into Abawi's office. She was as relieved as the others not to be sent to a penal colony, but this victory felt hollow.

Abawi entered the office and nodded. 'Good result, Agnar.'

'Is it?'

Abawi sat behind her desk. 'I think so.'

Agnar grunted.

'How much of what you told Ruthven was true?' the castellan asked.

'All of it.'

Abawi raised an eyebrow.

'It was. I just couldn't prove it was all true,' Agnar conceded. 'But it must have been close enough to rattle him.'

'Then what's wrong? The Lex has been served.'

Agnar looked away. 'The letter of the Lex, yes. But not justice.'

'I didn't have you down as an idealist,' Abawi said.

'I'm not, sir. But…' She paused. 'This was bigger than one cover-up. Tullian was targeting those gangs for a reason. Fenwick Ruthven is into something serious. The gangs are involved, and I'd be surprised if it wasn't something to do with their–'

Abawi interrupted her. 'Agnar, you're a good probator.' She ran a hand over her shaved head. 'Without your work we'd all be looking at transportation to Sacc-Five as a best-case scenario. The Lex has been served. Don't do anything to bring Ruthven down on us. That's an order. You've seen what he's capable of.'

Agnar frowned. 'I don't like it, sir. Tullian was a stupid kid, but he must have known what his father was capable of. He was willing to chase justice anyway.'

'And he died because he believed in perfect justice.'

'Maybe more of us should be willing to do that.'

Abawi shook her head. 'Don't wreck this, Agnar. I'm grateful to you, but I'm not going to let anything put my command at risk again. We all need to find a way of living with the justice we're given.'

'Understood.'

'That's an order.'

'As you say, sir.' Agnar stood. 'Now if you'll excuse me, I'm going to go home and get some sleep.'

'Do that. And Agnar – promise me you'll forget about this justice shit?'

'Already forgotten, sir,' Agnar said as she closed the door behind her.

CLEAR AS GLASS

DENNY FLOWERS

It was long past midnight when the Zalamar drew up. I stood pressed against a plascrete wall, shivering as I sheltered from the worst of the rain. The driver's door swung open and Stann emerged, his boots leaving ripples in the puddle-strewn parking strip. He met my gaze and managed a smile, even if its sincerity was questionable.

'Probator Raemis,' he nodded. 'Awful weather, ain't it?'

'You're late.'

He shrugged. 'Blame the scum. Had to bloody my baton twice on the way over here. And one of them dented the hood of my ride.'

'Is that a Zalamar?' I frowned, nodding to his vehicle. 'Not exactly standard issue.'

'Personal vehicle. I'm keeping a low profile.'

'You might succeed better if you weren't wearing blood-stained sanctioner armour.'

'A low profile whilst driving,' he said, grinning. 'Besides, the owner of this place prefers not to have a Rampart parked outside. Bad for business.'

'Is that right?' I said, glancing to the flickering neon sign above us. Upon it, the emerald glow barely visible through the rain, was escribed *The Broken Chain*. Or it would have been if half the letters weren't smashed to shards.

I looked back to him. 'You a regular then?'

'Part of the job. Probator Curris solved many an impossible case from this place,' he replied, looking me up and down. 'You should be able to crack a couple, providing you're old enough to drink.'

I glared at him. He sighed.

'Don't make a thing of it, kid. It's just banter, no offence intended. Curris always appreciated a little back and forth during escort duty. Kept us both sharp.'

'Curris is no longer deployed in this district.'

'Don't I know it.' He sighed again. 'Well, Probator Raemis, how do you wish to proceed?'

I glanced to the watering hole.

'In this instance I will follow your lead, seeing as you have experience with such places.'

'Haven't attended too many tavernae?'

'I prefer to launch my investigations from actual crime scenes.'

'Well, that's Paavo for you. When it's all domestic assaults and junkies stealing each other's stashes, it's simple enough to follow the trail of blood and stimm injectors until you trip over a body. Here? It's a little more complicated. Sometimes you need to talk to people on the other side of the Lex to uncover the big crimes.'

He strode past me, approaching the bolted steel door. He rapped five times, paused, then twice more. Moments later an eyehole slid open, though it was too dark to make out the figure behind it.

'Sanctioner Stann.'

'Evening, Jerri,' Stann replied. 'This is my associate, Probator Raemis. We have a little business inside.'

'Raemis? What happened to Curris?'

'Redeployed in the wake of the calamity. Lots of changes all around. Raemis has been called up in his stead. Don't let his youthful good looks fool you – he's a proper golden boy. Within ten years he'll be castellan. You'd be wise to make nice with him while you can.'

Jerri seemed unconvinced. My vision was adjusting to the half-light, and I could see his bloodshot eyes darting between us.

'I should check with Burgous,' he began, but Stann leant closer, till their noses were inches apart.

'He's with me, and we are here for a drink and a conversation. The deal is the same as always, Jerri – we don't see anything unless someone is dumb enough to show it to us. Now I've asked nicely, like I was addressing an actual person and not a sack of shit. But you're starting to annoy me, and if you don't open this door right now, I will retrieve my assault ram. And once I've finished battering down this door, I will commence flattening your face. Clear?'

The eyehole slammed shut. I heard bolts being drawn back.

'I'd be happier knowing the identity of our informant,' I murmured.

'It doesn't work that way.' Stann shrugged. 'Curris' network relies on intermediaries. They notify us that an informant has something to share, and I nominate a time and venue. Our contact is a cloaked woman with grey eyes. That's all we know. We figure out the rest from there.'

'And this qualifies as probator work?' I asked as the door creaked open.

'Why not? Every conspiracy begins as a conversation.'

Our informant was sitting alone, her table a stone's throw from the bar. About half the remaining booths were occupied by an assortment of clave scum, their whispers swallowed by encroaching shadows. When they saw us, they slunk even lower, doing their best to appear innocent and harmless, with limited success.

I glanced to my holster, already missing my pistol. Jerri had secured our sidearms in a lockbox beside the entrance. Stann insisted this was standard practice, that all patrons would be similarly unarmed. I might have found that reassuring, except Jerri had the blank expression of a topaz junkie and I doubted it would be difficult to slip a blade past him.

Stann was already at the bar. I joined him, still studying the room's layout. Only one entrance, unless the ablutions chamber had a window. No security beside Jerri and Burgous, the barman, and I counted fifteen figures dotted about the tables. Bad odds if the situation deteriorated.

'Evenin', Burgous. Two fingers of slatov,' Stann said to the barman, before turning to me. 'Raemis?'

'Recaff. Black.'

The man nodded, turning to the boiler. I pretended to watch him, studying the informant from the corner of my eye. She wore a once-black robe that was now a faded grey. Her hood was pulled tight, but I caught a glimpse of ashen skin and grey eyes beneath it. More tellingly, I saw the symbol adorning the collar of her undershirt. A pattern of thorned vines, entwined around a black-veined berry.

'You seen her?' I asked.

Stann nodded, taking up his glass.

'Khaadi?' I murmured as he knocked back the shot. He winced, setting it down and glancing over his shoulder. She must have caught his gaze because her head bowed further, as though she sought to disappear into the chair.

He shook his head. 'No. Not Khaadi.'

'That's their symbol on her collar.'

'Doesn't matter. You'd know if she was Khaadi. That whole damned bloodline's eyes are emerald green. It's a point of pride. Some junkies even claim they can poison you with a glance.'

'So why the symbol?'

'Could be a servant. Maybe even a H'ownd, though I'd have thought one of them would be smart enough not to flash their credentials in public.'

He caught my blank expression and sighed.

'Don't they teach you nothin' at the scholam?' he said. 'H'ownd are trusted servants. Considered broadly competent, which, in the eyes of a Khaadi, places them significantly above everyone else on the planet. Check the dataveil if you don't believe me.'

'Can't. The connection is still patchy.'

'The calamity has screwed everything up,' Stann said, motioning for Burgous to refill his glass. 'Well, I know the Khaadi, and if she's their servant, the kindest thing we can do is turn around and walk out of here. If her master knows she spoke to us, then it's a death sentence. He'll probably kill her slow, too, just to make a point. She's a dead woman walking.'

Burgous placed my recaff on the counter. I glanced to him. 'How much?'

'No charge,' he said, gaze flickering to Stann. 'The Lex drinks for free.'

'How much?' I repeated. He stared back. I produced a couple of slates, slamming them on the bar.

'Fix your sign,' I said, before turning away from him and towards the condemned woman.

Her table was central, the third-closest to the bar. Perhaps she felt a little safer under the glow of the overhead lumens, but her cloak cast her face in shadow. We positioned ourselves

either side of her, so between us we'd have a view of the surrounding tables. Not that we could do much if they rushed us.
The only vaguely defensible position was the bar itself.

Our informant had bowed as we sat but still hadn't spoken,
her head hung as though in prayer.

'You got a name?' I asked.

'Nateo,' she murmured, voice atremble.

'Just Nateo?'

'Yes. I am unworthy of the Khaadi name.'

I glanced to Stann, raising an eyebrow. But his gaze was fixed
on her.

'Nateo,' he murmured. 'I thought that was a male name?'

'Usually. There are exceptions.'

'Well, *Nateo*,' he continued, unconvinced. 'I hear you have
something to tell us. Do you want to get on with it, or do I haul
you in for wasting our time?'

'I have something,' she murmured, gaze fixed on the table.
Her lips barely moved as she spoke. I had never met someone
quite so still.

'Y'know what I think?' Stann continued. 'You have a death
wish. This meeting is some ritualistic suicide. Why the hell else
would a Khaadi servant dare speak to the enforcers?'

She shrank at his words.

'I serve my master,' she whispered. 'Even in betrayal.'

'You're H'ownd, then?'

'Yes. Though I won't be after this.'

Her hands were folded, one tucked beneath the other. But
something glinted between her fingers.

I reached out, seizing her arm. She offered no resistance as
I raised it, examining the ring on her finger. An emerald was
set in a mount of barbed silver vines.

'Expensive jewellery for a servant,' I noted.

'It was a gift,' she replied. 'And the gem is impure.'

She was right. The green was tainted by faint threads of crimson. I released my grip, her hand tucking back into place.

'So, you're a smile-girl?' Stann said with a leer. 'Probably a good one to get such prizes. Who's your lucky master?'

'Lord Laqui.'

Her voice was barely a whisper. I'd had few dealings with the Khaadi, but I recognised the name. Stann must have too, for he snorted, eyes rolling.

'You're telling me Lord Laqui's personal smile-girl has taken it upon herself to contact a couple of enforcers? How stupid do you think we are? Show me your feet.'

It seemed a bizarre request, but she did as he bid, slipping off her shoes and revealing a pair of mostly unremarkable feet.

Except the left was missing its smallest toe.

'One transgression?' Stann said, studying the long-healed wound. 'How long have you served him? I heard Laqui had his manservant's teeth ripped out merely for bringing him tepid water.'

'My lord is oft misunderstood.'

'We're getting distracted,' I said, glaring at Stann before turning back to Nateo. 'What do you have for us?'

'There is a threat to Varangantua.'

I raised an eyebrow. 'The entire city?'

'Possibly.'

'And this is a threat from the Khaadi?'

'No. They merely uncovered it. Or Lord Laqui uncovered it. I do not know if he has shared the knowledge with the other clans.'

'But you're all too willing to share it with us?' Stann said.

'Yes. The calamity saw to that.'

Her head was still bowed, and with her face hidden I was unsure of her meaning.

'This threat is connected to the calamity?' I asked.

'No. At least, I don't think it is. But it cost me something important, and I cannot risk a greater disaster unfolding because I didn't speak up.'

Her eyes met mine for a moment, but I could not read the expression. Despite the tremble in her voice, her face betrayed nothing.

'I know only what I overheard,' she began. 'A few months ago, a group of Khaadi performed a sea raid on an offshore platform. They sought to steal armaments, but the enforcers lay in wait. Though they slaughtered most of the clan, a handful escaped. They holed up in Saltstone for a few hours before being wiped out.'

'By whom?'

She looked at me, eyes grey as smoke.

'By a monster. From beyond Alecto.'

She spoke with every appearance of sincerity. Beside me, Stann set his glass down, wiping his mouth on his sleeve.

'A monster?' he said, sneering. 'From the void?'

'It tore them apart as though they were children.'

'I see,' he continued. 'Can you describe this monster? Did it have wings? Three heads? Stubbers in place of its nipples?'

'Lord Laqui did not provide such details.'

'I'm surprised he provided anything,' I said. 'It strikes me this is not something he would desire overheard. Is he often loose-tongued?'

'I am H'ownd,' she said. 'They sometimes forget we are there. Like furniture.'

'But he fears this void-born monster?'

'He fears nothing,' she replied with seeming certainty.

But her gaze flickered. Just a fraction.

'He is concerned, though?' I pressed.

'Yes. The most concerned I have ever seen.'

Stann opened his mouth to speak but caught my expression and closed it. His gaze flickered to the bar.

'I think this needs another drink,' I said. 'Stann?'

He nodded, glancing to Nateo, who shook her head. Her own glass was untouched.

As we rose, I risked a sideways glance at the other tables. They seemed caught in their own conversations, but every so often, nervous eyes would dart in our direction. Still, that proved nothing.

'What do you think?' I murmured as we reached the bar.

'Her story makes no sense,' Stann said. 'Even were it true, why come to us? What does she expect us to do? Put out an alert for a xenos monster?'

'You think she's lying?'

'Or mad. Or both.'

'Mad makes more sense. It's too strange a lie. Especially as she risks death by speaking to us.'

'It's a set-up,' he said, nodding to Burgous and motioning to his drink. 'She wants us chasing some fool's errand that serves her master's interests. Or distracts us from their actual goal so they can operate unopposed.'

'But why? I have no investigations that implicate the Khaadi. Do you?'

'I steer clear of them. For the most part they clean up their own messes.'

'Then why target us?'

'Maybe you busted Lord Laqui's half-nephew twice-removed years ago and they want revenge? They have weird ideas about family and honour.'

'Is Laqui dangerous?'

He chuckled. 'Yes, he's dangerous. He's an Ancient, one of a handful that are known. Even the vladar keeps out of his way. You really don't have a clue about them, do you?'

I met his gaze. His smile faded.

'If you keep disrespecting me then we are going to have a problem,' I said.

He sighed. 'Sorry, kid. I only meant that you don't understand the Khaadi like I do. No reason you should – they don't
operate everywhere. But Lord Laqui's smile-girl could not just
slip away to speak to us. It's beyond suspicious. We should bring
her in, see if the chasteners can loosen her tongue.'

'Perhaps,' I said. 'But first I want you to verify her account.
Find out about this sea raid she mentioned. Vox the Bastion.
See if we can confirm any of it.'

'I still say it's a waste of time.'

'Noted. Do it anyway. And watch my back.'

He held my gaze, and for a moment I thought he might
say something else. But instead he shrugged, glancing to the
barman.

'Burgous?' he said. 'Get me a drink and give me some privacy. Make sure nobody comes near me, else I might find cause
to look through your back office.'

'Stann is verifying your account,' I said, setting myself at the
table, back to the bar so Stann could cover it. 'We'll soon know
if you speak the truth.'

'You trust him then?'

My eye was on another table when she spoke, so I did not
see her face. But her tone gave me pause. It was different from
before, like something was missing from her voice. I could not
place it.

'He's a sanctioner,' I replied, glaring at her. 'I'd advise you
not to insinuate anything.'

'It was merely a question.'

'You're an informant. You don't ask questions, you answer
them,' I said, staring her down. But she did not flinch, and it
was then I realised what was missing from her voice.

The fear.

That flicker of uncertainty was gone. It sounded as though

she was smiling, though her face remained impassive. Her hood had fallen away, revealing dark hair secured in place by a silvered pin.

Did she look taller? Perhaps she merely sat straighter, for her eyes were now level with mine. But her gaze flicked over my shoulder, and my back suddenly felt very exposed.

I risked a glance behind me. Stann was seated at the bar, head bent low as he whispered into the vox.

My gaze shifted to the other tables, seeking any hint of Khaadi allegiance. Stupid, for any scum under her employ would likely be hire-knives, loyal only to their paymaster. And any one of the bar's clientele looked the sort who'd skin a family member for a modest price.

'I have no allies here,' she said from across the table. 'You have my word.'

'And what is that worth?' I asked, turning back to her. 'You're willing enough to betray your current masters.'

She smiled. 'You condemn me for providing testimony to the enforcers?'

'No. But I gather your masters will.'

'True. Khaadi are honour bound to never assist your kind. I am sure you swore similar oaths concerning the criminal classes. Yet here we are.'

'I do not assist criminals.'

'Not you, perhaps,' she said, her gaze flickering back to the bar and the seated Stann. 'But are all your kind incorruptible? I know of Khaadi who have violated their oaths. In fact, I heard it was one such traitor who led the ill-advised sea raid. Yet through his betrayal, this conspiracy was uncovered. Likewise, by making use of Probator Curris' network of informants, you have found yourself here. With me.'

Her voice was emotionless, her eyes like mist. I could not read her, and I was good at reading people. It was like an actor reading a script, her every word a message scribed by someone else. She was but the vessel, vacant and clear as glass.

Unless that was a front she chose to present.

I frowned. 'I was unaware you knew Curris' name.'

'Perhaps I heard it via the informant web.'

'Yet you were untroubled when I appeared instead?'

'I am trained to maintain my composure.'

'I'm beginning to think you're no smile-girl.'

'I never claimed to be. That was your partner's assumption.'

'He's not my partner.'

'I'm glad you see that.'

'All I see is someone dancing around a subject. You start with bizarre tales of void beasts, then progress to veiled insinuations. You requested this meeting for a reason. You can tell me what that reason was or you can tell the chasteners.'

She bowed her head and offered a smile.

'Very well, Probator Raemis. A fallen son of the Khaadi bartered with the enforcers, his intent to steal a consignment of bioweapons. Why they turned upon him I do not know. Perhaps it was always planned. Or perhaps they discovered what he sought and thought better of the allegiance. But, despite the massacre, the Khaadi managed to secure two devices from the hundreds being smuggled.'

'What sort of bioweapon are we talking about?'

'A stimm collar.'

I shrugged. 'There are plenty of combat stimms on the black market.'

'Not like this. This payload is beyond the ken of the sharpest Khaadi magi. Its alchemic elements defy classification. Even the housing, cobbled together as it appears, contains mechanisms forged from materials unknown to us.'

'You're saying its origins lie beyond Varangantua?'

'Beyond Alecto itself.'

I stared her down. Her gaze did not flicker.

'Let's pretend I believe some of this,' I said. 'Let's suppose an off-world-manufactured combat stimm has been smuggled into Varangantua. What do you expect me to do about it? Unless you plan on providing one of these devices as evidence?'

She shook her head. 'One was lost to us. Squandered and shattered. And the other is far beyond my reach. But despite its unique construction, core components of the device were manufactured here in Varangantua, from factorums in Korsk. The Khaadi were set to launch a raid to uncover their origin.'

'Until the calamity.'

'Yes. An unfortunate occurrence. It wiped out the trail.'

'You're suggesting it was deliberate?' I said, raising an eyebrow. 'Someone sacrificed two void-craft and an entire district just to destroy evidence?'

'I say nothing. But that is my master's assumption. His will has been thwarted and his blood is up. He now prepares for war.'

'With whom?'

She spread her hands. 'It has been an age since he has drawn his blade. He will find a reason to wet it.'

'And you oppose this?'

'I am H'ownd. I serve my master's interests. I do not consider war in his interests, not without knowing the true enemy. But there are no leads, bar one. The traitor who led our failed raid was working with your Bastion's enforcers.'

Her gaze crept over my shoulder again. I turned, followed it. Stann still sat at the bar, hunched over the vox.

He had his back to me.

'That's a serious accusation. Any evidence to back it up?'

'Only my word. And the fact I risk all even speaking to you. It would take but a whisper to the right Khaadi and my life would be forfeit. Perhaps that is what your sanctioner is doing right now. Or perhaps he is summoning his own underlings to do the job.'

I glanced back at her. She smiled, calm and cold as ice on water.

'I need a top-up,' I said, draining my cup. 'I suggest you use that time to conjure some evidence to back up these claims.'

'Or you will detain me?'

'Perhaps I'll just throw you out in the street, let the Khaadi deal with the problem. You have already wasted enough of my time.'

I rose, keeping my pace slow as I made for the bar, trying to unpick her words. Was any of it true? For a lie it seemed unnecessarily complex. If, as Stann suspected, it was merely a ruse or lure, why not claim something more believable? She risked death speaking to me – Stann himself had confirmed that.

The sanctioner was whispering into his vox, but he closed it as I approached and took a seat beside him. His drink still rested on the bar. Curiously, for the first time that evening, it seemed untouched.

'What did you find?' I asked.

'There was a heist that broadly matches her description. Seemed like a turf war between the Khaadi and another group. Someone tipped us off, and the enforcers took care of the problem. No reported survivors, but I suppose a few could have snuck away.'

'What were they stealing?'

'Armaments. Munitions. Usual stuff.'

'What sort of armaments? Guns? Explosives?'

'Just weapons. No other details.'

'There should be records. Itineraries of what was seized and whether the armaments were destroyed or repurposed.'

'What can I say? Our data-clerks are feckless little shits who don't do their job.'

'Who was the officer in charge?'

'You didn't ask me for that.'

He had yet to meet my gaze.

'Anything else?' I asked, watching him.

'Yeah. I know she's lying to us. That name she gave? Nateo? He was a pretty infamous Khaadi leader. Nasty piece of work. No way she would bear the name of someone like him. It's a message. She's playing with us.'

'Or merely a common name?'

'It's a message,' he insisted, finally meeting my gaze. 'What did she say to you? Anything we can use?'

There was sweat on his brow, despite the evening's chill. And when I looked at him, his eyes flickered. Just for a moment.

'Whispers and hearsay,' I said. 'But she thinks the Khaadi prepare for war.'

'They're always ready for war. They idolise a mythical time when their people rode the waves and conquered the world.'

'You seem very familiar with their culture.'

'It's my job,' he replied, looking away. 'I've had run-ins with their sort for years, and this reeks of a trap. Maybe of her making, or maybe she's just a witless pawn reading a script. But we need to bring her in. I've already contacted a couple of my squad. They're on the way.'

I felt a chill, as though the dank air of Varangantua had snuck into the bar. I glanced to the entrance, but it was sealed shut.

'You should have consulted me first,' I said.

He shrugged, nodding to Nateo. 'I tried to signal you, but you seemed distracted.'

'Are you insinuating something?'

'No. You're just not used to them. This one's probably been trained since birth to manipulate. She's playing you.'

'I doubt it.'

'All right. Well, if we get her back to the Bastion and she's in the clear, feel free to chew me out for jumping the gun. But until then I'm doing my job, which is keeping you safe.'

'You really think it will require four of us to subdue her?'

'Who knows?' he replied, nodding to the shadows. 'She may have allies hidden amongst this dross.'

I could not argue that point, in spite of Nateo's assurances to the contrary.

I sighed. 'Next time, you do not act without informing me first. Understood, sanctioner?'

He threw a sloppy salute. 'Sure thing, probator.'

'Nateo? We will continue this conversation at the Bastion. This venue isn't secure.'

We were seated again, flanking her. Stann had a view of the door and I the rest of the room. I expected her to argue, but she merely sighed.

'A shame,' she said. 'For you will learn nothing.'

'Really?' Stann replied. 'I think you'll find our chasteners adept enough in their arts.'

'And I am adept enough at holding my tongue. But it does not matter. I will not live long enough to confess anything. The Khaadi will silence me. Or your people will.'

Her gaze was fixed on Stann. He glared back.

'Wipe that look off your face or I'll do it for you.'

'You find me threatening?' she asked. 'A simple smile-girl? I thought your kind stronger than that.'

His gaze hardened, but he forced a smile.

'Trying to provoke me?' he said. 'Sorry, I'm a little too long in the tooth for that.'

'Or is it my name that bothers you?' she continued. 'Does it bring back some unpleasant memories? Did you provide Probator Raemis with the name of the Khaadi on that ill-fated sea raid? Or is that your little secret?'

'Shut your fucking mouth!' he roared. 'You are criminal scum! Your tales of monsters and void threats are just distractions! But you will not deceive us with your lies!'

He'd half risen, fists pressed to the table, voice thundering. I caught a dozen heads turning to watch us.

'Sit down and shut up!' I hissed, glaring at him. 'We're keeping a low profile, remember?'

He caught my expression, following my gaze to the surrounding tables, most of which had fallen silent. He nodded, taking a deep breath and returning to his seat. I glanced to Nateo. She was unmoved, though an echo of a smile haunted her lips.

'I'm not sure why you're smirking,' I said. 'Unless you have suddenly recalled some evidence that might support your rather questionable account?'

The smile faded. Her gaze fell to her folded hands. The emerald ring glinted on her finger.

'I might have something,' she said. 'If you're certain that's the only way.'

Before I could reply, there was a crash behind me. I turned to find a pair of sanctioners advancing into the room, the door hanging on hinges. They were fully armoured, and both had their stubbers drawn. One was shoving Jerri aside, an armoured fist smashing into his face. The other moved towards us.

Stann smiled, the tension flowing from him.

'Reinforcements,' he said, before surveying the room. 'Everyone remain calm. We have no interest in whatever business you're hatching tonight. We have one suspect to detain. That's it.'

The hulking sanctioners approached us, faces concealed by their helmets. Around us, I heard chairs scraping against the floor as a score of the bar's patrons rose, perhaps seeking a better view, perhaps reaching for concealed weapons.

Stann grinned. 'Good to see you, lads. This lady, and I use

the word loosely, is our suspect. Don't let her appearance fool you – she's a tricky one.'

The nearest nodded, turning towards Nateo. She seemed to have shrunk again, cowering in her chair even as Stann's smile spread across his face.

I glared at the sanctioners. 'What are your names?'

Silence.

Before I could ask again, Stann stepped in front of them.

'This is Parscal and Temis,' he said. 'Lads, this is Probator Raemis. One of the new recruits. Keep an eye on him – I don't want him getting hurt.'

The nearest, Temis, nodded to me, face still hidden, stubber drawn.

Parscal, meanwhile, reached for the cowering Nateo. But at the last moment she slid from his grip, falling to the floor and scrabbling backwards. Her voice once more faltered, yet somehow carried to the darkest corners of the room.

'No!' she wailed. 'The Khaadi will hunt us down, all of us. No witnesses! No survivors!'

Whispers came from the shadows, along with the clink of blades, confirming my suspicions about Jerri's lack of diligence. Stann heard them too, for he whirled around, his voice again booming.

'I repeat, stay where you are!' he bellowed as Temis cocked his pistol. 'We are here for this woman and this woman only. Mind your own business and you can spend tonight in your own bed instead of a holding cell. But anyone who makes a move will be put down!'

As he spoke, Parscal was making for Nateo, Temis covering the crowd. She had reached one of the far tables, hauling herself upright and grasping the collar of one of the drinkers.

'Please! Help me!' she said.

I saw the glint of her ring against his throat, just before the sanctioner struck her.

She folded, rolling neatly beneath the table. The drinker was still standing, swaying slightly, blocking the sanctioner's path.

'Move aside!' Parscal grunted, shoving him in the chest.

The man did not move. His hand was clasped to his neck, rubbing at something.

'Move, scum!' Parscal repeated.

The drinker raised his head, his gaze boring into the enforcer's faceplate. His lips twitched, receding from his teeth, until his mouth was stretched into a rictus grin.

'Stinkin' enforcers,' he slurred, voice thick.

Then his forehead smashed into Parscal's faceplate. I'd seen a few drunks and stimm-heads attempt this, with predictable results, as an enforcer helm was strong enough to repel stub-rounds.

But the faceplate shattered, the force of the blow almost knocking the sanctioner from his feet. He staggered, raising his stubber, but his attacker surged forward. A shot took him in the shoulder, tearing loose a chunk of meat but doing nothing to slow him, his hands closing around Parscal's throat. The screams lasted only an instant before the enforcer's head was torn from his shoulders.

'Shit!' Temis grunted, turning to fire. But as he spun, the bar's patrons surged towards him, scrabbling for the pistol, his shots firing wild. Before they could drag him down, Parscal's killer surged forward like a wild beast, tearing into them.

I saw blood, and limbs torn from their sockets, before I turned, sprinting for the bar, Stann doing likewise. I kept expecting a bullet to strike me in the back, but though I heard gunshots, the loudest sound was screams, and the wet snap of bone.

Ahead, the panicked Burgous was scrabbling beneath the counter, retrieving a hidden shotgun. I do not know what he intended to do with it, but I could not risk him firing upon us. As I vaulted the bar, I drove my boot into his face. He crumpled, but I had no time to follow up, snatching the weapon and spinning around. A score of attackers were closing upon us. I fired, the scattershot blasting them from their feet.

I expected a second wave. But none were standing.

None save Parscal's killer.

He was soaked in blood, flesh torn by blade and bullet, surrounded by the dismembered remains of the bar's patrons. One still lived, the killer lifting him one-handed by the throat. His other fist thrust out, shattering his victim's sternum.

I didn't wait for him to release his grip, unloading the shotgun into his back. He barely moved. I'm not sure he even felt it.

'Stann! Get to the lockbox!'

He was already there, scrabbling with the fallen Jerri's keys.

The killer looked at me. His face was still stretched into that rictus smile, the skin of his cheeks torn. The side of his neck was swollen and distended, and a growl emanated from his throat, reminiscent of an industrial engine. He bounded forward, impossibly fast. But I was ready, and as he hurdled the bar I fired, point-blank. The force of the shot catapulted him back across the room. At that range it should have turned him inside out. But he was already finding his feet, his face now a bloodied mess, the skin flayed by the scattershot.

He roared again, but a round hammered into his side, a second striking his chest. From the corner of my eye, I saw Stann advancing, stubber raised. Each bullet found its mark, two more in the chest, a third ricocheting from the torn brow. The beast staggered, momentarily dazed, gaze now shifting to Stann.

I bounded over the bar. Stann was still firing even as the killer advanced. His shot had torn the flesh from its forehead, exposing the skull beneath.

It only saw me at the last moment, intent on Stann. I ducked beneath a wild swing, thrusting the shotgun into the open head wound and squeezing the trigger.

Its head snapped back, blood and flesh spraying across my face. It swayed, almost remaining upright, until Stann unloaded three more shots into its head. Suddenly it went limp, collapsing, its bloodied fingers clawing weakly at the ground.

I pumped the shotgun, intending to unload whatever ammo it had left, just to ensure the damn thing was dead.

But something exploded in my side.

The armoured undersuit held, barely, but I was launched from my feet, the air driven from my lungs. I landed hard, shotgun tumbling from my hands. My chest was agony, every breath a struggle, but I managed to roll onto my side, and found myself staring up at Stann, clutching his still-smoking stubber.

'Traitor,' I spat, though my voice was barely a whisper. 'I knew you were crooked.'

'And I knew you were an idiot,' Stann said with a sigh, pistol still trained on me. 'I told you to walk away. I tried to protect you. But you're a naive fool, barely out of the scholam. All lofty ideals and zero understanding. You don't yet realise what it takes to get the job done.'

'Like working with the Khaadi?' I spat. 'Is that how you paid for the Zalamar parked outside?'

He laughed bitterly. 'Nobody works *with* them, you fool. You work *for* them. They use intermediaries, trick you into thinking you're serving the Lex, but all you do is further their ends until you are bound to them. When I was given the chance to get out, to lead them into a trap, I took it. Even brought down a clan in the process, which as far as I'm concerned makes me a hero. Who cares if there were a couple of survivors? The Khaadi disposed of them.'

I could see the shotgun. But it was beyond my reach, and Stann wasn't stupid enough to take his eyes off me.

'But what killed them?' I gasped, trying to buy time. 'Something like that creature? This is big, Stann, bigger than–'

'Not my problem,' Stann said, cocking the pistol. 'Goodbye, Raemis. May the Emperor show you mercy.'

I felt the growl reverberate through the floor. Stann must have felt it too. He spun, pistol raised, but a bloodied hand seized the weapon, crushing it along with his fingers. He screamed, staring at the abomination in disbelief. Half its face had been torn away, exposing an empty eye socket and cracked skull. It was dragging itself upright, left arm hanging limp and useless. But there was sufficient strength in the right to grind Stann's fingers into powder. Even as he screamed, he struck with his other hand, but his blows were like rain on flagstone. The beast wrenched him closer, forcing him to his knees before sinking its teeth into his throat, his screams choked by blood.

I could still barely breathe, each inhalation a blade in my side. The shotgun was scant feet away, but even as I clawed for it, I knew I would never reach it. Stann was still now, and his lifeless body no longer held much interest to his killer. Its remaining eye turned on me, lips torn back in a snarl.

But before it could reach for me, Nateo vaulted onto its back. Her cloak was now discarded, hair flowing freely, the pin that held it in place clasped like a dagger. The metal seemed to shimmer an instant before she drove it into the fractured skull, splitting the bone as she buried the blade into its brain.

Still the beast struggled, bucking and clawing at her. She twisted her wrist, wrenching the weapon back and forth. The creature spasmed, let out one last snarl and collapsed.

She dismounted it, glancing at me with those cold grey eyes.

'In the name of… the Lex Alecto…' I grunted, struggling to get the words out.

Nateo smiled. 'Your sense of duty is admirable. It is a quality we share. But you are in no position to detain me.'

She moved past me, stooping to retrieve the shotgun.

'I could kill you, probator,' she said softly. 'But I need your help. Our leads were consumed by the calamity's flames. The only remaining possibility is that your enforcers know something.'

I'd managed to drag myself into a sitting position, my gaze finding the fallen abomination. It seemed shrunken now, diminished by death and the absence of stimms. Its face was a ruin, body scored by shot and blade. But I could not take my eyes from its swollen throat, the flesh puckered and studded with tiny cuts, as though from barbed thorns.

Nateo squatted down beside me, blocking my view. She still held the shotgun, but I found my gaze fixed to the ring on her finger.

The gem, once bright, was now black, its barbed housing stained with blood.

She caught my gaze and smiled.

'You did this,' I gasped, my breath coming a little easier now.

She shrugged. 'You demanded evidence. If you need more, have a verispex examine the body, assuming you can find one you trust. But know that whatever lingers in its blood is but a pale facsimile, forged from dregs scavenged by the Khaadi magi. This monster is but a shadow of the beast that slew the Khaadi raiders. Imagine a score of such creatures unleashed across the city. Or worse, imagine an army of them directed with purpose. We cannot allow this.'

'We? You expect me to trust you?'

She lowered the gun, placing the weapon beside me. 'Trust that I saved you. And spared you. It is more than your enforcer allies offered.'

As I reached for the shotgun, she rose, striding calmly towards the door, only slowing to retrieve her cloak.

'Hold it,' I said, raising the weapon.

She glanced back at me. 'You intend to kill me?' she said. 'Then what? Who can you trust? Your Bastion is already compromised, your supposed allies ready to turn on you. Do you know how far the rot has spread?'

There was a horrid truth to her words. Killing her would eliminate the only lead I had. I thought about taking out a knee. But my hands were trembling, I could not aim with any certainty. And were I to miss, I had no doubt she would kill me.

'You think I would work for the Khaadi?' I spat.

She smiled. 'The Khaadi would never work with you. Lord Laqui would rather die than seek your assistance. But I am H'ownd. I have no honour to sacrifice. So perhaps we can work together?'

'I won't help you.'

'Then let me help you. See what you can uncover, and when you need me, I will be in touch.'

'Who are you really, *Nateo?*' I asked.

She paused in the doorway, glancing back, as though assessing the twisted bodies and blood-smeared walls. Her eyes glinted with the stolen light of the bar's broken sign. For an instant, they had an almost emerald hue.

'I am my lord's vessel,' she replied, slipping the hood over her head. 'When we next meet, please call me Glas.'

The darkness swallowed her.

I found my feet, surveying the carnage, the bodies so badly mutilated that I could not separate scum from sanctioner, death granting a horrible unity. Only the traitorous Stann and fallen abomination were identifiable amidst the carnage, their corpses entwined but torn faces laid bare.

Behind me, I heard Burgous whimpering.

I turned, staggering over to the barman. He was clutching his face, barely conscious.

'Get up,' I spat, pressing him with my boot.

'You broke my nose!'

'You threatened a probator,' I replied, pumping the shotgun. 'I could kill you right now for that. Not to mention the rest of the shit you're implicated in. This all happened under your watch. You're liable for every death.'

'No! Please!' he stammered, only now surveying the carnage. 'I wasn't going to shoot you! I don't know anything. Please, I never would–'

I let him babble awhile, pleas becoming sobs, before lifting the weapon away from his head.

He fell silent at once.

'Perhaps we can work something out,' I said, as though considering it for the first time. 'Perhaps you were just a bystander, and innocent in all this.'

'Yes! Yes, that exactly!'

'But I need something in return.'

'What? Anything!'

'You must get all sorts in here. Criminal scum. Corrupt enforcers.'

He nodded frantically. 'All sorts.'

'Tell me, do you know any verispexes who no longer serve the enforcers?'

SKELETONS

NICK KYME

They wore storm cloaks to ward off the rain, the neoplas shining like oil in the downpour. Twelve of them, bulky underneath those slickers. Bulky with tactical armour. Hard carapace with mesh under-weave. Enough to stop a solid slug at close range. Or a knife that was even closer. It was that kind of night.

Seraf Ciastro stood in the middle of the semicircle. She racked the slide of her Boyar. The crunch-clack of shotgun shells felt satisfyingly robust in her hands. Been a while since she was last in the field. Gooseflesh pimpled her arm.

'Let's get this done.'

Her voice grated through the rebreather filtering out the toxins of the Genovska wasteland. The dirt desert blew in over the edge of the district in a brown-and-ochre swathe, palling in the narrow crooks of manufactoria and cattleyards. Ciastro's hard gaze was on the storm bunker two hundred feet ahead. She marched on it through the rain, her sanctioners in lockstep.

Gench whistled, the sound tinny and nasal through his own rebreather.

'Size of it… Like a fortress.'

'It is a fortress, sergeant,' Ciastro reminded him, eyes ahead. 'And we're about to breach its defences and oust its king.'

'Right you are, captain…' Gench held his own shotgun low and across his body. Spare ammo had been attached to the Boyar's stock, a rack of seven stubby black shells. The wind spilling off the wastes opened up his cloak a little, revealing a bandoleer of grenades. He patted the explosives reverently. 'Right you are…'

Sixty feet from the exterior wall and the storm bunker loomed like some implacable edifice. It had been constructed as a civilian refuge and depot by the Erlon-Vant conglomerate, but all the really bad storms happened up in Polaris these days. Genovska just had the heat and the dirt squalls. It had been sealed by the Structures Committee once it fell out of regular use, its slab-sided walls forged of twelve-inch thick ferrum, with a single point of ingress and egress. A stronghold.

Twenty feet from the gate, which bore the abraded icon of Erlon-Vant, Ciastro stopped. She held out a gloved hand, the rain teeming over her outstretched arm as one of the sanctioners passed her a vox-horn.

The device emitted a faint crackle as she turned it on and pressed it to her rebreather. Then her voice boomed.

'Silas Heln, you stand accused of murder, extortion, blackmail, violence without a permit, and grand larceny against the Departmento Munitorum. In the name of the Lex Alecto you are to surrender yourself to our custody immediately. This will be your only warning.'

Static hissed while Ciastro waited ten seconds for an answer she knew wouldn't come. She handed back the vox-horn.

'Still think he's in there?' asked Gench, but the sergeant was already throwing off the hooded storm cloak in preparation for a fight.

'He's in there,' Ciastro replied.

'Trust that informant of yours?'

Ciastro shed her own cloak – they all did – rain thudding against charcoal-grey body armour now and pooling in the death's-head icon emblazoned on the chest.

'About as much as I can throw him, but he wouldn't lie about something like this.'

Gench snapped an underslung launcher to his shotgun. 'I hope you're right, captain...' he said, then slid a grenade from his belt into the tube.

'Jenezas are on me if it's empty,' Ciastro said, sinking to one knee. She gave Gench a savage smile as the others joined her in a braced position. 'As you were, sergeant.'

Gench smiled back. He lived for this shit.

'Fire away...'

Gas ignition plumed from the launcher and a split second later the grenade hit the gate and exploded. Then it burned, an inferno round made to core through metal. It did its job, searing a hole through the gate.

'Move!'

Ciastro led the charge, six in her wake, hoofing those twenty feet in double time.

Radev got to the breach first, an aperture large enough for her fist. She reached in with a latch-cleave, mag-clamping to the gate's interior locking mechanism. Muttering a benediction to its machine spirit, she let the insectile device do its work.

Thirteen seconds later, the rest of Ciastro's squad now flush against the wall and vigilantly checking sight-lines, the dull *thunk* of the gate locks disengaging echoed through the heavy metal.

The door lurched open just a fraction, wide enough for a body to pass through. It looked dingy inside, the lumens at low intensity. Heart pumping, Ciastro consulted a partial schematic of the storm bunker on the data-slate fixed to her vambrace. Twenty-one levels, tight corridors, numerous chambers. Plenty of places to hide.

She exchanged a brief glance with her squad. 'His Hand...'

Each sanctioner made a clenched-fist salute. 'His Hand...' they replied.

The rain was coming down like knives, hissing loudly against oil-black tarmac.

Ciastro led them in.

Then...

She clicked a runic key on the lectern where she stood briefing the squad in Bastion-G's strategium. A small hololithic projection coned into the dingy light, pulling back shadows in the dull, grey room. The image was monochrome yellow, a man – well groomed, imperious. He had a narrow face like a hook and long slicked-back hair, his image rotating through three hundred and sixty degrees as Ciastro talked.

'Take a good look,' she said. 'This is Silas Heln, gang lord of the Nine Devils Venetors. He's wanted in three districts for crimes against the Lex and we've cornered him in ours.' She paused, letting the prideful chests of the sanctioners swell just a little. They'd earned this collar. Heln was theirs. She would take him personally. 'I want him alive. His soldiers...' She made a dismissive gesture with her mouth. 'Either way. This is high profile. The highest. The gilded and the merchant-barons are all tied up about this scum.'

'Is that why you're joining us, captain?' asked Radev, a glint of something feral in her eye. Blonde haired with a left-hand side-shave, she had some scars, did Radev. Too many knife fights, although she was twelve to nothing in her favour on that score.

'I'm leading the mission, yes. Never let it be said that the castellan of Bastion-G doesn't get her hands dirty.'

They laughed at that. A good rapport. Trust and comrade-ship. Felt like coming home, like her old unit back in the day. The good parts at least.

'Rumour is, Heln is in possession of an old piece of tech,' Ciastro went on, 'something from the First Landings, if you can believe that. This part of the mission is low priority. Intelligence suggests the tech's probably a myth, but ours is not to reason why…'

'Ours is but to do and die. Only in death, right, captain?' suggested Radev with a sickle grin.

'That's the other band of shit-kickers, Radev.' Ciastro tapped the faded Guard tattoo on her arm. It read *105th Alectian* and was framed by a bird's wings. Underneath in a ragged scroll was the name *Helhawks*. 'Our comrades in the Militarum,' she said with savage pride. 'They can watch the stars and we'll look after the streets, so there's something for them to come back to.'

'What's this tech, captain?' said Kline, all business. Narrow-framed but strong with it, Kline wore a buzzcut and was taking notes with a stylus on his data-slate.

'Glad you asked.' Ciastro clicked off the hololith. 'No images of this, since it has about as much credence as those sight-ings of four-armed xenos with knives for teeth up in northern Polaris. Street name is "Skeleton Key", an old scrying device with a long reach. A vox-thief like no other. And for powerful people with secrets, something like that is scarier than any xenos, four-armed or not.'

A few chuckled at that; no one really liked the gilded or their ilk, but the rich bastards kept the city fed and in slate. Gench smirked. Bald scalp shining, the old veteran was like a fist of gnarled leather crammed into his strategium chair. Ciastro favoured him with a rueful smile.

'It's simple. We grab up Heln, ascertain whether this tech is real or myth. Then we get out. Expect heavy resistance. Any questions?'

Mannon raised her hand. Her squad name was 'Dead-Eyes' and it was apt. Thickly built, she had a faint dark ring around her right eye, stark against her pale skin from where she pressed the scope.

Ciastro jerked her chin in Mannon's general vicinity.

'Just one, captain,' she said, in that cold mortuarium cadence. 'When do we move out?'

'Immediately,' said Ciastro. 'Gear up and try not to get killed. His Hand...'

'His Hand...' they intoned in unison, and the strategium emptied in seconds.

The interior lobby was a vaulted space, wide enough for all twelve sanctioners abreast at least twice over and high enough with its soaring upper levels to induce a mild vertigo. Every lumen was a dull ghostlight in the gloom, a patch of watery grey that did little for visibility. It was also patently empty. Numerous balconies that led to doorways that led to rooms and corridors held the promise of something more. Something violent.

Ciastro took the squad across the lobby in two lines of six. Stained red carpet crinkled underfoot. She made for a statue of an Imperial saint towering at the far end. She didn't recognise which one. Sculpted out of marble, dressed in robes with a laurel about its head like a crown, it extended a hand benevolently. Three levels above was a lifter that offered a route to the higher floors, its operating lamp still green.

Two sweeping sets of stairs flanking the lobby peeled away from the statue, one leading to each second-floor balcony. Scuffed and made of synthwood, their sides flakboarded, the stairs had the look of barricades. She headed towards the left one, signalling the half-squad led by Gench to take the right.

'Eyes up...' she murmured, briefly checking her levels.

The air was good inside, good enough, so they shed the rebreathers for ease of comms.

'Can't be this easy...' whispered Radev thickly.

Ciastro agreed. She jabbed a finger at Harrok and then aimed that same finger at the quietly ominous balconies. After a low fizz of activation, a handheld stablight beam fanned out like a flare of white dust. Sanctioner Harrok swept it over the upper levels, slow and easy. He picked out worn bannisters, empty protein cans, tabac stubs and other refuse. Bare metal, shiny from use, gave the place the feel of a penitentiary more than a civilian shelter.

'Nothing,' he hissed, the edges of his dark skin fringed with pale light.

Ciastro shared a look with Gench; the veteran was panning his shotgun from shadow to shadow. He shook his head. The castellan's raised fist brought them to a halt. Soft bootsteps faded to silence. Slow, shallow breathing filled the space with an edgy susurration.

She whispered, 'Harrok...' and as he turned, she made a sharp cutting gesture across her throat. Harrok doused the stablight and the greyish dark flooded back. They were halfway across the lobby, the stairs close. Ciastro's eyes were on the second-floor balconies, focusing on the darker areas.

Subtle movement caught her eye, a shifting of the shadows too purposeful to be the light. Then she saw the glint of metal.

Ciastro roared. 'Eyes right!'

A burst of automatic fire ripped down at them, loud and flaring. It strafed the squad as Ciastro returned fire, heavy booms from her Boyar. Bannisters splintered, she cored a plane of flakboard sheeting. Then a low grunt of pain.

She yelled, 'Covering fire!'

Shotguns boomed in the darkness, spitting muzzle flash.

Ciastro was moving, running for the right-hand stairwell to

the second-floor balcony, when at least a dozen shooters opened up. They leaned out over the flakboard sides, aiming down with autoguns blazing. On instinct, the sanctioners hugged the walls to narrow the ambushers' arc of fire.

Vendt and Kilany were down, groaning as Gench dragged them by their collars but kicking their way into cover.

'Radev, Kline, on me!' Ciastro shouted above the rattle of gunfire to her two closest comrades.

They met her at the right-hand landing. She was hunkered down but gave a vengeful snarl of white teeth. A second later, an opportunistic sniper stuck his head over the lip of the stairs above. Ciastro had her sidearm and shot the Venetor through the cheek, shattering the ceramic mask he was wearing before he fell back out of sight.

She gestured to where she'd just killed the ganger.

'Balcony. Quick and close. Purge it.'

Kline nodded, and pulled a second pistol to join the first he'd already locked and loaded. Radev holstered her weapon and pulled a long knife from a sheath on her boot.

Below, the lobby was an utter shitstorm, hard rounds tearing up the floor and pinning the rest of the sanctioners. Gench had the squad fire on the first balcony at the stairs, keeping the gangers off Ciastro and her sortie.

Kline went in first. He was fast, twin pistols barking before he'd even mounted the final step. Radev followed, low like a viper. Ciastro swept in a few seconds later. Three lay dead, one with a hole in his cheek that she had tagged earlier and two more with crisp headshots. The gloom muddied the carnage and she almost missed the ganger with a hatchet coming at Kline from an alcove. Ciastro shouted a warning, Kline pivoted aside, and Radev cut the axeman apart with a flurry of rapid, efficient thrusts.

Four more seconds. Three more dead gangers and Ciastro's

party on the balcony hadn't taken a scratch. More Venetors emerged from other alcoves – the wall was lined with them. Radev dealt with these interlopers quickly. Every cut hit a vital organ. Kline took her leavings, one at point-blank range, who Ciastro barged and pushed over the railing. The scream was short-lived.

On the other side of the lobby, the shooters pulled their attention from the sanctioners below to the lethal bastards tearing through their comrades on the opposite side.

'Down, down!' cried Ciastro, dragging on Kline's belt and getting him behind the meagre protection of the flakboard. Radev stayed low, slitting throats of the mortally wounded, as the lifter doors at the junction where the two balconies met opened.

Ciastro noted the heavy stubber as its wielder heaved the weapon into place and *thunked* in the belt-feed. A door to her right offered sanctuary. 'Inside!' She shoulder-barged the door and it came apart at the hinges, nearly ripped right off. Radev and Kline followed on her heels as heavy-weapons fire engulfed the balcony outside.

Old memories returned.

That vine-choked world, Arrach. Those six miserable weeks in the hell-sworn jungle. Colonel Maggs pushing the greens hard, urging on the platoon: 'Only way out is through, only way out is through…' It became their mantra. Solid shot popping in the air like fireworks on Founding Day…

Eyes darting, Ciastro found an empty room and thanked the Throne for that. Just an iron bed-frame, basin, chair. She had her shotgun up, sidearm holstered. Even in the foul light, she could see Kline's grimace.

'Clipped me,' he lied. His right flank had a darkening, shiny patch. In better light, it would have looked red. *Like old man Maggs before the greens got him…* He staggered, and Radev rushed in to support him.

Ciastro was on the vox, the balcony lit up like hellfire beyond the broken doorway.

'Gench, respond...'

Throne, the light, the noise... It never left her. She regressed right back. *The scent of loam and sickly, cloying foliage. Maggs screaming as they took him by the legs. Dragging him like meat...*

A few lapsed seconds, though it felt longer, then: '*At your command, captain.*' Gench sounded stressed, breath huffing. Gunfire rattled across the feed. Ciastro held on to the present.

'Are you moving?'

'*Affirmative. Taking left stairs now.*' A thunderous report of shotgun blasts echoed down the receiver. Someone swore.

'Need cover on the right flank... See that cannon?'

'*I see it. She's chewing through that belt-feed like it's a last meal.*'

'It could be ours if we don't get some cover. Eighth door from the south end.'

A pause, then Gench's muffled voice as he turned to address another sanctioner. More gunfire. Heavier this time.

'*Smoke incoming...*' he said, and Ciastro heard the metal *clink* of a shell being slid into the breech.

The mortars loading up and laying down fire...

Ciastro cut the vox, turned to the others. Kline looked pale even in the low light but managed a grim smile. He patted Radev's arm and reluctantly she let him go.

'Rebreathers. Now,' said Ciastro.

The masks went back on, and breath loudened to a gale in an instant.

Outside there came a softening of the stubber's fusillade then a low *plink* of metal striking metal. Smoke ejected in a plume before spilling out in a violet cloud. Then came choking as the Venetors' fright-masks, so adept at intimidation, fell short of filtering out riot-control smoke.

Ciastro burst through the wrecked opening. 'Move, move!'

The others bulled right out after her. She'd flipped down her goggles. Body shapes hazed through the smokescreen in orange halos of heat-sight. She dropped one with her shotgun; it spun on its heel and was already fading to cold when she ripped up another.

Heavy fire coming in from the crew-served guns. Pulling the greens away. Maggs revealed, trussed to a spit. His legs hacked off at the knees. Slowly cooking. Still alive. Ciastro seeing it through the scope of her rifle. Maggs sees the glint of the sight through his agony. Nods his head as he grits his teeth. She takes the shot–

Kline fired off another burst, his pistol tuned to 'rapid', his other hand clamped to his side. Radev strafed with an autogun, knives sheathed for now, and pretty soon the balcony cleared.

So did the smoke. A few gangers still lived. Radev went back to her knives for these sorry bastards.

Kline slumped. Ciastro crouched to check him and after receiving a pat on the shoulder that he was stable, she stood and met Gench's wild eyes on the other balcony. The rest of the gangers were dead or in retreat. The reek of fyceline clung to the air like a shroud. Gun smoke lingered. The lobby was awash with shells, a beach of brass and copper.

'That all of them, captain?' Gench said, and levered a dangling Venetor over the side with his boot. The body hit like a meat sack, neck snapping on impact.

Ciastro looked down at the heavy she'd killed first in the smoke. A woman: the shotgun blast had torn through her ammo packs and cored her stomach like a stone-fruit. Her heavy stubber had Munitorum stamps. Militarum-grade weapons. Good, reliable ammo too.

'Not nearly all of them,' she said, jaw clenched. She wanted Heln for this. The lifters had turned dark after the rest of the Venetors had made their retreat. 'This was just a taste.' Then to herself, 'Just a taste...'

A vox-hailer, *all* the vox-hailers stationed around the lobby, suddenly crackled.

'You shouldn't have come here, enforcers. I warned them. I warned everyone,' said Silas Heln, his voice overlapping and reverberating with the slightly un-synched emitters. He sounded old, weary but knife-edge sharp. *'I was very, very clear. Leave Venetor territory alone. Stay out of my business.'*

Ciastro addressed the nearest vox-hailer, head up, voice like a clarion.

'Silas Heln, surrender yourself immediately to the custody of the enforcers, in the name of the Lex Alecto. Do so now and–'

'No, no, no,' he interrupted, *'this isn't an exchange, officer. There is no negotiation. I thought I had made myself very clear. No interference. No Lex. What happens now…'* He paused and the two seconds of dead air dragged like an age. *'That's all on you.'* The vox cut out, replaced by another sound, a mechanism, something grinding and deep within the structure.

Ciastro exchanged a glance with Gench, who shrugged, trying to locate the source.

A low tremble from below had her steadying her footing. She looked down.

'Are we… moving?' said Radev, and her gaze went to the entrance.

It was sinking, slowly. The gate had already shut, mag-locked fast.

A low wail of sirens cut the air.

'Fuck…' hissed Ciastro, and called out, 'Harrok! Get to that door. Stop the sequence.'

Harrok hustled. He was on the facing balcony with Gench, who had ordered the others into defensive positions in case this was a prelude to a second assault.

Ciastro quit the first balcony, helping Radev to hoist Kline at pace. Her eyes were on Harrok, who had practically flung himself down to the ground floor and hacked open a panel adjacent to the door with his knife.

'Harrok...!' shouted Ciastro, her tone firm but anxious. Time was running out.

The mechanism kept grinding, then the low shaft of light coming through a thin grate at the top of the door eclipsed to black. There was a dull, heavy *thunk* like a massive elevator platform reaching its terminus. The entire complex had lowered beneath the street surface.

'Shit.' Harrok banged his fist impotently against the wall.

Ciastro halted midway down the stairs, a few feet from the ground floor. She sagged a little.

'These old places,' said Gench, from above, looking the least perturbed of all the sanctioners, 'they were partly subterranean. Storm can't touch you if you're underground.'

'How deep does it go?' asked Ciastro. Kline could still just about walk, and with some analgesics might still be functional in an operational sense. Vendt and Kilany were on their feet, the former with a shot through his shoulder, the latter with a chestful of shrapnel that his armour had mercifully absorbed. They had a med-kit, enough to patch up their wounded, but Kline didn't look too good and Vendt cradled his injured arm.

'Three hundred feet, maybe more,' Gench replied.

Harrok suddenly frowned, tapping the comm-bead in his helm. 'Vox is out.'

'That's another thing about these old bunkers,' said Gench. 'Once you're under, no way to signal out.'

Leaving Kline with Radev, Ciastro brought up the building schematic on her data-slate. At the highest magnification, she went straight to the bunker's summit.

'Vox-mast...' she said, wearing a triumphant smile. She scrolled down a few levels to the opposite side of the building, where an ident marker pulsed softly. An overseer's station and the most fortified room in the complex. 'And that's our prey.' She regarded the squad, bloodied but unbowed. She'd have preferred to get Kline out. And resistance had been heavier than expected. They needed reinforcement. Heln was dug-in and surrounded by a fucking army, it seemed.

The jungle encroached, a shot echoing through the moist dark…

'What are your orders, captain?'

She looked up at Gench. 'Two teams, one for each objective. Sergeant, take five men. You've got the vox-mast. Confirm with Justicius Viandani, target is here and he's locked in. That should bring the Zurovs gunning. Rest are with me on Heln.'

'And the army he's got protecting him?' asked Gench.

Ciastro racked a fresh round into the Boyar's breech. 'The only way out is through.'

Then…

She didn't consider herself vain, but Ciastro checked her appearance in the mirror-glass pane for the fourth time. It took up most of the wall and gave a full-body reflection. Officer's attire, crisp lapels and silver brocade. The death's-head, serpent and coronet badge pinned to her jacket. Dressed in black, barring a flash of red here, a line of silver there. She filled out the uniform well, her Guard physique still evident despite the years since. Lean, hard, her face taut and angular. Short white hair, only slightly longer than the old Militarum buzzcut she used to have. The scar on her forehead a more permanent reminder of her service, pale and thin like a ragged vein. The rank of castellan afforded privileges; she could have had the scar removed, but Ciastro wanted the reminder. That it was real – all of it, and not just the nightmare it left behind.

That place, Arrach… That damned jungle…

She pulled at her collar, feeling the high sides encroach like a noose, the air mildly stifling–

'Castellan...'

A silky voice brought her back. The air cooled and Ciastro forced a smile as she turned to the well-dressed aide. Cybernetic from the waist down, the porcelain-faced figure gestured with metal fingers to a set of large bronze doors. The Lexmakers of old had been embossed onto the surface of the ornate doors, their raised edges tinted with verdigris.

'The Honourable Justicius Viandani will see you now.'

Ciastro bowed – ridiculous bowing to a half-machine but she had done it now and couldn't take it back.

She strode through the doors, which had opened the moment they registered her presence.

Like the outer corridor, Viandani's office sang with slightly faded grandeur even in the low light that cast shadows over everything. A statue in one corner, winged and looming, human and angelic. Terrifying. A huge, expansive window offering a glorious panorama of the city. A small library in an open anteroom, with scrolls and string-tied sheaths of vellum, as well as several well-worn tomes. Statutes of the Lex Alecto. Old case files. A recaff machine, the chrome catching the lamplight just so... And then the desk, a great sweeping hunk of heavy-looking synthetic wood. Faux-oak, if she was any judge. More papers and parchment here, well organised and neatly turned out, just like the man himself, who had left his plush throne to greet her.

Viandani smiled, his skin like rich, tanned leather under the soft lighting. His grey suit was well tailored. Expensive. He wore a gilded metal guard over the right shoulder, shaped into the head of an eagle. A high collar pushed up his chin made him look imperious. A haptic glove on his left hand and an oh-so-subtle bionic implant in his left ear, through which he could access the dataveil, were the only outward concessions to technology.

'Gauging threats, castellan?' That smile again, even wider as he reciprocated Ciastro's salute.

'Just habit, my lord.' Ciastro stood ramrod straight, like she was back on the muster field. 'His Hand, justicius.'

'His Hand.' He looked amused before returning to sit behind his desk. 'Now, what can I do for you?'

'Silas Heln,' she said. 'I have his locale.'

'The notorious gang lord of the Nine Devils Venetors.' Viandani lit an electro-pipe, the small flare of orange throwing a lustrous glow over his dark, well-groomed hair. 'Scourge of three districts. How long has he been on the list?'

'Three years, three months and eighteen days, my lord.'

Viandani regarded Ciastro with inscrutable neutrality, his bonhomie turned off like a tap.

'This isn't the first time someone has come to me on the hunt for Silas Heln. It has yet to pan out in our favour.'

'I need sanction for a raid.'

'Naturally. Why should I give it?'

'May I be frank, my lord?'

He gestured to her that she could.

'To say Heln has been elusive is putting it mildly,' Ciastro went on. 'He has evaded capture and put more of my fellow officers in the mortuarium than I care to count. I also think he is receiving high-level help.'

Viandani paused in tending to his pipe and quirked an eyebrow.

'Interesting. Elaborate. Does this have anything to do with the… ah… What are they calling it these days?'

'Skeleton Key, my lord.'

'Ah, yes. Prosaic, I suppose, but it suits.'

'I think the Skeleton Key is a pile of groxshit, if you pardon the expression, my lord.'

'Consider it pardoned.'

'Heln has influence. His gang has infiltrated the gilded. Extortion, bribery. I'm willing to bet he has vladars and merchant-barons in his pocket all the way to Polaris-Nul and back.'

'And castellans too?'

Ciastro didn't flinch. 'Anything is possible.'

Viandani chewed on that for a moment, deciding. 'And what makes this worth the bet, Castellan Ciastro?'

'An informant, an old friend from the Guard. He has eyes on Heln. I trust him, my lord. At least, I do in this.'

'Hardly a ringing endorsement.'

'This could be the best chance we'll ever have of bringing in Heln. Twelve men is all I need.'

'And backup if you find him, I assume?'

'Enough that I can keep the blood from spilling out onto the streets. And I lead the team.'

Viandani took a long draw on his pipe, the embers in the caged bowl flaring, his eyes on Ciastro as if searching for weakness. He blew out a luxurious purple plume. 'Very well. It's worth the risk. You'll have my letter of sanction via pneumo-tube by morning.'

Ciastro bowed again, the doors already opening behind her. 'My lord...'

'Alive, castellan,' said Viandani by way of a parting shot. 'If this corruption is as deep-rooted as you suspect, the chasteners will have their turn with him.'

She saluted, heels snapping together as she made to about-turn, when the smile returned, curved and sharp as a duelling dagger. 'And castellan...' he said. 'Good hunting.'

After the gunfight in the lobby, an unsettling silence fell over the Erlon-Vant bunker. Numerous rooms and corridors, every one of them needing recon, made for slow progress.

Ciastro, one man behind Harrok at the head of the group, clicked on the vox.

'Eighth level, north. No contact,' she whispered, eyes on the dark.

They were moving down a long service corridor, checking corners, blind spots. Mannon took rearguard, edging backwards with deliberate steps. Even though she had Radev, Kline and Enzo between her and 'Dead-Eyes', Ciastro still couldn't quell the itch at the back of her neck at having Mannon behind her. The woman had transferred from Bastion-U just over a year ago. Some trouble with another enforcer. Rumour was Mannon had shot him. Actually lured him out into the open and put two slugs in his knees with her rifle. Victim didn't walk again but had some marks against his record, also unearthed by Mannon. She put in papers the next day. Whenever Ciastro met those cold eyes, she was put in mind of something from the deep void, something adapted to the icy outer dark, something ophidian and barely human.

The vox crackled, the receiver engaging at the other end, and Gench's voice rasped, *'Tenth level, south-west. No contact. At this rate we'll stroll all the way to the summit.'*

'Don't count on it, sergeant. And take it easy. It's not a foot race.'

'Sooner we get that vox-mast in hand, captain, sooner the Zurovs will be in the air.'

'Not if you're dead and I'm stranded. I'm not fetching your corpse from up on that roof, Gench. You're thicker round the waist than you used to be.'

A chuckle at the other end. *'I can slow down for some sight-seeing.'*

Ciastro smiled. 'See that you do, serg–'

Movement at the junction ahead – something low, scurrying across their path. Harrok caught the tail-end with his stab-beam.

'Captain?' came Gench's hushed enquiry.

'We have contact,' she whispered back, and cut the feed.

Ciastro pulled up her shotgun, edging left to clear sight-lines for the others.

Then the floodlights hit.

Throne, it was like pure white fire poured into her eyes. A massive industrial lumen. Harsh as a blind-grenade. Geography wiped clean, drenched in awful burning light.

'I can't fucking see!' roared Harrok, plunging to a knee as the air rippled with solid shot and gunfire.

Ciastro felt a bullet shriek past her ear. Her Boyar spoke a second after Harrok's, and she fired into that magnesium flare that had turned her world into amorphous, searing white. She heard a grunt, and somewhere in those first few seconds Enzo took a hit. He took several, jerking back and forth as rounds punched his armour, hammering into him like rain. He went down amidst fyceline smoke. Kline got off a shot. Hit something.

Instinctively, the sanctioners hit the walls and went low with only the doorframes for cover.

Ciastro bellowed, 'Kill that damn floodlight!'

The gunfire kept on coming, zipping through the lumen flare. Kline took a glancing hit to his shoulder. Swore loudly. A rico-chet almost caught Ciastro in the neck, but the round whipped past her instead.

'Mannon, now!' she roared and heard the hiss-crack of Mannon's rifle and then shattering glass. It came from above them. How Mannon had scoped it, Ciastro would never know. Fright-masks loomed out of the shadows and the hazy after-glare as the Venetors closed. Cleavers and claw hammers in a ready grip. Short-range stub pistols and an auto-carbine all spitting metal.

Harrok got punched off his feet by a shotgun blast as Ciastro fired blind into the masses.

'Take them, Throne damn it!'

Mannon's rifle snapped three times in quick succession, each shot a kill. Headshots all.

After getting downed, Harrok was back on his feet, shotgun booming. Payback as three more Venetors fell. Five gangers reached the sanctioners, and came up swinging.

'Engage, close quarters!' shouted Ciastro, heart pumping, hooking the Boyar onto her back and pulling out her maul. She blocked a first wild swing, then leaned in to headbutt her attacker, breaking his nose, then curb-stomped his neck against a doorframe. She jammed the crackling electro-maul into another, cooking the perp inside out.

Harrok barged one into the wall, struggling to bring his pistol to bear, the two men wrestling for supremacy. A close-range blast went off – Ciastro didn't know from where, but her ears were ringing. She went over to Harrok, capping the knees of a ganger who had just got to his feet. He went down hard and Radev finished him with a headshot.

Barely slowing, Ciastro grabbed the shoulder of the perp who had pinned Harrok up against the wall, his forearm crushing the sanctioner's neck. With a grunt, she flung the ganger back and Radev shot him through the heart.

Kline finished the last with a pistol shot, right through the eye slit of a fright-mask.

'Not so scary now,' he murmured, putting another in the dead ganger for good measure. His gait had eased, less pained, but he still clenched his side. At least he was still breathing. Which was more than could be said for everyone.

As the dust and smoke settled, Enzo lay on his back in the middle of the corridor. Stooping to check his vitals, Mannon looked sombre as she met Ciastro's gaze.

'Dead.'

'Shit...'

Another shotgun blast went off. Harrok again. Then he was bolting down the corridor.

'Bastard's running!'

A glimpse, just a glimpse, of a lithe shadow limping hurriedly into the dark. A survivor. Must have missed one.

Ciastro gave chase even as a rifle shot blew out a chunk of distant doorframe ahead of the runner, but they slipped away only mildly scathed. She darted a glance over her shoulder, found Mannon and Kline. 'Stay with Enzo. Radev, with me.'

Ahead, Harrok hared after the ganger, pushing so hard Ciastro struggled to keep up.

The endless swathe of the jungle closing in as they fled from the greens...

Radev huffed alongside her. Her grimace to Ciastro warned of the potential trap the captain feared, but they pushed on. If the runner escaped, all the hells would rain down on the sanctioners. As they rounded another corner and entered a long stretch of corridor, Harrok slowed and pulled a bolas from his belt. He whipped it hard, two quick revolutions then release. The projectile spun like a rotor blade, striking the perp around the ankles and entangling their feet mid-stride. The ganger went down with a heavy thud, head striking the wall.

Gathering up his bolas, Harrok was standing over the body as Ciastro and Radev joined him.

'Neck's broken,' he said unnecessarily. The unnatural angle where it bent against the wall made it obvious.

Ciastro crouched by the corpse, tilting the mask aside where it had slipped during the perp's fall. Her eyes widened a little.

'She's just a juve.'

'And barely that,' added Radev. 'I saw a couple of the others just before we took off. Old-timers and juves. Every fucking one. What do you think it means, captain?'

Gaze lingering a fraction longer, Ciastro got to her feet.

'I don't know. Maybe this is the chaff. And Heln's softening us up. Maybe it's something else.'

Harrok nudged the body with his boot, gently easing the arm away from the torso.

'She's got something,' he said. 'In her hand.'

'That why she bolted?' asked Radev as Ciastro crouched again and came back up holding a wafer of metal. It had shapes cut into its surface.

'Looks like an access slate,' said Harrok, eyes narrowed as the ghostlight hit its edges and made them glint.

Ciastro had reached the same conclusion. 'Harrok, watch the perimeter – make sure we're not surprised. And get Kline on vox. Tell him what happened and to hold tight.'

Harrok saluted and hustled to the junction. His hand went to the vox-bead in his ear and Ciastro heard muted conversation.

She turned her attention to Radev, turning over the slate in her gloved hand.

'They were headed somewhere with this thing. Maybe a vault, a lockroom?'

Radev frowned. 'Why stand and fight only to run?'

'Maybe they weren't planning on fighting.'

'She was being guarded?'

'Not her. I think they were moving something,' said Ciastro.

'Important enough to keep sealed away...' ventured Radev. Her eyes narrowed. 'You think it's the Skeleton Key.'

'I don't think anything, trooper, but I do want to find out what's behind the door this access slate opens.'

She looked back down at the body. Not much older than a juve... She'd seen younger on Arrach and they'd died all the same.

They headed back to the others, leaving the dead girl where she'd fallen.

A cold-storage locker served as Enzo's tomb. It had long since been stripped of meat, the racks and shelves empty. They couldn't carry him and Ciastro didn't want to leave him slowly decomposing in some nondescript corridor, so this would have to serve.

She had done worse.

Maggs, his head broken open by the bullet and the greens enraged, sweeping through the mangrove like a plague...

Not long after, they reached an impasse.

A barricade, or more specifically a huge section of the upper floor, had collapsed the stairs between the fifteenth and sixteenth levels. Heavy slabs of overlapping debris closed off the way up, a tangle of shattered lumens and broken rockcrete.

'I've seen Guard redoubts that are easier to breach,' offered Radev, tapping a piece of rebar with the edge of her knife and eliciting a sharp *riiing*.

Ciastro took a look up the stairway, saw light from an open doorway higher up. They were inside a narrow shaft, having crossed level fifteen to reach this point. Down was just darkness, visibility ending after only a few feet. She pulled up the schematic on her vambrace.

'Another stairway... Here.' She jabbed her finger, the light graining where she touched it.

'That'll mean crossing open ground, captain,' said Radev.

So far, they'd stuck to service corridors and back stairways, skirting the fringes of the habitation levels where the civilians would have been during a storm. Ciastro was trying to tread fast but without making too much noise. Get in, take Heln. Get out.

Crossing a floor would draw unwanted attention.

They were down one already and Kline had deteriorated, leaning heavily on the wall, hand on his side.

'Kline, you good?'

He looked wan in Harrok's stablight. 'Think the mesh has split...' His hand came back red and shiny, and he staggered. Radev held him up.

Ciastro turned to Harrok. 'Can you patch him up?'

'I can but it'll just split again. It's meant for superficial wounds. He needs re-skin or a staple gun. I'm not a medicae.'

'No one's asking, Harrok,' snapped Radev. 'Just get him back on his feet.'

'And a few stimms for the pain,' suggested Kline with a weak smile.

'Keep your shit together,' Ciastro ordered. 'That goes for everyone. Kline, you can stay here, hunker down and we'll come get you when this is over, or you can come with, but no one here can carry you. Understand?'

'I'll pull my weight, capt–' He grimaced, teeth momentarily clenched as Harrok stabbed him with the pain stimm injector before reapplying spray-mesh to Kline's wound.

Ciastro regarded him appraisingly. 'At least you look less like a corpse now, trooper. Everyone, on me.'

Glass from the shattered lumens cracking underfoot, they moved on.

Returning to the fourteenth floor, the sanctioners reached a refectory, one of the civilian common areas. It was large, with too many places to hide and not nearly enough cover if you had to cross it. As soon as they hit open ground, they moved fast. Ciastro took point, Harrok a step or two behind, cutting a path through the shadows ahead with his stablight. The entire place was swathed in dust, layering tables and benches, serving stations and galley. Soft palls of it eddied in the air, disturbed by some unseen breeze. Garments had been discarded, left by the former occupants. They were threadbare and moth-eaten.

'Wait…' Ciastro hissed, and raised her clenched fist.

They were halfway across the hall when the dust motes gently swerved then realigned. Something cracked underfoot as she shifted her weight. A child's toy, a crude plastek gunship, lay broken by her boot.

The civilian colonies ravaged by the greens, their tools and belongings left behind. A doll flecked with blood...

There came the louder crash of a serving ladle dislodged from its hook.

'Down!' roared Ciastro as weapons fire tore through the hall.

Harrok upended a table, hauling it from its holding bolts and using it like a barricade. Solid slugs smacked its surface, and in the lull between bursts he fired around the edge. Ciastro was alongside him and blind-fired over the lip of the table, strafing in a ninety-degree arc. She heard a cry and someone fell.

Scratch one of the Venetors.

They were moving though. She could hear the gangers over the semi-sustained barrage of solid shot and las-beam.

'Radev, Kline,' she voxed, 'push up left and outflank.'

A curt vox-blurt confirmed the order had been received.

Ciastro snapped a burst around the right edge of the table. Three quick shots. She hit ceramic and cored the back of a chair, the other embedding itself into the wall. Damage wasn't the objective.

'I count six, right side,' she said.

'Same on the left,' remarked Harrok, darting out to fire off another round.

Radev and Kline had pushed up. Herding the gangers. Ciastro could hear the distinctive report of their weapons across the gunfight.

She clicked the vox. 'Mannon, are you in position?' Ciastro had lost track of the sniper almost immediately but knew she had an uncanny knack of finding a good vantage.

'I have eyes on, captain.'

Again, Ciastro suppressed a nervous itch. She glanced over her shoulder but there was just the refectory, dark and empty. Harrok met her gaze as she turned back.

'Any preference, trooper?' she asked.

'I say left.'

Ciastro eyed a servitor station on the left. The cyborg parts had been ripped out, but much of the mounting remained. Wide enough for two. Decent cover. Fifteen feet across the open aisle between here and there. She nodded and said into the vox, 'Baiting the hook on three... two... one...'

They ran, low and fast, firing wildly into the vague darkness that was spitting death right back at them.

A bullet clipped Ciastro's shoulder, tearing off a piece of fabric but nothing more. Another skidded off Harrok's helmet and he swore but kept on moving.

A flurry of shots rang out in rapid succession, their provenance hard to discern in all the chaos. Bodies fell. A pained shout echoed across the hall from one of the gangers. Scared, panicked. They ran, those that were left. Ciastro came up from behind the servitor station with her sidearm, but it was over before she had to fire another round.

'Dead-Eyes' Mannon had killed the rest. Cold, efficient. No mercy.

She emerged from a vaulted wooden pulpit carved into the face of an Imperial priest. She dropped back down onto the refectory floor with the silence and grace of a felid, her rifle resting against her left shoulder.

Ciastro gave an appreciative smirk. 'Lethal work, Mannon.'

'I incapacitated one,' she said by way of reply and jerked her head in the direction of a wounded Venetor who was clenching his leg and writhing in agony.

Harrok was first on scene, his foot on the perp's throat to prevent the ganger screaming.

'Let him up,' said Ciastro. She brandished the access slate in front of the perp's face as he clambered up onto his elbows.

Pain etched his face, and he eyed the morphia vial Ciastro had just taken from Harrok like it was a healing elixir. She held it and the slate, one in either hand.

'Simple exchange. Knowledge for pain relief,' she said.

The ganger's eyes widened as he bit down on his agony, glancing fearfully between the sanctioners. Without the mask, he looked small and unimpressive.

'What is this for?' Ciastro asked.

The perp began to shake his head when Harrok pressed his boot down on the leg wound, eliciting a pained yelp.

'Answer the captain,' he growled.

Like the others, this one was young and afraid. He started to shake his head again, recoiling as Harrok made to stamp down, but Ciastro's raised hand stopped the boot before it fell.

'I don't fucking know, man...' said the perp. 'Please... Throne... I don't know.'

Radev slid out one of her knives. 'I can make him talk, captain.'

A flick of the hand from Ciastro, more agitated this time.

'What's your name?'

He lifted his chin, sweating now and still shaking, his bluster as fake as his mask.

'Cutter.'

Ciastro scowled. 'You want to get stamped on again? Your *real* name, perp.'

His head fell, a tremble in his lip.

'Skeve... Just Skeve.'

'Skeve. You can talk to me or you can talk to them.' She repeated her question. 'What is this for?'

The perp was really shaking now. A faint ammonia stink wafted from his vicinity as a dark stain spread across his trousers.

'Please...' He was crying, terrified. 'I don't know what it's hiding... I don't know...'

Ciastro's eyes narrowed. 'But you *do know* where it is, don't you, the door it opens?'

His head bobbed, slow at first then more vigorous.

'Yeah... yeah, yeah. I know it. I know it.' Something like

hope in those young eyes, though Ciastro knew chastening and incarceration awaited this poor wretch even if he survived this moment.

She jabbed the morphia in his leg and he howled, but after a few more seconds appeared to calm, the pain's edge blunted.

'An act of good faith,' Ciastro told him. 'Now, your turn.'

He started to rise. 'I can take you, I can–'

Harrok put a vice-like hand on the juve's shoulder. Ciastro gave him a look and he eased off.

'Were you guarding it, whatever this thing opens?' she asked.

More head bobbing, slightly frantic, keen to comply. Nervous glances at the brute with the shotgun and the scary woman with the knives.

'How many outside the door?'

He shook his head. 'N-none. Zero.' He smiled, nodded. Eager to help.

'And inside?'

Skeve thought on that then held up some fingers. Then he did it again. And then again.

Radev let out a curt whistle.

Ciastro's gaze hardened.

Only way out is through.

'Take us there.'

Gench still wasn't responding. Either they were out of viable range or there was some interference. Or it was something else. She doubted the latter. Gench was, first and foremost, a soldier. He hadn't fought in the Guard as far as she knew, but he acted like ex-Militarum. Not as professional, say, as Kline, but brutal and uncompromising. A survivor. Ciastro clicked off the vox, silencing the dead air.

'Still nothing?' remarked Radev.

Ciastro gave a slight shake of the head, irritated but unworried.

'He could be vox silent. We don't know what's on the other side of the building.' She looked ahead.

Harrok had one hand on the perp's shoulder as he limped through the gloom, no doubt murmuring threats into his ear in case he was even thinking about bolting.

The rest of the squad fell into their usual positions.

Another corridor, wider this time, more like a gallery; another poorly lit space for them to cross, but only shadows and the old detritus of former human habitation greeted them.

'Permission to speak freely, captain?' asked Radev.

'Granted.'

'Strange, don't you think, that they've been hitting us like this?'

Ciastro glanced over at her. 'How so?'

'Reacting, retrenching, then retreating. What does it remind you of?'

Radev had served. Only Defence Corps, never off-world, but under Guard instructors and she was a good student of military tactics.

'Guerrilla fighters.'

'Exactly, skirmishers. The tactics of an inferior force against a superior one.'

'You think the Venetors are an inferior force in this scenario?'

'I don't know, captain. But this place is almost empty. Heln's gang are a bunch of old men and juves, barely a handful of hardened fighters amongst them, and they haven't tried to overwhelm us once. They must know where we are, or at least have a good idea. Why not attack?'

Ciastro had considered it. She had similar misgivings. A thought occurred. 'They're protecting something. Silas Heln for sure, but something else too.'

'Maybe it's not an urban legend after all.'

'Still doesn't explain the apparent lack of fighters or their ages.'

Ahead, Harrok raised his fist. They were here.

The door was large, easily wide enough for six abreast. A short corridor led up to it. The door was an addition, not part of the original design. The crude architecture holding it in place looked ugly, rushed. But it appeared solid enough and thick. Too thick for grenades or any handheld ordnance the sanctioners possessed. If Heln was behind that door and wasn't coming out, they needed industrial cutters, maybe something Mechanicus.

A second corridor abutted the short one, creating a crossroads. Ciastro had her squad spread half and half at either end facing the door. The perp had his back against the wall, and looked about ready to shit himself.

She put a hand on his shoulder.

'Tell me again what I need you to do.'

Wide-eyed, Skeve gave a nervous lick of his lips. 'Walk up to the door and tell 'em I need in. I got a message, something important. Yeah. Then soon as it opens, I hit the deck and don't move until you tells me.'

'Very good.' She pushed the access slate against his chest. 'This can still work out for you, Skeve. I will petition for leniency.'

'Yeah, yeah.' He was nodding again, only half listening. 'But can you get me a bullet farm or a manufactory gig? I don't wanna work in those grox pens or none of that agri shit. I hear that shit kills ya. Lung rot, I hear. Or fungus fever.'

He wrapped his spindly fingers around the slate – he looked so thin Ciastro wondered when he'd last had a decent meal – but she held on too for a few seconds.

'Betray us, betray the Lex, and the deal is off. You won't walk out of here, Skeve. I'll see to it personally.'

'Yeah, yeah… I ain't no snitch. I'm with you now. I'll get 'em to open the door. You'll see. I can do good. Yeah.'

She let go of the slate and off he went, sauntering down the short corridor.

Ciastro watched him intently, and the vid-picter lazily panning over the immediate outer threshold. As soon as it alighted on Skeve, a few feet out, it stopped moving. She pulled up her rebreather.

Across the aisle, Harrok and Kline primed grenades.

'Get ready...' voxed Ciastro.

Then Skeve started talking. He swaggered in front of the door, boasting at how he'd killed an enforcer, shot them dead through the neck. He even made sound effects, mimicked the gushing blood.

Radev in her ear. 'What the fuck is he doing?'

Ciastro tightened the grip on her gun.

'Steady...'

In the corridor, Skeve waggled the slate. Said he needed entry. That he had crucial information. That he'd taken something from one of the enforcers.

'We should move now,' voxed Harrok.

'Wait!' hissed Ciastro.

Mannon, crouching on the same side as Ciastro and Radev, hadn't moved. Her rifle edged around the corner by the smallest fraction.

Hand trembling, Skeve pushed the access slate into a slot in the door. It took him three tries and he glanced up at the vid-picter as he was doing it, face beaded with sweat.

'Shit...' muttered Ciastro.

The doors opened, swinging backwards into the room on hydraulic pistons. Skeve cut a solitary figure before the widening expanse, rake thin and pathetic. A lonely boy standing before a gulf. Scared out of his mind.

A rank of levelled autoguns and something bigger on a tripod greeted him.

He stood transfixed.

The seconds stretched.

Ciastro saw the future unfold before her eyes, powerless to prevent it. 'Shit!'

Muzzle flare rippled down the rank of guns and Skeve jerked and spasmed as the bullets hit him. They tore him apart, savagely, shredding him until there was nothing left but scraps of skin and blood.

Incensed, Ciastro roared. 'Move!'

Two grenades bounced into the fusillade, rolling to a stop just inside the room where they went off with loud twin bangs. Smoke and fractured light filled the space, and the gangers inside were choking, crying in agony. Eyes burning, blind; throats raw, suffocating.

The sanctioners pushed through it, breathing through their masks, goggles filtering out the harsh light.

Hurting and disorientated, the gangers died quickly.

Mannon took out the heavy gunner from back in the corridor, firing down her scope. She ended four more before the clip emptied and she had to reload. The rest died to shells and bullets, and the violent maul-armed justice of the Lex's finest. By the time the smoke was clearing, nineteen lay dead on the floor in various states of physical destruction.

'That seem too easy to you?' said Radev.

Mannon shrugged.

'I have no issue with easy,' Ciastro replied but privately conceded Radev might have a point. Nothing for it, though, but to press on.

A single ganger remained, another rangy juve with too many piercings and tattooed arms. He had a captive, a young woman. She wore plain clothes, typical of a civilian. Her eyes and much of her face were hidden by a cowl. The ganger had his arm around her neck, a stub pistol pressed to her right temple, and was backing off. Another figure sat towards the middle of the room. Head down so his face was obscured, his hands tied to the arms of a metal chair that was bolted to the floor. Beaten and stripped to the waist, his body was a mess of bruises, burns and ugly wheals. A single lumen swayed overhead, picking out first the man's brutalised condition then the hooded woman and then the ganger in low lazy sweeps.

He was shaking, the Venetor. A gasket poised to blow.

'I'll fuckin' kill her,' he swore, eyes darting from sanctioner to sanctioner, none of whom made any move with Ciastro's hand raised. She slowly stowed her weapon and held her palm out flat. The vox crackled in her ear, so soft only she could hear it.

'You let me walk, and she lives,' he spat.

'Let her go,' Ciastro said and calmly pulled down her rebreather so he could see her face.

'I'll do it! I'll shoot her right now.'

The woman showed no obvious sign of panic. In fact, she barely moved at all. Ciastro had seen statues more animate.

'Let her go,' Ciastro repeated. 'I won't ask again.'

He backed away, taking the woman with him, edging towards a doorway on the opposite side of the room.

It was a maintenance chamber, large, with plenty of exposed pipes. Crates lay about, some open. Old valves stood like lonely sentinels, caked in dust. Puddles of dirty water splashed under-foot, turned pink with blood. The ganger looked from them to the ruin of his comrades. He howled, *'I'll fuckin' do it! I'll kill the bi–'*

Mannon shot him through the throat and he fell away, stub pistol skittering into the filth, hands desperately trying to staunch the eager flow of blood. He died choking over several agonised seconds.

The hooded woman never moved. Not an inch.

Ciastro took charge, gestured to Kline. 'See to her.'

Radev had walked over to the man tied to the chair.

'Holy Throne...' she murmured. 'He's alive.'

Harrok confirmed it, wafting a wad of smelling salts under his nose. He jerked at first, twisting as he found his hands tied, and then slowly lifted his head. Encouraged by a shallow breeze, the lumen swung across his face.

Ciastro approached him, something curdling in her gut.

'Can't be...'

The man regarded her through strands of sweaty, blood-stained hair. Eyes brightening as they alighted on Ciastro, he gave a red-toothed smile.

'Oh hello, Seraf,' slurred Efrem Thade. 'It's good to see you again.'

Then...

Ciastro paced the room for the tenth time, rubbing her chin, trying to determine if he was lying to her again.

'And you're sure?' she asked. Again.

Efrem Thade sat on an iron bed-frame with a bare mattress, chewing on a piece of klay. The room was dingy, a low-grade hab in an even lower grade habclave. The partially boarded windows lit his narrow face in slashes of hazy red.

'I promise you, Seraf, this is–'

'I've told you not to call me that.' She grimaced. 'Do it again, and I shatter the other leg.'

Thade held up his hands plaintively. 'Mea culpa.'

He looked calm for a man about to lay dirt on the most notorious crime lord in three districts. Wiry to the point of unhealthy, pale, with frost-white hair, Thade was a jaeger, a freelancer, who would have looked unremarkable compared to every other malnourished, mildly drug-dependent citizen of Varangantua were it not for the slight glint of metal peeking out just below his left trouser leg. An augmetic leg, a good one he could scarcely afford. A parting gift from a long-ago war and a jungle they both cared to forget.

'Our shared history doesn't make us friends and doesn't afford you familiarity, either,' stated Ciastro.

'And yet here we are again, working together.'

'No, we are not. You are an informant, providing intel to a castellan of the Lex.' She glanced around, as if for the first time; sniffed. 'And where exactly is *here*, Thade?'

'An old safehold. I occasionally use it when I need to smuggle... ah...' He caught himself. 'When I need to keep someone or something safe.'

'It smells like shit in here.'

'Ah, that probably is shit. Having an issue with rats.'

'I know the feeling,' Ciastro groaned, rueful. She scowled. 'What the hells are you smiling for?'

'Nothing,' Thade lied, 'just that, last time we met I said I'd be seeing you.'

Ciastro rolled her eyes. 'If you're wasting my time, Thade, I'll send Gench to your domicile with a search-and-seizure warrant. Extreme prejudice. You haven't met Gench. He is unsubtle and he is not delicate. Tell me what you know.'

'I know where he is.'

'Elaborate.'

'Silas Heln.'

'Groxshit. No one knows where Heln is holed up. Or if they do, they're paid enough that they're not telling.'

'I know where he is and where he'll be. I've *seen* him.'

Ciastro scoffed, her patience ebbing. 'How?'

'Need to know.'

'I *do* need to know. Who's your source?'

'I can't tell you that.'

'Either give up your source or I can't get sanction to bring him in.'

'Yes, you can. You're a bloody castellan, Ciastro. Nothing is out of your reach.'

She folded her arms. 'Source.'

After staring at her for a few seconds, Thade gave out a demonstrative sigh.

'A client. Has history with Heln. Wants out of the district. She hired me to help, but let's just say she'd feel a lot better if Heln was incarcerated, instead of hiding out somewhere in Genovska.'

'Escort work? I thought you only did missing persons?'

'I do what the client asks. For a price.'

'Why should I believe you?'

'I suppose you won't accept old times' sake?'

'There's old and there's past life, Thade. You're out of favours.'

'Then let me do you one. This is legitimate. I know where he is and I can send you everything via tube. But I can only guarantee that he'll be there for a few days. After that...' He shrugged and made a 'puff' gesture with his hand. 'Smoke in the wind.'

Ciastro held his gaze, trying to determine if he was telling her the truth.

'What's in this for you? Heln has allies. Powerful ones. Lot of heat to bring down if this goes awry.'

'That's why it has to be you,' he replied, suddenly serious. 'Because I know you'll get it done. Just like on Arrach.'

'We all did what we had to do on Arrach.'

'You more than most, Seraf.' He rapped a knuckle against his augmetic and it rang a flat metallic note. 'You saved my life. And everyone knows what you did for Maggs.'

'Don't speak his name. Not in here. Not this place.'

Thade showed his palms, contrite.

'If you take Heln in, shackle him, feed him to the Lex, whatever it takes... I get to save a life too. *Her* life.'

Ciastro thought on it – she'd been doing little else since coming here to this verminous shithole – then decided.

'Send me what you've got. *Everything*, Thade. I'm warning you.'

Thade handed her a scrap of parchment. 'Here's the loc-ref where I'll send it. Tube code is on the back. I'll send it in two hours.'

Ciastro took it, and started to leave. She reached the dead-bolted door when she turned. 'Rumour says Heln has a device, some kind of high-end vox-scryer. Exposes secrets. You happen to know anything about that?'

Thade shook his head. 'Not really my expertise, I'm afraid. I heard it has a colourful name, though. Skeleton Key? A little dramatic, don't you think?'

'Most stories are, I suppose,' Ciastro conceded. 'The good ones at least.' She left, shutting the door behind her with a heavy thud of metal.

At Ciastro's order, Radev severed Thade's bonds. She did it none too lightly, making him wince and jerk in her grasp.

'Take it easy… I don't want to lose a hand as well as a leg.' He patted the bionic limb like it was an old canid he was still fond of. Clenching and unclenching his fingers, he looked strung out. Thade had always been an addict. Klay dulled the pain of his injury and the trauma of his past. Ciastro had her duty and service to the Lex Alecto to take the edge off. She hid or denied the blunt, abrading parts. The memories of the war.

She tossed him a leather jacket she found hanging off a pipe. It must have belonged to one of the dead Venetors, crimson and black in the gang's colours.

'Here… Cover yourself up.' She glanced around the room as Thade took the jacket, shakily pulling it over his sore and wiry frame. 'What in the hells are you doing here, Thade?' she asked as the rest of the squad fell back and maintained a perimeter. Mannon appeared from outside the room, her rifle at ease.

'An old friend?' she asked in a rare, unprompted utterance.

Thade paused in a state of half undress to emphasise the tattoo on his left shoulder.

105th Alectian, Helhawks.

'The oldest of friends,' he said unhelpfully, wearing a smile that dared only creep so far with Ciastro watching.

She groaned inwardly. 'A *very* long time ago. And I wouldn't call us friends. Answer the question.'

Thade finished putting on the jacket. It was a little loose around the shoulders but better than nothing. He winced as Harrok hit him with some morphia.

'I... ah... failed,' he said, rubbing at the puncture wound in his neck.

'Elaborate. Make it quick.'

'That client I mentioned... She's here. I thought I'd hid her well enough but Heln found us. Took us.'

She looked over at Kline, who was still with the woman.

'That her?'

'That's her.'

'Is she drugged? Traumatised?'

'Neither.'

Ciastro clenched her jaw, confused and irritated. 'What's Heln want with you? Why beat the shit out of a low-rent jaeger?' She gestured to the dead. They were slumped in corners or draped over crates and stacks of pipes, wherever they had fallen. 'And why all the guns?'

'They're not for me.' He craned his neck around to regard the woman.

'For her?'

Thade nodded as Kline was carefully pulling back the hood to get a better look at the woman's face.

'Why?' asked Ciastro. 'What's so special about her?'

He smiled, a half-smile really, tinged with sadness and a little fear. 'Her name's Elva.'

The hood fell back, revealing extensive augmetics buried in the woman's shaven skull. Her fingers ended in chrome tips, subcutaneous wiring faintly visible beneath her skin like varicose veins where it snaked up her wrists. Short and slight, she had a pale, almost grey pallor and rheumy eyes. Dead eyes that reminded Ciastro of pearls.

'She's the Skeleton Key,' said Thade.

She had turned up on his door one sweltering Genovskan evening. The city district had baked that day, he recalled, tempers fraying everywhere. Blood on the streets. Nothing new. But she had looked as frigid as a Polaris winter and not just her skin. Emotionally cold, like someone had excised some of the parts that made her human. Her name, she said, was Elva, and she needed his help. Hesitant at first – he'd been coming down off a klay binge – he noticed the augmetics and she told him about Heln, about being a prisoner, about escaping when her minders had tried to kill each other in the Varangantuan heat.

'I kept her safe for a few weeks. I've been working a contact in the Regio Custos, trying to secure passage across district borders.' Thade cinched up the jacket before spitting a wad of blood. He eyed the sanctioners around Ciastro warily before wiping his mouth and leaving a red smear across the back of his hand. 'It took too long. The riots, that disaster over in Korsk. And the fires that came after. Everything was locked down.'

'None of which explains the Skeleton Key,' said Ciastro. They really needed to move. Heln was the objective and she didn't want to lose momentum, but she also wanted answers and a little time to decide what she would do with Thade and his charge.

He rubbed his sore wrists where the ties had cut into the skin and sighed, resigned to his confession.

'Far as I can tell, she's a tech-savant. Or something like one.'

'Mechanicus?' asked Ciastro. She couldn't take her eyes off Elva. This… this *woman* was the Skeleton Key. It was real. She tried not to consider the ramifications. 'How did she get all the way from Nearsteel to Genovska?'

'She's not exactly indoctrinated,' said Thade. 'And she's not from Nearsteel – at least, I don't think she is.'

Everyone was looking at Elva now. She had yet to move an inch and stared catatonically into the room.

'What's the matter with her?' asked Kline, trying to find some spark of awareness behind her eyes.

'Nothing's the matter,' Thade said, and went to Elva. Ciastro ordered the others to stand down. Harrok stepped out of the way but looked none too pleased about it.

'We should move, captain,' he growled.

'Not until I know what's going on. What is this? What is she?' She looked pointedly at Thade. 'An explanation. Make it fast.'

'She's shut herself down. Her…' – he waggled his fingers around his head – '…brain, mind, whatever. It's augmetic. Data storage. She can… *deactivate* it.'

Ciastro's eyes pinched as she scrutinised the woman. 'Is she alive in there?'

'In every sense. But she won't come out of this state without a code to wake her.'

Realisation changed Ciastro's expression as she started to put it together.

'That's why the Venetors were torturing you. She gave you the code.'

A thin smile curved the edges of Thade's mouth. 'Always said you were a better detective than me.'

'I am,' Ciastro stated flatly. 'Give her the code and wake her up.'

Hesitant but with little other choice, Thade leaned in close and muttered something long and complex in binharic. He had to speak the numerics and it took time, prompting nervy glances between the sanctioners, who weren't accustomed to downtime whilst on mission.

When he was done, Thade stepped back.

Elva's eyes flickered, the dead grey pearl warming to iridescent blue before fading into something approximating a normal human cornea and iris. She blinked, once at him and then at the other occupants in the room.

Ciastro felt a mild chill run down her spine at her strange regard.

'Ciastro, Seraf,' Elva uttered in a soft, female voice that had the slightest mechanised reverberation. 'Castellan, Bastion-G. Former lieutenant, Alectian 105th Regiment, designation "Helhawks". Cited for bravery in the field, Arrach warzone, Denobar campaign. Lieutenant Ciastro received the Honorifica Imperialis for the mercy killing of–'

'That's enough,' Ciastro cut her off.

Elva blinked, betraying no emotion.

'Are you a prisoner here?'

'I am.'

'And this man is your protector?'

Elva shook her head. 'No, he is my hireling. I need to cross the border, leave Genovska.'

When she wasn't relaying cold data, she sounded much more human. Ciastro had never seen a cybernetic being like her, save perhaps in the Astynomia.

'Why not forge your own ident and border papers?'

'Part of my brain is a memcore. I can't manipulate the noosphere, only capture data from it. Though, I have some rudimentary machine skills.'

Harrok took a step forward. 'Captain…'

Ciastro flashed him an angry glance, but he was right. She held up her index finger. One further question. She directed it to Thade.

'Why keep you here? On this level?'

'This is the strongroom,' said Thade. 'Heln's not up on twenty-first. He's close. Fifteenth floor. He's holed up there, barricaded in. Those troops you fought. He has more. A lot more.'

Pieces were edging into place. Heln's reticence to attack. The lack of hardened fighters amongst his gangers. And now this. Ciastro frowned and considered everything she'd heard. She needed one more piece. She turned back to Elva.

'What do you have on Heln?'

Elva's mouth opened, almost mechanically, and a blurt of soft static emanated from within. It took a few seconds for the static to clear, like a radio homing in on a signal, and then suddenly she was speaking in Heln's voice. It was a vox-recording, covertly taken, discussing a bribe and what would happen if knowledge of that bribe were to be released. Ciastro recognised the other speaker. It was the district vladar. After another short blurt of static, there then followed a different conversation between the vladar and the baroness of a merchant-combine discussing the terms of an illicit trade deal. A third conversation followed this one, as two oligarchs made a pact to conspire against a rival and assassinate said rival if their initial plan failed.

When she was done, Elva closed her mouth again as if it had never happened.

'Holy saints...' uttered Ciastro, sharing a glance with Radev, who was similarly wide-eyed. She looked at Thade. 'Have you heard any of this?'

'Some,' Thade conceded.

'And there's more?'

'Reels and reels of it,' he said.

Elva put in, 'I have logged eight thousand, seven hundred and fifty-three hours, fourteen minutes and eight seconds of dialogue from four hundred and fifty-seven separate conversations.'

Stunned silence filled the room.

Heln had the hierarchy of Genovska and Throne knew how many other districts in his clenched fist. No wonder getting at him had been so difficult. Everyone wanted him dead but no one wanted to risk what would come to light once he was gone.

'You're coming with us,' Ciastro decided. 'Both of you.' She glanced at Kline. 'They're your responsibility, trooper. Watch them.'

Kline gave a curt salute as Ciastro turned her attention back to Elva and Thade.

'Soon as this is over, I want to hear everything. I'll take it to the damn Adeptus Arbites if I have to. For now, we need to get out of here. You know where Heln is, lead on. And know that us getting you out of here intact is contingent on your assistance. Understand?'

They both nodded.

Ciastro hefted the Boyar, checked her ammo.

'Let's move out–'

The sharp whine of the vox interrupted and she winced at the sudden and unexpected intrusion.

It was Gench.

'I thought you might be dead after all, sergeant,' said Ciastro.

Gench chuckled. *'No such luck, I'm afraid. Too stubborn to die. We've reached the vox-mast. It's intact, but this far out… we had some interference. Kilany reconfigured the signal and here I am. Relieved to hear your voice, captain.'*

Ciastro frowned. Gench was many things but he wasn't a particularly good liar. A twist of doubt knotted her stomach.

'Did you reach Viandani?'

'Imminently. Just wanted to confirm. Do you have Heln?'

'Not yet, we ran into something unexpected.'

'I see.'

That feeling of disquiet grew colder.

'And the Skeleton Key?' asked Gench.

Ciastro hesitated out of instinct. She glanced at Thade, then Elva and then at her squad, who stood ready, awaiting orders.

'No sign,' she lied. 'Must be an urban legend after all.'

'Ah, I see. That's a shame. Real shame.'

'How so, sergeant?' She heard the faint hiss of a secondary comms feed. She knew that sound. A vox-thief. Someone had been listening in. Someone close. She felt vulnerable all of a sudden, like plunging into a deep black ocean at night and not knowing what was out there. She tried surreptitiously to locate Mannon but the sniper proved elusive as ever. Her hand slid to her pistol. Gench still hadn't answered.

'You still there, sergeant?'

'Still here.' There was something absent in his voice. Distracted, like he'd silenced the feed and had been speaking to someone else off vox.

'Thought for a moment you'd experienced more interference.'

'No,' he said, tinged with resignation. *'That's over now.'*

Ciastro tightened her grip, pulling her sidearm and firing off a shot as Kline tried to kill her. She saw it late, but Kline's injury made him slow. A round hit her in the shoulder but the uniform took the brunt. Then she was diving for the ground and scrambling for cover as gunfire raked the air.

It happened fast. Her snapshot had caught Kline in the neck and he was prone, bleeding out. Radev shot Harrok, right in the face, through his cheek and out the back of the head. He died instantly. She got Mannon too: Ciastro saw the sniper reeling back with blood arcing from her chest. Of Thade and Elva, she saw no sign.

The Boyar lay useless feet away, Ciastro having dropped it when she took the slug to the shoulder. She still had her sidearm, though her chest and shoulder hurt like the Nine Devils. She lost sight of Radev and stood up tentatively from behind the stack of crates where she'd taken cover.

'I don't know what Heln's got on you, Radev, but–'

She flinched, crying out as something sliced her hand. Ciastro's sidearm went skittering away, while Radev's knife embedded in the wall like a nail.

'No way out of this, captain,' came Radev's voice.

Ciastro was already moving, biting down the pain, doubling back around the crates and trying to outflank the sanctioner.

'You're unarmed. Come out and I'll make it quick,' Radev said. She was trying to get Ciastro to talk, to give away her position. 'Make me hunt you and I'll use the other knife. It won't be pleasant.'

Head low, Ciastro crept through cover. She skirted around some pipes, another crate. Then she saw a shadow, heard the click of an autogun switching to 'rapid'...

With a roar, Ciastro barrelled out of hiding and hit Radev around the waist, bearing her down. Radev rolled, turned, got out from under her somehow. She landed a quick jab to the neck and suddenly Ciastro was choking, but she drove her knee up into Radev's midriff and was rewarded with a grunt of pain. Struggling to breathe, Ciastro blocked an elbow smash with her forearm. The bone jarred, sending white heat up into her injured shoulder. Then there was a flash of pale silver. The second knife glinted in the low light like a promise.

Radev snarled, her knee up over one of Ciastro's arms.

'I'm going to cut your fucking head off!'

The shot took Radev in the forehead, a high-calibre rifle round that blew out most of the back of her skull. She slumped back and Ciastro rolled her off, wiping the blood spatter from her face. Kline was dead too, his sightless eyes staring upward, his hand limp against his throat.

Shaking, Ciastro staggered to her feet and saw Mannon, deathly pale but alive, a rifle braced painfully over her arm. The sniper sagged almost immediately, and would have fallen had Thade not been there to hold her up. He looked as pale as Mannon. Evidently in shock.

Ciastro was still composing herself when the vox crackled again.

'Kline... Radev. Are they all dead?'

It was Gench.

'Why?' Ciastro asked simply. 'Was it slate? Something else?'

Gench hesitated. She thought she heard him mutter an expletive under his breath at a plan fallen foul.

'It's always something else,' he said.

'Kline and Radev are dead. Never betray the Lex, Gench.'

He gave a long exhale, then, 'Cavalry's coming, Ciastro. They're coming.'

She cut him off, hissed, 'Shit.'

Thade was still shoring up Mannon, his face etched with incredulity.

'What the fuck just happened?'

Elva held up a small metal shard in her silver-tipped fingers. She had kept her head down during the firefight, wisely staying out of the way. And keeping Thade alive, who still looked like he hadn't recovered from the near-death ordeal. Either that or his narco cravings had reached fever pitch.

'It's a listening device,' she said, allowing its triangular edges to catch the light. It looked like a flat arrowhead. 'You were being covertly surveilled, captain.'

Ciastro held out a hand and Elva passed her the vox-thief. She then dropped it on the floor and crushed it underfoot. She had fury in her eyes and the burning need for retaliation.

They'd patched up Mannon as best they could. She could

stand unaided, the rifle anchored to her grip. Thade had taken
a pistol, one of Kline's. That traitorous fucker wouldn't be
using it any more. Ciastro transfixed Thade with a look like
a spear-thrust.

'Which way to Heln?'

He checked his weapon, trying to still his trembling fingers.

'This is a death wish, Seraf.'

She racked her shotgun.

'Which way?'

Heln was waiting for them.

He was unarmed and had no defenders. He merely sat upon
a lonely throne, in a metal room, surrounded by contraband.

'Behold…' he said, 'my wealth.'

Ciastro saw guns and ammunition, narco of all stripes, even
open crates of illicit bionics. A veritable trove of illegal goods.
She edged warily into the large chamber. She kept her Boyar at
the ready, close to her body. She and Mannon checked corners,
blind spots. There was no obvious threat.

The doors had opened as soon as the vid-picter had alighted
on them, its scanning light bathing them in hues of grainy red.

It was a stronghold, bereft of strength.

'I see you've also returned my property,' Heln added with a
bloodshot glance at Elva, whose jaw stiffened in a rare display
of emotion. He looked wrung out, a far cry from the man who
cut such an impressive and imposing figure over the Bastion's
hololith. Even his attire was ragged and worn at the edges. It
didn't look like he'd actually slept at all for several days. Heln
was gaunt and grey of pallor.

'I've had enough of this,' Ciastro muttered. 'Silas Heln, you
are under arrest by the order of the Lex for the collusion and
conspiracy to murder city-sanctioned enforcers, and the actual
conspiracy-murder of one enforcer. Your other *numerous* crimes

are noted in the arrest log and will be relayed to you via data-slate as soon as you are remanded to my custody and in the Bastion-G holding cells.'

Heln held up his hands. 'Did that feel righteous, castellan?'

'It's justice,' she spat, teeth clenched. 'I should execute you right here for what you've done.'

'I have committed crimes. Many. I did not, however, conspire to murder or actually murder any of your men,' Heln said, unconcerned. 'Elva... Fifth of Octarum, eighteen hundred hours and sixth minute. Justicius Templum.'

Elva bristled at being so ordered but complied nonetheless. Ciastro wondered if she could refuse even if she wanted to.

A vox-recording played through her like it had before, her lips moving eerily to frame the words of the individuals who were speaking. Ciastro stifled a gasp when she heard Justicius Viandani's silken tones.

'...if it exists, if Heln has the Skeleton Key,' he was saying, 'bring it to me. And only me.'

Gench's voice replied. 'And what about Ciastro and the others?'

'No one must know about the Skeleton Key. If it's real and if they were to find out, there would be a full investigation. Every scrap of data it holds would have to be interrogated, logged and prosecuted. Many great men and women would be undone by those revelations. I include myself amongst that number.'

'I see, my lord.' Gench paused, weighing his next words as he often had with Ciastro when about to broach something delicate. 'And my own infractions?'

'If you do this right, consider them expunged.'

'Do you really think it's real? What if it's just an urban legend like they say?'

'Heln is getting his dirt from somewhere, but if it turns out to be false then that'll make things cleaner at least.'

'And the kill order?'

'*Still stands, regardless. Castellan Ciastro is entirely too loyal and too inquisitive. She dies, sergeant. They all die.*'

'*Of course, my lord.*'

'*A brave thing this, sergeant. Killing a known criminal underlord as justice for the murder of your senior officer, your comrades. I can see citations of honour, possibly even advancement. You need but do your duty.*'

Gench chuckled, the sound grating now. '*Consider it done.*'

The recording ended.

'And that's just a taste,' said Heln to a stunned Ciastro.

She swallowed, her mouth suddenly dry. This went far higher than she'd thought. She'd assumed Heln had compromised Gench and the others. That they had taken bribes or some lesser corruption was being leveraged against them. Not this.

Heln threw her a thin metallic wafer and she caught it, one-handed.

'It's a data-shunt. Everything you just heard is on there. I siphoned it from Elva as insurance. I'm trusting you with it, Captain Ciastro. Call it a good-faith payment.' That thin, odious smile returned.

Ciastro glowered. 'What do you want?'

'It's simple really,' said Heln with a slow, defeated sigh. 'I want out of here and some kind of immunity.'

'You are in no position to bargain.'

'I'll take a cell over execution. Besides, nor are you.' He turned his attention to a surveillance array as it flickered to life. Across a host of banked vid-screens a veritable army of sanctioners amassed on the roof around the vox-mast. Two Zurovs had touched down, turbine fans still kicking up dust and debris. Fifteen sanctioners in each, along with Gench and his troops.

'Damn it...' muttered Ciastro.

'What's left of my men are moving to intercept.'

Ciastro kinked an eyebrow, her weapon still on Heln.

'*What's left?*'

'Elva is a miracle. She brought me wealth and power at first, but then my enemies began to mount and others wanted what I had, or what they thought I had. Resources once plentiful started to dwindle. Those whom I once trusted turned coat, and increasingly I grew alone and paranoid. Most of my men are dead, by the hands of others or my own depending on the strength of their loyalty.

'I realise now she is a curse. That knowledge and secrets unbound are caustic. They erode the keeper, slowly but inevitably.'

Levelling her Boyar at the gang lord, Ciastro said, 'I am yet to hear the point, Heln.'

Heln smiled softly. 'I trust very few, but I am willing to place my faith in an uncorrupt enforcer's commitment to their duty. I have a way out of this storm bunker. And I'll share it if you take me with you. Even trade.'

'I'd rather take a stand here.'

'No, you wouldn't. Gench is a brutal bastard of the lowest order. He's part of the most violent and well-equipped gang in all of Varangantua. And he wants you dead. I do not expect my foot soldiers to survive. They are both entirely too long and too short in the tooth, my hardened fighters long expended in a war of attrition I never asked for but courted all the same. Hubris, thy name is human...'

It took all of her restraint not to put a round in Heln's knee. But he was right. Retreat now. Justice later. They had to escape. If she could reach Fort Gunlysk, one of the Arbites, then maybe...

She backed off, put up her weapon. 'If you cross me, Heln, I'll kill you.'

Heln spread his hands wide in a gesture of magnanimity.

'I swear it on the Throne.'

'He won't save you,' she vowed.

Heln grinned. 'Then I suggest you follow me.'

They took a private lifter. It was small, barely large enough to fit them all, an old rickety freight cage more used to crates than bodies.

Mannon leaned hard against the metal frame, her breathing shallow and her eyes perpetually on the verge of closing. Ciastro gave her a morphia shot and she perked up, that false sharpness from the drugs hitting her fast.

'Last one,' she told her, having now denuded Harrok's med-kit.

Mannon nodded her thanks, pale as ice.

The levels passed quietly, the doppler effect of their passage soothing. A yellow lumen flickered above and the hot breeze lapped at Ciastro's skin, heavy and stale. Thade stayed by Elva's side. He looked weary too, his eyes far away, clenching and unclenching his fingers.

'What will happen to me if we escape?' said Elva, and Ciastro turned to look at her, *really* look at her. She saw the woman, her dark shaven hair, her slightly over-wide eyes. Her sallow skin and thin arms. Despite her strange augmetics, she looked afraid.

'We're getting out of here.'

'Will I remain a slave, only to a different master? Or will I be given to the priests of Steelmound?'

Ciastro didn't have an answer for that. 'That won't be up to me to decide.'

'I think I will end up a prisoner, or dissected for parts and study. This' – she gestured to the machine elements in her skull – 'dulls my emotional sensitivity, but I am scared.'

Ciastro flicked a glance at Heln but he was studiously ignoring the conversation, standing in a corner of the lifter, eyes forward, hands behind his back. If he had any thoughts, he wasn't sharing.

'Is that why you reached out to Thade?'

'I wanted to escape. To live. Stay hidden.' Something like pleading touched her eyes. 'Do not let them take me.'

'You are a threat.'

'I am a victim.'

'I can't just let you go.'

'Yes, you can.'

'I won't,' Ciastro replied but lacked conviction.

Heln absently checked the chrono on his wrist. An antique piece, bronze with silver drum numerics. Expensive. It was the first time he'd moved since entering the lifter.

'Late for an appointment?' Ciastro sniped.

That smile again.

'Any moment now...' he uttered.

Ten levels down and the lifter died. The gears slowed and ground to a stop. The lumen *plinked* to darkness.

Gench had cut the power.

Ciastro seized Heln by the scuff of the neck, but he maintained his poise.

'Could he know? About your backdoor?'

'I sincerely hope not, but...' Heln gestured to the dead lifter, 'Regardless, we're on foot from here.'

'If you're lying to me, Heln...'

'Oh, captain, I may appear at ease but I do not wish to die. And make no mistake, your sergeant has two outcomes in mind for me. Death or torture. And I do not care for either.'

Letting Heln go, Ciastro raked open the lifter door. She glanced at Elva when she turned to spur on the others, saw her staring back.

They carried on.

They reached the lowest level of the storm bunker and only here did Heln begin to betray his nerves.

'This is it,' he said, hurrying off. 'It's close. A gate. It leads to the catacombs under Genovska.'

Ciastro held him back, seizing his arm.

'Slowly does it.'

'I would not trust this piece of groxshit if I was wiping him off my boot,' muttered Thade.

Heln gave him a sour look but continued, 'The gate is slaved to my bio-imprint. Even she can't open it.' He glanced at Elva, who stared back with indifference. Then he looked down at his arm.

Ciastro let him go.

It was some kind of depot, perhaps a vehicle yard once. It had been used for storage, more of Heln's plunder, only the less obviously valuable or tradable kind. Machine parts in the main, pieces of fuselage, tank tracks and hold interiors. Even the remnants of a partially decommissioned Kastelan.

Ciastro eyed the robot, rust-edged and missing one of its arms. The other limb ended in a clenched metal hand. 'If Nearsteel knew you had this...'

'They'd want my head on a spike. Broken down, these machines fetch a lot of slate. Rogue tech-priests, pit-fighters looking for an edge, the overbosses who run the chrono-gladiators over at the Spike. Very nice business.'

Thade whistled, murmured something about slate. He was looking over some of the merchandise.

Heln stopped as if to find his bearings anew. It was an expansive space, low-ceilinged with thick rockcrete columns holding up the levels above. Strip lumens lit the path at irregular intervals, several broken or shorted out.

'Here...' he said, and went over to a stack of crates lined up against one wall. 'Help me with this.' He started pushing, his desire for survival providing a verve he had otherwise lacked. Shouldering her weapon, confident Mannon had them covered, Ciastro dragged one of the crates. Slowly, as the hefty boxes parted, a door was revealed. It looked strong, like a blast door. Dust caked the access panel. Heln smeared it clean with his coat. Then he peered at it, leaning in as if scrutinising some unfathomable detail.

'Something's amiss...' he murmured, and Ciastro drew in alongside him.

She realised her mistake too late. And felt the gun pressed against her side.

'This is a shot pistol,' said Heln calmly. 'It has six chambers, each filled with an armour-shredding round. It'll tear up that carapace of yours like it's parchment.'

Ciastro gave him a questioning look.

'Told you,' said Thade, his pistol coming up too late, 'he's a mendacious old fucker...'

Heln gave an indulgent smile. 'Oh, you don't survive as long as I have in my profession without learning how to conceal a weapon,' he said.

She backed up at Heln's urging, his steady aim covering all four of them. He wagged the pistol. 'Drop the weapons. Belt too.'

Ciastro obeyed, signalling to Mannon and Thade to do the same.

'Now what?' she said, unarmed.

'Elva comes with me,' Heln said, beckoning her with the other hand.

'Thought she was a curse.'

'And one I want rid of, but for a price. The Lex can't have her or me.'

'You'll be leaving us to die, Heln. Gench is coming.'

As if summoned, the flat thud of many booted feet echoed throughout the basement.

Heln licked his lips, eager to be gone. 'I think he's here, captain. Elva... come here now.'

She didn't move.

'Either I kill you here, or she comes with me and you at least have a fighting chance.'

Heart thumping, Ciastro's old memories returned. Of Arrach...

The jungle, the sweat and the fear, the trap that Maggs failed to notice. The clearing and the firepit. Skin slowly roasting, the greens baying... Her rifle pressed up against her shoulder. The first shot... a slip, Maggs screaming as his ear exploded in a welter of gory skin and muscle. Reload, readjust... Shoot again. Shoot to kill.

Ciastro saw Elva walking towards Heln. For the briefest moment, she came between Ciastro and the gang lord, and the shot pistol lowered the barest fraction. Elva lunged, caught Heln's arm and pulled it wide. In the same moment, Ciastro swept up her sidearm from the ground and fired.

The shot reverberated around the basement. Heln lay dead, a ragged hole in his chest, shot through the gap between Elva's arm and body, a perfectly threaded needle of a bullet.

Elva turned, her face ashen.

Releasing the breath she had been holding, Ciastro turned to Thade and Mannon. The sniper regarded her with something approaching awe.

'A damn fine shot.' She had already retrieved her rifle.

'Sorry you didn't take it yourself?' Ciastro asked, picking up the rest of her gear.

'I would have had to shoot you through the head to hit him, and right now I am barely worthy of the range, let alone combat.'

It was the most she had ever heard Mannon say.

'I'll take whatever you can give me.' Ciastro looked at Thade. 'That goes for you too.'

The haggard jaeger managed a thin smile. 'Like old times.'

'Old times. Keep her alive,' she said, but Elva's gaze was wandering, her thoughts distant. Some kind of post-traumatic fugue, Ciastro assumed. It didn't matter now. They'd rake through all of that later. If they lived.

Stablights pierced the gloom not so far ahead and the tramp of booted feet rose to a clamour.

Gench had found them.

Ciastro and Mannon took a position behind a section of disused fuselage large enough to cover them both. It had Militarum stamps. Part of an old Valkyrie.

'Shoot to kill, confirm?' said Mannon.

'They are corrupt enforcers of the Lex,' Ciastro replied. 'Execute with extreme prejudice.'

They hunkered down, Mannon's rifle braced over the makeshift barricade, Ciastro with her shotgun.

It took a few more seconds before the first of the sanctioners appeared out of the shadows. Mannon let them advance before she shot the first through the neck. She'd killed a second before the grunts scattered, taking cover wherever they could find it. And firing back.

Ciastro blasted a third, injured or dead the dark made it hard to tell, before hurling herself fully behind the Valkyrie. Heavy fire roared from the other sanctioners, Gench bellowing in the midst of it all for them to push up and overwhelm.

The armour plate between Ciastro and certain death was being chewed up like tin. Mannon got off another shot, chalking up a kill before a ricochet clipped her and she spun on her heel. At the same time, part of the fuselage caved, surrendering to the sheer attrition of bullets, and cored through. Right through Mannon. The woman spasmed, her body erupting in sputtering geysers of blood. Ciastro reached out to grab her hand, as if she could hold on to Mannon's life if she just gripped tight enough. But the sniper was spitting blood, her uniform a ragged mess of holes. Her nerveless fingers went limp in Ciastro's grip.

She let Mannon go and ran, firing blind behind her into the bellowing mob, wishing death on Gench with every fibre of her being. But it was she who wouldn't be walking out of here, she knew. Diving over a crate, trusting to its solidity to repel hard rounds, she fired off half her clip in a blaze of muzzle flare and took down two more of her enemies. The maul fizzed at her hip and she wrenched it off as it briefly caught fire, a bullet lodged in its powercell.

'Shit...' she hissed.

Goaded by Gench, the sanctioners kept on coming.

Sparks flashed where bullets hit metal, Ciastro firing back through the chaos, bellowing her defiance. From somewhere behind her, Thade was firing too.

And then the ground shook, a flex of pressure and then release. Something large, something fast, barrelled past Ciastro. It took her a moment of disbelief to realise it was the Kastelan. Shots hit the robot, solid slugs pinging off its armour, then a shouted expletive before it was amongst the sanctioners, tossing bodies and crushing them with its fist and its bulk.

There was screaming, sanctioners torn apart and pulped.

Throne, it's monstrous.

Ciastro thought of Mannon and her pity evaporated.

For almost a minute there were shouts of agony, shotgun blasts, muzzle fire and the wrench of abused metal.

A grenade went off, a low, dense *crump* of explosive. The Kastelan fell back, riddled with holes, oozing smoke and missing half of its cranial section. It landed with a heavy metallic clang.

Only Gench emerged out of the carnage, though far from unscathed. His weapon *clacked* empty and he tossed it, wiping blood from his mouth at the same time as drawing a knife.

Ciastro had no ammo left either. She set down the Boyar and

holstered her sidearm. She didn't carry a knife and the shock maul was wrecked, so she put up her fists and rolled her shoulders.

'Come on then, you traitor dog.'

'At your heel no longer,' Gench replied and lunged.

Ciastro sidestepped the first jab, then deflected a second before landing a blow to Gench's jaw. He retreated, momentarily punch-drunk, but like a prizefighter came back swinging. The knife screeched a jagged line across her armour and she lashed out with the flat of her boot. Gench screamed as Ciastro stamped down, fracturing his shin. He lunged again, and this time she trapped his wrist, swinging the burly veteran around with his own momentum and launching him into a crate. Gench bounced off, dazed, bleeding, and unleashed a savage flurry of blows at Ciastro, who fell back against the onslaught. She hissed as a hot spike of pain ran down her arm, the blade tearing through her ballistic armour. Blood flecked the ground, cast off by Gench, who grinned at her murderously.

A deft kick, driven hard and into his midriff, caught him by surprise. Gench doubled up, hacking wildly to fend her off, but Ciastro stepped inside his guard and smashed her elbow into his neck. It crushed his collar piece, bent the light armour inwards and into his throat like a punch dagger. He choked, still clinging to the knife, every slash more desperate and deadly than the last. Gench staggered to one knee, flailing now, his breath a choked rasp, then fell to both knees. Bloodstained teeth clenched like a barricade.

Ciastro had retrieved Mannon's sidearm and held it unfalteringly to Gench's head as he knelt in front of her.

'Drop it,' she ordered, hard as stone.

Gench, who had begun to recover, obeyed, and the knife clattered to the ground. It took effort for him to clear his damaged throat and he slowly raised his hands, about to plead his case when Ciastro shot him through the head.

'Never betray the Lex,' she said, breathless.

Her aim swung up, alighting on Thade standing with Elva before the door. Heln's hand was pressed against the access panel. Thade, who at least had the decency to look guilty, had heaved the corpse up to the door.

'Not so injured then,' uttered Ciastro, the gun unwavering.

Thade offered a wry but pained smile. 'Oh, I'm pretty hurt.' At the pressurised hiss of pneumatics, he let Heln's hand drop. The door let out a dull *chank* of heavy locks disengaging.

Elva stood stock still as it creaked opened, her eyes on the gun.

'That you?' asked Ciastro. 'With the robot?'

'I have some rudimentary machine skills.'

'So you said.'

A few seconds passed, each one heavy with decision.

Ciastro lowered the gun, much to Thade's surprise.

'Heln's dead,' he said, 'but what about her?'

'Haven't you heard, there is no Skeleton Key,' Ciastro told him. 'It was an urban legend. A myth invented by the underworld. Heln's death proves it.' Her gaze met that of Elva, who said nothing but didn't need to. Gratitude was all over her face. 'Otherwise, he would have known we were coming.'

She flicked the safety with her thumb then turned the pistol around in her hand, flipping grip to barrel before throwing it to Thade, who caught it one-handed.

The jaeger stared at it like it was a foreign object.

'You'll have to shoot me,' Ciastro told him.

Bemused, he glanced from the gun to Ciastro.

'I can't let you leave unless you shoot me,' she said, and realisation dawned. He shot her in the shoulder, a clean shot, through and through. She swore, hard, gritting her teeth against the pain.

'Be seeing you,' said Thade, as Elva led them through the doorway.

'No, you won't,' Ciastro replied, hiding a rueful smile.

'No,' said Thade. 'Suppose not.'

They broke down the door with a powered ram, the artful bronze yielding to thirty thousand pounds of concerted pressure.

Viandani was standing behind his desk, hastily reaching for his pistol, an outraged look on his face. His anger turned to incredulity when he saw who had come knocking. She wasn't in her finery this time. Her arm in a crude sling, armour scuffed and dirty. It still had Mannon's blood on it.

'Ciastro?'

She wasn't alone, either. An Arbites judge from Fort Gunlysk loomed behind her, armoured in black, cloak draped over one shoulder. A more severe and stolid man you would never meet. He was armed, so were the two arbiters in the corridor, and so was Ciastro.

As she listed his many crimes, his corruption against the Lex being the most dire in the eyes of the Arbites, the justicius kept glancing at her holstered pistol and tried not to balk at his visitors in black.

Then she played the data-shunt Heln had given her, and a second data-shunt that had mysteriously arrived at Bastion-G for her eyes only that sealed Viandani's condemnation.

Listening to the crackly but unequivocal evidence being played for his edification, and no doubt seeing his bleak new life set out before him, he went for his pistol after all.

His fingers had wrapped around the fine leather grip, the brushed chrome of the barrel glinting in the light as he raised it up, before the bullet took him in the chest and he slumped back down in his chair, dead.

'Guilty as charged,' said Ciastro, lowering her weapon. 'Sentence delivered.'

As the arbiters moved in to secure the scene, the dawn was

rising red and beautiful through the expansive window. For a moment, and only a moment, Ciastro allowed herself a rare smile before heading out of the office to face the violence and depravity anew.

ONCE A KILLER, ALWAYS A KILLER

MITCHEL SCANLON

Captives

The sky above the Dredge was a shard of dull crimson, crowded out by the needle-peak spires of the city. It looked like an old wound, the edges ragged, damage stubbornly refusing to heal. On another world, it might have felt like a bad omen. On Alecto, it was just another day.

I was in the front seat of my patrol groundcar, by the open air refectoria on Heroes Prospekt, doing my best to enjoy the flavour of warmed-over recaff, triple strength to keep me awake, when the alert came in over my helmet vox.

'Bastion HQ to Rampart patrol five-nine-omega-nine.' The voice hissed with static. *'Gunfire reported, Zaranghast Commercia. Advise status.'*

I knew the location. Zaranghast Commercia was a down-at-heel collection of food stalls, tonsurists, apothecaries and other tabernae of various stripes, set under the communal roof of a cathedral-sized indoor trading space, situated on the western side of the district.

I threw away the recaff and gunned the engine.

'Five-nine-omega-nine receiving, Bastion. Sanctioner Kirian Malenko responding. Estimate arrival at eight minutes.'

I made it in seven, the early-morning traffic scattering like frightened birds at the sight of the Rampart groundcar and its insignia.

Once at the alert destination, I parked beside the front entrance and drew my sidearm. The weapon was a Zev Arms semi-automatic stub pistol in .55 calibre, the Penitent model. A portable hand-cannon, it was proof positive of a common adage in Varangantua – downclave, there was no such thing as too much gun.

Weapon at the ready, I proceeded into the commercia.

It didn't take any great genius to locate the source of the alert. A man's body lay halfway down a parade of storefronts, his life bled out onto the tiled floor of the inner courtyard. The blood trail led back to the doorway of a nearby provisioner's.

'Bastion, this is five-nine-omega-nine. One body found at Zaranghast. Suspected homicide. Offender at large.'

'Affirmed, omega-nine. Do you need backup?'

'Negative. I'll handle it. Send a meat wagon for the body. I'll let you know whether one's needed for the offender.'

There's an art to moving quietly in body armour. Most sanctioners never learn it. It's not just the bulk of the standard uniform, with its full-face helmet, oversized boots and layers of flak armour, all designed to be as intimidating as possible. As the uniformed branch of Alecto's enforcers, we're supposed to be the visible presence of the Lex – whether it's on the streets or in the nightmares of criminals. For the most part, that involves kicking down doors and making arrests with no time for stealth or any other kind of subtlety.

I work patrol, though. There, things are different. Don't get me wrong. I can kick down doors with the best of them. But on patrol, sometimes you need a few more tools than are kept in the standard sanctioner's toolbox. Not every problem needs a hammer. Not unless you've got a nail waiting to be hit.

In this case, with a body down and no sign of fleeing civilians in the vicinity, I had to wonder whether I was dealing with plain murder or a hostage situation.

I took a sideways route towards the provisioner's, careful to stay out of sight of anyone who might be watching through the big display window in front. As I passed the audio emporium next door, I saw a nervous commercia worker with blue face tats peer over the stacks of reel-slugs towards me.

I gestured to him to stay down. The safety off on my stub pistol, I eased to the edge of the provisioner's, planning on snatching a fast look through the glass.

There were hostages all right. As I drew closer, I could hear some of them crying. My first glimpse confirmed one offender inside, a scrawny, jumpy scuzz-stain waving an autopistol around with menace as he stood in the middle of one of the aisles. He had grabbed a young woman as a shield, the crook of his arm tight around her throat as he threatened the other hostages with the pistol. He was screaming so loud his words were audible, even through the glass.

'It ain't my fault!' His voice was petulant. 'You saw it – all of you! If he'd just opened the strongbox like I told him, he wouldn't have got himself hurt!'

I counted six captives inside, including the woman whose neck he was holding. One of them, a balding, middle-aged man in an apron marked with the provisioner's sigil, stood ahead of the rest, his hands raised as he tried to placate the gunman.

'He didn't have the code. Please! Only the owner can open the strongbox, and she's not here!'

'You're lying!' the scuzzer yelled, pointing the autopistol at him. 'I already told you! Keep lying to me, it'll be your fault what happens!'

Even from a distance, I could see he was a stimm-head. He had the telltale signs – skin flushed, profusely sweating and, most incriminating of all, twitchy, spasmodic movements like he had a live wire hidden somewhere, giving him the occasional jolt.

Most stimms were legal, with the right slate, but there was a thriving shadow trade in super-concentrated, toxic-level mega-stimms with names like Crystal Emperor or Heisengrad Blue. I couldn't know for sure, but I assumed one of them was the killer's habit of choice. He'd probably decided to rob the provisioner's to get the slate to buy more drugs.

I was tempted to take the shot from where I was. Put him down before he hurt anyone else. But the window presented a problem.

I could detect a slight distortion in the view through the glass. It was a magnification layer, intended to make the goods on sale appear larger and more attractive to people passing by. I could try to compensate when I took the shot, but any misjudgement and I'd hit the hostage. The stimm-head's constant involuntary movements didn't make it any easier.

I would have to get inside.

Moving while the scuzzer was distracted, I eased the door open. The gunman was oblivious, too busy arguing with his hostages to notice the presence of a sanctioner even as I advanced into the premises. I aimed my gun, waiting for his next twitch to lift his head far enough away from the woman for a clean kill shot.

If I had learnt one thing in Varangantua, it was never bet against the Imperial citizenry to do the most stupid thing imaginable while picking the worst possible moment to do it.

'A sanctioner?' The balding man looked at me in relief. 'Thank the Holy Throne!'

Alerted, the stimm-head jerked around to face me, bringing his human shield with him.

So much for stealth.

'Drop your weapon!' I commanded. 'You are under arrest in the name of the Emperor!'

That works more often than you'd think. Most people are so scared of sanctioners they'll do anything you tell them as long as it's said with conviction, and/or you are pointing a gun at them. Scuzzhead, though, was made of sterner stuff. Or, more likely, he was so wired on stimms he wasn't afraid of anything.

'No, you're lying!' He squinted like I was out of focus. 'The Emperor didn't send you. If He did, He would have told me. I'm His messenger. I am the Chosen One, come to redeem the city of its sins.'

I made a mental note to add blasphemy under the influence of a proscribed substance to the other charges he was facing.

He still had the woman, and I didn't have a clear shot. I know some sanctioners would have fired anyway, shooting through the hostage if needed. They'd argue losing one civilian when another five lives were at stake wasn't too bad. Me? I'd like to think I'm not that much of a bastard.

'What's the message?' I asked.

The question caught him off guard. 'What?'

'The message. You said you were a messenger. That means there must be a message.'

'Yes.' He nodded in understanding. 'Yes. The Emperor told me where we went wrong. Varangantua is cruel. Ugly. But it shouldn't be that way. We shouldn't be that way. We should be beautiful. Golden. Instead, we let our souls become trapped in these vile bodies. That's what causes the corruption.'

'Corruption, right.' I tried to sound persuaded. 'And you decided to start here with your message? Inside a provisioner's?'

'What? No!' He scowled like I was stupid. 'The Emperor only

talks to me when I take the pills, the blue miracles. That's why I came here. I need slate to buy more.'

'Right. You want in on the strongbox. But these people don't know the code–'

'That's what they say!' Anger flared in his features, the poison coursing through his brain making him volatile. 'But they're lying! This city is full of liars. That's why the Emperor says I have to clean it! Make it beautiful again!'

Filled with sudden zeal, he pulled the woman closer and pressed the pistol to her temple.

'Do you want to see the beauty? I can open this vessel – show you her soul!'

'Wait!'

I lifted the muzzle of my gun, flipping the weapon around in my hand to present the grip end towards him.

'Wait! You've convinced me.'

I inched forward to narrow the distance between us, drifting towards the shelves on the side of the aisle closest to him.

'I can see you're telling the truth. I want to join you. Become your first disciple. Here, let me give you my gun so you can see I'm with you.'

He removed the autopistol from the woman's head and jabbed it towards me.

'This is some kind of trick.'

'No trick. Look, I'll put my gun down.'

I took another step closer. It seemed the staff had been in the middle of restocking when the gunman entered. The metal shelves on one side of the aisle were empty, with a selection of goods stacked in neat rows on the floor nearby, ready to fill the gaps.

Each movement careful and deliberate, I laid the pistol on the shelf nearest to me.

'I'll slide it to you,' I said. 'That way, you'll have all the guns. You'll be in charge. Then, you'll know I'm not lying.'

It was breaking half a dozen regs to surrender my weapon. If things went wrong, I could end up on a charge. Then again, if things went wrong, getting punished for breaking regs would be the least of my sorrows. Odds were, I'd be dead.

Either way, I knew it was a dumb move. Blame the woman he held as a hostage. She had long blonde hair, with her head shaved on one side, and eyes so blue they might almost have been shining pieces of cobalt ore.

Guess maybe she reminded me of someone. It was the only reason I had for taking the chance I did.

I pushed the stub gun away from me, sliding it down the shelf towards the stimm-head. He reached to pick it up, only to realise both his hands were already full. After a moment's indecision, he transferred the autopistol to his other hand, awkwardly attempting to keep me covered while maintaining his grip on the hostage.

Eyes wide, he stretched his now free hand towards the weapon on the shelf. No doubt he couldn't believe the turn his day was taking. A sanctioner giving up his gun and offering to be his disciple? The Emperor really was on his side.

The scuzzhead's fingers closed around the body of the stub gun. Contact.

All the while I was offering up my gun and sliding it to him, my own free hand had been busy working behind me. I had lifted the shock maul out of its loop on my belt, thumb hovering over the activator that powered the weapon. I touched the maul to the shelf behind my back, triggering it to send Emperor alone knew how many volts surging through the metal.

His hand in contact with both the stub gun and the shelf, the stimm-head began twitching for a different reason. Mouth clenched in a rictus grin that showed missing teeth, he jerked and convulsed, the autopistol falling from nerveless fingers to clatter harmlessly to the floor.

'Down!'

I yelled at the woman, only to see she had caught some volts by virtue of her connection with her captor. Electricity streaming through her, she joined him in the same shuddering, jittering dance.

Already moving, I closed the distance and pushed her out of the way. Protected from the juice by the insulation in my gloves, I lifted the shock maul from the shelf, sweeping it in a rising arc straight into the side of the scuzzer's head.

He went down like a cold sack of dreck. I don't care what kind of stimms he was on, there aren't many can take a head-shot from a shock maul and stay conscious.

In case it didn't last, I worked fast. A swift kick propelled the autopistol out of his reach before I turned him onto his front and manacled his wrists behind him.

Once the restraints were on, I retrieved my gun. Nearby, the other hostages had gathered around the blonde to check she was all right.

Rendering assistance to shaken civilians wasn't part of my job, not when there was an offender to be dealt with. I secured the autopistol, tucking it into the back of my equipment belt.

The Bastion maintains a drop-off for confiscated guns. The weapons are examined to check whether they've been used in any unsolved cases before being recycled. The good-quality ones end up with the Defence Corps, to see better service doing the Emperor's work. The dreck – and the ones from downclave are mostly dreck, as likely to kill the user as whatever they are aimed at – get melted into slag. Only to be turned into new guns in the forges later, some of which end up on the streets via the black market, starting the cycle all over again.

With the offender subdued and arrested, public order was restored. My work there was done.

In a few hours, a probator would be along to take statements from the provisioner's staff. The Bastion might even send a verispex to go over the forensics, but it was unlikely. The local justicius probably wouldn't even read the report.

It was an open-and-shut case. The only question was sentencing. The justicius would decide whether to send the offender to the penal legion, condemn him to the prison colony on Sacc-5 or let the Ecclesiarchy have him on account of the blasphemy charge. That last would be the harshest option – the Ecclesiarchy had its own ways of punishing miscreants.

Sometimes, the local news-sheets carried details of the verdicts, but mostly I didn't follow the cases. Not any more. I didn't care what happened once my part was done.

I had started to drag the dead weight of the stimm-head out of the provisioner's when I heard the vox in my helmet crackle back into life.

'Bastion to Rampart five-nine-omega-nine. Advise status.'

'Bastion, this is omega-nine. Status is clean. Offender arrested and awaiting transport.'

'Affirmed, omega-nine. I'll put your prisoner on the list for pickup. There's a new alert in your patrol area. Male fugitive spotted fleeing scene of a suspected homicide, Valdov Office Plexus. Can you respond?'

I glanced down at the prisoner, still unconscious. He wasn't going anywhere. I fastened his manacles to one of the lumen-poles outside, ready for the pickup wagon.

'Affirmed, Bastion. Show me responding.'

An Uncommon Weapon

There was no sign of the fugitive by the time I reached the new alert. To make matters worse, it had started raining.

When it rains in the Dredge, it rains hard. The water fell in great, rolling, relentless torrents, reducing visibility to little more than a few feet. If the fugitive had left behind a blood trail or any other clues as to his direction of travel, they were gone, washed away by the deluge. The rain had even chased away the gawkers who usually congregated near any crime scene. They might, at least, have pointed which way the suspect had fled.

Even with the quarry gone, it remained a hot pursuit. Normal procedure was to perform a sweep of the area, the search radiating outwards in a series of concentric circles starting from the last known sighting.

If you kept your eyes open for anyone acting suspicious or anything out of place, sometimes you got lucky. The offender might have blood on his clothes or could still be carrying an obvious weapon. Although, given the downpour, he could have wandered past carrying a votive banner proclaiming his guilt. The rain was so heavy, I wouldn't have been able to see a thing.

I decided to check the crime scene itself, hoping to find evidence to help me track him.

That kind of detective work was supposed to be left to the probators. But it was a choice between pushing against lines of demarcation or blundering around aimlessly in a rainstorm, hoping the fugitive would jump out in front of me.

Besides, you'd be surprised how often a basic search can achieve results. Most criminals in Varangantua aren't geniuses. Sometimes, they leave things behind that lead you right to them.

I'm not talking about forensics. I'm talking about ID fobs, personal slate cards, even clothing with their name and address written on tags inside.

I headed for the doors of the office plexus. It was a typical enterprise of its kind. A multi-storeyed sub-building latched on to the side of a nearby spire like a sludge-leech clamped to its host, housing rented office space for a variety of small local businesses.

Once inside, it wasn't difficult to spot the route the offender had taken out of the building when he fled. I followed a series of bloodied boot prints left on the synthwool cover tiles of the foyer and corridors, all the way back to their origin point at the scene of the crime.

The alert from the Bastion had identified the fugitive as male. From what I could see, the marks on the floor all but confirmed it. The pattern of the soles matched a popular men's style of bootwear, while their dimensions and the killer's stride length suggested he was pushing abhuman in size. Based on a comparison to my own stride, he was at least six foot eight. Maybe taller.

The trail led to an office whose half-open door showed a shiny, blood-splattered brass plaque that read *Erek Zorn, Fiscal Tabulator*. Stub gun drawn, I pushed inside.

The interior looked like an explosion at a haemo depository. Blood was sprayed in patterns on the walls, bathing every object in the room, and had soaked into the deep pile of the floor's luxury cover tiles.

It was the kind of crime scene that might have caused even a sanctioner to retch. But I was made of sterner stuff. Besides, I had seen worse, long before I was ever an enforcer.

There were two victims. The first was a young woman, lying face down with her throat cut in an anteroom just inside the door. The other, an older man, I found dead within an inner sub-office.

You didn't need to be a probator to see which one of them had been the intended victim. The body of the man was all but hacked to pieces. He had been struck with multiple blows, some administered after he had fallen, based on the position of the wounds. In contrast, the woman had been dealt with almost as an afterthought, killed by a single cut and left to bleed out after she hit the floor.

Even then, the blow had nearly taken her head off. The blood-spatter patterns on the walls were familiar enough that I knew the attacker had been armed with some kind of chain-weapon. A chainsword, most likely.

It was an uncommon weapon, at least in the Dredge. Putting aside the fact that chainswords were expensive and difficult to obtain, most people preferred a weapon they could easily conceal. Not to mention one that didn't make quite so much mess.

A quick check for ID turned up an automotive licence in the man's pocket identifying him as the same Erek Zorn whose name was on the door. The woman, a personal scribe based on her ID, was Rula Katenova.

There was another sub-office next to Zorn's. I gave it a cursory check for victims. It was deserted, stacked with packing crates filled with furniture and personal oddments as though someone was in the process of moving out.

I could see nothing to help track the offender. I was about to call in to update the Bastion when something occurred to me.

A chainsword was a long weapon. I had never seen one shorter than three feet in length. Maybe you could make them smaller than that, but it would have made it even more rare and costly – likely out of the price range of anybody living in the Dredge.

The ceiling within Zorn's office was fairly low. I couldn't see how a man standing over six foot eight, presumably with long arms based on his height, could have used a chainsword without hitting the ceiling on his backswing.

When I double-checked it, the ceiling appeared undamaged beneath the blood spray. It seemed strange, given the frenzy of the attack. I could think of only one thing to explain the discrepancy.

The weapon was an augmetic.

It fitted the facts. The length of a man's arm made less

difference if part of it had been replaced with an augmetic weapon. Although that raised another question – what kind of man had his arm replaced by a chainsword?

Almost as soon as the question came to me, I thought of an answer. One that caused a creeping chill at the base of my spine.

With an abrupt hiss of static, my helmet vox squawked into life.

'Bastion to all units vicinity of Zmeya Prospekt! Reports of violent rampage in progress at Kerensky Bathhouse! Offender is reported as armed with a chainsword. All available units, respond!'

Returning my gun to its holster, I raced for the exit. Coincidences can happen in a city the size of Varangantua, but two killers running amok with chainswords within a few miles of each other would have been nothing short of freakish.

'Five-nine-omega-nine to Bastion! Show Malenko as responding!'

Convinced I was on the trail of the same killer, I headed for my vehicle.

Joy house

Zmeya Prospekt was two miles north. A broad, open square, dominated by an elaborate serpent-shaped fountain at one end, it was the kind of place that gave the Dredge a bad name. Given the Dredge was downclave to begin with, you can guess how disreputable that made it.

Zmeya was a local hub for the black market. Whether they manned the storefronts ringing the prospekt or were among the street hawkers who thronged every accessible space within it, most of the traders there were up to no good in one way or another.

They said you could get anything you wanted in Zmeya – if you knew where to find it. Given its reputation for criminality, enforcer raids were commonplace. Not that it made much difference. No sooner had the manacles clicked shut and the sanctioners left with their prisoners than the prospekt opened for business once more.

Even this early in the day, I would have expected Zmeya to be a hive of activity. Instead, the square was deserted by the time I arrived. As I pulled in, I saw upturned stalls and discarded merchandise left abandoned on the paving. It takes a lot to make the kind of street sellers who gravitate to Zmeya flee. Even more to make them leave their goods behind. Whatever had happened, it had been enough to create a panic.

The Kerensky Bathhouse was on the other side from the fountain. I parked the Rampart out front, careful to check the safety was off on my stub gun as I exited the vehicle.

The double doors into the building were shattered, left hanging off their hinges. Blood and broken glass littered the ground outside, along with the occasional torn bathing shift or lost piece of footwear.

It looked like a lot of people had tried to escape all at once, breaking through the doors and trampling each other in their desperation to get away from whatever had scared them.

I stepped inside the bathhouse, careful to give my eyes enough time to adjust to the dim light of the interior.

The Kerensky wasn't the kind of place where anybody wanted to see anything too clearly. It called itself a bathhouse, but that was a polite fiction. I don't say bathing didn't happen on the premises, but its real business was as a joy house.

Murals of men and women in varying states of undress decorated the walls, the bronzed and muscular depictions looking nothing like the average Kerensky clientele. Wary in case of ambush, I followed a line of poorly carved nude statuary further into the building. Just because the people inside had fled didn't mean the killer wasn't still in there.

As with the office plexus earlier, it wasn't difficult to tell which way I should go. Even without the damage caused by fleeing patrons and the occasional lost piece of clothing as markers, the blood spills staining the floors and walls told their own story.

The killer had been busy. I found a body at the foot of the stairs leading up to the special VIP section on the third floor. The victim was a blond, chubby-faced man wearing a winged-heart sigil on his tunic. I recognised him vaguely from the last time Kerensky's had been raided as one of the bathhouse's stewards.

There was another body at the next landing. This one I didn't know, but I could guess his job title from his appearance. He was broadly built and well muscled, with a neck so thick it was all the top fastener of his tunic collar could do to hold it back. He had ganger tattoos on his earlobes and below his left cheek, the ink old and faded enough to suggest he was no longer a member. In contrast, there was a more recent tattoo on his right cheek, showing the sigil of one of the securitor companies that supplied bodyguards for the lower end of the market.

He had a stub gun in his hand. Unfortunately, somebody had separated said hand from the wrist it once belonged to, leaving it lying on the floor a few feet away from its former owner.

I continued towards the VIP section. The floor was stained with the bloody impressions of what looked like the same boot prints I had found at Zorn's. I followed them into a corridor with a series of doors on either side, most lying open to reveal the vacant rooms beyond.

A chainsword isn't a quiet weapon. The patrons in the VIP rooms had likely fled at the first opportunity, once they heard what was happening.

The blood trail led to a steam room at the end of the hall, wispy clouds of vapour drifting out through the open doorway. Unable to see through the steam, I removed my helmet and laid it on the floor, cautious in case the moisture in the air fogged the eyepieces, blinding me.

Even without the helmet, it was impossible to see more than a few inches in front as I entered the room. I hugged the wall and moved sideways in search of the controls, half expecting to hear the roar of a chain-weapon above the quiet hiss of the steam pipes at any moment.

The heat was stifling inside my uniform. Sweat pooled at the open neck of my flak armour and ran downwards, soaking through my undershirt.

At last, I found the controls. I pressed an adjuster to shut off the steam, before pushing a second one to trigger the hidden exhaust fans in the ceiling, clearing the room.

As the haze receded, I got a first good view of the crime scene. It resembled something out of a nightmare. There was even more blood than at Zorn's, the humidity keeping the gore wet and slick as it clung to every surface.

I counted five bodies. Two men and three women, although in truth it was hard to be sure. Not all of them were intact. I figured matching up the missing parts to their owners would give the verispexes a headache when they arrived.

Somehow, it made it worse that the victims were naked. I guessed the two men were clients, while the women were smile-girls, caught in the wrong place at the wrong time. As with the murders at Zorn's earlier, the killer's real target was clear from the savagery he had inflicted on one particular victim. The others were cut up, but one had received special attention.

Despite the mutilations, I was able to recognise the dead man by his augmetic eyes. They were oddly mismatched. One eye was ludicrously oversized, resembling a magnifying glass, while the other was small, as though it had been created for a child or an animal, only to be repurposed later.

There was only one man I knew in the district whose

augmetics matched that description – a bookmaker called Argus 'the Eyes' Hadenzach.

Hadenzach had been renowned for the brutality with which his leg-breakers collected debts from anybody who owed him. I suspected there would be wide celebration among local gamblers once the news of his death spread. The funeral would likely be well attended, if only from the number of people wanting to see for themselves that the bastard was really dead.

One of the bodies belonged to a fat man who I assumed was either Hadenzach's friend or somebody he had bribed with a trip to the joy house. He lay slumped face down against a bench inside the steam room, his bulk half on the floor.

As I moved closer to inspect the body, I saw a sudden movement. A tremor quivered through the flesh. My vision obscured by the remaining steam, at first I thought the fat man was alive despite his wounds. The body moved as though attempting to rise. I was about to help him when I realised it wasn't the fat man who was moving. There was someone concealed beneath the body, trying to lift it off themselves.

Unsure what to expect, I levelled my pistol at the figure underneath with one hand, while I helped roll the body to the side with the other.

There was a woman beneath it. A smile-girl, covered in the fat man's blood. I saw big, frightened eyes looking up at me, an expression of relief spreading across her face as she realised I was a sanctioner and not a madman with a chainsword.

'Throne, I thought he would…' She peered at the room around her as though expecting the killer to leap screaming from the shadows at any instant. 'Is he gone?'

She was naked except for some torn intimates. I retrieved a towel from a nearby laundry basket and gave it to her. It wasn't very clean, but it was the only thing in the room not covered in blood.

'He's gone,' I said as she wrapped the towel around herself. I helped her to her feet.

'What happened here?'

'We were jubilating with Argus and his guest.' The words came out in a jumble, breathless, her eyes casting nervous glances around the room like a hunted animal. 'He was celebrating a big deal, he said. That's why he wanted four girls. He asked for Oksana specially, and she recommended the rest of us – me, Taisina and Elina. Argus said four was his lucky number. Taisina said her lucky number was four hundred and one, since she was born on the four-hundredth-and-first day of the year. Elina said she was stupid – nobody's lucky number was four hundred and one, she didn't care when they were born. It was too big a number. Then they both started arguing and I said–'

She was babbling, in shock. Maybe a little high as well, on topaz or some other narco. I held a hand up to silence her.

'What is your name?'

'My name?' She blinked as though the question surprised her. 'Ludmila.'

I jabbed a thumb at the sigil on the chestplate of my uniform. It was a skull wearing a five-pointed coronet, set against the backdrop of a serpent eating its own tail – the symbol of Varangantua's enforcer corps.

'Do you know what this means?'

'Death...?' She seemed uncertain.

'It means I enforce the Emperor's peace. You pray to the Emperor, don't you, Ludmila?'

Her eyes widened. 'The Emperor...? Yes.'

'You believe He is merciful and all powerful. That He guards the Imperium and its citizens, keeping them safe from harm?'

'Yes.' She nodded, with more vigour this time. 'Oh yes.'

'Then you know you are safe now. A man broke in here, didn't he?'

'Yes.' The fear was back. She took a step backwards, almost seeming to shrink in size as she remembered what had happened.

'He was a big man with a chain-weapon. He killed Hadenzach and your friends. But you escaped, didn't you? You hid under the fat man and played dead until the killer was gone. Right?'

'Yes.'

'But it's over. I'm here. A servant of the Emperor. I will keep you safe. In His name. Do you believe me?'

'Yes.' She nodded again, still afraid but more resolute. 'I believe you.'

'I need you to describe the man you saw. The killer. Tell me everything you can remember about him.'

'Describe him? But I can tell you his name.'

'You can?'

'Everybody knows him. He's famous.'

The cold feeling at the base of my spine was back, spreading upward with freezing fingers like winter frost climbing a spire.

'It was the old pit fighter. The one with a chainsword for an arm. "Ripper" Revnik. Everybody knows him.'

Revnik.

She was right, of course. Everybody knew him.

Me included.

Knucks

'Citizens of Varangantua! Sons and daughters of the Imperium! Tonight, you are blessed! You are engraced! Tonight, you will see a spectacle to thrill the heart. Two of the finest specimens ever to draw breath in the pits will meet here, to make war on each other in the name of your entertainment. I tell you, there are men and women across Alecto tonight who will weep bitter tears – who will curse themselves! – that they were not here to see it. On this night of nights, this glory of glories!

This great and wonderful spectacle of combat, known across the galaxy by these six simple words. Two will enter! One will leave!'

When I thought back to my time in the pits, the years of training, the hardships, the struggles, the cruelties, it was always the fight nights I remembered most.

I remembered sitting in the staging area, checking my gear again and again as the annunciator whipped the crowd in the arena into a frenzy. I remembered the chant, the sound growing louder until it was as though the audience were a single screaming beast, hungry for blood.

'Two will enter! One will leave! Two will enter! One will leave!'

By the time the chant reached a crescendo, I was ready. I'd head for the entry gate, alongside whomever I was down to fight that night. Sometimes, it would be someone I didn't know. Or better yet, someone I hated. They were the good nights, the easy nights.

The hard nights were the ones when I had to fight someone I knew and liked. Lucky for me, the masters tried to avoid putting those kinds of pairings together. There was too much chance the fighters would make a bad show of killing each other, or else refuse to even fight at all.

In consequence, the masters did their best to keep friends apart. Sometimes, they'd go even further. The praeceptors who trained us were told to watch out for fighters who didn't get on. They would work on that dislike, repeatedly pairing the men together in training, doing their best to make sure the animosity grew, turning initial distrust into outright hatred. All for a simple reason – when the pair met in the arena, that hatred would show. The crowds loved a grudge match.

I remember the time I fought Ivo Ivanov. Ivo 'the Flayer', they called him.

Ivanov was a strong man. Built like a blockhouse, with muscles on his muscles. Most people fought in the pits for no other reason than to survive, but he was different. There was a sadist's gleam in his eyes every time he was in a bout. Ivo liked the killing.

Maybe that enjoyment was part of the reason he used the weapon he did, an electro-lash. Armed with the lash, Ivanov could flay the skin from an opponent at distances up to fifteen feet.

A lot of fighters liked to taunt each other while they were waiting for the gates to open. They'd try to undermine their opponent with scorn and ridicule, hoping to dent his confidence. Convince a man he's about to lose and you've won the fight before it begins. That was the theory, anyway. Personally, I liked to do my talking in the arena.

'What's it feel like, Malenko?' Ivanov asked, leaning in as we waited by the gate. 'How's it feel to know you're about to die?'

'I wouldn't know.'

'No?'

He held up his weapon, making a show of the coiled length of the whip line.

'I got this lash. It's got fifteen feet of line. Fifteen feet of pain that will tear the flesh from your bones before you can even get close to me. What you got?'

I was wearing spiked metal knuckles over my gloved fists, the skin beneath them protected by layers of leather and a special blend of plasweave fibre. Compared to the electro-lash, they seemed meagre weapons.

'Knucks? You got knucks? Guess your master must've got tired of you. Probably decided to cut his losses and take some side action on how quick you'll fall. He sent you here to die.'

It was the tradition in the pits that every fighter had their own signature weapon. Ivanov had the lash. Drillbit Tavovich used a converted rock drill. Gerod 'the Savage' Savic used a glaive. Adil 'the Axe' – well, you can guess.

It was part of the theatre of the pits. Each man was given

his own individual fighting persona, crafted by his master to make sure he stood out among his brethren. Not just a signature weapon but signature armour and clothing, sometimes even in signature colours.

To cap it off, there was the cognomen. The fighter's nickname. Ivanov was 'the Flayer'. I was Kirian 'the Killer' Malenko.

One thing was different about me, though. I didn't have a signature weapon. I used a different one each time I was sent into the pits, picking something I thought would give me an advantage against my opponent.

This break with tradition gained me extra attention from the crowd, as well as bringing kudos to my master. In truth, though, it was as much of a matter of theatre as all the rest. Not having a signature weapon was my signature.

That night, I had considered long and hard before choosing the knucks. I hoped they would give me an edge on Ivanov.

I wasn't about to tell him why, though.

'What's the matter, dead meat?' Ivanov leant in closer, trying to crowd me. 'Fear got your tongue?'

'Just don't see the point talking to a dead man.'

The gate buzzed and rattled open, the baying of the crowd growing more deafening as we advanced into the pit and took our places in the ring at its centre. The annunciator, a little man wearing a faux uniform with shining metal epaulettes and covered in glister, announced our names before exhorting the crowd to roar once more. After that, he beat a hasty retreat.

Maybe they started pit fights in a different way elsewhere in Varangantua, but in the Dredge they liked a countdown. There was a serpent mural set into the middle of the pit floor between the two fighters, the only place free of sand and sawdust in the entire arena. Each segment of the serpent was a different colour, with ten segments in all. One by one, they lit up as the crowd chanted along with the countdown.

'*...Four! Three! Two! One!*'

Ivanov was the first to move once it ended. With a sharp twist of his wrist, he sent the lash spitting towards me, the end of the whip making a noise like an angry swarm of insects as it seethed through the air.

I jumped backwards, dancing out of range of the strike.

The crowd cheered. The fight had begun.

I feinted a charge towards the Flayer's left, before leaping sideways as he snapped his weapon into another strike.

Another feint, then sideways again as I avoided the whip. I knew the weapon's effective range. I kept to its outskirts, dancing back and forth on the boundary between safety and the lethal touch of the lash.

The Flayer grew impatient. He whirled the weapon above his head, making another strike. Each time the lash changed direction, it made a cracking sound like a snapping neck. Unable to land a hit, he advanced towards me, attempting to push me back against the pit walls to reduce my room for manoeuvre.

It didn't work. Even as Ivanov whirled the lash around him in a wide arc, I ducked and leapt and danced my way free.

'Stand and fight, damn you!' yelled the Flayer amid a stream of curses.

The crowd was growing restive, frustrated by the lack of blood. Some fighters might have let it pressure them into attacking, afraid of angering the audience. But I continued as before, biding my time, staying just out of reach of the lash. I wasn't worried about the crowd – there would be blood enough to satisfy them soon enough.

Ivanov lacked my patience, however. In an effort to gain a little more reach, he started to extend his arm further into every strike, putting more of his weight on his front foot each time.

Before long, the moment I had been seeking arrived. The Flayer misjudged his strike, losing balance for a split second as the tip of the lash hit the arena floor and the line went slack. I pounced, putting my foot down on the played-out whip line, capturing it. At the same time, I activated the shock unit concealed inside my knucks.

Earlier, as we'd waited by the gate, Ivanov had been too busy trying to spook me to take a closer look at my weapons. If he had, he would have realised I was wearing shock knuckles, designed to deliver a powerful burst of electricity with each blow – just like the Flayer's lash.

I used the knuck on my left hand to make contact with the line as I grabbed it with my right. In any ordinary circumstance, the electric charge from the lash would have fried me. But the insulation concealed in my gloves and boots protected me, even as the charge of the electro-lash met the charge from my knucks.

Unlike me, the Flayer was grounded. Ivanov shrieked as his weapon shorted out, the grip exploding in his hand. The destruction took a couple of his fingers with it, even as it prevented his electrocution. No matter, I preferred to finish him up close anyway.

With Ivanov's main weapon gone, I moved in for the kill. His eyes wide in sudden fright, the Flayer went for the dagger he wore on his belt.

Too late. I was on him before he could even halfway draw the blade. I disarmed him with ease, before hitting him with a combination to gut, throat and face. My knucks hadn't shorted, but I chose not to activate the shocks. I didn't want to finish him too quickly. Better to play to the crowd. Give them the show they had come to see. That way, they might remember and decide to spare me in future on the day I finally lost a fight.

Another blow and Ivanov fell. I wasn't done. Even as he begged for mercy, I rained blows down on his head as the crowd cheered. Once he fell silent and it was clear he was knocked out and defeated, I paused, taking a step backwards.

I raised my hands, showing the blood-covered knucks to the crowd. But the ritual of the fight wasn't over yet. I turned to the ornate observation booth above the pit as the crowd noise subsided, looking to where the masters and their guests liked to watch men and women fight and die for them.

A hush spread across the pit. Behind the reinforced arma-glass of the booth's viewing window I could see the bloated form of my master, Syrus Volantich. He stood, spreading his arms wide, before cupping a hand to his ear in a gesture to the crowd. In answer, they began to chant once more, delivering sentence.

'Mortem!' went the chant. 'Mortem! Mortem!'

Volantich signalled thumbs down. I stepped forward and knelt beside Ivanov, before driving my shock knuckles into his face once more.

'You did good out there, Lenko,' Orvo Revnik told me in the aftermath of the fight. 'Real good. I liked that trick you pulled with the knucks, shorting out his lash. You were smart.'

I shrugged. 'Smarter than Ivanov, anyway.'

We were sitting in the fighters' quarters after the bout. Two old friends, side by side on a bench, sharing a bottle of slatov to celebrate my victory.

It was a post-fight tradition, dating back to our earliest days in the fighting pits. We passed the bottle back and forth, each taking a deep draught in turn.

'Yeah, he was a dumb one,' Revnik agreed. 'And a scum-wipe. Can't say I'll miss him.'

Compared to many of the fighters in the pits, Revnik's appear-ance was low-key, even spartan. He didn't believe in elaborate costumes or hairstyles. His head was shaved bald, his clothes dark, his appearance lacking any of the efforts others made to stand out for the crowd.

Then again, he didn't need them. He stood almost seven feet tall, with an inordinate amount of his bulk made up of thick slabs of muscle. His face was heavy-browed and square-jawed, his features covered in the lines of old scars left by the fighting pits. As if that weren't enough to guarantee attention every time he stepped out into the arena, his right arm had been replaced by an augmetic, sporting a removable chainsword in place of a hand.

We had known each other since we were kids. Through the years, fate had kept us together. First, in the foundling home where we had grown up. Then, in the mines, where they had sent us once we were old enough to work as 'grease-rats'.

The excavators, conveyors, ore-crushers and other machinery in the mines used to suffer frequent breakdowns. Most of it was for minor reasons that didn't rate the time or expense of having the tech-adepts repair them. Instead, they sent in children to apply votive oil, tighten loose helicals, clear debris from the mechanisms and the like. Because we were smaller, we could fit into tight spaces, allowing us to work in places the adults couldn't reach without having to remove the machines from the pithead.

It was dirty, dangerous work. You could be in the middle of a task when something you did caused the machine to roar back into life. If you were in the wrong place, or were too slow, you could get dragged into the workings. I had seen a lot of people die that way.

'Yeah, it was clever what you did with the knucks,' Revnik said, passing the bottle to me. 'But your reflexes were the key. If not for them, Ivo would have flayed you like every other fighter he ever faced.'

'Maybe.'

I took a drink from the bottle. The liquor inside burned like fire going down. It was good slatov.

'For sure. Your reflexes have always been your strongest asset. That's what's helped you win so many fights. You shouldn't rely on them too much though. You're fast, Lenko. But one day, you could meet somebody faster.'

'You got anybody in particular in mind?' I raised an eyebrow.

'Me, for one.'

'Really?' I handed the bottle back to him.

'Really.' He took a healthy slug of slatov, smacking his lips in pleasure afterwards. 'Folks look at me and they think a big guy like that can't be fast. Makes 'em underestimate me. How do you think I've won so many fights?'

'The chainsword helps.'

'I'm not saying it doesn't. But it's about more than just having a weapon. You gotta know how to use it. You gotta be good with it. And I am.'

I couldn't argue with that. He was an artist with that thing. Assuming you could be an artist and a butcher at the same time.

'Yeah,' I said. 'Modest, too.'

He creased his face into a smile. 'Just being honest with an old friend. My oldest friend, when it comes down to it. Don't think I'm forgetting you were the one taught me how to steal extra rations back when we were foundlings.'

'I felt sorry for you. Day after day, you'd go up to the overseers after every meal with your bowl licked clean and ask them for more food. You'd tell them you were still hungry. And what did it ever get you other than a beating? I figured if I didn't show you how to pick the lock on the refec-cart, they'd beat you to death one day.'

'They probably would have, too.' He scowled. 'There's a lot of bad people in this city. But I reckon the overseers in the foundling home had to be some of the worst. You know what I regret?'

'I'm sure you're going to tell me.'

'I think it's a shame we never got to meet any of the over-seers down here in the pits. That would be something to enjoy. All the times I've killed in the arena, you think I'd get to let loose on a few of the people I've wanted to see dead ever since we were kids.'

'That isn't the way it works, Orvo. There ain't no vengeance in the pits. There's just more killing.'

'How about you?' He gave the bottle back to me. 'Who'd you like to see down here? It can be anyone. Anybody you want to kill.'

'Nobody.'

'Come on. There's got to be someone.'

'Nobody. You said Ivanov was a scum-wipe, and you were right. But that's not why he's dead. I didn't kill him because I didn't like him, or because I thought he deserved it. I did it because if I didn't, he would have killed me. It's the same with every other fight I've ever been in. I've only ever killed any of them for one reason. Survival. All the rest of it – honour, glory, the acclaim of the crowd, vengeance? It's a load of dreck. All of it.'

I tipped the bottle back and took another swallow. After a fight, I liked to get good and drunk. It was my way of forget-ting that I'd be back where I started soon enough. There'd be another fight in a few days. Then another, and another. Until one day, I would be the one who died in the pits.

It was Revnik's turn for the bottle. This time, though, when I passed it back, he paused before drinking and shook his head.

'You're kidding yourself, Lenko. Nobody's that good at some-thing unless they've got a taste for it. You're good at killing. You can say it's about survival, but you ain't fooling me. Like it or not, there's something inside gives you a talent for it. You ask me, the praeceptors talked truer than they realised the first time they called you Kirian the Killer.'

I watched him take another drink, but I wasn't really watching him. I was thinking about the fight earlier. About the soft, wet sounds as I punched Ivanov in the face again and again and again. I had kept punching him even after I knew he was dead, reassuring myself I was doing it to play to the crowd. I had felt joy at that moment, but I told myself it was only relief. It had been either him or me in the fight, and I wasn't going to let it be me.

'You're wrong,' I told him. 'It's about survival. It has been ever since we were foundlings.'

'Uh-huh.' Revnik made a face, letting me know he didn't believe it. 'Don't get me wrong. I ain't criticising. I'm just saying you were born tough. Good thing for me, too. If you weren't, I wouldn't be here today.'

One day in the mines, when we were about twelve, Revnik and I had been working on a stalled excavator when it suddenly sprang into life, catching his right arm in the gears. I moved fast when I heard him scream, pushing a broken shovel deep into the machine's workings to stop it before it chewed him to pieces.

There had been no saving the arm. I had been forced to cut it off just below the elbow joint to free him, otherwise he would have bled to death long before the medicae arrived. I could still remember his screams, begging me to kill him before, finally, mercifully, he lost consciousness.

After that, neither of us was considered any good for rat work any more. Revnik was left with only one arm, while I had damaged a machine. An unpardonable sin, given it had caused the loss of working time and forced the mine owner to pay for the repair.

In the ordinary run of things, our employer might have looked to reduce his losses by auctioning our contracts of indenture off to the Mechanicus or one of the trade syndicates. But he already had a lucrative sideline selling the contracts of some of his workers on to the fighting pits. He reasoned anyone tough enough to cut a friend's arm off had the makings of a future pit fighter, as did the friend who had survived having the arm cut off.

Our contracts were sold to different men. I ended up with Syrus Volantich, while Revnik was indentured to a man named Adrik Kuznetski. It was Kuznetski who had paid to have an augmetic fitted in place of Revnik's missing arm, giving him a chainsword and the fighting name of 'the Ripper'.

Despite having different masters, we had not been separated. Both Volantich and Kuznetski kept their fighters in the same training stable. Together, we had risen through the ranks in the pits, winning dozens of bouts.

Still, the pits had a way of destroying friendships. Even if the masters preferred to avoid matching friends together, the longer any two fighters survived, the more likely it was they would meet in time.

It hadn't happened yet to me and Revnik. But it was inevitable. We both knew it.

'Do you ever think about those days?' he asked. 'In the mines, I mean?'

'Sometimes. I try not to dwell too long on the past.'

'What about the future? You know we'll have to fight one day, right? The way we both keep winning bouts, it's bound to happen. Eventually, there'll be nobody else left for us to fight. Nobody good enough anyway.'

'I try not to dwell on that either.'

'Do you ever wonder who'd win?' Revnik asked.

'No,' I replied. 'Let's hope it never comes to it.'

'Just so you know, when the day comes, I'll drink a toast to your memory after I kill you. In good slatov, if I can find it.'

'Just so you know, I make the same promise. Good slatov, if I can find it.'

Revnik took another drink before passing the bottle back to me.

Backup

'You're sure?' I asked Ludmila. 'It was "Ripper" Revnik? The pit fighter?'

She quailed and pulled back. Without realising what I was doing, I had grabbed her arm, my fingers closing tight enough to hurt her. A little ashamed, I released her.

She nodded, still subdued. 'Course I'm sure. Ain't like he's hard to recognise, with a chainsword for an arm and all. Argus even yelled out his name before Revnik killed him. Then... Oh, Emperor... I saw what he did...'

She started crying. Unsure how to react, I hovered in unease for a moment before the sound of approaching footsteps alerted me to potential danger.

I turned and aimed my gun at the doorway, gesturing to Ludmila to move to the side of the room, out of the line of fire. Careful to avoid the bodies underfoot, I moved to intercept the new arrivals.

It was a pair of sanctioners, a man and a woman, advancing down either side of the corridor with guns drawn. When they saw me, they relaxed.

'Ho! Is that you, Malenko?' the woman called out. 'Bastion said you'd responded to the alert. But when we saw a sanctioner's helmet on the floor over there, we figured someone had killed you.'

Her name was Mika Vorozov. Even if I hadn't recognised her voice at once, I would have known her from the ident number embossed below her sigil. We worked some of the same patrol routes together. I didn't know her partner. He wore a plainer, more austere version of the standard uniform, marking him as a sanctioner-novus – an apprentice enforcer.

'I'm fine. More than can be said for the patrons. There are seven dead here, including the two on the stairs. One survivor.'

'His Hand protect us.' Vorozov took a sharp intake of breath as she reached the doorway and peered inside the steam room. 'Looks like somebody went crazy with an axe in here.'

'Chainsword,' I told her. 'Suspect is Orvo "the Ripper" Revnik.'

Vorozov holstered her weapon before removing her helmet, revealing short dark hair, along with a face whose features were only slightly marred by a broken nose that had healed askew a long time ago.

'The pit fighter?'

'The same.'

'He retired, didn't he? A few years back. There was some kind of big event?'

'King of the Mountain,' I said. 'That's what they called it. To celebrate Emperor's Day, a group of the masters pooled their resources. In place of two fighters going into the arena to battle it out, they sent in twenty at once. It was a free-for-all, with the prize that the last man standing would be released from his contract of indenture, earning his freedom.'

'And Revnik won? Guess we shouldn't be surprised he's so dangerous.'

She turned towards me, a smile half in jest on her lips even as her eyes narrowed to size me up.

'I didn't know you were such a follower of the pit fights, Malenko. You do realise they are illegal?'

'A lot of things are illegal in this city, Vorozov. Doesn't mean a sanctioner shouldn't maintain an interest. Otherwise, we'd never know what the criminals were up to.'

'Makes sense, I guess.' Her eyes flicked to Ludmila in the corner of the room. 'Who's the sweetmeat?'

'A witness. She saw Revnik kill the others.'

'She'll need to be sent to the Bastion to make an oath of statement.'

Without removing her gaze from the smile-girl, she clicked her fingers at the novus behind her.

'Hey, fledgling. Escort the girl to the groundcar and take her preliminary oath. And see if you can find some clothes for her on the way. We don't want to give the boys in the Bastion too much of an eyeful.'

If the recruit objected to being ordered about at the snap of her fingers, he gave no sign of it. He hurried to Ludmila and bustled her away, trying his best not to glance at the places the towel did a bad job of covering.

'Girl's a bit fragile,' I told her. 'She'll need careful handling.'

'That's up to the chasteners back at the Bastion.' Vorozov shrugged, indifferent. 'As I remember, this Revnik is something of a giant. Scarred face, shaved head, a chainsword for an arm, not to mention he's a local celebrity. Shouldn't be too hard to track.'

'You'd think so. But this is the second place he's hit this morning.'

'What was the first place?' She cocked an eyebrow.

'Office of a fiscal tabulator named Erek Zorn. Revnik killed two there, before heading here. Seems he's on a rampage.'

'Not for long. With so many dead, the Bastion are bound to send backup, probably move in people from the raid teams to help with the search. That's a lot of extra eyes. We'll get him.'

I didn't share her confidence. Varangantua was a big city. Hunting a fugitive, even one who stood out from the crowd as much as Revnik, was like looking for a needle in a sludge pit.

'It would help if we had some idea where Revnik was headed.' I retrieved my helmet from the place where I had left it. 'This isn't random. There's got to be a reason behind it.'

'How do you mean?'

'Revnik has been out of the fighting pits for five years, without so much as a blemish on his record. You said it yourself, he's a local celebrity. Everybody in the Dredge knows his face. For that matter, most people in Varangantua have probably heard of him – anyone who follows the fights, at least. If he'd been breaking the Lex in any way – getting into fights, working as muscle for one of the crime combines, running his own fighting pit, anything – we would have heard about it.'

'Sure. Guy like that is too famous to keep his business secret for long. I get that. But I still don't see your point.'

'Revnik went five years without doing wrong. Then, today, he explodes into a killing spree. Goes on a rampage. Kills nine people. If we don't find him, he's going to kill a lot more. Makes you wonder what set it off.'

'Not me it doesn't. That's probator work, Malenko. Kind of thing you and me are supposed to leave alone. Anyway, you ask me, you're overthinking it.'

'How?'

With a grimace, Vorozov indicated the scene of slaughter inside the steam room.

'You're asking how come a man with a name like "the Ripper" started murdering people? The answer's obvious. Think of how many he killed in the fighting pits. It's always the same with these types. After a while, it becomes a habit. The killing gets into their blood. You know what they say...'

She lifted her own helmet, ready to put it on once more.

'Once a killer, always a killer.'

Oath of Service

I had been a pit fighter once. And a grease-rat. And a foundling. But I wasn't any of those things now. Not any more.

Ten years before the massacre at Kerensky's, I had found myself manacled at the wrists and ankles as I sat at a table in a small, grey, dimly lit room.

My captors had placed me there with the chain of my wrist restraints looped through a metal anchor ring set at one end of the table in front of me. The table itself was made of pla-steel, bolted to the floor.

I wasn't going anywhere. Couldn't run. Couldn't escape. They had left me alone in the room for what seemed like hours. Probably hoping to break me.

I knew why I had been brought there. Knew there was only one way it would play out.

They had brought me there to die.

After an eternity, the door opened. The influx of light after so long in the gloom was a little blinding. I saw a figure silhou-etted in the doorway. Broad-shouldered, wearing body armour.

A sanctioner. He had a cup of recaff in one hand and a folder filled with parchments in the other. With a free finger, he pressed twice on the lumen activator on the wall, raising the lighting to a more comfortable level.

He sat down, placing the folder and the recaff on the table on either side of him.

He wasn't wearing a helmet. I had never seen a sanctioner without one before. I don't know what I had expected. A cruel-faced and bloodless fanatic, perhaps, unflinching in his devotion to the Lex Alecto? Instead, I saw a man who looked like any other. Close-cropped hair, dark but greying at the temples, clean-shaven, with deep-set eyes that were a steely blue-grey but not unkind. The face was worn and well lived. I had no idea whether sanctioners had access to juvenat, but he looked to be in his late forties.

'So.' He took a deep breath and flipped the folder open. 'You can call me Sladek. Ah, I almost forgot.'

He dug in one of the equipment pouches on his belt and retrieved a key. Leaning forward across the table, he took hold of my right wrist, before pausing.

'Before I unshackle you, understand this. If you attack me, or try anything, if you even spit at me, I will break the bones of your right hand one by one. All twenty-seven of them, starting with the tip of your little finger and moving across. Nothing personal, you understand. You're from downclave, so maybe you don't know this. We have a simple rule here. One that's more important than all the codes and sections of the Lex combined. Nobody can be allowed to disrespect a sanctioner without retribution. Do you understand?'

I glared at him, saying nothing.

'Yeah. I think you do. I've been glared at by experts, son. You should know you're not as intimidating as you think.'

He put the key in the lock, releasing my hand, before placing the cuff of the manacle around the anchor ring and closing it until it clicked. Satisfied, he leant back and pushed the cup of recaff towards me.

'Help yourself. I had one earlier.'

I was tempted. It had been hours since I'd had anything to eat or drink. Still, I held back.

'You think it's drugged, maybe? Or poisoned?' Sladek smiled. 'You have an overinflated sense of your importance in the world if you think we'd waste interro-drugs on you. Here.'

He reached for the cup and took a sip, before breathing out a sigh of pleasure.

'One good thing about this floor of the Bastion, they make decent recaff. Not like that swill in the armoury.'

He placed the cup back within my reach.

'It's up to you whether you drink it. Although bear in mind, if you get sent to holding after this, there's no guarantee they'll give you anything. And recaff is better when it's warm.'

A part of me hated myself for giving in, but I lifted the cup and drank some. For all I knew, it might be the last one I would ever have.

He was right. It was good recaff. Rich and bitter, the way I liked it.

'Andrei Kirian Malenko,' the sanctioner read from among the parchments inside the folder. 'For reasons unknown, you prefer not to go by your given first name, using Kirian or Malenko instead. Parents both believed dead. You are first recorded in our system at the Light of Terra foundling home. Transferred to the mines at age eight to work as a grease-rat. Somehow, you ended up as a pit fighter, where you compete under the name Kirian "the Killer". Captured in a raid on the pits twelve hours ago.'

The enforcers had shown up as I was in the middle of a bout, announcing their arrival with a barrage of stun grenades and choke gas. Blinded by the gas, unable to see either the crowd or the opponent I had been fighting, I had kept low, crawling on the arena floor in the hope I could sneak out unseen.

It hadn't worked. The screams of the panicking crowd ringing in my ears, I had come face to toe with the boots of an advancing sanctioner. The last thing I remembered was the pain and involuntary muscle spasms as a shock maul hit me. Then, only blackness.

'I watched the vid footage of some of your old fights before I came in here,' Sladek continued. 'Impressive.'

He removed a few pages from the folder and spread them on the table in front of me. I saw grainy pict-caps of my fights. Me, crouching beside Ivo Ivanov as I beat him to death. The time I fought Andreas the Grox and smashed his head to pulp with a mace. An action shot, with me stabbing Rock-Claw Jonovich in the guts with a sword, shortly before I administered the mercy cut. It seemed pointless to protest my innocence, or claim it was a case of mistaken identity. It was all there in black and white.

None of which explained why I was in the room with Sladek.

My guilt was clear. Sanctioners were renowned for the dispatch with which they dealt with criminals. I was sure at some point they would take me to another grey room, somewhere nearby, to finish matters. Perhaps a place with drainage channels in the floor, making it easier to wash away the blood after they put a bullet in my brain.

I had expected them to execute me hours ago, performing the deed without ceremony or fuss. For reasons I didn't understand, I was still alive. Maybe they were playing with me.

'Of course, the fights aren't sanctioned,' Sladek said. 'So that makes each one of these a murder. Nice of the people who run the arena to record it all on vid. It reduces the paperwork when you can hand this kind of evidence to the justicius. I know that wasn't the reason they did it, but it worked out well in that regard. For me, at least. Not for you.'

'Why don't you just get it over with?' I asked.

'Get what over with?' His brow furrowed.

'The execution. Why don't you take me to wherever it happens and get it done?'

'Execution?' He stared for a moment in genuine confusion. 'Ah, I see. You think we brought you here to deal with you expeditiously? A quiet corner, a gun to the back of the head, that kind of thing? I'm not saying it never happens. But this isn't one of those instances. Lucky for you.'

He began to tidy the table, collecting the picts together and placing them back in the folder.

'The justicius has issued a preliminary judgement in your case. He's sentenced you to penal servitude. Although it remains to be decided whether you'll serve your time at the prison colony on Sacc-Five or in the penal legion. Either way, the life expectancy isn't great. But there is a third option.'

He pulled another parchment from the folder, laying it on

the table between us before turning it around to give me a better view.

I saw a page filled with densely packed script, written in ornamented and painstaking calligraphy. The words, while vaguely familiar, were gibberish. The only part I could understand was the date, written next to an empty signature line at the bottom, alongside the death's-head sigil of the enforcer corps and the seal of the local vladar.

'What is this?' I asked.

'Don't you read?'

'Yes. They taught us in the foundling home.' I gestured at the parchment with my free hand. 'But not this... whatever it is.'

'It's Old High Gothic. Very formal, very exact, and written in the traditional style. They've been writing these documents the same way on Alecto for thousands of years. It's an oath of service. It says you agree to become a sanctioner.'

I gawped at him. 'You're crazed.'

'We get a lot of our recruits among people like you. Offenders with the right skill set who are given a second chance. Officially, you'll still be a prisoner. But you'll be granted reprieve of sentence as long as you volunteer for the enforcer corps. Makes sense when you think about it. It can be difficult for us to get recruits. Enforcing the Lex is a dangerous job. The pay is dreck. The hours are long. Any friends you had before you put on the sigil don't want to know you any more. Not once they think you might arrest them at any time to make monthly quota. Once you become a sanctioner, you're about as popular as a bodily emission in an elevation carriage.'

'You're doing a good job of selling it.'

'I don't have to sell anything. It sells itself. We both know, whatever the hardships, however tough the life, becoming a sanctioner is better than any of the alternatives you're facing. What's say we stop fooling around?'

He delved into another equipment pouch, removing a self-inking stylus from inside.

'Just so you know, once you're a sanctioner you'll have to follow regulations to the letter. No exceptions. Otherwise, they'll revoke your reprieve and turn you back into a convict. No third chances, Malenko.'

Withdrawing the cap to reveal the nib, he laid the stylus on the table next to the oath.

'Now, make your mark so we can get you out of here. First, to the refec-hall to get food and some more recaff. Next, to the training hall so you can begin getting ready for your new profession.'

Mind still reeling, I looked down at the oath. Throughout my life, I had hated sanctioners. To me, they were no better than the overseers, mine owners or masters. They were all part of the same corrupt, rotten system that made sure people like me stayed downclave, a system that had kept me poor and miserable.

If I joined the enforcers, it would be a betrayal of everything I had ever believed. But I could see no other choice. At least, no choice that wasn't worse.

In the end, it came down to survival.

As I reached out to pick up the stylus and sign my name, Sladek smiled.

'You made the right choice. We'll see if we can put that talent for violence you learnt in the pits to better use keeping the Emperor's peace.'

Lines

Revnik was long gone, but I checked the rest of the bath-house along with Vorozov just in case there were any more victims. Finding none, we separated. Vorozov stayed to protect the crime scene until someone arrived to handle the forensics. I headed for the exit.

En route, I updated the Bastion, hitting a recessed control stud on the side of my helmet to connect the vox.

'Bastion, this is five-nine-omega-nine. Multiple homicides confirmed at Kerensky Bathhouse. Seven dead. Witness at the scene identifies offender as Orvo Revnik, cognomen "the Ripper". Fugitive is described as six foot eight inches tall. Muscular build. Shaved head. Facial scars. Right hand and lower forearm missing, replaced by a chainsword augmetic.'

'Chainsword? Clarify on offender's identity, omega-nine. Sounds like you're talking about the ex-pit fighter "Ripper" Revnik?'

'Affirmed on that, Bastion. Request district-wide alert, as well as backup to search the surrounding area.'

'Affirmed on the district-wide and backup. Command will want to supervise the search from the Bastion.'

'Understood. It's been raining hard here, hampering visuals. Request cyber-mastiff squad to help with hunt.'

'Request received and forwarded. But I wouldn't hold your breath. There's a big narco sweep in the South Dredge this morning. All mastiff units currently engaged. Wait... Orders incoming from command. Hold for update, omega-nine.'

The vox switched to dead air as the operator received new instructions on another channel. After a pause, the voice returned.

'Bastion to five-nine-omega-nine. Your orders are to search the line west of the Korovoi Transitway for the fugitive. Standard sweep pattern, with search corridor terminating at Yubilev Railer High-Line.'

'Affirmed on that, Bastion. However, request dispensation to conduct further investigations here first. If I work the prospekt, try to find witnesses, I might be able to pick up the offender's trail.'

'Negative on that, omega-nine. You have your orders. Command

will dispatch probator to question witnesses if deemed necessary. Bastion out.'

The vox went back to dead air, forestalling any further discussion.

Outside, the rain was beginning to ease. As I emerged from the bathhouse, I saw people had started to return to the prospekt. Gawkers for the most part, driven by their curiosity at the presence of sanctioners, doubtless hoping for some free entertainment if we arrested anyone. But given the quantities of trade goods lying abandoned across the square from the earlier panic, it was only a matter of time before the street hawkers came back as well.

The same hawkers could be a goldmine of information. By nature, those who worked the black market had to be keen-eyed and always on the lookout for danger, whether from gangers, sanctioners or their fellow traders. Anyone who had been in the prospekt when Revnik attacked the bathhouse might have seen something important.

I wouldn't expect them to cooperate, not without persuasion. But as a sanctioner, I had plenty of ways to make people talk.

There were a lot of questions remaining about the case, even now I knew Revnik was the killer. For one thing, I hadn't determined his means of transport. Was he on foot or using a vehicle? It made a difference to the size of the search perimeter, not to mention the kind of places we would look for him.

I didn't even know which direction he had taken once he had left the building. The lexators back at Bastion would be working on that, trawling through the public surveillance feeds, trying to identify Revnik among the footage so they could track him. But that could take hours, even assuming the vid-feeds in Zmeya and its vicinity were working. Given the amount of illegal business that went on in the prospekt, there were no guarantees. Corruption was rife among enforcers. At any time, someone might have been bribed to disengage the local feeds, leaving a hole in the coverage.

If I waited around the prospekt for an hour or so, maybe even as little as another few minutes, there was a chance I could find a lead. Roust some of the hawkers once they returned, offer a few snitch fees to grease the wheels, break a few heads if needed. Chances were, I'd be able to find somebody who had seen something. Instead, I had been ordered to leave the area to work a search pattern on the other side of the transitway.

It was frustrating. But it was the nature of life as an enforcer. Procedure was all important to the Bastion. They weren't interested in initiative or bright ideas, only complete obedience. Particularly when it came to the lines of demarcation. Sanctioners were the hands and fists. And Emperor help you if you crossed those lines. Especially if, like me, you were a man on reprieve, able to be bounced into penal servitude at any time if you broke regs.

Swallowing my discontent, I headed for the Rampart. Along the way, I saw Ludmila. She was sitting in Vorozov's groundcar, parked nearby. Vorozov herself hadn't returned from the bathhouse, but her novus was in the front of the grounder, guarding the girl while Ludmila sat glum and despondent in the prisoner compartment at the back. She looked desolate, probably starting to think of the friends she had lost, now the initial shock of the attack had worn off.

She wasn't alone in that. Orvo Revnik was one of the few friends I had in the world. At least he had been, once.

I hadn't seen him in a long time. Not since the day I was arrested.

Revnik had escaped the raid that day. While I became a sanctioner, his life in the fighting pits had continued as before. In the years that followed, he had won every bout, claiming victory after victory. Over time, he had become renowned as one of the greatest pit fighters of his generation – a reputation only further enhanced after he won King of the Mountain.

I had watched it all from afar, cheering every triumph even as I avoided seeing him, knowing it would be my duty to arrest Orvo if we ever came face to face.

King of the Mountain was Revnik's last fight. After that, he had retired – undefeated to the last. But even after he left the arena, I had continued to avoid him. I was pleased for Revnik's success. Pleased he had managed to put the pits behind him. From what I heard, he had retired with a useful sum. Found a wife, bought a hab. He had built a happy life. Or, at least, as happy as anything ever could be for somebody from the Dredge.

Still, I kept my distance. As kids growing up, the two of us had always hated sanctioners. I figured if he had been the one captured in the raid, Revnik would have spat on the oath of service and told Sladek where he could stick his reprieve.

Call it shame, call it embarrassment. In the end, my motive for continuing to stick clear of Revnik was simple. I never wanted him to see me in a sanctioner's uniform. Never wanted to see the look of disgust on my old friend's face when he realised what I had become.

Back behind the wheel of the Rampart, I updated the nav-console on the dash. Setting a course for Korovoi Transitway, I triggered the ignition, knowing Bastion could use the ground-car's transponder to track my coordinates. If I delayed heading out towards my assigned search location, even for a few minutes, I could end up facing a charge. As a reprieved prisoner, I spent every day walking the razor's edge. It wouldn't take much for command to declare me a recidivist and order my sentence reinstated.

I pulled out through the prospekt, the Rampart's engine making a low, angry noise like a captive beast unable to escape the confines of its cage.

I knew how it felt.

* * *

The rain had stopped by the time I exited the transitway to begin the search.

In theory, the streets of Varangantua are laid out in well-ordered and regular lines, making the city simple to navigate. In practice, thousands of years of continuous building and rebuilding had long ago erased the original template, leaving behind a disordered mess of conflicting and competing architecture, all pushed together in ways that made little sense.

It was not yet midday. Overhead, the clouds were starting to clear, allowing the red sun to peek through the forest of buildings. Even at its most radiant, the sun was never that bright in Varangantua, especially not downclave. The tall spires of the city cast long shadows, bathing the streets in gloom.

If the sun made one difference, it was in its palette. The scarlet blush of the sky was reflected in the puddles left behind by the rain. A poet might have said they resembled pools of washed-out blood staining the rockcrete as proof of the city's crimes. But there wasn't much room for poetry in Varangantua. Not in the places I knew.

As I eased the Rampart through the search zone, I saw the panoply of life in the Dredge play out before me. Citizens hurrying through the streets. Hawkers peddling their wares. Street preachers and other zealots exhorting passers-by to seek repentance. Then there were the others, the ones who might as well have been wearing their desperation as a sigil. The vagrants. The broken-down. The destitute. The crave-cases addicted to any of a multitude of different drugs, both legal and illegal. The smile-workers, male and female, forced to sell themselves for a handful of slate.

There was no sign of Revnik. Not that I found it surprising. A man would have to be crazed or stupid to wander around in the open after killing nine people. I knew Revnik wasn't stupid. Although, whether or not he was crazed remained to be seen.

I was heading south along the Via Grevski when an idea occurred to me. Just because I was complying with command's orders, it didn't mean I couldn't perform two tasks at once.

I activated the vox. 'Bastion, this is five-nine-omega-nine. Request patch-through to data retrieval, extension three-seven-one-eight.'

'Is this an approved call, omega-nine?' The voice on the other end was snide and waspish. *'I don't see that extension on the list of authorised contacts for patrol.'*

'It's a personal matter, Bastion. I won't be long.'

'See that you are not,' the operator harrumphed. *'The enforcer corps isn't paying you to gossip with your drinking confederates.'*

There was a click as the call transferred, followed by the rapid modulations of the alert chime. After a short pause, a gruff male voice answered.

'Retrieval. Archivist Sobol speaking.'

'Sobol, it's Malenko. I need you to run some names.'

'Authentication code?'

'I don't have one. I'm following a hunch.'

'Hmm. We don't do hunches here, Malenko. Only approved requests backed up by the proper auth code.'

'Call it a favour. Part of the payback you owe me. Remember the time you had trouble with those gamblers?'

'All right, all right,' he said, presumably wary as to who else might be listening to the channel. *'I'll mark it as an exigent circumstance request. That way you don't need a code. Give me the names.'*

'There's three of them. The first is Erek Zorn.'

'Home address and ID number?'

'I don't have either. But Zorn operated as a fiscal tabulator out of Valdov Office Plexus. Shouldn't be too hard to find him. The second name is Argus Hadenzach, cognomen "the Eyes". Again, no home address or ID. But he was a bookmaker. Probably got an arrest record big enough to choke a grox.'

'And the third name?'

'Orvo Revnik.'

'The fugitive? I just saw the district-wide on him.'

'Any sightings yet?'

'A dozen. All mistaken identity so far. Including at least one citizen shot in error because someone thought he was the Ripper. Right now, it's a dangerous time to be a bald man with any kind of augmetic in the Dredge.'

That was the problem with a district-wide alert. People got overeager, started seeing the offender everywhere. Made it hard to verify the real sightings amidst all the dross.

'I'll run your names,' Sobol said. 'What am I looking for?'

'Some kind of connection between Revnik and the other two. They were his real targets. I'm sure of it. If we can establish Revnik's reasons for killing them, it could help identify any future victims before he gets to them.'

'You are assuming he didn't just murder them because he was high on narco. Plenty of pit fighters end up addicted to combat drugs or other enhancers. Or maybe he took a few too many blows to the head during his fights and now his brains are addled. You ask me, it's a waste of time.'

None of that sounded like the Revnik I knew. But I couldn't say Sobol was wrong. A lot might have happened in ten years.

'Humour me. Vox me back when you've analysed the files.'

'It could take a while. There's a lot of requests backed up. We've been having problems with the feeds for the dataveil.'

'Fast as you can. I doubt Revnik has finished killing.'

'I'll see what I can do.'

The call cut off.

Ahead, the roadway branched in two directions. The left side joined a transitway that sped on through the district, while the right side led into a series of prospekts and connecting alleyways. In line with my orders, I headed right to search each location, street by street, alley by alley, eyes open for Revnik.

I hoped Sobol's data-work might give me a better chance of finding him. If command ever questioned me on it, I would tell them what I had told Sobol. I was following a hunch.

The truth was more layered. I was chasing Revnik for more reasons than simple duty. Once upon a time, we had been friends. Whatever Revnik had become in the interim, I was gambling that enough of our friendship remained that I could bring him in alive. At the very least, I intended to try.

It was more than any other sanctioner would do. Nobody was going to be gentle when arresting a suspect in nine homicides. They'd shoot first and ask questions later. The unfortunate citizen shot in error was proof of that.

Right then, I figured I was Revnik's only chance of being alive by the end of the day.

Time would tell whether or not he would take me up on it.

Hand of Mercy

'Bastion to all sanctioners vicinity Divine Hand of Mercy Infirmary, off Kadutsey Throughway! Fugitive wanted in district-wide alert spotted near main entrance! Offender name Orvo Revnik, also known as "the Ripper". Shaved head, scarred face, with a chainsword augmetic in place of right arm. Suspect wanted in multiple homicides. Believed highly dangerous. All available sanctioners, respond!'

I was conducting a street-by-street search in my Rampart when I heard the alert. The Divine Hand of Mercy was a little over a mile away. I pressed the transmit activator on the side of my helmet.

'Bastion, this is five-nine-omega-nine! Show me responding. Estimate arrival at infirmary in two minutes!'

I pulled the groundcar into a tight turn, the tyres screeching in protest beneath me. Foot pushing down on the acceleration pedal as the vehicle straightened, I sped in the direction of the infirmary with clarion wailing.

It wasn't hard to spot the source of the alert once I reached the location. Even if I hadn't known the infirmary by sight – or had been unable to recognise the enormous skull-headed caduceus on its side – the horde of panicked citizens streaming from the building would have given it away.

The empty parking places by the entrance were jammed with fleeing staff and patients. Unable to get any closer, I left the Rampart on the street and continued on foot.

It was a struggle to make headway through the crowd. In ordinary circumstances, people from the Dredge did everything they could to avoid sanctioners, giving the uniform a wide berth. But panic had pushed them together into a heedless throng. Buffeted by elbows and shoulders, I drew my maul, ready to shock anybody who didn't give way.

That did the trick. Wary of the blue fire crackling from the end of the maul each time I squeezed the activator, the crowd parted on either side, giving me room.

The worst of the exodus had thinned out by the time I made it through the front entrance. Inside, I was greeted by a reception area littered with the crushed and injured bodies left trampled by the crowd, along with broken walking frames, bent crutches, overturned aid-chairs and other medical detritus.

In search of information, I grabbed a passing medicae. 'The man with the chainsword, where is he?'

For an instant, I thought he might try to break out of my grip and continue his flight. Instead, the habits ingrained by a lifetime of acquiescence to Imperial authority kicked in.

'Floor tertius! The chirurgical wards! He's killing everyone!'

He scampered away as I released him.

The elevation system was clogged with people. I made for the stairs, activating my vox as I ran.

'Bastion, this is five-nine-omega-nine. Mass panic and disorder at Divine Hand of Mercy. Multiple casualties. Request backup, as well as Bulwark support for crowd control.'

'Backup is on its way, omega-nine. Closest units to your location report estimated arrival at five minutes. I'll forward your Bulwark request.'

'Affirmed, Bastion. Let backup know suspect is reported on floor tertius. I am in pursuit.'

'Affirmed on that, omega-nine. Good hunting.'

Ahead, people were coming down the stairway in a steady stream, but in nothing like the numbers I had seen at the entrance.

I ran up the steps two at a time, pushing aside anyone too slow to get out of the way.

As I emerged onto the third-floor landing, I swapped the shock maul for my stub gun. I wanted to bring Revnik in alive if I could – I owed him that much. But I wasn't about to risk close combat with a man armed with a chainsword. If he wouldn't surrender, I'd shoot low, aiming to hit him in the legs.

It didn't take long to find evidence of my old friend's presence. Two securitors lay dead inside a corridor, their blood splattered on the walls and ceiling. They had probably recognised him from the alert. Or had thought a man wandering the halls of an infirmary with a chainsword could be suspicious. Either way, Revnik had made short work of them.

One advantage to hunting a man with a chainsword was that it wasn't difficult to pick up his trail. I tracked a set of familiar, bloody boot marks as they followed a winding route along the white-tiled floor.

The infirmary was a maze of branching, anonymous corridors, lacking much by the way of signposts or markers. Based on the meandering pattern of the footprints, I got the feeling Revnik had quickly become lost.

Where I might have asked for directions, he favoured more violent methods. I found another dead body, a medicae this time. Nearby, a group of patients sheltered inside a medical bay, hiding behind a bed. I motioned for them to leave, directing them to use the stairs. I didn't need to ask which way the killer had gone. The blood trail he had left behind told me all I needed to know.

The tracks led through a set of double doors marked *Medicae Personnel Only*.

The doors opened out into a refec-room filled with tables and auto-dispensers. Once inside, I discovered the leavings of another rampage. Six bodies in all, some ripped apart, a great pool of blood beneath them.

A medicae-auxilia in a pale uniform sat slumped in despair on the floor next to one of the bodies, her hands and clothing covered in blood. It was clear she had tried to treat some of her dying colleagues, but to no avail.

She looked up as I entered, her face a study in sorrow. Before I could say anything, she pointed with a bloodied hand at a doorway on the other side of the room.

'There. The monster went that way.'

In truth, I had little need for further directions. Even without the continuing blood trail, I could hear the distinctive, grating hum of a chainsword in the distance.

The corridor out of the refec-room led into a cramped office packed with writing tables and archive cabinets. A much larger chamber lay beyond it, the two sections separated from each other by a low partition wall topped by an opaque sliding glass screen. The sliding screen was shattered halfway along its length, leaving a two-foot-wide hole in the middle. Below it, the surface of the partition was chewed up by the teeth of a chainsword, making it clear which way Revnik had gone.

The space beyond the partition widened out into a cavernous waiting area, big enough to hold as many as a thousand individuals at once. There were several hundred people inside, some standing while others cowered behind serried rows of plastek chairs.

I couldn't see Revnik through the crowd, but the incessant roar of a chainsword motor told me he was at the other end of the room, the people in between blocking my view of him. I heard voices praying and begging for mercy, the pleas playing out against the threatening counterpoint of the chainsword's drone.

At first, I wondered why no one had fled. Until, pushing myself through the hole Revnik had left in the glass screen, I found a trio of bodies slumped by the foot of the partition on the other side. They had been cut down from behind, most likely killed while trying to flee. Looking over the heads of the intervening crowd, I saw the only other exit from the room was at the other end of the waiting area, guarded by Revnik and his chainsword.

No one noticed me as I eased into the room. All eyes were on Revnik. I caught a flash of him through a momentary gap in the crowd. Face enraged, he was gesticulating with the chirring blade of the chainsword even as he held a terrified medicae by the tunic and shook him.

Revnik was yelling something, but I couldn't make it out.

The opening in the crowd closed before I could draw a bead. I moved closer, searching for an angle of fire that would let me wound Revnik rather than kill him – although regs would have had me end him then and there.

I thought about the stand-off with the stimm-head earlier. Maybe Sobol was right about Revnik. His behaviour seemed unhinged, deranged. Maybe he was an addict, like that scuzz-stain at the provisioner's. It would explain a lot of things.

I couldn't draw a clear line of sight. Too many people were in the way. Deciding it was time to improvise, I lifted my gun and aimed it at the ceiling. With silent hopes that there was nobody standing above me, I pulled the trigger.

The gunshot reverberated through the room's yawning interior, briefly drowning out the sound of Revnik's chainsword.

'Enforcer corps!' I shouted. 'Everyone on the floor! Now!'

A ripple passed through the crowd. Some complied with the order, throwing themselves to the floor, while others turned to gawp at me in dumb shock.

The numbers blocking my vision had thinned. I took advantage of the change, sighting in on Revnik even as he dragged the medicae into position as a shield. I fired once, hitting Revnik in the left shoulder and breaking his hold on the hostage.

I was about to shoot again, aiming lower this time, but the crowd intervened. Spooked by the second bout of gunfire, they burst into pandemonium. People ran blindly in all directions, breaking my line of fire.

I tried to re-aim, but Revnik was fast. I caught a glimpse of him as he turned to dive headlong through the doors behind him. I gave chase, vaulting onto a line of nearby chairs and running across them as a shortcut through the crowd.

It only took seconds for me to reach the door, but Revnik was already at the end of the corridor by the time I followed him through it. Passing a trolley stacked high with oxygen cylinders, he slashed at one of the valves with his chainsword before pushing the trolley over.

The contents broke free as the trolley overturned, sending a dozen cylinders bouncing along the floor towards me.

The canister Revnik had damaged rolled to a stop right in front of me. I leapt for cover and braced for the explosion.

It never came. The ruptured valve emitted a small, feeble hiss before falling quiet. Lucky for me, the damned thing had been empty.

Back on my feet in a heartbeat, I resumed the pursuit. Revnik had gained a lead while I was busy, disappearing from view into the next room. I rushed after him, ready for anything.

I found myself in another waiting room. The people inside were huddled in frightened groups, trying to stay as distant from Revnik as possible as he stood, partially out of sight, behind a support pillar at the far end of the room.

The chainsword was roaring in high gear. As I moved around to get a clean shot, I saw Revnik had his weapon buried deep into the substance of the wall in front of him, almost to the base of the blade.

For a second, I wondered whether he had succumbed to insanity.

'Orvo Revnik!' I aimed my gun at his back as I shouted orders. 'Hands in the air! Turn off the chainsword and turn around. Slowly! Don't make me kill you.'

Revnik made a show of complying. He withdrew the chainsword from the wall, the buzzing of the blade dying as he switched off the mechanism. Arms raised, he began to turn around.

'All right, breaker,' he said, using a downclave slang term for sanctioners. With my helm, I was as anonymous to him as the next ground-pounder. 'Don't get nervous now. You've got me.'

As he changed position, I was able to see past Revnik's body to the wall he had been attacking. The movement revealed yellow-and-black warning stripes painted on the surface, along with large red letters reading *Incendiarius*. I caught a glimpse of a small silvery object nestled in the palm of his left hand as the method to his earlier madness became clear.

'Yeah. You got me *right* where you want me.'

I became aware of the hiss of escaping gas. Realising Revnik had cut into the infirmary's gaseous fuel system, I dived for cover even as he worked the flint wheel of the igniter in his hand.

The sparks turned the broken gas pipe into an impromptu flamer. Revnik leapt to one side as a jet of fire exploded from the wall like a burning finger.

In an instant, the place was an inferno. An alarm sounded as hidden sprinkler heads activated overhead, water falling from the ceiling like rain in an attempt to douse the conflagration. Meanwhile, the fire from the pipe itself subsided, the building's safety systems acting to choke off supply to the ruptured line.

Wincing in pain, I got back to my feet. I had caught enough of the blast that I could feel burns across my skin. Glancing down, I saw the upper section of my uniform was covered in soot and pitted with holes where the heat had burned through it.

Ahead of me, the room was now divided in two by an impassable curtain of fire as flames danced along the rows of burning chairs. I saw Revnik on the other side, running for the far door. Unable to follow him, I went for my gun – only to realise I had lost it when I landed.

The weapon was nowhere to be seen, its resting place on the floor obscured amid the murk of smoke and falling water. Around me, civilians fled in panic, terrified by the blaze.

Revnik was nearly at the door. I had no way to stop him. Frustrated, I tore away my helmet, revealing my face as I yelled after him.

'Orvo!'

He glanced in my direction, our eyes meeting as he paused in the doorway. I saw an expression of surprise, followed by a smile of recognition. He turned away.

In another moment, he was gone.

Firewatch

'You were lucky,' the medicae-auxilia said as she placed a dressing over the burn on my shoulder. 'Your uniform stopped the worst of the heat getting through to your skin.'

'Luck has got nothing to do with it,' I told her. 'Getting shot, stabbed, burned – it's a regular day for a sanctioner. They make the uniforms with that in mind.'

I was sitting on the hood of my Rampart, my helmet and tunic off, as the auxilia tended to my wounds. My upper body was peppered with small burns, though she had assured me none were serious enough to require a dermal graft. With care, she worked through them one by one, adding a layer of healing salve and some sprayed-on synthskin before fixing a dressing to each in turn.

It was the kind of medical work that might have ordinarily been done inside an infirmary. But the infirmary was on fire, the heat intense enough that we could feel it even from where my Rampart was parked.

The fire Revnik had started had spread fast. By the time the firewatch had arrived to deal with it, the blaze had engulfed much of the third floor.

Given the scale of the emergency, I had been forced to put the hunt for Revnik on hold for a while. The pursuit of a killer, even a multiple murderer, paled compared to the present disaster. By all accounts, Revnik had gone to ground anyway, with no sightings since he fled the infirmary, and no leads. Once I had recovered my gun from where it had fallen, I had spent the better part of the last two hours helping to evacuate the building. Then, once the place was clear, I had joined with the Bulwark squads dispatched by Bastion command to work crowd control around the infirmary grounds.

Disasters always brought out the worst of the city. Any time the enforcers were busy, there were those who tried to take advantage. Crime would be up all across the district, with outbreaks of looting, even rioting a real possibility.

If there was one thing that made the enforcer corps sit up and take notice, it was any threat to public order. In such circumstances, the sanctioners were sent in hard, to break heads and smother the offenders with as much choke gas as was needed to subdue them.

Once the public order situation at the infirmary was judged under control, I had been rotated out of secondment with the Bulwarks and sent back to patrol, with orders to have my wounds treated along the way.

By that time, I was under no illusions about the difficulties I faced in picking up Revnik's trail again. Events had given him two hours to make good his escape, with the disorder and confusion created by the fire only adding to his advantage. Worse, any forensics inside the infirmary were lost, burned up in the fire along with the vids from the building's internal surveillance feeds.

Despite the setbacks, I refused to give in. Instead, I tried to use my time wisely. Not least when it came to which auxilia I had asked to treat my injuries.

Her name was Marina Glinka. She was the same woman I had encountered in the refec-room on the third floor earlier, surrounded by bodies. The one who had called Revnik a monster.

Based on what I had seen so far that day, it didn't feel like I could argue the point.

I hadn't considered it at the time, but when I thought back to the murdered bodies I had seen in the refec-room, it occurred to me that one of them had suffered much worse mutilations than the others. Like the bodies of Zorn and Hadenzach at the previous crime scenes, one of the victims had been attacked with special ferocity, suggesting the man in question had been Revnik's real target. With the body itself burned to ash on the third floor, along with the dead man's ID, I had gone looking for the auxilia in the hope she might identify the victim.

Turned out she was able to do a whole lot more.

'You were telling me you knew Revnik?' I said as she continued to work on my wounds.

'Yes. His wife was a patient here, about a year ago.'

'What was wrong with her?'

'Progressive heart failure. She had an inherited disease that disrupted her sanguinary system, creating toxins in her blood. Over time, it had damaged her heart.'

'Who treated her?'

'Chief Medicae Berisov. He gave her a transplant.'

'This Berisov, was he one of the men Revnik killed in the refec-room?'

'Yes.'

'Was he the one Revnik chopped up the worst?'

Her mouth tightened. A bad memory. 'Yes.'

'Why did Revnik hate him?'

She paused for a moment, as though wondering how much she should say, before releasing a frustrated sigh.

'Everyone knew the woman was dying. Everyone but her husband. He came in promising he'd pay anything to the person who could save her. He didn't care about the cost.'

'And Berisov took him up on the offer?'

'He offered to perform the transplant. Replace her damaged heart with a vat-grown one. But it was never going to work. Not when we couldn't cure the underlying disease. Replacing the heart made no difference. Not in the long term. Eventually, the toxins would have destroyed the new one just like the original. Everyone on staff knew the operation would fail. But he did the operation anyway.'

'Why?'

'The slate. You have to understand, Dimitry Berisov was a great medicae. He did extraordinary work as a chirurgeon. Saved a lot of lives. But as a man... he was greedy. He knew Revnik was desperate. Knew he could gouge him for a small fortune.'

'I didn't know Revnik was that wealthy.'

'He must have had some kind of money. It was the only

way Berisov would have done the operation. Revnik said he'd do anything, spend anything, to keep Sharna alive. He'd go broke, sell his hab-unit, anything. Even go back to fighting in the pits if he had to.'

'That was his wife's name? Sharna?'

She nodded.

'What happened to her?'

'The transplant was successful at first. But she was weak from all the toxins. She died two days later.'

I glanced at the burning infirmary. I didn't know whether Revnik had come intending to set fire to the place or had only done it to escape. Whatever the case, it didn't really matter. The consequences were the same either way.

'I'm guessing Revnik didn't take it well?'

She shook her head. 'I don't think I've ever seen anyone so angry. When we told him his wife had died, I thought he was going to kill Berisov right there and then. He only stopped at the last moment. Told Berisov he was lucky. Revnik said his wife had never liked him hurting people. He'd honour her memory by sticking to the vow he had made her – a vow that he wouldn't hurt people any more. After that, he left. I didn't see him again. Not until today.'

She fixed a dressing in place over the last wound. Her ministrations completed, Auxilia Glinka removed her plastek gloves and cleaned her hands with an alco-wipe, before fishing a cotin inhaler from her surcoat pocket.

'There. You are done. You'll need to change the dressings every day, making sure you keep the wounds clean. Only plain aqua, though. No harsh ablutives. They dry out the skin. You should come back to the infirmary in three days to get the wounds checked and–'

She stopped herself. Another sigh. Her eyes moved to her former place of work, now wreathed in smoke and flame.

'Well, maybe not *this* infirmary. I'm guessing you have medicae services available in your Bastion?'

'We do. Thanks for the help.'

She walked away, puffing on the inhaler as I dressed myself once more in my uniform. The tunic was a mess, its surface singed and blackened beyond my ability to clean it, with holes burned through the outer materials in places that exposed the pressed plates of the flak armour inside it. Given the damage, I doubted the armour still functioned as intended. Made brittle by the heat, it would probably give way at the first good shot or blow, offering little protection.

It would have to do. I wasn't about to return to the Bastion for a replacement. Not when I had made my first real breakthrough.

It was only one part of the puzzle, but the auxilia's story had confirmed the reason for Revnik's attack on the infirmary. He had been after Berisov – the man he blamed for his wife's death. But other questions remained. Why had Revnik waited a year before killing him? And how did it relate to the murders of Zorn and Hadenzach?

I knew what a probator would do to try and solve the mystery. Interrogate the people who had known the dead man. Friends, family, business partners – anyone who could speak to the nature of any connection the victims had with Revnik and each other. The connection was vital. It could explain Revnik's actions. More important, it could also reveal where he intended to strike next.

It didn't feel like Revnik's killing spree was over. Unless he was stopped, there would be more innocents left slaughtered in his wake. Already, the fire at the infirmary showed just how far he was willing to go.

As a sanctioner, it was my job to bring in killers. But this was about more than duty. It was personal. It had been ever since I learnt Revnik was involved.

I was about to get back in the Rampart when I heard the buzz of an incoming call over the vox. I answered it.

'Malenko?' It was Sobol. *'Sorry it's taken me so long to get back to you. There's so much going on in the district the vox-system is becoming overwhelmed. Command has rationed all Bastion calls to priority comms only.'*

'I understand. What have you got for me?'

'Not much. I ran the first two names you gave me, looking for connections to Revnik. But I couldn't find anything.'

'What about the victims themselves? Anything interesting there?'

'Plenty. You were right about Hadenzach having a long record. I found surveillance files and person-of-interest reports going back more than twenty years, all indicating his suspected activities as a bookmaker. No arrests, however.'

'That's not hard to explain. He must have known the right people to bribe.'

'Right. The situation is similar with Zorn. Lots of surveils and reports indicating criminal activity. But no action was taken.'

'Wait. Are you telling me Zorn was also a criminal?'

'Suspected criminal. No arrests.'

This was new. Up until that point, there had been no reason to believe that Zorn was anything other than an honest citizen.

'What crimes was he suspected of committing?'

'Unclear. Some of his record has been purged. Though whether that was for legitimate reasons or because he greased the right palms, I couldn't say. Most of what remains is small stuff. Failure to complete fiscal documents. Failure to update fiduciary records. That kind of thing. There is repeated evidence, however, of the firm of Zorn and Jorgev having widespread criminal connections – including with your bookmaker, Hadenzach.'

'I see. Wait a minute... Did you just say Zorn and Jorgev?'

'That was the name of the firm. Zorn and Jorgev, Fiscal Tabulators.'

'Not when I went there. The name on the door was Erek Zorn. There was no mention of any Jorgev.'

I thought back to the blood-splattered brass plaque I had seen on the door at the office plexus. Beneath the blood, it had been shiny and brand new. Then there was the sub-office next to Zorn's. It had been empty, except for packing crates filled with furniture and personal effects, as though someone was moving out.

'That may be. But all the financial reporting says the firm's name is Zorn and Jorgev. The fiscal regs follow a thirteen-week reporting cycle, though. If they dissolved the partnership in the interim period, it wouldn't show up in the record yet.'

'Right. So there's a former business partner of Zorn's still out there? Is there a home address for this Jorgev in the records?'

There was a pause for several seconds while Sobol checked.

'Here it is. Daniul Jorgev. Hab-unit forty-three-beta, Macharietski Hab-Complex, off Arkadin Prospekt.'

'Run me through everything else you know about him,' I said, hurrying to the Rampart. 'I'll listen while I'm driving.'

'Where are you going?'

'Where do you think? To have a friendly talk with the surviving partner of Zorn and Jorgev.'

Turn of Fate

'Open up in the name of the Emperor!'

I banged on the entryway with my shock maul, the reinforced synthwood of the door vibrating in its frame with every blow. Around me, the denizens of the hab-complex hurried through the hallway to the safety of their own units, just in case a sanctioner at a neighbour's door was a prelude to gunfire.

'Open up, Jorgev! If I have to break this damned thing down, it will be worse for you.'

I was getting ready to make good on the threat when I heard the clicking of a series of locks on the other side. The door crept open, revealing the face of a frightened middle-aged man in the gap.

'Yes?' He blinked at me like a sewer rat caught in the beam of a luminator.

The restraint chain was on the door, limiting the degree to which it opened. I glowered down at him.

'Are you Daniul Jorgev, of Zorn and Jorgev?'

'I... Yes. I mean, we dissolved the partnership... What seems to be the problem, sanctioner?'

I kicked the door, hard, breaking the chain.

The impact forced the door into his face, sending him tumbling backwards. I crossed the threshold and hit him with the maul while he was on the floor. It was the lightest of touches, shock only. A love-zap, to keep him from mischief. I grabbed Jorgev by the tunic and turned him onto his front, pushing my knee into the small of his back as I put the manacles on him.

A fast pat-down revealed he was armed – a snub-nosed, small-calibre rotary stub gun, tucked into his waistband. I took the weapon, sliding it into my belt for later.

After closing the front door, I checked the rest of the hab-unit, clearing each room in turn.

There was no one else there. From the looks of it, Jorgev lived alone. His hab was cheaply furnished, the interior austere and much more monastic than I would have expected from a tabulator. I found a small bottle of narcos in a night-stand, along with some prophylactics. That, along with a list of joy house addresses, nightdance pamphlets and a closet full of clothing twenty years too young for him, suggested where his money went. Seemed Jorgev liked to jubilate in search of his lost youth.

Satisfied, I picked up a chair from the refec-chamber and took it to where I had left its owner. Once there, I dragged Jorgev into the chair and set him upright.

He was unconscious, but I carried a small vial of ammoniac salts for that very reason. It was an old sanctioner's trick, taught to me by Sladek. I took the cap from the vial and waved it underneath Jorgev's nostrils.

Even through the helmet, the ammoniac smell irritated my nose. The effect on Jorgev was almost instantaneous. With a cough and a splutter, he jolted awake.

He shook his head to clear it as I replaced the cap and put the vial back in one of the pouches on my belt.

'I... What happened?' He gave me an accusing stare. 'You hit me!'

'The door hit you, Jorgev. You just didn't get out of the way fast enough. You know why I'm here?'

'I... No... I have no idea.'

I tutted. 'Bad answer. An innocent man would say it must be because of what happened to poor Tabulator Zorn earlier. You must have heard about it by now. Otherwise, you wouldn't have had the gun.'

'I keep that for protection.'

'I'm sure you do. Particularly from angry ex-pit fighters, I suspect. Is that why you were so slow to answer a sanctioner at your door? You wanted to be sure I was really an enforcer. Not a madman with a chainsword for a hand.'

'I don't know what you're talking about.'

'That's what they all say. I'm guessing you'll tell the justicius that you didn't know about the narcos I found in your night-stand. The good news is that I only counted four pills left in the bottle. Not enough for an intent-to-distribute charge. But still worth four years' penal servitude for possession of an illicit narcotic. Of course, the sentence gets doubled if you don't have a licence for that stub gun – which I'm sure you don't.

Then it becomes going armed in the commission of an infraction. Still, if you beg the justicius, maybe they'll go easy on you. Cut thirty days from your sentence on account of your previous good record.'

'But the pills aren't mine! I'm just holding them for someone!'

'You're a bad liar, Jorgev. But today is your lucky day. I'm less concerned by your violations of the Lex than I am interested in information.'

I removed my helmet and placed it on a small table nearby.

'I want to know about Zorn's dealings with Orvo Revnik. As well as his connection to a bookmaker named Argus "the Eyes" Hadenzach.'

Jorgev's left eye gave a little twitch.

'I can see you know that name. It's a shame we're not playing cards. I suspect I'd win every hand.'

'You're mistaken. About the name, I mean. I don't know anything about Erek's business.'

'Uh-huh. Sounds like we're going to have to do this the hard way.'

I took the snub-nose from my belt and made a show of opening the rotary cylinder. One by one, I removed the bullets from the gun until I held them cupped in my hand.

'Understand me, Jorgev. I don't care about whatever illegal or illicit business you and your partner were about. I'm only interested in knowing why Orvo Revnik killed Zorn this morning.'

'You said it yourself. He's a madman!'

'Possibly. But we both know there's more to it.'

I placed the bullets on the same table as my helmet, spinning the cylinder of the gun repeatedly back and forth.

'The very fact you had this gun close at hand tells me you know something about what's going on. Innocent men don't cower behind the door with a loaded firearm when a sanctioner comes knocking. That's a sure sign of a guilty conscience.'

Still spinning the cylinder, I moved back to Jorgev's chair. Then I snapped the cylinder in place inside the gun frame as I stood over him.

'I told you!' he protested. 'There's been some kind of mistake!'

'Well, then your imminent death will be a senseless tragedy. I'll remember to send votives to your funeral.'

I pressed the gun to Jorgev's forehead and pulled the trigger. Despite knowing the weapon was empty, he jumped.

'Ah, what am I doing here?' I made a chiding noise. 'I'm playing the game all wrong.'

I returned to the bullets. My hand drifting through the pile as though choosing one, I brought it to rest before lifting a single round, holding it between my thumb and forefinger to give Jorgev a clear view.

'You're familiar with the game, I assume? People call it Emperor's Mercy or Turn of Fate.'

'Please, this is a mistake. It's all a mistake. I don't know anything!'

'You take a rotary gun, just like this one.' I held the gun up, performing a series of actions in turn. 'You open the cylinder. Make sure it's empty. Then you load a single bullet... like so.'

Again, I made a show of it, loading the bullet before slamming the weapon shut.

'You spin the cylinder,' I said, doing so. 'I suppose that's why they call it Turn of Fate. Assuming a six-shot weapon, like this one, you end up with one bullet and five empty chambers.'

'Please! I was only ever the junior partner! Erek kept me in the dark about everything!'

'Still lying, I see. Normally, I'd hit you with the maul until you started telling the truth. But it has been a long and frustrating day. Beating a confession out of a man is hard work. I thought we'd play this game instead. Although, of course, I won't be the one actually playing it.'

I put the gun to his head and pulled the trigger. It clicked on an empty cylinder. Jorgev shrieked and jumped again, the movement unbalancing the chair and sending him crashing to the floor.

'Please! Please! I was only the junior partner!'

'One shot down.' I pulled Jorgev upright and placed him on the chair once more. 'Five more to go. As a tabulator, you're good with numbers. Next time I pull the trigger, what are the odds it comes down on the bullet? Is it still one in six? Or do the odds change with each trigger pull? I know, why don't we find out?'

There was an unpleasant odour in the room. Glancing down, I realised Jorgev had sullied himself. I pointed the gun at his head, my finger tightening on the trigger.

'Erek was stealing from him,' Jorgev said, the sound a plaintive sob. 'Please, I'll tell you anything you want to know!'

'Anything?' I lifted the gun away as though considering the matter. 'All right. But understand this – if I think you're lying or trying to hold back, we'll start the game again. No one back at the Bastion will shed any tears if I kill a crooked tabulator. Understood?'

'I understand. I promise, I'll tell you everything.'

He was almost crying, relieved the gun had been taken away.

In reality, the weapon was empty. I had palmed the bullet before snapping the cylinder shut. It was another trick Sladek had taught me. One of many things I had learnt after becoming a sanctioner.

'Start with Revnik's connection to Zorn,' I told him. 'We'll see where we go from there.'

Confessions

Once Jorgev opened up, there was no stopping him. The words came in a flood, the man barely pausing for breath in his confessions. It was something I had seen before. Sometimes, once a prisoner decided to give up their secrets, it was like a dam had broken. The secrets came out as a torrent, not a trickle. If I had wanted, I could have made Jorgev confess to every misdeed he had committed since learning to walk.

My focus was narrower. I asked questions in an attempt to keep him on track.

'You say it was Hadenzach who introduced Revnik to Zorn?'

'That's right. Erek had known the bookmaker for years. He was his laundryman.'

'His what?'

'He washed his slate for him. So the enforcers wouldn't know where it came from. That was Erek's real business. He cleaned money for a dozen different illegal operations. Nothing brings the enforcers to your door faster than dirty money. Some of them want to bust you for it. Others come wanting bribes.'

'So Revnik was involved in illegal business?'

'No.' Jorgev shook his head. 'He was the only honest client on our books. He made a lot of money from side bets in the fighting pits.'

'Really?' I raised an eyebrow. 'I'm surprised that he made that much. It's not like you can throw a fight in the pits. Most often, the losing fighter dies.'

'You don't need to throw it. All the fighter needs do is make bets on things he can control. Say there's two fighters. One is stronger than the other and knows he's going to win. He makes a bet that he's going to defeat the other fighter in the sixth minute. Then he makes sure it happens. Even if it means going easy on his opponent for a while, playing to the crowd to make it look like more of a contest.'

'And Revnik did this?'

'It helped that he was such a good fighter. Nobody could touch him in the arena. Course, it wasn't always about when the fight would end. You can make side bets on anything. Who'll strike the first blow. Whether both fighters will get wounded. How many limbs will the defeated fighter end up losing. Anything.'

'Revnik couldn't have made those bets himself. No book-maker would take them.'

'That's where Hadenzach came in. He handled the betting side. He used shills to place the action with other bookmak-ers so the odds wouldn't come down too low. Although he'd always lie about that to Revnik, telling him the payouts were lower than they really were.'

'He was cheating him?'

Jorgev nodded. 'They were supposed to split the pot from each bet sixty-forty, with the larger share going to Revnik. In reality, the split was more like eighty-twenty in Hadenzach's favour. But Revnik was making so much slate from side bets, he didn't realise what was going on.'

'What about the fighters' masters? Did they know what was happening?'

'Revnik's master, Adrik Kuznetski, didn't know anything. Not at first. Not until Revnik's woman got involved and ruined everything.'

'You're talking about his wife? Sharna?'

'She wasn't his wife yet. But yeah. She told Revnik she didn't like him killing people. Persuaded him to get out of the pits.'

'What was wrong with that?'

'You mean besides all the money he was making for Haden-zach? Money that me and Erek were getting paid to clean, by the way. The real problem, though, was the way Revnik did it. He went right up to Kuznetski one day and told him he wanted to buy himself out of his contract.'

I could imagine how that was greeted. I played dumb, though, to encourage Jorgev to continue with his story.

'I don't see the problem.'

'How is a pit fighter supposed to have that kind of slate? Of course, Revnik wouldn't tell Kuznetski where he got it. But that didn't stop Kuznetski from digging.'

He sighed, exasperated.

'When I think of all the different ways Revnik could have handled it. Hadenzach offered to use one of his shills. Make it look like the man was a wealthy aristocrat eager to get in on the fight game. If one of the gilded had showed up at Kuznetski's hab with a bag full of slate, offering to buy out the contract, no questions asked, Kuznetski might have gone for it. But Revnik insisted on going to Kuznetski in person. Sharna didn't like him being dishonest, he said. You ask me, he was thinking with his–'

'Keep to the point, Jorgev. I haven't got all day.'

'Right. At first, Kuznetski turned him down. Said he didn't care how much Revnik offered – Kuznetski wouldn't sell his contract. But then Revnik told him he wouldn't fight any more. He didn't care if Kuznetski had him killed. He wouldn't hurt anybody in the arena ever again.'

'I'm guessing that went down well.'

'Kuznetski went crazed. Threatened to have Revnik tortured to death. But the big lug wouldn't budge. And that left Kuznetski with a problem. He didn't want to sell the contract. But if Revnik refused to fight, the contract was worth nothing.'

'What's this got to do with Hadenzach and Zorn?' I was starting to lose patience.

'I'm getting to it. Eventually, Kuznetski offered him a deal. He'd sell the contract, but only if Revnik agreed to one more fight. Revnik didn't like it – probably afraid about what his girl would say. But he realised Kuznetski was trying to save face. At least, that's what everybody thought. Revnik took the deal.'

'And this last fight was King of the Mountain?'

'Yeah. A final act of spite. After the deal was agreed and Revnik handed over the money, Kuznetski let him know that the last fight was going to be the biggest slaughterfest of all time. King of the Mountain. Twenty men went in, only one walked out. And just to really rub it in, Kuznetski said whoever won the fight would have their freedom. This after Revnik had already paid for his own freedom.'

My own days as a pit fighter had long ended before any of this happened, but I wasn't surprised to hear of it. As I remembered him, Kuznetski had been a real piece of work. It went without saying he was a bastard – all the masters were. Based on Jorgev's story, it sounded like he was petty alongside all his other failings.

'Why'd he do it?'

'Kuznetski? Spite, like I said. Plus, it let him save face with the other masters. He didn't want them to know he'd allowed a fighter to buy himself out of his contract. If rumours got around about a thing like that, it might have started giving people ideas. But in the meantime, Kuznetski found out that Revnik was in business with Hadenzach. It didn't take long for him to put two and two together.'

'What happened?'

'Kuznetski went to Hadenzach and threatened him. Said he'd tell the other masters what Hadenzach had been doing, unless he cut him in for a piece of the action. What else could Hadenzach do? They negotiated for a while, but eventually he agreed to give Kuznetski fifty per cent of any bets Revnik made on King of the Mountain.'

'But he couldn't have known Revnik would win?'

'He didn't have to know.' Jorgev tried to shrug, only to find the manacles constrained his movement. 'He'd already made a bundle when Revnik bought out his contract. Anything else was extra. As it happened, though, Revnik did win. But he never knew most of his winnings from the side bets went into Hadenzach's and Kuznetski's pockets. Hadenzach lied to him about the odds and the payout, just like always.'

'And Zorn? What was his part in all this?'

Jorgev shifted in his chair, a little uneasy.

'That could be where we got a little greedy. Even if he didn't realise how small his own cut really was, Revnik retired from the pits with plenty of slate. Erek got Hadenzach to introduce them, so he could offer to help Revnik look after his money. Invest it for him.'

'Let me guess. He started stealing Revnik's money.'

'Not at first. In the early days, all he did was manage it – just like they'd agreed. But, over time, Erek made some bad investments for the clients whose money we were washing. People like that, you don't tell them you've lost their funds. Not unless you want to end up in a corpse shroud. Erek said all we had to do was take some of the slate from Revnik's accounts. The first time we did it, the plan was to pay it back almost immediately. But we kept losing money on investments. Over time, we robbed Revnik blind. Erek said he'd never catch on. Said the guy was as dumb as a lobotomised grox. But I guess he wasn't so dumb after all.'

'Maybe it wasn't a good idea to be cheating someone whose nickname was "the Ripper".'

'Figure you're right.' He sighed. 'Things began to go bad a few months back. It was Revnik's wife being sick that started it. All those medical treatments cost a lot of slate. By then, Erek had all but cleaned out Revnik's accounts. We made up some of the shortfall, moving money around and making excuses whenever things got tight. We managed to cover the medical bills, and the funeral. But then, a couple of months ago, Revnik got sentimental. He decided he wanted his wife's body moved to a nice sepulchre upclave. You know how expensive that can be? Erek tried to put him off, claiming he didn't have enough money. In the meantime, I had decided I wanted out. Erek said everything was fine, but I could see it was only a matter of time before the business collapsed. Or worse, some of the people we had stolen from realised what we had been doing. I thought Erek would fight me when I told him I wanted to dissolve our partnership. But he didn't. Probably figured, when it came to dividing the operation, he'd cheat me like he had been cheating everybody else.'

'When did Revnik find out you'd been stealing from him?'

'Today, I'm guessing. I got a panicked call from Erek yesterday. He said Revnik had started asking questions about where his money was going. Turned out Revnik understood the figures better than either of us had ever realised. He knew how much slate was supposed to be in his accounts. And when Erek told him he had less than that, he knew something was wrong. The meeting today was supposed to sort it all out. Erek wanted me to go to it, even though we were no longer partners. To give him moral support, he said.'

'But you didn't go?'

'All the time Revnik was a client, I hardly had any dealings with him. Erek wanted it that way. He'd always handled Revnik's account personally. I knew why. So he could steal a little bit extra without having to split it with me. Erek was like that. He stole from everybody. Like it was a compulsion. Anyway, I knew Erek's game. The only reason he wanted me involved at this late stage was so he'd have a scapegoat ready. He would have blamed it all on me. Told Revnik I was the one who stole his money. So I just didn't show. Way things turned out, guess I was lucky.'

'Lucky? You helped your partner steal from Revnik, then left him to face it alone when things got hot.'

Despite his confession, and the fact he had sullied himself

earlier, Jorgev tried to make a display of outraged dignity. He drew himself up to his full height in the chair, his face a picture of offended innocence.

'Yeah, well, if you put things that way, you can make anything sound bad.'

Upclave

'Bastion, this is five-nine-omega-nine. Heading out of Dredge, en route to home of Adrik Kuznetski, Karnak Luxury-Hab Enclave, off Elysian Prospekt.'

'Omega-nine, this is Bastion. That is not within your assigned patrol route.'

'I know that, Bastion. This is a hot pursuit. Acting on information from an informant, I have reason to believe fugitive offender Orvo Revnik is on way to named location. Request backup.'

'Backup? To an upclave lux-hab? You know what kind of dreck storm it will cause if you're wrong about this one?'

'Not as bad as it will be if Revnik goes on a rampage in a nice upclave neighbourhood and you could have prevented it. Your choice, Bastion. You'll be the one explaining it to the castellan.'

'All right, omega-nine. You've made your point. Backup notified, but the nearest unit is at least twenty-five minutes away.'

'Affirmed, Bastion. Tell them to step on it.'

I had left Jorgev manacled to a lumen-pole outside his hab-tower, awaiting pickup, while I sped upclave. He was facing a long list of charges, particularly once the lexators sorted through the records of Zorn and Jorgev. Not that it felt like much of a victory to have arrested a crooked tabulator. Jorgev might have helped start this whole mess, but I was on the trail of bigger game.

Kuznetski would be Revnik's next target. I was sure of it. As best as I could figure, Zorn must have laid everything out for Revnik earlier that morning. Probably tried to bargain for his life once Orvo got angry and the chainsword's blade started whirring.

It hadn't saved Zorn, but whatever secrets he had spilled had sent Revnik after Hadenzach. The medicae, Berisov, was a side project. By that point, Revnik had already killed nine victims. Any vow he had made to his wife about not hurting people was out of the window. It stood to reason he would take the opportunity to kill a man he had wanted to murder a year earlier. Revnik always had a taste for vengeance.

I headed upclave with my Rampart's clarion screaming. Other groundcars got out of the way, even as the traffic thinned.

The further you went upclave, the less traffic you saw. Cramped roadways gave way to wide-open highlines. Dirty, dented automotives were replaced with gleaming luxury machines – the kind the folks downclave only ever saw on the vid-projector or in their dreams.

I was lucky that Kuznetski lived at one of the less prestigious addresses of his district. If you went too far upclave, you had to deal with checkpoints and guard posts, manned by either sanctioners or private securitors – depending on the location. Fortifications, designed to guard the borderlands between rich and poor, keeping the people in the gilded districts safe from the rest of us.

The checkpoints were more than just a hassle. They were time-consuming, and that could mean the difference between life and death. I had to figure Revnik had a big lead on me.

For all I knew, he was already bearing down on Kuznetski. Driven by the weight of years of glowering resentment against the man who had once owned his contract of indenture, making him a slave in all but name.

In some ways, it was a surprise Revnik hadn't tried to kill Kuznetski before. Sharna's influence, I supposed. Whatever Zorn had told him about his former master, it hadn't been the source of Revnik's hatred – only the spark that started the fire. The kindling for Revnik's rage-fuelled murder spree had been laid much earlier, over years of hardship and maltreatment.

I understood the impulse. If Revnik had been on his way to kill my own former master, Syrus Volantich, I wasn't sure I could have found it within myself to stop him. For that matter, it was hard to work up too much in the way of eagerness to save Kuznetski.

I was forced to remind myself of the scenes of slaughter I had witnessed at each of Revnik's murder sites. Zorn might have been a scumbag. Hadenzach definitely was one. Even Berisov might have deserved it. But there had been people killed who had no involvement with any of it. Innocent bystanders, if innocence of any kind existed in the city. Zorn's scribe. The smile-girls at Kerensky's. The medicae, securitors and patients killed at the Divine Hand of Mercy.

Revnik was responsible for the deaths of people who had nothing to do with his vengeance. He didn't get a pass for that. Never mind the fact that, as a sanctioner, it was my job to stop him.

As I pulled onto the egress ramp leading to Kuznetski's hab, I could see Revnik had beaten me to it. The gates to the hab's outer wall hung open, left twisted and damaged by a tremendous impact.

The cause could be seen crashed into an ornate marble fountain further inside the hab's gardens. It was a Raxis cargo hauler, a common ground-freight vehicle used throughout the city. Revnik had put it to use as a battering ram, barrelling through the gates into Kuznetski's sanctum.

There were bodies in its wake – securitors who couldn't get

out of the way in time and had ended up pulped. There were more bodies on the gravelled walkway leading to the hab. I counted five in total. More entries in Revnik's kill book. More people who would never make it home to their families.

I parked the Rampart and drew my weapon, making sure the safety was off.

'Bastion, this is five-nine-omega-nine. Violent disturbance confirmed underway at Kuznetski hab. Multiple victims down. Request that backup ASAP.'

'Affirmed, omega-nine. We're working on it. But right now, you're on your own.'

The front entrance into the hab was open, blood staining the delicate fretwork of the ornamental lion inlaid into the substance of the door as though standing guard for its owner.

I stepped into the hallway atrium to find three more bodies. They looked like servants rather than securitors. Revnik had been busy. And indiscriminate.

The roar of a chainsword grinding against some hard object reverberated through the open confines of the hall. The inner precincts of the hab were so wide and spacious it was difficult to identify the sound's point of origin. It rebounded around the atrium, bouncing off decorative statuary, the echo seeming to come from everywhere and nowhere at once.

Unable to pinpoint a location, I had no choice other than to work room by room until I found Revnik by process of elimination.

The noise stopped without warning, replaced by deathly silence. Given the hush, and Kuznetski's apparent love of statues, I might have been in a votive garden or place of remembrance.

I called out, scanning around me for signs of movement. 'Orvo! It's Malenko! Surrender now! In the name of the Emperor!'

No answer.

Despite its broad, airy expanse, the atrium was filled with

hiding spaces. The hallway was lined with alcoves on either side. There were statues in them, each one a study of pit fighters in various poses, represented as though they were the gladiators of ancient Terra, moulded slightly larger than life-sized to make them more impressive.

There were statues of gladiators wearing half-armour and armed with swords. Others of men equipped with net and trident. Gladiators with large square shields and smaller round ones. Men fighting other men, and men fighting animals.

I advanced across the hallway, wary of ambush.

There was an elaborate staircase, rising up three storeys almost to the upper reaches of the atrium, with more statues set along the balustrade. These ones were shaped like wrestlers in different stances, arms outstretched to grasp the empty air.

As I passed within the shadow of one of the upper levels, I heard a sound from above.

Eyes snapping up, I saw Revnik emerge from hiding behind one of the wrestlers. I raised my gun, only for him to push the statue before I could fire.

It became clear what Revnik's chainsword had been working on. Cut loose from its moorings, arms cast wide as though to enfold me in its embrace, the statue hurtled downward.

I leapt for safety. The falling wrestler missed by a hair's breadth, exploding into flying pieces as it smashed against the floor. A solid chunk of marble smacked me in the face, the force of the blow shattering the front plate of my helmet and breaking my nose. No longer able to see through the shattered eyepieces, I pulled the helmet away even as a shadow fell across me.

I looked up to see Revnik had followed the statue down. He landed on top of me, foot descending in a powerful kick before I could bring my gun to bear. It hit the ground, the weapon knocked from my hand by the impact and sent skittering across the smooth tiled floor.

Revnik had a shock baton in his good hand, presumably taken from one of the dead securitors. Before I could draw my own maul, he hit me with the shock in the side of my exposed head.

For an instant, the world lit up with coruscating blue fire. Then, nothing.

Everything faded to black.

King of the Mountain

I awoke to throbbing pain and the taste of blood. The world was a blurred patchwork of colours and shapes, none of which made any sense.

'There. I knew you wouldn't be out long. It takes more than a buzz from a shock baton to put down Kirian the Killer.'

As I homed in on the voice, my eyes started to focus. Revnik stood next to a writing table, a makeshift gauze dressing on the shoulder where I had shot him earlier.

The writing table was a showy, grandiose thing carved from a single oversized piece of black volcanic stone. Nearby, a man sat dead in a chair behind the table, ribs peeking through the gouges cut into his clothes and flesh. I recognised him as Adrik Kuznetski, Revnik's former master.

'I always hated that name,' I said, trying to get my bearings. 'I see you've been busy.'

'Him?' Revnik glanced at the body. 'Not really. You'd think a man who owns pit fighters might have picked up a thing or two. But no, he spent the last seconds of his life begging rather than defending himself.'

'What about Zorn? And Hadenzach? And the medicae, Berisov? Did you make them beg as well?'

'I didn't make them do anything,' the big man said. 'Oh, they begged. And pleaded. Hadenzach even prayed a little.

As though the Emperor has any time for bookmakers and leg-breakers. Lot of good it did them. Anyway, they deserved it.'

'And the rest? The scribe you killed in Zorn's office? The smile-girls at the bathhouse? All those people dead at the infirmary? The securitors and servants here? Did they deserve it?'

'No, you have me there. They probably didn't. I killed a lot of people today. Many, many more than I intended. That's the problem when you have a chainsword in place of an arm. It makes the killing too easy. After a while, you do it without thinking.'

We were in the dead man's study. That much became apparent as my head started to clear. I was lying in the middle of the room – dragged there by Revnik, I assumed.

Kuznetski wasn't the only one dead. There were four more bodies scattered about the room, their blood coating the polished wooden floorboards. Servants, based on their uniforms, who had tried sheltering with their master in the hope that he might save them. It hadn't worked.

My gun was nearby, lying on the floor halfway between me and Revnik. I gauged the distance, calculating whether I could get to the weapon before Revnik got to me.

'Don't try it, Lenko,' Revnik said, reading the direction of my gaze. 'Not yet, anyway. Give yourself a little time to recover from that crack you got in the face. I wouldn't want to have an unfair advantage.'

There was an open bottle of slatov on the writing table next to him. An expensive brand, the kind that came in a hexagonal crystalline bottle with a fancy gold label. Revnik turned and poured a measure into a shot glass.

'We can fight later. For now, I thought we could talk.'

'Talk? About what?'

'Old times, maybe? Like how it is an old friend ended up as a sanctioner?'

'It's a long story.'

'Probably not enough time then. I'm sure you've got backup on the way. Guess we'll have to think of something else.'

He lifted the shot glass and emptied it in one gulp.

'Throne, but that's good slatov. Feels like it's trying to burn its way through your throat while you're drinking it. I'll say this for Kuznetski. He may have been a miserable piece of dreck and an affliction to the world, but he had some good booze.'

He poured another measure.

'Sorry if I'm being selfish, not sharing some. But we both know you'd only take advantage of any kindly gesture on my part. You'd break the bottle over my head, or throw slatov in my face, or some other clever manoeuvre. You always were a tricky one. It's what kept you alive all those years in the pits.'

He raised the glass in a toast.

'To the pits, and all the people we killed there, just to stay alive.'

He drank the slatov, before slamming the glass down hard on the table.

'I remember in the old days you drank your slatov straight from the bottle,' I said.

'That's right. I did. But Sharna cured me of my bad habits.'

'Not all of them.'

'No, not all.' He sighed. 'Maybe if she was still alive, none of this would have happened. I didn't intend to kill Zorn when I went to see him this morning.'

'Why not? He was cheating you.'

Revnik gave a sharp look of surprise. 'You know about that? Guess maybe you're a better enforcer than I ever would have thought.'

He poured another glass.

'Yes, he was cheating me. And I knew it. I went there figuring we'd have it out. I thought I'd shake him a little, get him to pay it back, even if it was only in instalments. But when Zorn got frightened, he started babbling. He told me about Hadenzach and Kuznetski, about how they had cheated me as well. He tried to blame it all on them. That was a mistake.'

'You didn't know about that part of it until then?'

'No. When I realised they had all been playing me for a fool, I got angry. I thought about Sharna, about how she died. With the amount of slate they had stolen from me, maybe I could have saved her. Found better medicae. Gone to the cogmen. Anything. Instead, those three had been laughing at me while poor Sharna suffered. I saw red, like I did sometimes back in the pits.'

'So you killed Zorn and the scribe?'

'The woman was a mistake, of sorts. After she saw what I did to Zorn, she wouldn't stop screaming. I was trying to quiet her and, well… things got out of hand.'

'And afterwards, you decided to go after Hadenzach and Kuznetski? Not to mention the medicae, Berisov.'

He nodded. 'It was too late to go back by then. Once I killed Zorn and the scribe, I knew the enforcers would be coming for me. It don't matter whether you kill two people, or five, or twenty. The punishment is the same. I decided before I was arrested I'd settle up with every bastard I ever knew who was due a reckoning.'

He drained the glass, tossing his head back to swallow it.

'Course, I didn't expect to see my old friend Kirian Malenko. Not as a sanctioner. My jaw almost dropped when I saw you at the infirmary.'

'It didn't make you surrender. You kept running.'

'Yeah, well, I had to settle with Kuznetski. He was the last of them. I'm done now. Not that I'm planning on surrendering.'

He lifted the augmetic weapon in front of his face, staring at the chainsword as though seeing it for the first time.

'It's detachable, you know. The chainsword, I mean. I could have got rid of this thing years ago. Sharna asked me to, more than once. I could have had a whole new arm fitted. I've got the money.'

He corrected himself with a bitter smile.

'I *had* the money.'

A frown creased his scarred features.

'One time, I even went to a medicae who specialised in fitting new augmetics. He had a fancy consulting room. Not in the Dredge. Way upclave.'

He jabbed a thumb into his chest.

'Nothing cheap for this guy. For half a million in slate, he said he could fit one of the upscale models. It wouldn't look like the arm I lost, but it would feel almost the same. They put all these sensors in 'em, wired to your nerves, so when you touch something it feels like a real hand touching it. For an extra half mil, he said he'd throw in some decorative gemstones, a little scrollwork, maybe a chrome coating to make it gleam. "As befits a man of your standing." That was how he put it.'

Its teeth turning, the chainsword whirred into life. Revnik ran it along the edge of the writing table, trimming the uneven carving from the stone as delicately as a man might shave his face. Just as quickly, he switched it off once again.

'A man of my standing? I thought about it for a while. But in the end, I told him to forget it. I might not have been born with this chainsword, but it's as much a part of me as anything I was born with. All those years in the pits, it was with me. All those fights. All those victories. It gave me those. It even gave me my name. "The Ripper". Even after I retired, I was still somebody as long as I wore this weapon. When I was out on the street, people would recognise me. They'd ask me to sign things for them. Sharna didn't understand it, but I couldn't give that up. I didn't wear the chainsword around our home 'cause I knew she didn't like it. But I couldn't get rid of it like she wanted. It was a part of me in ways she couldn't understand.'

His face grew sad.

'It's funny. The day I walked out of my last fight as a free man, I felt like the world was wide open. I could do whatever I wanted. Anything was possible. But I was forgetting. I was born downclave. It don't matter how much slate you get. When you begin life downclave, this city will always drag you back there again. It will never let you win.'

He picked a small piece of grit from between the chainsword's teeth with his fingers before turning towards me.

'Anyway, that's enough talking. Time we got down to it.'

'Down to what?'

'The killing. You and me. This room, it's our arena. "Two will enter. One will leave." Just like in the pits.'

'I don't want to kill you, Orvo.'

'No? That's a shame. 'Cause I'll kill you. Don't think I won't.'

'We don't have to do this. You could give yourself up.'

'And what? You gonna tell me you can get them to go easy on me after I'm arrested? You never lied to me before, Lenko. Don't start today.'

He activated the chainsword again, revving the weapon into high gear, before pointing at the fallen stub gun in no man's land between us.

'I think of you as a friend, Lenko. That means I'm gonna give you a sporting chance. I figure it's fifty-fifty whether you can get to your gun before I can get to you. If not, you're gonna get ripped, like Zorn and all the others.'

Behind my back, out of sight, I hunted for a weapon. The shock maul was gone from its belt loop, presumably taken away by Revnik. But, opening one of my belt pouches, I found I still had the ammoniac vial I had used to revive Jorgev earlier. I crushed it in my gauntlet, hoping the roar of Revnik's chain-sword covered the noise of breaking glass.

'Last chance, old friend.' Revnik put on his fight face. It was an expression I had seen him wear a hundred times in the fighting pits, a mask of implacable and deadly purpose. I had no doubt he would kill me when it came down to it. 'I'll give you to the count of three. One...'

Before he could finish counting, I sprang to my feet and ran for the gun.

Revnik ran to meet me, the chainsword drawing backwards, ready to strike.

We would meet in the middle, leaving it a close-run thing whether I would reach the gun first or Revnik would get to me.

I had another idea. As we neared each other, I threw the remains of the vial at Revnik, ammoniac and broken glass hitting him in the face. At the same time, I dropped low, sliding along the polished, blood-slick floor.

Blinded, Revnik tripped over me, his chainsword swooping in a wild swing above my head. Sent sprawling, he went into a roll, somehow avoiding eviscerating himself with his own weapon. With none of his skill or reflexes lost from his days in the pits, he righted himself almost immediately. He turned, charging to close the distance once more.

I had already retrieved the stub gun. I fired a single shot.

It hit him in the centre of his chest. Momentum fading, Revnik dropped to his knees. The chainsword continued whirring for an instant, then stopped, falling silent.

He looked at me, eyes blinking, his face red and inflamed.

'What... what was it? The stuff you threw at me?'

'Ammoniac,' I explained. 'Smelling salts.'

'Hurt like hell. Though not as much as when you shot me. I knew you'd try something. You always were a tricky one, Lenko.'

'Take it as a compliment. You were always too good for me to beat in a fair fight.'

He smiled.

'Now you're just trying to make me feel better.'

He stared down at the wound in his chest.

'Throne, but that hurts. You shouldn't feel bad about this. Truth is, I was hoping you'd kill me... Didn't want to spend the rest of my life in a penal colony. It's better this way... Cleaner, too.'

He collapsed, falling on his side. His eyes starting to glaze over, he peered in my direction, trying to focus.

'Always knew it would come to this one day, ever since the pits. Congrats, Lenko. Looks like you are the only guy to ever beat "Ripper" Revnik in a fight.'

Eyes closing, he breathed his last.

'Guess that makes you King of the Mountain...'

Good Slatov, If I Can Find It

Backup arrived a few minutes later, their clarions wailing.

I sat on the floor of the study, my back propped against the overgrown monstrosity of Kuznetski's writing table, listening as they pulled into the grounds. I heard the crunch of tyres on gravel, then boots and shouted orders.

The bottle of slatov was in my hand. I took a deep draw, straight from the neck of the bottle, drinking a silent toast to an old friend.

Revnik was right. It was good slatov. The kind that burned just right. Perhaps it was because I was relieved to be alive, but it felt like the best slatov I had ever tasted. A fitting libation to celebrate the passing of a former champion.

The other advantage of drinking alcohol was that it helped clean some of the taste of blood from my mouth. Not that it could do anything for the blood caked on my face and uniform from the broken nose, the splatter from shooting someone at close range or the gore Revnik had left all about the room – both his own and other people's.

There and then, it didn't feel like any of it was my problem.

Footsteps hurried through the hallway, coming nearer. I heard the sound of distant retching. A sanctioner with a weak stomach, I assumed, unaccustomed to seeing at close range what a chainsword could do to a human body.

'His Holy Hand! Is that you, Malenko?'

I looked up at the sound of a familiar voice. Three fellow sanctioners stood framed in the doorway on the other side of the room, guns drawn. I couldn't see their faces through their helmets, but as their heads turned to take in the bodies and the blood, I sensed a disquiet, even unease.

Maybe it was because we were upclave. It was unusual to see blood spilled in such a rarefied setting. They were probably worried some aristocrat somewhere would complain to the lexmarshal about the failure of local sanctioners to keep the peace.

A citizen upclave was dead in his own home, along with his servants and securitors. It didn't matter that Kuznetski was a son of a bitch who, without doubt, deserved what had happened to him. He was a man of means. In Varangantua, that made him sacrosanct.

'Malenko? Are you injured?'

It was Vorozov. Doing her best to avoid the blood pools congealing on the floor, she crossed the room towards me.

'A broken nose.' I used my fingers to test my face, wincing as I touched my cheek. 'And maybe a few other things busted. Nothing too serious. Compared to everyone else here, I'd say I came out of it pretty well.'

'So I see.' She holstered her gun, then removed her helmet. 'What happened here?'

'Revnik wouldn't surrender. I had to kill him.'

'I can see that. What's with the bottle?'

'I knew Revnik a long time ago. In the fighting pits. We grew up together.'

'You were a pit fighter?' She raised an eyebrow.

'Kirian the Killer.' I hoisted the bottle in mock salute. 'As I say, a long time ago. I promised I would drink a toast to Revnik if I ever had to kill him. Today was that day. Hence, the bottle.'

I took another drink.

'You should probably get rid of that,' she said. 'News of killings this far upclave is bound to stir things up among the brass. Command staff are en route to the scene. There's even a rumour the castellan may join them.'

'Don't worry. It'll be gone by the time they get here.'

I inspected the bottle. Revnik had drunk a goodly amount before I even got to it. There were barely a few swallows left.

'Not that it will take much longer. You were right, Vorozov, in what you said earlier. Back at Kerensky Bathhouse.'

'What I said?'

'Killing becomes a habit. It gets into the blood. Yes, you were right. How did you put it?'

I looked over at Revnik, though I wasn't thinking about him as I repeated her words.

'Once a killer, always a killer.'

GRIT IN THE WHEELS

GARETH HANRAHAN

The laud hailer crackled, then boomed, cutting in midway through another rant from the self-proclaimed Prophet of Man.

'–isten not to the blandishments of the liars and heretics! The Emperor has turned His eyes from this sinful WORLD and forgotten us! We ARE unworthy of his love! We must make a grand gesture, a grand sacrifice!' The Prophet's words reverberated through the canyons between the towering hab-blocks.

'If these scrags are going to get themselves killed anyway,' muttered Sanctioner Erix, 'how 'bout we head home to the Bastion and let them at it?'

Laris scowled. 'Sergeant said clear this traffic before the Bulwarks get here.' She stomped off down the street, brandishing her combat shotgun at the tangle of carts and groundcars that blocked the intersection alongside Hab-block 12998, or as it had been renamed according to the graffiti on its walls, the Cathedral of the New Prophet.

Erix made a rude gesture at Laris' back. Who was she to tell him what to do? If she wanted to lick boot and do the Castellan's scut-work, fine, but why drag him along, too?

''Warks are coming?' rumbled Big Joach, the third member of their squad. It was supposed to be a five-strong unit, but the Bastion's budget was stretched thin. Either way, Joach probably out-massed three average-sized sanctioners combined. Saint's bones, the Imperial Guard recruiters missed a mark when they hadn't taken him. The standard-issue sanctioner shotgun was like a child's toy in his absurdly large hands.

'They're going to seal this whole area off,' muttered Erix. 'Panthera units are coming down too, to break some heads and discuss theology. They say the whole hab-block's run by the Prophet's crazy followers, and they're all armed, so, yeah – Bulwarks to close off the roads, and then...' He shook his head, unable to convey the depth of his scorn for the fools up in the hab. The city was not kind to those who struggled against it.

Joach grinned broadly, which reminded Erix of the time he'd seen a roadway collapse. A widening crack in the ferrocrete and lots of twisted rebar and sewage. ''Warks. I like 'warks.'

'And we,' continued Erix, 'will be safe on the far side of the barriers.'

'A BEACON! A FIRE TO LIGHT THE WAY TO HOLY TERRA! A FIRE TO BURN AWAY–'

Off in the distance, Erix saw a laud hailer explode in a shower of sparks as Laris snapped off a shot at it, but the Prophet's voice continued to echo from the dozens of others hanging from the sides of Hab-block 12998.

'*Sanctioners, I need your assistance. Now!*' she hissed over the squad vox, her voice fading in and out. Weak signal.

Joach moved forward, unhurriedly taking out a dispersion-gas grenade and rolling it into the crowd. Some poor street vendor was too slow to get out of the big man's way, and out came the shock maul. The intersection emptied.

Erix took his time strapping on his rebreather, blinking as
the leading edge of the dispersion cloud irritated his eyes. This
was all just Laris trying to impress the superiors to get a pro-
motion. She was low-born, scraped out of the Dredge – no
family connections, no way to advance except on merit. Erix,
though, came from... well, not wealth or nobility, far from it,
but enough money and standing that he could have got into
the Ecclesiarchy instead of the Sanctioners, if only he'd had the
patience for learning the litanies. Study and drudgery, though,
were not part of Erix's makeup.

But whatever else you could say about the life of a sanctioner, the job was rarely boring.

Laris' voice hissed in his ear. He couldn't make out the words
over the static, but he got the meaning. He shook his head.
He'd almost felt sorry for her there for a moment, but–

A patch of road in front of him exploded.

Another, at his feet, then a hammer to his ribs.

He moved, dodging for cover as the ground was chewed up
around him. 'Shooters!' he gasped into the vox. 'Up high!'
Glimpses of muzzle flashes, high on the flank of the hab-block
as autopistols cut traces through the thinning gas cloud.

They were caught in the open.

'Get to cover!' Erix sprinted towards the hab, trying to get
under the edge of the tower's jutting superstructure. He was
vaguely aware of Joach thundering after him, of Laris spraying suppressive fire at the sky.

He made for the darkness of the alleyway that ran alongside the hab-block. Once an access route for service vehicles, it
was now choked with refuse. Erix flung himself into the waste
pile and rolled until he was sure he was out of the immediate
line of fire.

Joach and Laris landed next to him. 'Are you hit?' Laris
asked.

'Armour took it.'

'Not shooting at us,' said Joach. 'Shooting at the Bulwarks. Look.' He pointed back down the street, which was now blocked off by a blast shield as it unfolded from the prow of one of the vehicles. The Bulwark riot-control tanks had sealed off the hab-block from the rest of the city. Small-arms fire ricocheted off the armoured barriers.

'We're on the wrong side!' said Erix.

Joach shook his head slowly. 'Cut off.'

'Bastion, Bastion,' said Laris into her vox. 'This is squad Gamma-Eight-Four, taking...'

But another transmission drowned her out. 'I SEE! I SEE! I SEE THE FALLEN ONES! THEY SURROUND OUR TEMPLE!'

'The Prophet's damn preaching! It's jamming our comms,' snarled Laris. 'We'll have to climb up the block until we get a clear signal.'

'JUDGEMENT IS UPON US! NOW IS THE TIME OF TESTING!'

'Why bother?' Erix stood and wiped the filth off his uniform. 'The 'warks are in place. No one's going anywhere for a while. We sit here until reinforcements show up, they clear out the block and we mop up the...' His voice trailed off as he noticed that the laud hailers weren't the only thing the Prophet's followers had wired to the outside of the tower.

On the wall above him was a package the size of Joach's fists, striped yellow and black and stamped with warning sigils. A wire ran from it to another identical package further along the alleyway, and from that to another, and another, and another...

'They're a suicide cult,' whispered Erix.

'NOW IS THE TIME OF FIRE!' proclaimed the Prophet.

Laris knew this city. She knew Varangantua as a shambling monster of steel and rockcrete; a half-tame beast. As long as you stayed clear of its hooves, avoided its line of sight and didn't bite it in a sensitive spot, then maybe it wouldn't trample you.

The best way to survive the monster was to be part of a gang, and the enforcers were the biggest gang of all. When she was young and stupid, she'd assumed that the enforcers were the richest, that they were in charge even in places like the spires.

Now she knew that there were other gangs in the spires, gangs she'd never be a part of. Nobles, plutocrats, Administratum officials. They saw the city as a different sort of beast – one that you could ride for a while and milk for money. A small beast, too. Though Laris could scarcely believe it, she'd heard stories that Varangantua was just one city among dozens on Alecto, and Alecto but one world among millions.

Still, big or small, the city was a monster.

Now she felt like she was climbing up through its guts. An access shaft ran up the south face of the hab-block. Pipes around them carried water into the hab, while others took away waste, or shielded electrical and data cables from the elements. Over the centuries, rust and hasty repairs had turned the whole shaft into something that seemed disturbingly organic to Laris – a clogged artery, one that was dripping wet and softly rotting. Unmentionable fluids spattered down from above as she clung to the rungs of the ladder.

She passed another package of explosives, identical to the ones outside. A squishy brick of fyceline clay, wrapped in black-and-yellow paper. A mining charge, she guessed. Wires connected it to the rest of its kin. Maybe cutting them would disarm the charges. Maybe it would set them all off.

The Bastion had a specialised bomb disposal verispex unit. If they could get the vox to work she could call the Bastion and request them to placate the machine-spirits in the detonators.

'WE WILL LIGHT A BLAZING BEACON IN THE NIGHT! WE SHALL CRY OUT WITH ONE VOICE TO THE EMPEROR, AND

TELL HIM THAT THIS WORLD MUST BE CLEANSED. WE SHALL RISE AS SPIRITS, PURIFIED IN OUR FAITH, AND RETURN AS HOLY BOMBARDMENT! WE SHALL RETURN AS THE SWORDS OF HIS ANGELS, AS THE LAS-BEAMS OF HEAVEN THAT SEAR THE CORRUPTION FROM THIS CURSED CITY.'

'They're going to kill themselves,' Laris said.

'We should let them,' muttered Erix from behind her as he hauled himself up the ladder.

'Shut up.' Laris tried her vox again, but got only static. 'The Prophet's followers aren't the only people here. There are thousands of innocent bystanders in this block. We can't let them all perish.'

Erix stopped climbing. 'We absolutely can. When the Bastion learns that the Prophet is running a suicide cult and not an armed insurgency, you know what they're going to do? They're going to stand back. They're going to let it burn. There may be thousands of people in this block, but this is a big city, Laris, and there are millions more blocks just like this.'

'I SEE JUDGEMENT! I SEE THE CORRUPTED ONES!' The Prophet's words echoed down the shaft.

'So why did you come with us?' hissed Laris.

'Because they were shooting at me!' Erix pointed up the shaft. 'They're all heavily armed madmen! We climb to the top, we call for extraction. Only we get out of this alive!'

'We get to the top, we warn the Bastion. Our orders were to secure the hab, not to let it burn,' said Laris.

'I SEE THREE HERETICS! I SEE ENEMIES IN OUR MIDST!'

'These prophecies are getting worryingly accurate,' said Erix.

Laris pulled out her magnoculars and scanned the darkness of the shaft above them. Nestled among the pipes were more laud hailers, more explosives... and the eye of a vid-picter, staring back at her.

She threaded her arm through the iron rung and brought

her shotgun to bear on the distant oculus, but Erix grabbed her belt and tugged it before she could pull the trigger.

'Don't shoot in here, some of these are promethium pipes! Anyway, they've already spotted us!'

'HERETICS!'

Joach grunted as an access hatch slid open in the wall next to him. Laris glimpsed a masked face and the barrel of a slug gun before Joach grabbed the cultist by the scruff of the neck, yanked him forward and dropped him down the shaft. The big man looked at his squadmates and shrugged. 'Resisting arrest.'

'Come on!' Erix said, motioning to the opening in the wall. 'They definitely know where we are now!'

'We have to keep climbing!' said Laris. 'Until the vox works!'

'We have to get out,' hissed Erix, and he dived into the hatch, wriggling through it and into the corridor beyond. Joach looked at Laris and shrugged again, then began making his way through the opening.

Knowing it would be suicide to split up, Laris relented and followed them, crawling through the tunnel before spilling out into the corridor.

Erix led them down the hall that ran along the outer wall of the hab-block. On the right-hand side stood a row of nine statues with windows between them. Doors littered the wall opposite, presumably leading to individual habs.

Through a cracked window Laris could see the sanctioner cordon behind the massive armoured barrier of the Bulwarks on the street below. She hammered on the window, but they didn't notice her. Desperately, she tried the vox again, praying that the Emperor would carry her words of warning to her fellow officers below.

A nearby laud hailer crackled before giving voice to the Prophet once more. 'I HAVE SEEN IT, MY CHILDREN! KNOW THAT THIS IS THE TIME OF TRIAL!'

A cultist came around the corner, his face hidden behind a rebreather. 'The time of trial!' he echoed. More followed after him.

Some well-meaning bureaucrat had once purchased untold numbers of identical statues to adorn the lower city hab-blocks and bolster the civic faith of the populace – millions upon millions of cowled figures, each one eight feet tall and clutching a human skull. The statues were cheap foamstone and wouldn't stop a bullet, but Laris knew there were hiding places in the folds of their cloaks. Now, she dragged Joach into one and breathed a prayer of thanks to that long-dead bureaucrat. The cultists hadn't spotted her.

Even with her weapons, even with Joach's sheer might, there were too many foes to risk a direct confrontation without backup. Maybe she could keep going to the auxiliary stairwell, or smash a window open and signal the sanctioners below with a flare. Just hide here until the cultists passed, then come back and show them the meaning of justice. Show them not to challenge the Lex.

A hab-unit door opposite her hiding place opened a crack. Laris glimpsed the face of an old man staring fearfully out at her. Slowly, silently, she tapped the crowned serpent-and-skull embossed on her armour, mentally pleading with the man to stay silent.

His eyes widened. He raised one trembling hand and brushed it against an old scar on his forehead.

The city trampled him, Laris thought, *and he blames us.*

'Here! Over here!' screeched the old man. He pointed across the corridor at Laris, then slammed his door.

'Sanctioners!' shouted Laris, desperately. 'Move! Move!'

She stepped out from her hiding place, sprayed a hail of fire down the corridor. Behind her she heard Joach roar as he charged. She couldn't see Erix.

Then they were on top of her, pawing at her. Her shotgun was torn from her hands as she was knocked to the floor.

The city had turned on her, and now it trampled her too.

It took six of them to drag Joach up the stairs. Another three to bind him as his arms strained against the cables. Ahead of him, two more cultists carried Laris. She was barely conscious, her helmet shattered.

Joach was amazed he was still alive. When the cultists had finally dragged him down, he'd assumed the next thing he'd feel would be a gun barrel against his face and then nothing, forever.

Instead, they'd been taken alive.

'The Bastion will not bargain for our lives,' he said. 'The Lex forbids it.'

'Shut up!' shouted one of the cultists, cuffing him across the face. As an expert in punishment beatings, Joach could have offered tips on how to inflict more pain for less effort.

'Where's Erix?' muttered Laris.

'I think he got away.'

'The coward ran off?'

It was a mark of Joach's strength that he was able to shrug while tied up. He had never been one for complex thought but, better than his two fellow sanctioners, he understood his place in the Imperium. There were billions of people in this one city alone, a blind horde swarming over one another. Joach had once heard Laris compare the city to a monster, but he knew better.

It was a machine – a factory that churned out materiel for the Imperium's distant wars. People were part of this machine – fuel at best, or maybe lubricant.

But sometimes they clogged up the works.

Joach knew there were far too many people for the system to

promise anything like justice. Order was the best that could be managed. It was the task of wiser, keener minds than his – for probators and castellans – to identify problems with the machine. Sanctioners like him were the tools to remove the grit from the gears. The machine of Varangantua kept spinning on through endless night, and his job was to scrub its blood-choked cogs.

Joach would never be able to articulate such thoughts, but they came to him instinctively nonetheless. As they were brought before the Prophet, Joach felt a wave of anger rise up from within him. Here was a speck of grit that threw off sparks, a malfunction that threatened to start a fire in the machine.

The cultists shoved the two sanctioners to the floor before the Prophet. Joach tried to rise, but the bonds holding him were too strong even for him.

The Prophet stood in front of a huge window looking out over the city. He was a small, hunched man, with eyes like cold and distant stars. He raised his arms in benediction.

In his right hand he held a detonator. In his left, a vox. 'I said unto you,' he proclaimed, his voice echoing from a thousand laud hailers, 'that this was the time of trial. This world is so sinful that the Emperor will no longer look upon it. Listen not to the lies of false priests! Know that you are corrupt, and trust in me to save you! I will burn away your sins!'

He removed Laris' broken helmet and pressed the vox to her cheek. 'You speak for this corrupt city. Do you repent?'

Laris spat a gob of bloody spittle onto the floor, then took a deep breath. 'Enforcers, be warned!' she yelled. 'The building's rigged to burn!'

'Silence!' shrieked the Prophet. 'The time of trial is at hand!'

Two masked cultists rushed forward to muffle Laris, wrestling her to the ground and stuffing a rag into her mouth. Another cultist knelt by Joach and whispered in his ear. 'Get 'im.' Erix's voice. The bonds gave way, cut with a knife.

Joach rose, his hands clamping around the Prophet's wrists. He tore the detonator from the madman's grasp as he shoved the Prophet hard towards the window. The glass shattered and the prophet smashed through it, screaming, his body flailing until it burst far below.

The cultists surged towards the three sanctioners, but stopped short as a Zhurov gunship emerged from the smog clouds over Varangantua. It hovered in place outside the smashed window, the barrels of its underslung machine guns tracking the cultists' movements. From its own laud hailer thundered a voice, clearer and louder than the Prophet's had been. 'IN THE NAME OF THE LEX, STAY WHERE YOU STAND. COMPLY OR PERISH.'

Soon, Joach thought with satisfaction, they'd hose the Prophet's remains off the street, and there'd be no trace of the grit in the wheels of Varangantua's endless, grinding engine.

They fell back to a taproom. Outside, they could hear the rumble of the Bulwark tanks driving away as the cordons came down. The riot-control tanks were always needed somewhere in the city.

'Look, when they rushed you, I had a chance, right?' said Erix. 'Got one of 'em with my shock maul, ditched my uniform, took his mask.'

'And followed us into the Prophet's sanctum?' asked Laris.

'Not by choice. Got caught in the crowd, didn't I? They were eager to show off their prisoners.' Erix took a gulp of his drink. 'Close call. Too close.'

'The Prophet is dead,' rumbled Joach.

'That'll just make it worse,' said Erix. 'He's a martyr now, yeah? And he said this was "a time of trial", so in their eyes his prophecies came true. Mark my words, those scrags will be back on the streets tomorrow, wiring up more buildings to burn. They'll be back.'

Laris shrugged. 'Then so will we.' She stood and drained her glass. 'See you back at the Bastion. Next shift starts in six hours.'

HABEAS CORPUS

JUDE REID

Editor's Note: The events of this story take place before the Korsk calamity and Probator Calix's involvement in that tragic event, as detailed in *The Vorbis Conspiracy*.

'And how do you like the Via Aquae Magna, Probator Calix?'

'Very scenic. I have to say, though, I generally prefer my canals with fewer corpses.'

Calix adjusted the volume on her vox-bead, then took the right-hand path at the lock gates, following the line of the branch canal deeper into the Zoransk estate. It was rare she ventured so far into Korsk's prosperous northern sub-districts, and every time the wealth on display came as a fresh surprise. For one thing, there was a clear view of the sky, and the air was filled with the crisp scent of imported evergreen trees.

'You might be out of luck, then.' The usual wry amusement was dripping from Verispex Orestes' voice, underscored with a shrill positronic whine that set Calix's teeth on edge. *'It's a popular way out for the desperate and the doomed. There's a local legend that says its waters can wash away even the most mortal of sins. Pre-Imperial superstition, of course.'*

'Fascinating, I'm sure. Can you do something about that vox feedback?'

'Sadly no. The mortuarium equipment here doesn't agree with the vox-system. Can't blame it, really. Anyway. What was it you wanted to know?'

'Whatever you can tell me, starting with how Tymon Zoransk ended up on your slab.'

'Ah, that's easy. They dredged him out of the canal this morning. Unseasonal rains caused flooding–'

Calix rolled her eyes. 'I'm more interested in the part where he walked out of the cells through a locked door and past a sleeping enforcer.'

'It's not a verispex you need for that, I'm afraid. Try a diviner.'

Calix brought the dead boy's file up onto her iris augmentation display. The ident-pict taken at the time of his arrest showed a solemn young man in his late teens, his thin face framed by curls of fashionably dishevelled black hair. The second set of images had been taken a week later, after the denizens of the canal had nibbled away his soulful brown eyes and exposed the blade of one high cheekbone through the rotting remains of his face.

'What's your plan, then?'

'The usual. Talk to the family, tell them their son's dead. See if there's anything else I can find out.'

'Isn't that below your pay grade?'

'Apparently, Ortsgrave and Lady Zoransk requested me by name – they're hand-in-glove with the burgrave here. More than just a business relationship, too – their children shared a tutor, that sort of thing.'

'Ah, yes. Burgrave Grahl. Not a woman I'd be eager to cross.'

'I'm under strict orders to tie everything up neatly before the gilded start kicking up trouble,' Calix sniffed. 'You know what they're like.'

'Not as well as you do, I believe. Congratulations on the betrothal, by the way. You can send the wedding invitation to the mortuarium. Can I bring a guest?'

'Only if they're still breathing.' Calix looked up. Ahead, the great stone face of the Zoransk residence loomed stark against the dull grey sky. 'I need to go. Vox me if you find anything.'

'I certainly shall.'

If the outside of the mansion had been gloomy, inside was even worse. Heavy velvet drapes covered the reinforced windows, reducing the available light to the glimmer of a few hooded lumen-globes. The electro-chimes at the front entrance summoned a top-of-the-line servitor draped in the family's livery, which escorted her to a lavish reception room and furnished her with freshly boiled caffeine in a delicate boneware goblet. She took a sip of the scalding liquid – strong and bitter, with a tarry chemical aftertaste that was enough to make her wince. Even so, it was better than the muck they served in the refectorum at Bastion-K.

She hadn't quite finished her cup when Ortsgrave Kazmar Zoransk burst through the door, the collar of his military-styled tunic half-undone as though he had dressed hastily in the dark. 'Probator – is it Tymon? Have you found him?'

A stooped woman in a heavy mourning veil and a girl of four-teen or fifteen followed him into the room. The veiled woman whispered a few words in the girl's ear, and the latter nodded, stepped back through the door and closed it behind her.

'I'm sorry.' Calix steeled herself to deliver the hammer blow. Breaking news like this never got any easier, but there was no sense in prolonging the agony. 'Tymon's body was recovered from the canal this morning.'

'You're certain?' the ortsgrave asked.

Calix waited for the hope in his eyes to die before she answered. 'I'm afraid so.'

'May I... see him?'

'I'd advise against it.'

Silkweave skirts rustled softly by the door, where the boy's mother was leaning against the wall with her hands clasped in the sign of the aquila.

'Are you aware of the circumstances of my son's arrest, probator?' Lady Zoransk's voice was perfectly steady.

'Witnesses reported' – Calix paused, choosing her words with care – 'possible psychic epiphenomena in the warehouse district. Ice covering the canal, unnatural lights in the air.' She brought up the report on her iris and scanned the details. 'Several figures were seen fleeing the scene, your son among them. He was arrested after refusing to give a statement.'

'We were told he was taken to the cells, awaiting transfer to a more secure facility.'

'Except the following day, the vigil-enforcer was found unconscious at his post, and your son's cell was empty.'

'We had no idea he was capable of such things.'

'Have you any idea how he ended up in the canal?'

'No. Nor do I care.' Hard black eyes looked out from beneath the heavy veil, meeting Calix's gaze unflinchingly. 'The God-Emperor has passed His judgement on Tymon. I am content.'

'What my wife means to say is that she would prefer a dead son to a living psyker.' The ortsgrave's voice dripped bitterness.

The door opened a crack, but the dead boy's parents seemed too busy glaring at each other to notice the single brown eye that peered through the gap.

'Please forgive my husband,' Lady Zoransk said stiffly. 'I fear grief is clouding his judgement.'

The face vanished from the doorway. Calix got to her feet. 'I've taken up enough of your time. I'll be in touch if I need anything else.'

She didn't bother waiting for the servitor to let her out. Instead, she followed the sound of footsteps towards the main entryway. The girl she had seen before was waiting outside, her arms folded, lips pressed in a bloodless line.

'I need to speak with you.'

Calix raised an eyebrow. 'Here?'

'Further away. Where the augurs don't reach.'

They walked to the end of the boulevard in silence. Calix checked Tymon's file for siblings and found a match: Ivara Zoransk, fifteen years old, now the sole surviving heir to her father's dynasty – though the resemblance alone would have been enough to make the familial connection.

'Is this far enough?' Calix asked.

The girl nodded. 'They didn't want me to talk to you.'

'They?'

She jerked her head towards the house. '*Her,* mostly. She wants all this to go away. I'm supposed to keep my mouth shut and be grateful that we haven't all been sent to the pyre for harbouring an unsanctioned psyker.'

'It's not the worst advice I've heard.'

'Except Tymon wasn't alone the night he was arrested.' Ivara took a deep breath, visibly steadying herself. 'I caught him going out to meet Karlyn Grahl.'

'The burgrave's daughter?'

Another nod. 'They've always been close. Closer, lately, though the burgrave doesn't approve.'

Calix studied the girl's face, searching for any signs of deceit. If the girl was lying, she was damn good at it. 'You think she's involved in his death?'

'I don't know. Tymon worshipped the ground Karlyn walked on, but I...' Ivara shot another glance towards the house. 'She's full of secrets. Always has been.'

'You don't trust her?'

Ivara's mouth twisted, as if the words tasted bitter as hot caffeine. 'Oh, I trust her. I trust her to look out for herself any chance she gets, and Throne help anyone who gets in her way.'

* * *

'What's your theory, then?' Orestes asked. The grinding whine of an osteotome was mixed with the vox feedback, providing a grating counterpoint to his words.

'I don't know.' Calix twisted her betrothal ring absently back and forward. 'The father's devastated. The mother was… resigned to it. Maybe even relieved. Not what I was expecting. Maybe Tymon broke out, went to her for help and she decided it would be better for them all if he vanished.'

'Wouldn't be the first of the gilded to prune their family tree.'

'And to complicate it further, apparently Tymon was with the burgrave's daughter the night he was arrested. Please tell me you've got something that's going to make my life easier?'

'Don't get your hopes up. Still no evidence of struggle or restraint. Nothing to say that young Master Zoransk walked into that canal at anyone's behest other than his own.'

'Perhaps knowing he was a psyker was too much to live with, and he decided to let the water wash away his sins.'

'Can't blame the boy for seeking atonement.' The osteotome gave another sharp whine. *'I'm just about to examine the intracranial contents. That's the brain, in case you were wondering.'*

'Enjoy. I'm going to head downtown for a word with Karlyn Grahl.'

The young woman was nervous. Calix could see that from the moment she opened the door to the hab-unit, her face grey and her eyes unnaturally bright, like she had just chewed down a mouthful of stimms. With her dirty blonde hair hanging in rat-tails about the shoulders of her oversized robe, she looked more like a hungover scholam-girl than a burgrave's heir-presumptive.

Calix flashed her holo-seal. 'Are you Karlyn Grahl?'

The other woman frowned. 'Who's asking?'

'I'll take that as a yes.' Calix jammed her boot in the doorway just in time to stop it slamming shut in her face. 'I'd like to talk to you about Tymon Zoransk.'

'I've got nothing to say.'

'I have a witness saying you were with Tymon the night he was arrested on suspicion of warp sorcery.' Calix took half a step forward. 'We can speak at the Bastion if you prefer, it's all the same to me.'

Karlyn's eyes narrowed. 'Come in.'

The hab-unit was lavishly furnished, but no attempt had been made to keep it tidy. Leftover food and unwashed utensils were stacked haphazardly beside an expensive radiation oven, and dirty clothes lay discarded on every surface. Calix removed a crumpled silkweave tunic from a high-backed wyrwood chair, and sat down facing the door.

'Do you live here alone?'

'My mother is very keen that I develop my independence.' The young woman's shoulders stiffened. 'But I don't believe you're here to discuss my domestic arrangements.'

'Only insofar as they relate to your relationship with Tymon Zoransk.' Calix plastered on her most winning smile. 'Would you say you were close?'

'We were friends.'

'Did you ever have reason to believe he might have unnatural abilities?'

'No.'

'When did you see him last?'

'A week ago.' Karlyn glanced at the door, fingers tapping out an inaudible rhythm on the skirts of her robe. 'We took a walk together, after dark.'

'Were you there when he was arrested?'

Karlyn shook her head. 'I panicked. Ran. I thought he was with me, but when I finally looked round he was gone. I assumed he'd gone home. I only learned he'd been arrested the next morning.'

'Why didn't you come forward to speak in his defence?'

'My mother didn't know we were out together. She doesn't approve of me spending time with him.' Karlyn met Calix's gaze without flinching. 'I was afraid.'

Calix's iris display flashed a distracting, insistent red. Incoming vox-call, urgent. 'Throne damn it. Excuse me a moment. What is it, Orestes?'

'I've found something.' Feedback squealed through the call, but the verispex ignored it. *'Micro-haemorrhages scattered throughout the brain, especially in the auditory receptive cortex. I compared the pattern to the vigil-enforcer's tomogram, and it's a perfect match. Whatever happened to one of them happened to both.'*

'One of them inexplicably fell asleep at his post, the other one walked into a river.' Calix glanced at Karlyn, and found the other woman staring back intently. 'That sort of behaviour seems pretty out of character. Could that be related to these changes in the brain you're seeing?'

'Maybe.' Orestes sounded uncertain. *'I've checked the mortuarium's cogitator records, and there's only one reference to anything remotely like this – in the brain of a suspect who was brought down by enforcers after he murdered a stranger, seemingly without motive. The case was never solved, but there was a suspicion of psychic control. Unproven, of course. Let me run a few more tests, I'll let you know what I find out.'*

Orestes cut the vox-link, and a shiver went down Calix's back. She let her hand drift down casually towards the holster on her belt. Karlyn had moved so that her back was to the door, her breath pluming silver in air that had suddenly turned ice cold.

'Stay in your chair, probator,' Karlyn said. 'It's time for us to have a little talk.'

Calix tried to stand, but her legs felt as though they had been frozen in blocks of ice. 'I'm listening.'

'This isn't my fault. You understand that, don't you?'

'No one would choose to be born a psyker, but we all have to live as the God-Emperor ordains.'

'Easy for you to say.'

'There are people who can help you.' Calix tried to move her legs again, but the muscles refused to respond, like the limbs of a puppet with its strings cut. She forced a slow, deep breath in, then out, fighting down the panic that threatened to overwhelm her.

'I don't want help. I just want to be left alone.' Two bright spots of colour had appeared on Karlyn's cheeks. Her hands were shaking.

'You trusted Tymon, though, didn't you?' Calix fought to keep her voice casual. 'Was that what you were doing that night? Showing him what you could do?'

For the first time, genuine emotion showed on the psyker's face. 'He understood. He promised me he would never tell. We were going to run away together.'

'Except something went wrong, didn't it? You ended up attracting the sort of attention that could bring the full weight of the Lex down on you. So you ran, and you let Tymon be arrested in your place.'

Karlyn's face flushed scarlet. 'It was his idea. He said it would give me time to get away. He said the Lex would never convict an innocent man.'

Calix edged her hand closer to her belt. The snub-nosed Mauros Astrapi in its tooled synthleather holster was inches from her fingertips. All she had to do was reach it before Karlyn decided it was time to finish their conversation in the most terminal way. 'Except you changed your mind. You broke him out, then he drowned in the canal.'

'I didn't want to do it! But – what if they'd brought in the chasteners? I've heard about what they do. There's no way he'd have been able to keep my secret. I had to make sure. I had to.' Karlyn's fists were clenched so tightly her knuckles had gone grey. 'This is a waste of time. Put your gun to your head, probator.'

The muscles of Calix's arm spasmed suddenly, as if shot through with electrical current. Her hand closed involuntarily around the Astrapi's grip, then, to her horror, she felt the freezing metal of the muzzle against her temple. Karlyn stepped closer, staring intently into Calix's eyes. 'I can't let his death be for nothing.'

'Then honour his sacrifice. Hand yourself in. Serve the Emperor in the task He has chosen for you.'

'I won't spend my life in chains.'

Calix closed her eyes, and subvoxed a command to her iris. The line crackled in her ear, followed by Orestes' querulous tones. *'My favourite probator again! What is it this time?'*

She ignored him. 'Don't you think a dead probator in your hab will attract attention, Mamzelle Grahl?'

'Interview not going so well, I take it?' Orestes said.

'The canal isn't far. I'll use more weights this time.'

'What do you need, Calix?'

There was no point in asking for backup; the psyker would have the hab redecorated in grey matter long before help arrived.

'Deafen me,' she subvoxed, focusing all of her attention on Karlyn. It was all about playing for time, now – that and keeping the psyker distracted while Orestes caught up with what was going on. 'I'm willing to speak on your behalf. Advocate for you. Your mother's contacts alone should be enough to see you're treated fairly.'

'What?'

'I know what happens to psykers, high-born or not. I'd rather die.' Karlyn Grahl's voice was ice cold. 'Put your index finger on the trigger of your pistol–'

Calix's finger twitched. *'Feedback, through the vox.* Now!' The final word came out as a shout.

Grahl's mouth opened to deliver the fatal command as a polyphonic shriek seared through Calix's eardrums. The psyker's lips were still moving, but her words fell on suddenly deaf ears, and the iron grip around Calix's mind eased.

She wrenched the Astrapi away from her skull, and fired.

The pressure on her mind vanished as the psyker darted out into the hallway. Ears still ringing, Calix sprinted after her, down the narrow passageway and through the front entrance. Outside, Karlyn was fleeing down a vennel between two warehouses. She was less than a hundred yards away. Calix fired a warning shot, but the psyker kept running, her bare feet splashing over the cobblestones, heading straight towards the canal at the end of the lane.

It was a dead end.

Calix slowed to a walk. At this distance she couldn't miss, not even on a bad day. Karlyn had stopped running and was standing with her toes curled over the quayside stones, staring into the canal.

'Give yourself up, Karlyn. You haven't got a choice.'

Frost was forming around Karlyn's bare feet, spreading out across the flagstones, creeping down to form a thin layer across the water. Motes of light danced in the air like tiny sparkling snowflakes.

'There's always a choice,' the psyker said, and stepped back into the canal.

For a second it seemed like the ice might hold her weight, but then it gave way, plunging her into the freezing water, the ice around her thickening and spreading to form a glacial crust across the surface above her. Calix caught one last glimpse of Karlyn's wide-eyed face, her desperate hand clawing up at the impermeable barrier above her as though she had changed her mind, as though drowning was far worse than any torment the Sanctum Psykana might have in store – then the ice clouded over, and she was gone.

'Calix! Can you hear me?' Orestes was still on the vox, real anxiety in his voice. Calix shook her head, as if partial deafness was something she could physically dislodge.

'I'm fine. It's over.'

Orestes sniffed. *'Your idiot plan worked, then. How's your suspect?'*

'Dead, at the bottom of the canal.'

'The Via Aquae Magna claims another victim.' Orestes gave a theatrical sigh. *'Ah well. If they dredge her out, perhaps I'll have a psyker to dissect after all.'*

A crowd was starting to gather. Calix turned up the collar of her longcoat and retraced her steps up the vennel.

'Case closed, I suppose,' Orestes said. *'Though I imagine you'll have some explaining to do before too much longer.'*

There was no way to tell how long the burgrave and her entourage had been waiting outside Bastion-K, but their appearance didn't come as a surprise. In the hours since Karlyn Grahl had taken her fatal plunge, Calix had been braced for a vox-call, a summons, maybe even a knife in the back. The burgrave's reputation preceded her, and it was a formidable herald.

'Probator Calix, isn't it?' The burgrave offered a gloved hand to Calix. She looked only a few years older than her daughter – clearly the rejuvenat treatments were working well – but while Karlyn had been a whirlwind of nervous energy, this woman radiated stillness like the heart of a storm.

'I'm sorry about your daughter, Burgrave Grahl.'

'Regrettable.' The burgrave waved the apology away. 'I wanted to convey my personal thanks for all your hard work on this difficult case. Your skills and dedication are a credit to your Bastion.'

Calix nodded, every nerve on edge. The burgrave was making

her wary in a way that had nothing to do with the threat of physical violence. One of the entourage stepped forward, a heavy vellum scroll held in both hands.

'I'd like you to take this formal commendation to your superiors. I'd also like you to consider accepting the formal offer of my personal patronage.'

It didn't make sense. An offer like this was as rare as an honest ratling. The burgrave's patronage could take her career to heights she'd never dared dream of, and here it was, offered up for the taking.

'However...'

And there we are, Calix thought. *Nothing comes without a price.*

'You will appreciate that my patronage has value only as long as my position remains secure.'

'What exactly are you saying, burgrave?'

'A simple request. Omit my daughter's name from your report.'

A laugh forced its way out of Calix's mouth. 'I appreciate your situation, ma'am, but I'm not going to lie to my superiors.'

'Not *lie*. Merely omit the unnecessary details. For the good of Korsk.'

The attendant offered Calix the scroll. The acrid tang of hot wax still clung to the blood-red seal, imprinted with the aquila-and-serpent of the burgrave's signet ring. She could imagine the weight of it in her hand, the luxurious smoothness of the vellum's creamy surface.

Calix folded her arms across her chest, a ward against temptation. 'No.'

'How disappointing.' The burgrave's lips curved like a sickle. 'You're recently betrothed, are you not, probator?'

A prickle of unease crept down Calix's spine. 'What's that got to do with anything?'

'To Adept Sevastyan Tzemerov, as I understand it – another

young citizen with a glittering career ahead of him. At this time of day he'll be leaving the Winter Palace, down those white marble steps.'

Calix shot a glance around the burgrave's guards – six of them, fully armed and armoured. If they decided to make trouble, she wouldn't stand a chance.

'A young adept's career can be such a fragile thing at this early stage, don't you agree? Like a hothouse flower, it can be nurtured into a magnificent blossom, but it takes only a little rough handling to blight it forever.' The burgrave's sickle-smile sharpened. 'Bearing that in mind, probator, can I ask you to reconsider my offer?'

Calix drew herself stiffly upright and took a deep breath, a leaden weight forming in the pit of her stomach. 'It appears I misspoke before. I should be honoured to accept your offer, lady burgrave.'

'Excellent.' The burgrave motioned to her adjutant, who placed the scroll in Calix's unresisting hands. 'This city is full of our enemies, probator. I do so like to make friends where I can.'

Calix waited until the burgrave had gone before she voxed Orestes again, cutting him off as soon as he drew breath to speak.

'I need you to destroy all the evidence relating to the Tymon Zoransk case. Cerebral specimens, scans, data-logs. All of it.'

There was silence on the other end of the line. When Orestes spoke, there was no trace of the usual levity in his voice. *'It's already done.'*

'Good. I'll send you a copy of my report before I submit it. Make sure the details match.'

Calix rubbed at her eyes. At the far end of the street, the wind was stirring the surface of the canal into tiny, glittering peaks, leaving the depths below undisturbed.

If water could wash away guilt, she thought, the Via Aquae Magna would be so thick with sin by now you could walk from here to the sea.

'She got to you as well, then, did she?' Orestes said, his voice flat and tinny in her ear.

'I don't know what you mean,' Calix said, and severed the connection.

ABOUT THE AUTHORS

JONATHAN D BEER is a science fiction and alternative history writer. Equally obsessed with the 19th century and the 41st millennium, he lives with his wife and assorted cats in the untamed wilderness of Edinburgh, Scotland. His Warhammer Crime stories include 'Old Instincts', 'Service' and 'Chains', and the novel *The King of the Spoil*.

MIKE BROOKS is a science fiction and fantasy author who lives in Nottingham, UK. His work for Black Library includes the Horus Heresy Primarchs novel *Alpharius: Head of the Hydra*, the Warhammer 40,000 novels *Rites of Passage, Warboss* and *Brutal Kunnin*, the Necromunda novel *Road to Redemption* and the novellas *Wanted: Dead* and *Da Gobbo's Revenge*. When not writing, he plays guitar and sings in a punk band, and DJs wherever anyone will tolerate him.

VICTORIA HAYWARD is a trained historitor who spent her youth serving as an acolyte in a Games Workshop store. She writes about black holes and the palaces of despots in her day job as a science communicator and her favourite corners of the 40K universe are those occupied by the Inquisition – which is all of it. Her work for Black Library includes the short stories 'The Siege of Ismyr' and 'The Carbis Incident'. She resides in Nottingham, where she keeps birds and practises printmaking.

DENNY FLOWERS is the author of the novels *Fire Made Flesh* and *Outgunned*, the novella *Low Lives* and several short stories. He lives in Kent with his wife and son, and has no proven connection with House Delaque.

NICK KYME is the author of many Horus Heresy novels, novellas and audio dramas, including *Old Earth*, *Promethean Sun* and *Nightfane*. His novella *Feat of Iron* was a *New York Times* bestseller in the Horus Heresy collection *The Primarchs*. For Warhammer 40,000, Nick has written *Volpone Glory* and the Dawn of Fire novel *The Iron Kingdom*. He is also well known for his popular Salamanders series and the Cato Sicarius novels *Damnos* and *Knights of Macragge*. His work for Age of Sigmar includes the short story 'Borne by the Storm', included in the novel *War Storm*, and the audio drama *The Imprecations of Daemons*. He has also written the Warhammer Horror novel *Sepulturum*. He lives and works in Nottingham.

MITCHEL SCANLON is a full-time novelist and comics writer. His previous credits for Black Library include the Horus Heresy novel *Descent of Angels*, *Fifteen Hours*, the background book *The Loathsome Ratmen*, and the comics series Tales of Hellbrandt Grimm.

GARETH HANRAHAN's three-month break from computer programming to concentrate on writing has now lasted fifteen years and counting. He lives in Ireland and has written more gaming books than he can readily recall by virtue of the alchemical transmutation of guilt and tea into words. For Black Library he has written the short stories 'Castle of the Exile, 'The View from Olympus' and 'Rites of Binding'.

JUDE REID lives in Glasgow with her husband and two daughters, and writes in the narrow gaps between full-time work as a surgeon, wrangling her kids and failing to tire out a border collie. In what little free time she has, she enjoys tabletop roleplaying, ITF Tae Kwon Do and inadvisably climbing big hills. Her many stories for Black Library include the Warhammer 40,000 novel *Creed: Ashes of Cadia*.

YOUR
NEXT READ

Bloodlines
by Chris Wraight

An investigation into a missing member of a wealthy family leads Probator Agusto Zidarov into a web of lies and danger amidst the criminal cartels of Varangantua. As the net closes in, Zidarov falls further into darkness from which he may never return…

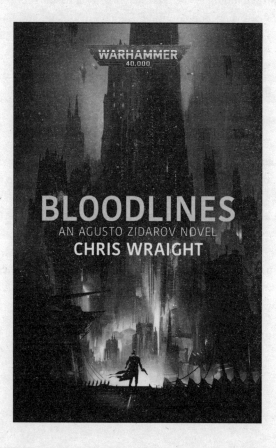

An extract from
Bloodlines
by Chris Wraight

Down, down below, down under the flyovers and the transit arches, down to where the lumens floated on wheezing suspensors and the windows were steamed with condensation. People packed in on all sides, some high on topaz, some exhausted, all smelling of euphoria.

She breathed it in. She let her fingers graze along the rockcrete of the close wall, feeling its coldness against the wet heat of the night. She looked up, and saw the smear-glow of private club entrances, vivid in neon. She heard the rumble of turbine traffic overhead, and the hiss of groundcars on damp asphalt.

She'd taken it. Topaz. It was as good as she'd hoped – she was giddy, enjoying the freedom. Every face she looked at was one of a friend, smiling back at her, rouged, whitened, darkened, flared with photoreactive pigments, glittering with augmetic baubles. Music thumped away, spilling from the open doorways of the sanctioned haze dens, threatening to drag her in, smother her in the heat and the noise.

She could have walked along that street forever, just drinking it in. She liked the smells, overlapping one another, competing like jostling suitors for her attention. She stuck her hands in the pockets of her overcoat, pushed her shoulders back, slipped through the crowds.

She didn't know what time it was. The deep of the night, for sure, a few hours before dawn. It didn't matter. Not any more. That was the point of freedom – make your decisions, stupid ones, good ones, get out, do your own thing.

A man lurched into her way, grinning and drunk. He shoved up against her, and she smelled his breath.

'Hello, young fish,' he slurred at her, swaying. 'Come to swim with me?'

He had plastek-looking hair, too clean, too sculpted. She kept on going, sliding past him, out into the middle of the street. The press of people swept him away, giving her more faces to gawp at. Fireworks went off in the sky, dazzling, smelling of chems, picking out high arches overhead engraved with skull-clusters and fleur-de-lys finials. Commercia chameleon-screens flashed and whirled, spinning pixelated images one after the other – a woman smiling, a man gazing at an altar, a Navy drop-ship wheeling across a starfield, troops in uniform marching under a crimson sky on another world.

For the first time, she felt a spike of danger. She had walked a long way, away from the friends she had come with. She had almost forgotten about them entirely, and had very little idea where she was.

She looked back and saw the plastek-hair man following her. He was with others, and they had latched on to her.

Damn.

She picked up the pace, skipping on her heels, darting to the street's edge, to where the grand avenue, scarred with twin steel ground-tracks, met another one, cobbled and glinting, that ran steeply downwards.

If she hadn't taken topaz, she'd have stayed, by instinct, with the crowds, where the press of bodies provided its mute kind of safety. But it got darker quickly, and the lumens faded to red, and the old cobblestones underfoot got slippery. The beat of the music felt harder – dull, like the military dirges they transmitted every evening over the communal prop-sets.

Down, down, down.

She felt a bit sick. She shot a glance back and saw that they were still coming, only jogging now, four of them, all drunk on jeneza or rezi or slatov. They all had those sharp, fake haircuts, smart dress, clean boots. Defence-corps trainees, maybe – officer-class, full of entitlement, untouchable. She'd come across the type so many times before. Hadn't expected to find them down here – perhaps they liked to slum it from time to time as well, to skirt against the grime for fun, see whether it stuck to their uniforms.

Just as she began to worry, someone grabbed her by the arm. She pulled back, only to see a girl smiling at her, a girl her age, pale emerald skin, orange hair, a metal serpent-head stud in her cheek.

'Come on,' the girl said, her irises glittering. 'I saw them too.'

She followed her. She went down a narrow passageway between two big hab-blocks built of dark, crumbling prefab slabs. It soon smelled of urine and old sweat, of drains and discarded carb-bars. As she wound further down the alley, the noise of the men's footfalls, their laughter, faded. Perhaps they'd gone straight on past. Perhaps they'd never really been that close.

It got hotter. She felt the boom of the music well up from under her, around her, as if the walls themselves were vox-emitters. She needed a drink. For some reason she was very thirsty.

The girl brought her to a door – a heavyset door in a block-work wall, one with a slide panel in the centre. She activated a summon-chime, and the slide opened, throwing out greenish light from within.

'Elev in?' the girl asked.

'He is,' came a man's voice.

The door clunked open. Warm air billowed out, and music came after it, heavy, thumping music. She felt it move through her body, make her want to get going, to get back to that place she'd managed to reach a while back, where everything was forgotten save for the movement, the heat, the heartbeat of escape.

The girl pushed her inside. They were at the head of a long flight of plastek-topped stairs. The walls were bare cinder blocks, the floor sticky with spilled drinks. It was hard to hear anything at all over the music, which seemed to be coming from everywhere at once.

'Down,' said the girl, smiling at her again, encouragingly.

They went together. Soon they were in a bigger chamber, one full of bodies moving, throwing shadows against lumen-scatter walls. What had this place once been? An assembly chamber? A chapel, even? Not now. The light was lurid, vivid, pulsing in time to the heavy smack of the music. She smelled sweat fighting with commercial fragrances. She smelled the acrid tang of rezi. There was a high stage with murals half-hidden in a haze of coloured smoke, men and women dancing on platforms surrounded by kaleidoscopic lumen flares. The floor was jammed, crushed with damp bodies in motion. It was hard to breathe.

'Just keep moving,' said the girl, taking her by the hand.

They somehow threaded through the crowds. A drink was passed to her and she took it. That made her feel better. She started to look for the source of the music. Faces swelled up out of the dark, flustered and glowing, all grinning at her. They were nice, those faces, and interesting, with their slim metal exo-frames and their holo-halos that waved and flashed like prisms. Where had they all come from? Did they work in the manufactories she had heard about, during the drab day? Or were they all the sons and daughters of the gilded, writhing down here until they collapsed into narc-induced sleep? They were like exotic beasts, feathered, horned, wrapped in silks and sequins, coming in and out of the flickering shadows, fragments of strange bedtime stories, moving in unison under old gothic arches.

She danced for a while. The girl seemed to have gone, but that was fine. She thought back to the past, to the rules that had kept her in her chamber every hour, all the hours, at her studies, learning the catechisms and the rotes, and wanted to scream out loud for the joy of being free of it. Her limbs moved, clumsily, because she had never been able to do this before, but she learned fast, and the topaz made it easier.

They pressed around her, the others – reaching out for her hair, her arms. She lost track of time. More drinks appeared, and she took them again.

And then, much later, the girl came back. She led her from the chamber of lights and heat, and down some more narrow, slippery stairs. That was a relief, for she was getting tired. It would be good to rest, just for a moment. Away from the music, it was cooler, and she felt the sweat patches on her shirt stick to her skin.

'Where are we going?' she asked, and was surprised to hear how the words slurred.

'Time out,' said the girl. 'I think you need it.'

It was hard to follow where they went. Some stairs went down, some went up. At one point she thought they'd gone outside, and then in again, but she was getting very tired and her head had started to hurt.

'Do you have any water?' she asked.

'That's where we're going,' came the reply. 'To get some.'

And then they were through another heavy door. She had the impression of more people around her, though it was very dark, and increasingly cold. They went down yet more stairs, a well so tight that it scraped against her bare arms, even though she wanted to stop now, just sit on the floor, clear her head.

Eventually they ended up in a narrow, empty room with bright overhead lumens that hurt her eyes. She really wanted a drink.

A man was there, one with sallow skin, a tight black bodysuit and collarless shirt, a knotwork tattoo just visible at the base of his neck.

'What's your name?' he asked, pleasantly enough.

'Ianne,' she replied.

'Ianne. That's unusual. I like it. Are you having a good time?'

'I could use a drink.'

'Fine. Come with me, then. We'll get you something.'

By then, the girl seemed to have gone. She felt hands on her arms, and she was heading down again. The lumens were turned down low, and she struggled to make anything out.

She had the vague sense of being surrounded by people again. She heard a noise like breathing, in and out. She shook her head to clear it, and saw metal shelves, many of them, all with glass canisters on them. She saw tubes, and she saw machines that had bellows and ampoules and loops of cabling. She saw the padded couches, in rows, running back into the dark, and it looked like people were sitting on them.

She felt a lurch of worry. There was no music. It was quiet, and cold, and she didn't know the way back out.

'Where am I?' she asked.

They found a chair for her. It was a recliner, but it was hard and uncomfortable. She thought she should struggle then, but it became hard to think about anything clearly. She felt something wrap around her wrists.

'Where am I?' she asked again, more urgently, suddenly thinking of all those catechisms, and the rules, and home, and its certainties.

A face loomed up out of the shadows. She didn't recognise this one. It was a hard face, with hollow cheeks, and the smile it gave her made her feel suddenly panicky.

'You're Ianne? Just relax. You're in the right place.'

She tried to kick out, but something had tied her ankles down. She looked up, and saw a collection of needles hanging over her, glinting in the cold light. Fear welled up fast, as if she would drown in it.

'Get me out.'

'Don't worry about a thing,' said the man soothingly, reaching up for one of the needles. It was connected to a slender tube, which looped down from a bag of clear fluid. 'It'll all be fine.'

'I want to get out!' she cried, starting to struggle.

'Why would you want that?' the man asked, tapping the needle and preparing to insert it. He looked up and down the rows on either side of her. Her eyes had adjusted. She could see that the other couches were all occupied. No one lying on them was moving. 'You'll do so much good here.'

He set one of the machines running. The device beside her started to whirr, with a thud-tick-thud that sounded like some monstrous heartbeat.

'Wh– what are you doing?' she asked, her throat choking up with a thick sense of horror.

'Just relax,' he said, reaching over her. 'I say the same thing every time. This is a place of dreams. So I'm going to give you something now. Something good. And after that – believe me when I say this – you're going to live forever.'